The Renovation

on

Hollyhock Hill

AUTUMN LAKE BOOK 4

BECKY DOUGHTY

BraveHearts
Press

1
Candy

"GOOD MORNING, HEARTH BREAKERS! It's Candy Needham coming to you on a fabulous Monday morning, and folks, it's Demolition Day!" Candy beamed at her phone mounted on the dashboard as she pulled into the driveway of the charming two-story house on Hollyhock Hill. She put her SUV in park and reached for her framing hammer from the passenger side floorboard. Holding it aloft in front of the camera, she asked, "Are you ready? I know I am!"

She took a moment to appreciate the lake house's potential. The home had that classic character that made her heart flutter, with its natural limestone foundation, tall windows, and a deck that looked out over the lake. Sure, the flaking paint on the eaves and the overgrown garden beds showed signs of neglect, but she could already envision how stunning it would look once she worked her magic.

It was perfect showcase material, Candy thought, the butterflies in her stomach doing a happy dance. After working so hard to salvage her reputation, this project could be the cornerstone she needed.

And maybe, just maybe, if the renovation went well enough to truly launch her business, she could make Maeve an offer on the place. The thought had been growing in her mind over the past few weeks, that she could transform this lakeside gem into not just a portfolio piece, but her own home. It was almost too perfect to imagine: living in a house she'd renovated herself, waking up to that lake view every morning.

But she hadn't breathed a word of this dream to anyone, not even to her cousin, Liz. It was the kind of thing to keep close to her heart until she knew if it was even possible.

She unclipped the phone from the dash and slid out of the car, trying not to jostle her camera too much. "I can't wait to show you the transformation we're about to begin." She panned slowly to capture the house and the property it sat on. "This beauty has so much potential hiding under her dated façade. We're going to honor all that gorgeous character while bringing in some modern touches."

She flipped the camera back to herself, the early morning sunlight glistening on the lake behind her. "Wait until you see the floors, you guys. There's original oak underneath the decades old Berber carpet!"

Candy ended the recording and posted it to her social media accounts, resisting the urge to look for that first heart or thumbs up. Her follower count had been steadily climbing again since the TV scandal a couple of years ago, but she still had a long way to go. Every like, every comment felt like a small victory in reclaiming her reputation from the ashes.

After tucking her phone away, she grabbed her tool bag from the floorboard behind her seat and headed toward the house. The owner, Maeve Lewis, had given her the keys to the castle, so to speak, and had granted Candy carte blanche to renovate and restore to her heart's content. Although the property had once been Maeve's family home, it had been a summer rental for years, and had slowly become too much for the older woman to manage. Having decided it was time to sell, Maeve had assured Candy that she had no compulsion to be involved in what was going on. "Do with it what you would if you were the owner," she'd told her.

For Candy, who'd been living under the dark cloud of the fallout of her DIY home improvement show scandal, Maeve accepting her offer had been nothing short of a miracle. A full renovation would bring the home up to modern standards in order to fetch the best price on the market, and would also allow Candy to showcase her talents to potential clients. It was the perfect way to launch her new renovation and restoration company.

She pulled out her phone, fluffed her blonde ponytail, straightened her "Hearth & Home Renovations" t-shirt, and hit record.

"Let's take a little tour before we start tearing things out," she said, keeping her voice upbeat as she pushed open the front door. It creaked a little, sending a shiver of excitement up her spine. "That's the sound of a warm welcome from a house like this one," she said, panning her camera around the foyer. Inside, the air was musty with disuse, but sunlight streamed through the tall windows that faced the lake, illuminating the home's beautiful bones.

"Hello?" she called, her voice echoing. To the camera she said with a chuckle, "Just in case the critters haven't heard I'm coming."

She wandered through the open plan downstairs, careful not to move too quickly, lest she make her viewers seasick. "Check out these gorgeous crown moldings. And look at that fireplace with the original stone surround!"

She continued her tour into the kitchen, with its off-white appliances and worn linoleum. "This kitchen is going to be our biggest transformation. I'm thinking glass paned upper cabinets with low watt lighting inside to display the contents, a butcher block island, a farm sink with granite countertops in—" She stopped abruptly, her ears picking up a sound from upstairs. A thump, followed by what sounded like... growling?

Candy froze, her pulse racing. Great. Was she going to have to deal with a crazy raccoon or an angry possum today? She'd been joking about the critters a moment ago, but the idea of actually coming face-to-face with an animal who might see her as a threat was not appealing to her.

Putting on a brave face, Candy grinned into the phone. "Did you guys hear that?" She pointed toward the stairs. "I think we might have a visitor to oust. Maybe I'll have to add wildlife removal to my list of services."

She wasn't afraid of mice or spiders; she'd had to accept them as part of her career choice. But something larger? *Please let it be a squirrel that's more afraid of me than I am of it,* she prayed silently, not wanting her viewers to pick up on her trepidation. She squared her shoulders and started toward the stairs, her camera facing outward. "Let's investigate, shall we? This house has been empty for quite some time, after all."

She climbed the stairs, still narrating quietly. "All three bedrooms are on the second floor. Two share a Jack and Jill bathroom between them, but the largest bedroom has an en suite bathroom with an enormous claw-foot tub. We're keeping that fabulous tub, but the rest of it needs a major overhaul. I'll show you that in a minute, but first—" She approached the first of the smaller rooms where the soft growls seemed to originate. "Let's see what's making that noise, shall we?"

Was it growling? The sounds were almost... rhythmic.

Wait. Was that—could it be snoring?

A flicker of unease passed through her, but she dismissed it. This was Autumn Lake, not Chicago. Animals snored, too, right?

Surely, it wasn't a squatter. She'd just been in the place two days ago, and there'd been no evidence of anyone but herself in the house.

The sound stopped. She held her breath and listened again. Was the creature on the other side of that door holding its breath and listening for her, too?

She grabbed the hammer she'd tucked into her tool belt and gripped it at the base of the handle, giving her swing an extra sixteen inches if push came to shove. Being barely five-feet-two, she'd take it.

She flipped the camera to herself and whispered, "Let's do this."

She raised her hammer boldly and stepped closer to the door. She pressed her ear to it. Something rustled inside, then let out a snort.

Her heart was pounding in her ribcage. Was she being stupid? Should she call the police? Should she be recording this?

Why, yes. Yes, she should be recording this. All of it. This was her renovation site. If some stray—or squatter, heaven forbid—had broken in, they needed to leave. Now.

She flipped the camera again so she'd capture footage of whatever was in that room and rapped a knuckle on the door. "Hello?" she called, hoping with all her might that no one would answer.

When there was no other sound, she tapped the door with her boot. It wasn't latched and drifted partially open. She stepped back, peering cautiously into the six-inch gap, but she couldn't see anything except the far wall of the room where an empty bookshelf stood.

"Hello?" she called again, louder this time. "Is someone there?" She nudged the door open the rest of the way.

The room was dim, curtains drawn against the morning light. As her eyes adjusted, Candy started violently, the phone jerking in her hand.

A large shape was sprawled on the twin bed under the window. Not an animal, but a human form in a sleeping bag, a bedraggled head of dark hair protruding from the opening, facing away from her toward the wall.

A filthy backpack rested against the foot of the bed, alongside a pair of well-worn, even filthier boots.

Her heart thrashed around inside her ribcage. "Hey!" she shouted, instinctively raising the hammer higher. "This is private property!" Her voice came out with much more authority than she felt.

The figure grunted and rolled over. A shaggy-bearded, disheveled man glared at her through slitted eyes from across the room. He was clearly displeased at being awakened, but she didn't back down.

Well, she didn't run screaming, which was what she *wanted* to do, but she did back up so that she was outside the room. "I don't know who you are, but you need to leave right now."

He closed his eyes and burrowed back into the sleeping bag.

"I said, wake up!" Candy flipped the light switch on the wall on and off several times, hoping the flickering would irritate him even through his closed eyes. "You're trespassing! I have you on camera right now, and thousands of my followers are seeing this. I'm calling the police!"

That got his attention. The man pushed himself up into a sitting position, the sleeping bag slipping down around his waist to reveal a threadbare t-shirt that might have been white at one time. In spite of his broad shoulders, the shirt hung on his slender frame.

Candy's grip on her phone tightened. If everything worked out, this would make for some potentially viral footage. If things got ugly, she'd have evidence to turn in to the police. *If you survive,* a small voice in her head whispered. The guy was definitely hostile.

"Lady," he growled, his voice rough with sleep. "You're the one who's trespassing. Since you let yourself in, you obviously know where the door is, so you can let yourself out again." Then he flopped back down and turned his back to her, drawing the sleeping bag up over his head as if to shut out both the morning light *and* her.

"Buddy! Hey!" She raised her voice. His dismissive tone sent an ever ready spark of anger through her. She'd dealt with enough condescending men in her career to recognize the type.

"I'm not your buddy," came the muffled retort.

"I don't care who you are, but you need to leave," she repeated, growing angrier by the second. "Now."

He flipped back the top of the sleeping bag but didn't roll over to look at her. "This is my house," was all he said before drawing the cover up over his head again.

"No, it's not." Good grief. Was she arguing with a squatter over ownership of the house? On camera? This guy was making her look like a fool to her viewers.

"That's it," she said. "I'm calling the police." She stopped filming and put the phone on speaker so that he could hear just how serious she was.

The phone rang twice, then was answered by a calm male voice. "911. What is your emergency?"

The man in the bed sat bolt upright and threw back the covers again. "Is this some kind of a joke? Who are you?" He pulled his legs from the covers and pushed to his feet, causing Candy to take another step back. She also raised her hammer again. The man snorted with derision. "You planning to club me with that thing?"

Candy straightened her shoulders defiantly and brought the phone a little closer to her mouth. "I'm at 1432 Hollyhock Hill and there's an intruder here. I need the police."

The operator paused a moment, then asked, "Ma'am, are you safe? Are you in the home with the intruder?"

Candy shot a challenging look at the man who now stood in the middle of the room in only his t-shirt and boxers. "Am I safe?" she asked him, refusing to look away. All the important bits were fully covered, and since he didn't seem to be embarrassed by his state of dishabille, then she refused to let him think it bothered her. Besides, what if he lunged at her the moment she turned her back on him?

"Ma'am?" The operator spoke a bit more urgently. "Do you know the intruder?"

"No, I most certainly do not," Candy exclaimed. "Please send the police as quickly as possible." She gave the dispatcher her name and promised to stay on the line with him until the police showed up.

The man was shaking his head, his tangled hair and beard wild from sleep, giving off major irritated sasquatch vibes. "Idiot," he snarled, turning away from her. As if suddenly remembering that he was only in his underclothes, he reached for the backpack and withdrew a pair of cargo pants with holes in both knees and one back pocket nearly torn off.

"Did you just call me an idiot?" Candy demanded, offended by his belligerence.

"Nope," the guy grunted, his back to her as he unceremoniously stepped into his pants. He was almost gaunt, Candy noticed. She could practically count his ribs through the thin fabric of his shirt as he bent forward to root around in his pack again. He stumbled a little when he straightened, but placed a hand on the wall to steady himself.

He looked like he needed to eat something. Was he sick?

Oh, no, no, no. Don't start feeling sorry for him, Candace Needham. He just called you an idiot.

Because she doubted he'd called himself an idiot. Obviously, this guy was gunning for a fight, hoping to get a reaction out of her.

"Ms. Needham?" It was the dispatcher trying to get her attention. "I'm advising you to remove yourself from the situation while you wait for the police. Get out of the house, maybe into your car and lock the doors."

But Candy wasn't about to give up ground. Sure, she was being stubborn, but after sizing up her opponent, she figured she could take him. She was armed with a hammer, after all.

Besides, she was finished with men dictating her every move.

"Thank you," was all she said in response, but she did acknowledge to herself that she didn't have to loiter in the doorway and stare at the guy. She moved to the top of the stairs where she could see the front door below, while still keeping an eye on the open bedroom door just a few feet down the hall. "So much for a smooth first day on this project," she muttered under her breath.

The man didn't emerge from the room, which was almost more unnerving than if he'd tried to flee, especially with the police coming. Either he was completely delusional and truly thought he owned the place, or he was the most confident squatter in Indiana history.

Within ten minutes, a police cruiser pulled up outside. Candy hurried downstairs to meet Officer Wayne, a clean-cut man in his mid-thirties, and a familiar face to most of the Autumn Lake locals.

"Hey, Bobby," Candy greeted him, holding the door open. She said goodbye to the dispatcher on the phone and hung up. "He's upstairs. Unless he's crawled out a window. I have no clue how he even got in."

The officer eyed the hammer she still clutched in one hand.

"Oh," Candy said, flushing under his questioning gaze. "Yeah. Effective, don't you think?" She shoved the thing back into her toolbelt like she was holstering a gun.

"Why are you still in the house?" Bobby asked, scanning the large open floor plan beyond her. "Why didn't you wait in your car for me?"

Candy drew herself up, trying to look a little taller. "I didn't think he was dangerous."

"And you could tell that by looking?" Bobby frowned. "Was he armed?"

"He was sleeping," she shot back, not appreciating what sounded to her like a condescending tone.

"I know a lot of guys who sleep with their weapons."

Candy took a steadying breath. She would not fight with Bobby Wayne. Not today. She had a renovation to tackle, and the sooner she could get both men out of the house, the better. She'd put herself on a strict schedule, having already posted her open house weekend online and in the local Courier newspaper, and this was not the kind of delay she'd accounted for.

Instead, she waved a hand toward the staircase. "Will you please go deal with him? I'm not the one trespassing. I'm supposed to be here, remember?"

Bobby was a good cop. He was a good guy in general. Candy knew he wasn't belittling her, that she was just being defensive, and so she conceded a little ground to him. "I'll wait down here."

Bobby nodded, grim-faced. "Good idea. I'll go take a look."

"Holler if you need me," she added, as he started up the stairs.

Bobby shot her a long-suffering glare over his shoulder, and Candy fluttered her fingers at him, grimacing in acknowledgement that maybe that might have been a little much.

2

Jonathan

"HELLO? POLICE OFFICER COMING UP."

Jonathan had just finished lacing up his boots when he heard the deliberately friendly voice of the officer coming up the stairs. He pushed up from the edge of the mattress, his head pounding. Not only had he not gotten nearly enough sleep, but he hadn't eaten since noon the day before, and with his current metabolism, he was pretty sure his stomach would start cannibalizing itself if he didn't feed it something soon. He snatched up the house key he'd found under the flower pot at the back door, just as instructed, and stepped into the hall, half-marveling at the absurdity of the situation he found himself in.

He raised both hands when he saw the muscle-bound officer waiting for him at the top of the stairs. "I'm Jonathan Burkhardt," he said, his voice scratchy. Great. Was he getting sick, too? "My aunt, Maeve Lewis, owns this house. I am here at her invitation." He held out the key as if that might explain everything.

The officer nodded in greeting but kept a respectful distance. "I'm Officer Bobby Wayne. You can put your hands down. Mind if I see some ID?" His hand rested casually near his holster, but his tone was conversational.

From the bottom of the stairs, the blonde woman's voice rang out.

"Your aunt? That's a crock. Maeve never said a thing to me about you."

Jonathan looked past the officer to the woman at the foot of the stairs. She might not be much more than five feet and a couple of inches, but there was nothing fragile about her, he decided. The fiery determination on her face matched the defiant stance she'd taken. She was cute, too, and that only irritated him more.

"I've got this, Candy," Officer Wayne called back, his eyes never leaving Jonathan. "Maybe you could wait outside?"

Candy? The name fit her with an irony that wasn't lost on him. Sweet on the outside, but really bad for your health.

"Not a chance," the woman shot back, crossing her arms over her chest.

The officer, still locking gazes with Jonathan, grinned at the woman's impudence, and for the first time since the blond whirlwind had swept into his bedroom, he thought he might get out of this situation unscathed. Maybe he could even go back to bed. Although now that he was fully awake on his feet, he doubted his stomach would let him do so without a meal. He hoped there was a good diner in town.

"ID?" Officer Wayne repeated.

"It's in my wallet," Jonathan said, gesturing over his shoulder. "In my backpack by the bed."

Officer Bobby nodded. "Mind if I take a look?"

Jonathan stepped aside. "Go ahead."

The officer entered the room and located the backpack.

"Side pocket," Jonathan told him, then added, "And no, there are no weapons or sharps or anything else illegal in there."

"Well, well," Candy said scathingly from below, plenty loud enough for him to hear. "Someone's been searched before."

Jonathan shot her a look, taking in her petite frame—she couldn't be more than five-two—and the tool belt slung low on her hips. She looked like she should be selling cookies door-to-door, not swinging that hammer notched into her belt.

Officer Wayne carefully extracted Jonathan's wallet. He examined the driver's license and compared it to Jonathan's face. "Your last name is Burkhardt. How are you related to Ms. Lewis?"

"My dad is—was her brother. I'm her nephew." Jonathan moved to stand against the rail, turning his back to Candy. Sure, he knew it was a little rude, but she'd called the police on him, for crying out loud.

"Maeve never said anything about a nephew," the woman called up the stairs, and then she started up, herself. "If she knew you were coming, she would have told me."

Officer Wayne moved to stand on the top step, essentially blocking her from joining them. "I told you to wait downstairs, Candy."

"I know, but he's obviously lying," she said, gesturing wildly at him.

Officer Wayne sighed. Turning to Jonathan, he said, "Can you please give me a few more details about why you're here, Mr. Burkhardt? Let's start with this invitation you mentioned."

Jonathan shoved the housekey into his pants pocket and ran his fingers through his hair, pulling it back from his face. He tugged a rubber band from his wrist and wrapped it around the tangled mess. He knew it wouldn't be pretty, but at least it would be out of his eyes. Candy's eyes widened as she watched him, but he looked away before he saw the inevitable transition in her expression. Pulling his hair back also showed off the jagged scar that ran from his left eyebrow over his cheekbone, ending at the misshapen remains of his earlobe. Most people went from surprise to pity to pretending not to have noticed, which was worse than if they'd pointed and laughed.

Candy pointed, but at least she didn't laugh. "My goodness. What happened to you?"

He shook his head. Really? "None of your business," he shot back.

"Candy, am I going to have to call in backup to remove you from the scene?" The officer was only half-joking, Jonathan thought.

"Remove me?" she all but gasped, pressing a hand to sternum. She'd somehow managed to maneuver herself around the big cop and was standing on the landing with them. "I'm not the trespasser, remember?"

Jonathan had had enough. "Listen, lady. I don't know who you are or what you're doing in my aunt's house, but I am tired and hungry and I need a cup of coffee, and then I'd like to come back here to and empty house, the rooms echoing with nothing but peace and quiet."

Candy's mouth dropped open and Officer Wayne shot Jonathan a warning look. "Hooey, buddy. You're playing with fire on multiple counts. I can vouch for Ms. Needham being here. It's you I'm not so sure of."

Jonathan pointed at the backpack at the officer's feet. "Can I get my phone? I'll call my aunt right now."

"I can call her, too," Candy declared, holding up her phone, but Officer Wayne stepped in front of her again.

"Candy, please." He was serious, his tone firm. "You called me to come deal with this, remember? I need you to let me do my job."

"You can turn off the camera, too, Miss Toolbelt," Jonathan snapped, his patience wearing thin. "We adults will take it from here."

She blanched at his dismissal and leaned sideways so she could glare at him. "My camera isn't on, Squatch," she retorted before Bobby blocked her view again. That didn't stop her from adding, "Besides, you don't deserve air time with my fans."

Fans? Jonathan almost laughed. She had fans? For what—wielding a hammer and harassing exhausted hikers?

"Mr. Burkhardt," Bobby said in a voice that meant business. "As I've already said, Miss Needham has business here. She has permits; I've seen them. So, why don't you get Mrs. Lewis on the phone right now. I'd call her from mine, but I don't want her worrying if she sees an ALPD phone number pop up on her screen." He narrowed his eyes at Candy when she opened her mouth to speak, and the woman—for once—wisely didn't speak. "Right now, you're here on your word alone, which isn't saying much since I don't know you from a hole in the wall, but I'm quite familiar with Candy." He handed Jonathan his backpack.

Quite familiar? What on earth did that mean? Were these two dating? Jonathan wasn't sure he liked the way that notion made him feel. But then, again, nothing really felt good right now.

Candy, apparently deciding she'd been exonerated, shot him a triumphant look.

He felt a surge of irritation, both at her smugness and at himself for noticing her at all. He dug out his phone and found Maeve's number in his contacts. He dialed, then held the phone out to the officer. "It's ringing. You want to talk to her, or shall I?"

The officer took the phone and stepped toward the bedroom door for some privacy. He pointed at each of them in turn. "Can you two behave long enough for me to take this?"

Jonathan lowered himself to sit on the floor, too exhausted to remain standing any longer. He rested his arms on his knees and lowered his head to his forearms. The last three months had pushed his body to its limits, and yesterday's long drive from Atlanta had drained what little energy he had left. He hadn't even bothered with dinner, just collapsed onto the first bed he found.

He caught fragments of the conversation. "Yes, ma'am... Claims to be your nephew... About six foot, full beard..." The officer was describing him to her. Jonathan sighed in frustration, but didn't try to interject. He could feel Candy's eyes practically boring into him, but when he lifted his head briefly to glance at her, she was thumbing something into her phone. Nice. Telling her *fans* all about him, no doubt.

"All right. Sure thing, ma'am. Bye now."

When the phone call ended, Jonathan quickly got to his feet, then had to grip the banister to keep from falling over when he got lightheaded from the sudden movement. Hopefully, this whole ordeal could be wrapped up now, and that crazy woman standing on the top stair practically boring holes into him with her glare would take her toolbelt and get out.

Officer Wayne's voice brought him back to attention. "Mrs. Lewis is on her way. She hasn't exactly confirmed your identity, but she did say she'd sent *someone* an invitation. She'd like to talk to you in person, make sure you're who you say you are, since she never heard back from her nephew."

Jonathan wanted to punch something, but objectively, he understood. He and his aunt had never met in person, and there were all kinds of scams carried out against the vulnerable elderly. And even if she had seen photos of him, she certainly wouldn't know him based on the description the officer had given her. The Jonathan Burkhardt Maeve Lewis was probably expecting didn't do beards and wild hair. He didn't do tattered clothes and ratty hiking boots. That Jonathan Burkhardt had his hair trimmed every three weeks. That Jonathan couldn't remember the last time he'd had more than a five-o'clock shadow, and he rarely left the house in anything but his tailored suits and dress shoes. The Jonathan Burkhardt that Officer Wayne had described to Maeve Lewis likely had her very concerned indeed.

"You look like you've had a rough couple of nights," Officer Wayne observed not unkindly, handing him the phone back. It was like he'd been tracking Jonathan's thoughts.

"Rough couple of months," Jonathan clarified. "Right now, I just need some coffee."

The officer nodded. "Mrs. Lewis should be here in about fifteen minutes. In the meantime, why don't we head downstairs? I could use a cup, too." Turning to Candy, he asked, "Got any coffee you can whip up for all of us?"

Candy's eyes widened, clearly affronted. "Excuse me? You want this little lady—" She paused pointedly and narrowed her eyes at Jonathan, to whip you boys up some coffee? Is that what you're asking, Bobby Wayne?"

Officer Wayne closed his eyes, and Jonathan had to turn away so neither of them would see the smile he couldn't bite back.

"I meant that as a collective 'us,'" the policeman said, the muscles in his jaw twitching. "If you show me where things are, I can make *us* a pot of coffee. It may not taste like it came from Juno's, but it'll put a little kick in this guy's keester."

Candy seemed not to know how to respond to his offer, and she turned on her designer boot heel and marched toward the kitchen. "Are you coming?" she called, but she didn't deign to look over her shoulder at them.

Officer Wayne and Jonathan exchanged a wary look and followed at a safe distance behind her.

Miss Toolbelt refused to let the officer touch her fancy French press after he admitted to never using one, so while she brewed fresh-ground coffee, the two men took seats at the vintage gold Formica and chrome table.

"So, tell me how it is that you ended up in Autumn Lake," Officer Wayne said, sounding friendly and casual, like they were two old acquaintances catching up. Jonathan wasn't fooled; he knew the man was probing for information. "Mrs. Lewis said she sent out that invitation last April."

But he had nothing to hide, either. "I've been hiking the Appalachian Trail since May. I had a neighbor hold my mail for me, and I just got back last week. I only read Aunt Maeve's letter a few days ago." Her name, particularly combined with the familial label of 'aunt,' felt almost like speaking in another language. His father had never referred to the woman as anything but Maeve, and he rarely even acknowledged that he had a sister at all. But he felt compelled to stake his kinship to Maeve Lewis sitting across from these two. They were clearly ready to judge him harshly.

Or protect someone they cared about, he reluctantly admitted to himself.

Candy studied him from across the room. It was obvious that she wasn't sure if she should believe him or not. "Why didn't you call her to let her know you were coming?" She crossed her arms. "I mean, obviously, you didn't, or she would have told me to expect you."

"Mrs. Lewis was not expecting you," Officer Wayne confirmed.

Jonathan nodded. "I had a lot on my plate when I got back from the AT. I hadn't realized it was a limited time offer. In her letter, she'd written that the place was no longer able to be rented out and was now just sitting empty. She made it sound like on open-ended invitation, and since we'd never met, I thought it might be a good idea to come speak to her in person." He cleared his throat. "This was where my father grew up, and I want to know what she intends to do with it."

"So, you came to introduce yourself to your long-lost aunt looking like a—like a—" Candy flapped her hand up and down at him, evidently taking offense in his appearance. Not that he blamed her. He knew what he looked like. He'd taken one look in the bathroom mirror last night and turned off the light so he wouldn't have to see the dark circles under his eyes, or the sunken hollows of his cheeks, the way his collarbones protruded from the stretched-out collar of his t-shirt.

"Like a bum? A dirty squatter?" he suggested. "A good-for-nothing-"

"Yes," Candy interrupted him with a sharp dip of her chin. A timer went off on her phone and she began to slowly press down the plunger on the coffee press. "Exactly like that. I mean, Maeve is a classy dame, Mr. Burkhardt." She made it sound like Maeve's status in life should directly determine his own.

"Well, that's nice for her," Jonathan shot back, kind of liking the way she said 'Mr. Burkhardt.' It made him think of the way Keira Knightley as Elizabeth Bennett said 'Mr. Darcy' in *Pride and Prejudice*, one of the movies that he'd been required to watch for a film class he'd taken as an elective in college. Not a movie he'd brag to his friends about enjoying, but he'd watched it twice in twenty-four hours, so enraptured he'd been by the cinematography, the music, the acting, and the effervescent Ms. Knightley.

Sometimes he longed for the rules and expectations that dictated Elizabeth Bennet and Mr. Darcy's conduct and interaction. How was anyone supposed to know how to behave toward each other these days?

Candy set a cup of coffee down in front of him, the dark liquid sloshing a little as she did. "Hope you like it black and strong. I don't have any cream or sugar." She gave him a challenging look, like she thought he might balk at that, but before he could explain that he'd been without any but the most basic necessities for the last several months, she'd turned her attention to the police officer. She was still glaring, though.

"I can't believe you're making me serve coffee to a criminal."

If the coffee didn't smell so good, if he wasn't practically salivating for that first sip, is his body wasn't anxiously awaiting that first jolt of caffeine to hit his bloodstream, Jonathan might have poured the cup down the sink, just to spite her. Instead, he made a show of taking a sip of the dark brew, his eyes closing in ecstasy—it really was a heavenly elixir—sighed with pleasure, and then opened his eyes to find her watching him.

A kind word turns away wrath. He could hear his father's steadying voice in his head. *Be grateful. Be kind, Jon.*

The expression didn't come easy, but he smiled and said, "Thank you, Ms. Needham. This is an excellent cup of coffee."

Kill her with kindness; that's what he'd do.

Officer Wayne shook his head slowly, almost like he'd figured out exactly what Jonathan was thinking.

"I have Maeve's letter," he added after he took another sip. He glanced back and forth between Candy, who still stood, and the officer sitting across the table from him. "It's out in my car if you'd like me to get it."

"And where is this car of yours?" Candy drilled, her arms crossed again. She hadn't made a mug for herself, he noted. Then again, she was already way too amped up. "I didn't see any car out front."

Did he have to answer her? The officer didn't speak, but he looked at Jonathan with his brows raised, obviously waiting for a response.

"It's parked in the garage."

Candy smirked. "So that no one would know you were trespassing?"

Jonathan took another sip of coffee and willed himself to remain calm. "So no one would decide to take it for a joyride while I was passed out upstairs." To the officer, he added, "My dad's '67 GTO."

His eyes widened in appreciation and he let out a low whistle.

"Original inside and out," Jonathan added, knowing his next words were going to rile the not-so-sweet Candy up even more than she already was. "Wanna take a look?"

"You have got to be kidding, Bobby," Candy declared when the officer scooted back his chair. "He's going to take you out to the garage and strangle you or something."

Jonathan couldn't help it. He let out a guffaw, his laugh also sounding foreign to him. "Now I'm a strangler, too?"

"Come on, Candy," Bobby said, cajolingly. "We're just waiting around, anyway. You can come, too."

"I have work to do, remember? In fact, why don't you boys run off and do your thing. I'm going to get my day started, so that when Maeve shows up, I'll have something to show for the time I've been here." She lifted both hands in a shooing gesture. "And if that man does something vile to you out there, don't call for my help. I'm putting my headphones on so I won't be able to hear you scream." And with that, she turned and marched out of the room.

3
Candy

CANDY STOOD IN THE hallway bathroom, snapping some 'Before' pictures on her phone, but really just trying to get her breathing under control. The morning had gone from excitement to disaster in the space of an hour, and she wasn't sure if she should pack up and leave or stick around to see what Maeve had to say.

She ran her fingers along the edges of the vintage porcelain sink, studying the way the four-inch pale yellow tiles surrounding it were cracking, the once-white mortar stained and crumbling. In any other circumstance, she'd be thrilled at the prospect of revealing what might be hiding beneath—maybe beautiful hexagon tiles from the 1920s, or even original hardwood. But now she hesitated, not wanting to start demolition until she got the official go-ahead from Maeve.

It was looking more and more like Jonathan Burkhardt was, indeed, who he said he was. The fact that he wasn't trying to come up with some excuse to hit the road now that Maeve was on her way over to identify him sure bent things in his favor. And if what he was saying turned out to be true, if Maeve was going to give him the house, then Candy might find herself without a job, or worse, sued for property damage if she started ripping things out without permission. The last thing she needed was another scandal attached to her name.

"This was supposed to be my fresh start," she whispered to herself, taking a photo of the cracked mirror above the sink.

Hearth & Home Renovations had been born from the ashes of her television career, and this project on Hollyhock Hill was meant to be its crowning achievement. She'd poured everything into this opportunity—her finances, her professional reputation, and the fragile remnants of her self-confidence.

Candy had worked so hard to rebuild after the TV disaster. She'd gotten her contractor's license and spent eighteen months taking on smaller jobs to build a portfolio of legitimate work. But people still saw her as that perky blonde from 'Drills and Thrills,' even when she showed up with proper permits and professional tools.

This lakeside renovation was supposed to change all that. A complete overhaul of a classic home with good bones, documented from start to finish, followed by a three-day open house event that was being marketed across the tri-state regions; this would show everyone what she could really do. Was all of this going to be pulled out from under her now?

The sound of a car pulling into the driveway shook her from her thoughts. Maeve had arrived. Candy tucked her phone into her back pocket and took a deep breath.

She stepped out of the bathroom just as the front door opened. Maeve Lewis stood in the doorway, her normally composed face looking flushed and anxious. The woman's silver bob gleamed in the morning light, and even in her distress, she looked elegant in her pale blue sweater set and perfectly tailored slacks.

"Candy!" Maeve exclaimed, obviously relieved to see a familiar face. "I am so sorry about all this confusion. I had no idea."

"It's okay," Candy said quickly, noticing that Maeve's hands were shaking. The morning had clearly rattled Maeve, and Candy felt a rush of protectiveness. She guided the older woman into the kitchen where she could sit down. "Let me get you a cup of coffee. I just made some."

Maeve sat in one of the chairs at the table and pressed her palms to her cheeks. "I'm completely discombobulated, Candy. I never imagined..." Her words trailed off as the door from the garage opened abruptly. Officer Wayne entered the kitchen, followed by Jonathan Burkhardt.

Candy glanced up from the mug she was filling, noting the change in Maeve's posture. She'd started to rise when the door opened, but upon seeing Jonathan, she sank back down, her face draining of color.

"Maeve?" Candy asked, concerned by the woman's reaction. She hurried to her side and put a protective hand on Maeve's shoulder.

Jonathan stood awkwardly in the doorway, his tall frame filling the space. Despite her irritation with him, Candy couldn't help noticing the discomfort etched on his face. For someone claiming to be reconnecting with family, he looked like he'd rather be anywhere else.

"Oh my," Maeve whispered, her eyes fixed on Jonathan's face. Her voice shook as she added, "You look just like Troy."

The name hung in the air between them, and Jonathan shifted his weight, but didn't come into the room. Candy felt like an intruder in a private moment, and she glanced over at Bobby to see a similar expression on his face.

What was happening here? Candy had expected a joyful reunion, or at least some kind of connection between aunt and nephew. Instead, the two regarded each other with caution, as if each were afraid the other might implode with the wrong word.

"Mrs. Lewis," Officer Wayne broke the silence. "This is Jonathan Burkhardt. He's who he says he is, I presume?"

Maeve nodded slowly, still staring at Jonathan. It was apparent to anyone watching that she recognized him. "Yes, this is Troy's son." Her voice had a slight tremor that Candy had never heard before.

"So, he *is* your nephew?" Candy had still been holding onto hope that he'd been lying.

"Yes," Maeve confirmed, finally tearing her eyes away from Jonathan to look at Candy. "I wrote to him several months ago about the house, just like he said, that I was going to sell it unless he thought he might be interested in it." She turned back to Jonathan. "When I never heard from you, I assumed you weren't—that you didn't want—" She broke off, her emotions overwhelming her for a moment.

Jonathan finally approached the table and slid an envelope toward Maeve. From beside the older woman, Candy leaned forward so she could read it, but she recognized the elegant handwriting immediately. Indeed, the letter was addressed to Jonathan Burkhardt in Atlanta, Georgia, and Maeve Lewis' name and address were in the upper left-hand corner.

"That's why I accepted your offer, Candy," Maeve continued, reaching out to touch the envelope with the tip of one finger. She didn't pick it up.

Candy was beginning to feel a little lightheaded. Well, not really, but she thought she should be with the speed her thoughts were zipping around inside her skull. Even so, she pulled out a chair and dropped into it, just in case her knees decided to start wobbling. "I see." Why hadn't Maeve ever told her this? That there might be the possibility of some long-lost family member showing up to claim his rights to the place? That bit of information might have been useful.

Jonathan nodded. "I'm sorry. I should have called first." He tugged on his beard, his brow furrowed. "I didn't read your letter until just a few days ago. I've been traveling," he said, his voice softer than Candy had heard it before. He cleared his throat and started again. "I was hiking the Appalachian Trail." He stopped talking abruptly, almost like he thought he might be admitting too much.

Maeve squared her shoulders and smiled weakly up at him. "I did tell you there wasn't any rush for you to make a decision, that the house needed work before I could sell it." She gestured at Candy. "But when I didn't hear back from you after several months, I accepted Candy's offer."

When Jonathan didn't immediately respond, Maeve asked, "You hiked the entire trail?" There was a note of something in Maeve's voice—pride, perhaps, or wonder.

"I did." He hooked his thumbs in his pockets, his eyes locked on the letter rather than meeting Maeve's. It appeared he wasn't comfortable talking about the trail. He changed the subject. "When I read your letter, I thought it would be better to come speak with you in person rather than just call and say yes to something that my dad said 'no' to."

Maeve blanched at his words, and Candy stiffened at his tone. She was still perturbed at Jonathan on her own account, even thought she'd been wrong about him. Bobby stepped closer, his frown showing that he'd heard it, too. She couldn't contain herself. "Hey, now. You might be here by invitation," she said, using Jonathan's own words. "But if I'm understanding correctly, this is still your aunt's house. You'd better be careful how you talk to her."

Maeve put a hand on Candy's arm. "It's okay, sweetie. He doesn't know what kind of person I am, not like you do."

"And we don't know what kind of person he is," Candy shot back, although she kept her voice calm so as not to upset Maeve further. "Except that I'm starting to find out." To Jonathan, she added, "Maybe your dad should teach you how to respect your elders, Mr. Burkhardt."

The kitchen fell silent. Maeve pressed a hand to her mouth, and Jonathan's face hardened into an expressionless mask as he stared a hole in Candy's forehead.

Uh-oh. She had no idea what she'd just done, but somehow, in her vehemence, she'd just stuck her new leather work boot in it.

"My father died in May," Jonathan said finally, his voice flat. "Which is why we're all gathered here today."

The weight of his words settled over the room, and Candy felt her cheeks burn with shame. She'd been so wrapped up in her own plans, she hadn't bothered to consider that the house might represent something more than a renovation project to Maeve. This wasn't just a rental property the older woman was unloading; this was her family home, one she was letting go of after losing her brother.

And Jonathan wasn't just some random intruder, or even just a long-lost nephew come to visit. He was a grieving son, sleeping in what might even have been his father's childhood bedroom.

Candy turned to Maeve, mortified by her own behavior. She took the woman's hand in both of hers and squeezed. Maeve was already shaking her head, dismissing Candy's apology, but she had to say something anyway.

"I am so sorry," she said, looking first at Maeve, then up at Jonathan. "I had no idea. I've made a lot of assumptions, and I—I'm sorry for your loss, both of you."

"None of this is your fault, dear," Maeve assured her, squeezing back. "There's no need to apologize. You've done nothing wrong."

"Except for the part where you threatened me with a hammer," Jonathan added dryly. Coming from anyone else, Candy might have thought he was joking, but the look on his face told her in no uncertain terms that he was dead serious.

To Candy's surprise, Maeve turned to look at her with newfound respect. "You did what?"

Before Candy could respond, Bobby's radio crackled and a staticky voice said something unintelligible. It was turned way down, but Bobby listened, waited, frowned.

"I need to take this," he said. He turned to Jonathan. "Listen, Mr. Burkhardt."

"Jonathan. Or Jon."

Bobby stepped forward to pull out another chair at the table. "Okay, Jon. Will you do me a favor and take a seat? It might be better for all parties involved if everyone is at least in a posture of communication." He wasn't smiling anymore, and Candy saw Jonathan stiffen at the tone of reprimand in Bobby's voice. "Invitations aren't binding agreements and can be rescinded at any time. You are here because of the good graces of Mrs. Lewis, and if she wants you to leave, that's her prerogative."

"Of course," Jonathan said, lowering himself into the proffered chair but keeping his back ramrod straight. Candy got a cheap thrill out of watching Bobby giving the newcomer his comeuppance. She shouldn't, she knew, but it was true all the same.

"How are you ladies feeling about this situation?" The officer looked between Maeve and Candy. "Would you rather I stay or are you comfortable with me leaving? I can always come back and check on things a little later, too."

"We'll be fine," Maeve said, waving a hand at him. "Thank you, Bobby. You've been very helpful. Please don't let us keep you."

might want to remember that you are here to get something, so it might behoove you to show a little humility."

He motioned for Candy to follow him outside. "Walk out with me?"

On the porch, Bobby lowered his voice. "I don't feel great about leaving yet, but I've got a fender bender across town I need to handle."

"I was just thinking I should probably go too," Candy admitted. "Let them have some time to catch up. I feel terrible about his dad. Her brother." She grimaced. "Why didn't you kick me out of the house the moment you walked in, Bobby? Me and my big mouth."

He chuckled. "Like you would have gone without a fight? I did suggest it; remember? And you said—"

"Not a chance. Yes, I remember." Candy nodded, put out with herself, but also not exactly sorry. "Well, you needed backup."

Bobby snorted, but then grew serious. "Speaking of backup, it's up to you, Candy, but I'd feel better if you stayed with Maeve until things are completely sorted. This is obviously a family matter, and since there isn't really even a dispute, there's not much more I can do, at least as far as the law is concerned, other than play referee if things take a turn. The guy seems pretty chill, but there's clearly some bad blood there. Maybe not between the two of them, but something happened to keep them apart all these years. Atlanta is less than a day's drive away, so it's not like they were living on opposites sides of the world." His radio crackled again. "I'd feel better knowing she wasn't alone with him, nephew or not."

Candy glanced back at the house. "You think he's okay with me staying?"

"You going to threaten to assault him again?"

Candy patted her hammer. "Absolutely. But only if provoked."

Bobby shook his head. "Look. You're a good judge of character." He said it like he believed in her, even after this morning's misjudgment. Although, she had decided Jonathan wasn't actually that scary by the time Bobby arrived, hadn't she? "Just keep an eye on things until they sort things out. I can stick around if you need me to, but..."

"No, go ahead," she assured him, but knots of trepidation tightened in her belly. She had the feeling that once she headed back inside, things were going to change for her all over again. "I'll stay," she told him, putting on a brave face.

After Bobby drove away, Candy couldn't bring herself to go back inside right away. Her car wasn't locked and she climbed in, staring up at the lovely old home. This place needed her. She needed this place. They both needed the transformation that she'd so carefully mapped out.

Tears welled up unexpectedly as the reality of the situation sank in. If Jonathan took the house, her dream project would be over before it began. The months of planning, the materials already ordered, the marketing she'd already done—all of it potentially for nothing.

She wasn't just grieving the loss of a project; she was grieving the loss of what it represented. A chance to prove herself. A chance to be taken seriously. A chance to finally put the past behind her and move forward with a business of her own making.

And what hurt even more than the professional setback was the personal loss. In her mind, she'd already started to see herself living here, had imagined her furniture in these rooms, pictured herself drinking coffee on that deck overlooking the lake. It was a pipedream, perhaps, but she'd been nursing that secret hope that once the renovation showcased the home's true potential, and offers for more jobs like it came pouring in, she'd be in a position to make an offer. Now that dream seemed to be slipping through her fingers before she'd even had a chance to reach for it.

Candy wiped her eyes with the back of her hand. She'd bounce back. She always did. But right now, sitting alone in her car with the weight of disappointment pressing down on her chest, it was hard to remember that.

4
Jonathan

JONATHAN SAT AT THE kitchen table, staring into his now-empty coffee mug. The haphazard reunion with his aunt wasn't going at all how he'd pictured it. Not that he'd had much of a picture in his mind; his father had said very little about his older sister, other than that they'd exchanged terrible words back before Jonathan was born, and there was no coming back from them. His father had talked about his childhood, about the lake town where he'd spent many happy years, but once he'd left home, it had been with the intent to never return. The few conversations about what had happened had been terse, clipped affairs that had left Jonathan with more questions than answers.

The silence between him and his aunt now was palpable. He looked up briefly, wondering if Maeve was waiting for Candy to return. The blonde spitfire had excused herself with Officer Wayne nearly fifteen minutes ago, and Jonathan was starting to think she might not come back. He wouldn't blame her if she didn't.

His stomach rumbled loudly in the quiet kitchen, reminding him that caffeine alone wasn't enough to keep his body running. Jonathan had grown accustomed to the constant hunger on the trail, the hollow feeling that never quite went away no matter how many MREs or protein bars he consumed. Now, after months of pushing his body to extremes, it wasn't just sleep he couldn't get enough of, but food, too. He was always hungry.

He was tempted to look in the refrigerator to see if Candy had stocked it with anything to eat, but he knew that would just cause more trouble. He wished he'd thought to check last night when he'd stumbled into the place; his conscience would have bothered him, but he'd have been happy to replace whatever he took. Now, after their confrontation, he was a little afraid to go near anything that belonged to Miss Toolbelt.

And that had nothing at all to do with the way her big blue eyes had flashed when she'd brandished that hammer, or the pretty flush that had crept up her neck when she'd realized she'd put her foot in her mouth about his father. It had nothing to do with how her smile, brief as it was, lit up her entire face when spoke with Maeve or Bobby.

She had yet to smile at him. *Yeah, and you have yet to give her a reason to,* came his father's voice in his head again.

At the thought, Jonathan pushed back his chair and stood up, hoping there might be enough coffee left for another cup, even though he knew he should probably wait for food. As he passed the window, he halted. Candy sat in the passenger seat of her car, staring up at the house. She looked like she was... crying.

He closed his eyes and tried to put himself in her shoes. It must really have been a shock to come in here and find a strange guy crashed in one of the bedrooms. She'd been stupidly brave, he had to admit. And now she was sitting out there alone, clearly upset, probably because she thought her renovation project was about to be taken away.

"She's good, you know," Maeve said, breaking the silence. Jonathan turned to find his aunt watching him. "At what she does. Renovations."

He nodded noncommittally and made for the carafe, pouring the last quarter cup into his mug. It was cold and muddy and he grimaced.

"She's been through a lot since the fiasco over her TV show," Maeve continued, her eyes still on his face. She seemed unable to look away from him for long, and he imagined she was cataloging all the ways he resembled her brother.

"TV show?" Jonathan hadn't expected that. "Is that why she filmed me?"

Maeve's lips curved in a small smile. "Not for television. She has a popular social media account where she documents her renovations. It's how she markets her business."

"Oh." Of course she wasn't some kind of TV star; she was just a contractor with a phone.

But Maeve contradicted his thoughts. "A few years ago, Candy was the star of a DIY renovation show for two seasons," she explained, seeming glad for a neutral topic of conversation. "It ended rather abruptly under... unpleasant circumstances. She's been rebuilding her reputation ever since."

Jonathan leaned against the counter, curiosity getting the better of him. "What happened?"

"There was embezzlement going on, then the production company cut corners by using substandard materials and bypassing inspections, all to keep within budget and on schedule. When one of the renovated homes developed serious structural issues, everything came to light." Maeve shook her head. "Candy took most of the blame publicly, even though she was the host and not the one calling the shots. She was young, beautiful, personable—exactly what they wanted for the show. But she didn't have real construction expertise then."

"And now she does?" Jonathan couldn't hide his skepticism.

"Oh yes," Maeve nodded firmly. "She went back to school, got her contractor's license. She's been taking on projects around the area for over a year now, building a legitimate portfolio. But this place is her first top-to-bottom renovation. She's doing the work at cost, Jonathan. I'm getting quite a bargain out of her, which means, if you are interested in this place, you will, too."

Hm. It didn't sound like Miss Toolbelt was going anywhere anytime soon.

Maeve gave him a pointed look. "I'm afraid your arrival has her worried."

Jonathan glanced out the window again. Candy was still in her car, her head now resting in her hands, her fingertips pressed to her eyes. He felt a pang of something uncomfortably close to shame.

"She's just sitting out there," he said after a prolonged silence. She was starting to worry him. He glanced over at his aunt.

"I'd better go check on her." Maeve started to rise from her chair. "I'd like to work this out with both of you here."

Jonathan held up a hand to stop her. "I'll go," he said, feeling badly about how he'd treated the woman. He might have been exhausted and caught off guard, but that was no excuse for his rudeness. "I think I owe her an apology anyway."

He didn't miss Maeve's pleased nod as he left the kitchen.

Outside, the August morning sun was heating up, which meant Candy had to be sweltering inside her car. What was she doing? Jonathan approached the SUV cautiously, noting the "Hearth & Home Renovations" logo on the door. She didn't see him coming; her head was still bowed.

He knocked gently on the window, startling her so badly that she jerked upright, banging her elbow on the door panel. Her eyes were red-rimmed, mascara smudged, and she quickly swiped at her cheeks before lowering the window just enough to speak.

"What do you want?" she asked, her voice rough with emotion.

In the sunlight, the freckles across her nose gave her a youthful appearance that contrasted with her wary expression.

"Maeve would like you to come back inside," he said, feeling awkward. "She wants to talk to both of us."

Candy nodded, pulling down the visor to look at her reflection. She let out a little yelp at the sight of her smudged makeup, then rooted around in her console for a packet of wipes.

Jonathan glanced away, unsettled by how deeply he felt her embarrassment. When she spoke, he looked back at her.

"I was coming back in," she said, her pronunciation odd due to the way she was holding her mouth while she dabbed the dark smudges from around her eyes. "I'm sure you two have a lot to catch up on. I thought I'd give you a little time to discuss... you know, family stuff."

"I appreciate that," Jonathan added, surprising himself with the sincerity in his voice.

Candy studied his face for a long moment, as if searching for some sign of deception. Finally, she nodded and reached for the door handle.

As she climbed out of the car, Jonathan noticed how petite she really was. The top of her head barely reached his shoulder, yet she carried herself with a confidence that made her seem taller. She straightened her work shirt and adjusted her tool belt before looking up at him.

"I really am sorry about your dad," she said quietly.

Her directness caught him off guard. "It's okay. You didn't know."

"But I'm not apologizing about the hammer. You really freaked me out, and I was just defending myself." Then she flipped her ponytail over her shoulder and started toward the house. "Are you coming?"

Jonathan let out a snort of laughter, but he followed her nonetheless. "Defending yourself from what? A sleeping man?" Walking behind her wasn't so bad, he thought to himself as he watched her march ahead of him. There was something alluring about a woman in a pair of jeans and wearing a toolbelt. He caught up to her. "You know, most people would have just called the police and let them handle it."

An impish grin touched her lips. "Yeah, well, I'm not most people."

"I gathered that," he replied, matching her tone.

As they walked back to the house, Jonathan kept a respectful distance between them. Candy seemed to be assessing the property with every step—her gaze traveling over the stoop rail, the chipped paint around the windows, the uneven walkway stones. Her professional eye was cataloging problems and solutions, and he wondered what kind of vision she had for the place.

He'd been too tired last night to notice much about the house beyond finding a bed, but now he could see that it needed significant work. The lakeside location was stunning, but the house had suffered from years of minimal maintenance.

Inside, they found Maeve still at the kitchen table, her hands wrapped around her now-empty coffee cup. "Come sit," his aunt said to both of them, smiling warmly. "Jonathan, I called over at Juno's Coffee Bar, and she's sending breakfast." She held up a hand when he started to protest. "I heard your stomach. Let me do this for you."

"You'll find no better breakfast sandwiches in town," Candy offered in defense of Maeve as she sat down beside her. Despite her earlier tears, she'd composed herself completely, offering Maeve a reassuring smile. It was a practiced look, he thought—the smile of someone used to putting others at ease regardless of her own feelings.

"I got one for you, too," the woman told her, patting her hand. "Juno said to get you roasted pepper and asiago on ciabatta. I hope that's right."

"You didn't have to do that," Candy exclaimed. "I already had breakfast this morning."

Jonathan spoke without thinking as he dropped into his seat across from the two ladies. "A half a cup of yogurt topped with fruit and a few too many cups of coffee?"

Apparently, he'd just hit a nerve. She narrowed her eyes at him. "Um, no. I work hard, I'll have you know. Three eggs, a couple of slices of bacon, a piece of avocado toast, *and* some Greek yogurt topped with blueberries, thank you very much." She counted the items off on her fingers.

Jonathan's brows shot up. "Wow. You like your breakfasts, do you?" Ugh. That had sounded much more like a compliment in his head. He practically saw her hackles rise.

"Well, I'll donate mine to you; you clearly need it more than I do." She actually tipped her head back so she could look down her nose at him. "You need to put some meat on your bones. A good lake breeze could blow you over, if you're not careful."

Maeve cleared her throat to get their attention, and both of them straightened in their seats like reprimanded schoolchildren. "I ordered more than enough to go around," she said in a motherly tone. "Enough for both breakfast and lunch."

"Sorry, Maeve," Candy was quick to apologize, but she shot Jonathan a side-eyed glare.

He'd offended her good, and this time, it hadn't even been intentional. He'd been jealous of her breakfast, which had, in fact, made his mouth water. "Me, too," he said. He should apologize to Candy, too, but maybe he'd wait until he'd eaten something first. Talking on an empty stomach and not enough sleep wasn't doing him any favors.

"Well, I've been thinking," Maeve began, looking between them, "and I believe I have a solution that might work for everyone."

Jonathan sat back, bracing himself. A solution to what? He hadn't come here expecting to walk away with a house. He'd wanted to meet his aunt, to see the place where his father had grown up, to try to understand the family history that Troy had never shared. The house was peripheral, as far as he was concerned. He'd just needed a place to stay, having come in so late the night before, and he hadn't wanted to wake Maeve up in the the pre-dawn hours. He could only imagine how that would have gone over. Officer Bobby Wayne might have shown up with reinforcements.

"Jonathan," Maeve turned to him first. "When I wrote to you, I offered you this house because it was your father's childhood home. I thought you might want that connection to him, especially now that he's gone." Her voice wavered slightly. "That offer still stands."

Jonathan started to speak, but Maeve held up a hand.

"But," she continued, "I also made a commitment to Candy. She's going to renovate this house, and I intend to honor that agreement."

Candy's shoulders relaxed, though her expression remained guarded.

"So, here's what I propose," Maeve said. "If you're interested in the house, Jonathan, then it will be yours—after Candy has finished renovating *and* showing it."

Jonathan and Candy exchanged wary looks.

"That way," Maeve explained calmly, "Jonathan can still have the house to do with as he pleases, but he'll have much better options after Candy works her magic on it. And Candy will have her showcase project."

Jonathan frowned. "You know, I can do any repairs that need to be done." He wasn't entirely sure that was true, but he didn't want to be beholden to Candy or anyone else. "You don't need to spend the money on a renovation."

"That may be so," Maeve said diplomatically, "but it's still my house until I sign it over, and I've already contracted with Candy."

Jonathan felt a stir of frustration. This wasn't at all what he'd expected when he'd decided to drive up from Atlanta. He wasn't sure he even wanted the house—he certainly hadn't come here intending to claim it. And now his aunt was suggesting he receive it only after allowing Miss Toolbelt to transform it? And exactly how long was that supposed to take?

"There's one more thing," Maeve added, looking between them. "Since Jonathan will be the new owner, Candy, you will need to get his input on the design."

"What?" Candy's voice rose an octave.

"I'll still have final say over everything," Maeve clarified. "But you will need to have Jonathan on board with the changes. After all, he'll be the one living with them."

Jonathan caught the flicker of dismay that crossed Candy's face before she smoothed it over. Clearly, she wasn't thrilled about having to consult with him on every decision. He couldn't blame her; they'd hardly gotten off to a stellar start.

"I'm not sure I'll be living here," he felt compelled to point out. "I haven't decided—"

"Of course not," Maeve interrupted gently. "But whether you choose to live here or sell it or rent it out, you should have a say in how it's renovated."

Candy cleared her throat. "Maeve, I'm thrilled that I can still do the project, but I have some concerns about working with..." She gestured vaguely in Jonathan's direction.

"With a bum? A dirty squatter?" Jonathan raised an eyebrow.

"With someone who isn't my employee," Candy clarified, her tone professionally neutral. But he could tell she was trying very hard not to rise to the bait. "There are liability issues to consider. Safety protocols. Technical decisions."

"Jonathan won't be working for you, dear," Maeve said. "He's family. He'll be working with me." And with that, she pushed back her chair and rose. "I am going to leave you two to discuss plans over brunch, if you don't mind. I have a hair appointment at ten."

Candy pressed her lips together in a grim smile, obviously holding in whatever she'd been about to say.

Maeve added, "Will you two be okay after I'm gone? Can you manage to work things out without me here?"

"As long as she doesn't whip out her hammer," Jonathan muttered.

"Only if provoked," Candy sing-songed sarcastically as she got up, too. "I'll walk you out to your car, Maeve," she said. "I have questions about the project timeline."

5
Candy

Candy looped her arm through Maeve's as they walked to her car. The older woman seemed more frail than usual, and it worried her. The morning's revelations had clearly taken a toll.

"Are you okay to drive?" she asked as they reached the woman's silver Buick. "I could take you to your appointment."

Maeve patted her hand. "I'm fine, dear. Just a little shaken up. It's not every day your long-lost nephew shows up looking so much like your brother the last you saw him." She sighed, her eyes misting over. "It's like seeing a ghost. Although the last time I saw Troy, he was a decade younger than Jonathan."

Candy nodded, understanding a little better now why Maeve had reacted so strongly. "I can only imagine. But are you sure about this arrangement? About him being here? I mean, you don't really know him." She hesitated, then added, "I can ask him to leave, if you'd like me to. Or Bobby can come back."

"No, no, sweetie." Maeve patted her hand. "I knew his father," she said simply, as if that explained everything. She unlocked her car door but didn't open it, turning to face Candy instead. "Troy was my brother. We were very close once..." She trailed off, then shook her head. "The point is, Jonathan is Troy's son, and this house will one day be his."

"Are you sure he can be trusted? You said you'd never met him before today," Candy pointed out gently.

"I've never met him in person. You're right about that." Maeve's hands trembled, making the keys she held jangle. "But I've stalked him on social media, and somewhat followed his career. From what I can tell, he's a good son and a hard worker, and he's had a good role model in Troy. Thankfully,

Jonathan has posted a few pictures of him and his father over the years, and I've devoured every one of them." Her expression grew wistful, and in a quieter voice, she said, "I've made a photo album of father and son; perhaps one day, Jonathan will tell me more about each picture."

Candy's heart ached for her friend. "When was the last time you saw Troy? Spoke with him?"

"It's been more than thirty years, now. It was before Jonathan was born." Maeve blinked quickly, and Candy could tell she was fighting back tears. "And now it's too late to fix what broke between us."

"Oh, Maeve," Candy said, stepping forward to give her a comforting hug. "I'm so sorry."

Maeve returned the hug, then stepped back, determination straightening her spine. "But it's not too late for Jonathan. He is here for a reason, even if he doesn't fully understand it yet. I believe God brought him to Autumn Lake because this is where that boy needs to be."

Candy bit back her immediate response—'that boy' probably came for the free house—knowing it would hurt Maeve. Instead, she nodded, and said cautiously, "Well, he's a lucky guy to have you, Maeve. and I hope he doesn't try to take advantage of you."

"I don't think he will," Maeve said serenely. "He's searching for something, for answers. He's hurting, I believe. I can see it in his eyes."

What Candy had seen in his eyes was wariness and exhaustion, but she didn't say so.

"About the renovation," Candy began, anxious to establish some ground rules. "I'm happy to have Jonathan's feedback, if that's what you want."

"It is," Maeve stated, her voice gaining resolution.

Candy forged ahead, determined to not relinquish the reins of this project so easily. "But you've already approved of everything I've got planned, so I'm asking you to back me up if he starts making unreasonable demands. I've already ordered materials, hired subcontractors for the specialized work—" She broke off; the list could go on and on.

"I don't believe that he'll interfere with your vision," Maeve assured her. "I just want you to take into consideration his wants and needs since the house will eventually be his."

"And if he chooses to turn around and sell it when this is all over?" She hadn't intended to voice the question outright, but she was worried about Maeve's expectations. They didn't seem realistic to Candy.

Maeve pressed her lips together, then grabbed Candy's hand and squeezed it. "Then that will be his choice. I can't take it with me when I go, and if he doesn't want to stay here in this wonderful place, then I'm not going to stand in his way."

She couldn't help but wonder if Maeve had said something similar to Troy Burkhardt thirty years ago. She wanted to reach back in time and shake the man, to make him see how much pain his leaving would bring to his sister, to give him a glimpse of how difficult this reunion between Maeve and Jonathan was because of Troy's decision to walk away.

Candy nodded again. "Okay. And you're still good with the open house at the last weekend in September? That gives us just under eight weeks to complete everything."

"Yes, the date still stands. That also allows Jonathan time to figure out what his plans for the house will be." Maeve opened her car door but paused before getting in. "Candy, I know this isn't what you signed up for. I'm truly grateful that you're willing to adapt. This project meant so much to me already, but now that Jonathan is here? Well, it's even more important that all of this works out for everyone involved, including you, my dear."

"I'd do anything for you, Maeve. You know that." Even if her own hopes for the house were colliding with Maeve's family obligations.

When Candy's TV show had gotten flushed down the toilet, she'd come running to Autumn Lake to stay with her cousin, Liz, desperate for a safe place to hide away and lick her wounds. Candy hadn't had any knowledge of the embezzlement and subsequent cutting corners that had created the fiasco, but for a while, there had been a lot of fingers pointing at her. Even after her name was cleared and she'd received a settlement that would help her get her feet back under her, she'd still hardly been able to hold her head up in Chicago where the show was filmed, so she'd tucked her tail between her legs and run to find refuge with her cousin.

To her surprise, it wasn't just Liz who welcomed her with open arms, but a wonderful group of friends, too.

The Garden Variety Lovers Club, they called themselves, even though they didn't garden together or have any actual club activities, other than to get together and catch up on each other's lives at least once a month. They'd met the first time out at Hazel Poleman's guesthouse, which had since been converted into The Garden Gate Bed & Breakfast by Penny St. James, née Anderson, and her husband, Ward St. James. Penny moved to Autumn Lake shortly after Candy had, and she, too, had been taken in by Liz and her friends, Juno Thomas, who owned Juno's Coffee Bar and Cafe, Claire Maitland, the proprietress of The Cracked Spine Bookshop, and Addison Stewart, née Wedgewood, who now ran a lovely flower shop over on Larkspur Lane.

But it wasn't just the Garden Variety Lovers Club ladies who embraced her and made her feel like she belonged. Word got around the way it does in a small town, and soon, Candy was getting offered general repair jobs around Autumn Lake that she was more than comfortable doing. She wanted to more than just installing fans and fixing stair rails, but without any goals, she'd been floundering.

While replacing a bathtub faucet at Maeve's condo one day, the woman had asked Candy what her plans were, and she'd admitted that she didn't know, that she was still trying to find her way out from under the black cloud that had hovered over her since 'Drills and Thrills' was cancelled. It was Maeve who'd encouraged her to go back to school and get her general contractor's license, to show them all that she was bigger than what she'd left behind, that her past didn't define her. "You're so good at what you do," Maeve had told her. "I never have to worry about cleaning up after you or wondering how long the repair will last or if you're going to take advantage of a trusting old lady."

That's what she'd done, and now, here she was, having come full circle, preparing to do some of her best work on Maeve's family home.

If the woman's long-lost, gold-digger nephew didn't throw a wrench into the works and mess everything up.

Candy chewed her lip, not sure if she should say what was on her mind.

"What is it, Candy?" Maeve asked, sensing her hesitation.

Candy let out a sigh. "I've worked my tail off for this, Maeve. You know that better than most. I just hope he isn't going to make this harder than it needs to be. "

Maeve's eyes twinkled. "He might surprise you. He might actually be a help to you, if he sticks around. Troy was stubborn as a mule, but he had a good heart underneath all that bluster. I suspect Jonathan's the same."

With a final squeeze of Candy's hand, Maeve slid into her car. She rolled down her window. "The food should be here any minute. I'll give you two a chance to circle the room a little; maybe find some middle ground."

Candy snorted. "I'm just here to do my job, Maeve. He's the one who's going to have to circle the room to get around my busy backside."

Maeve chuckled. "Oh, dear. Try not to antagonize him too much." She patted Candy's cheek. "I'll drop back by this afternoon after I visit my attorney. I have a few things I need to speak to her about before I move forward with Jonathan, but it has nothing to do with what you're doing, so forge on, my dear."

"I'll be on my best behavior," Candy promised, crossing her fingers behind her back like a child.

As Maeve's car disappeared down the driveway, Candy turned back toward the house, her enthusiasm for the project warring with her dread of working with Jonathan. Could she really pull this off with him looking over her shoulder at every turn?

She took a deep, fortifying breath and let it out in a huff. The sun glinted off the lake beyond the house, and a gentle breeze scented the air with pine and fresh-cut grass from the neighboring property. It was a perfect summer day in Autumn Lake, and this was still her dream project, Jonathan Burkhardt or no.

"Lord, give me patience," she murmured, glancing heavenward. "And maybe a muzzle for that man."

She marched back to the house, refusing to let her steps drag. This was her project, her chance. Jonathan might have his name on the deed eventually, but right now, this renovation belonged to her.

Inside, she found him studying her design boards in the hallway. He looked different in the natural light streaming through the windows—still too thin, still unkempt and scruffy, but less threatening than when she'd first discovered him. She couldn't see his scar from this angle, which made him look less like a roguish intruder and more like a man who didn't quite know where he belonged.

Candy pushed those observations aside. It didn't matter what he looked like or what had happened to him. All that mattered was that he not derail her carefully laid plans.

6
Jonathan

As THE WOMEN HEADED for the door, Jonathan remained at the table, trying to process this unexpected turn of events. He hadn't woken up this morning thinking he'd be involved in a home renovation, much less one led by a pint-sized, hot-headed contractor.

Yet something about the house tugged at him. This was where his father had spent his formative years. A place Troy had left and never returned to, for reasons he'd never fully explained. If he closed his eyes, Jonathan could imagine his father pointing out the dock he'd jumped from, the lawn he'd kicked a soccer ball around on, the wide driveway where he and his friends used to shoot hoops into the basket that had once hung above the garage door. The woods where he'd hiked....

Maybe there were answers here that Jonathan couldn't find elsewhere.

Maybe he should stick around for a while.

He pulled out his phone and stared at the screen for a long moment. Then, with a sigh, he opened his email and sent a brief message to his boss in Atlanta, extending his leave a little longer. He knew he'd get flack from Mitchell, maybe even a termination threat, but he didn't really care. "Go ahead," he muttered. "Make my day." Whatever was happening here, he needed time to figure it out.

When Candy returned a few minutes later, she found him studying the design boards she had propped against the walls in the foyer. Her proposed changes were ambitious but thoughtful, preserving the character of the house while updating its functionality.

"Design concepts for each room," she said, startling him. "To show color palettes, textures, mood."

Jonathan straightened up and turned to face her. She stood with her arms crossed, her expression professional, but wary.

"They look good," he said honestly.

"Thanks." She didn't sound convinced of his sincerity. "Listen, I need to be clear about something."

Jonathan waited, bracing himself for whatever boundary she was about to establish.

She made a sweeping gesture at her plans. "I have worked very hard on all of this. Too hard for some long-lost, ne'er-do-well nephew to just show up and rip it out from under me. I'm a nice person, and I get along with everyone—and I mean, *everyone*, Mr. Burkhardt—except, apparently, you. I'd like to think for Maeve's sake that you will try to see things from my perspective, and for Maeve's sake, I will go along with her wishes and let you sign off on my designs."

Jonathan snorted. "*Let* me? And did you just call me a ne'er-do-well nephew? What are you; some kind of Victorian bricklayer?"

Candy's jaw dropped, but before she could respond, he continued.

"You know, how about you try to see things from my perspective? For Maeve's sake," he added, trying not to mock her, but failing miserably, he was certain.

"And just what exactly *is* your perspective, if not that of a long-lost, ne'er-do-well nephew here to mooch of the aunt he's never even bothered to meet?" She planted both hands on her hips and glared up at him. "Atlanta, Mr. Burkhardt? That's a leisurely seven hours' drive from here. I looked it up. You could have come up here and visited her long before now. Was your father, God bless him, keeping you a prisoner? You're not a child that you can't make decisions for yourself, regardless of what went on between him and your aunt. Weren't you at least curious about her? You clearly knew of her existence before she wrote to you."

Jonathan opened his mouth to defend himself, but his tongue seemed to have forgotten how to function.

"Do you know that she has been alone for nearly two decades since her husband died? Alone, with no family to look after her. Almost twenty years, dude. And then her only brother dies, and you still don't bother coming to see her? Nope. Where have you been? Traipsing along the

Appalachian Trail? Galivanting around the country, pursuing your own interests?" She shook her head dramatically and clucked her tongue. "But then the moment she has something to offer you, you just happen to show up, unannounced, on her doorstep, and yes, like a long-lost, ne'er-do-well nephew. Is that the perspective you want me to see things from?"

He took a step back in an effort to deflect the blast of her words. When she put it that way....

Candy kept going. "I'm sorry your father died. I really am. And I'm especially sad about it because it's obvious that there were things left unsaid and unresolved between him—and you, by association—and my dear friend, and that's heartbreaking on a whole new level."

Jonathan started to thank her, but he snapped his mouth shut again when she swept an arm out as if to encompass the house, the town, maybe the whole world. She still wasn't finished?

"I don't know why you're here. I don't know what made you decide to haul your bedraggled, sketchy—" She broke off like she couldn't think of the right word for a moment. But then she found one that seemed to work for her. "—squatty sasquatch self to Autumn Lake after all this time."

Squatty sasquatch self? Did she actually expect him to take her seriously? Jonathan would have laughed if he wasn't afraid that she might kick him with her fancy steel-toed boots.

"And honestly, I don't really want to know any more about you than I already do." She lifted a finger and shook it at him, her cheeks bright with the heat of her emotions. With a tight jaw, she wrapped up her tirade. "But if you do anything—and I mean, *anything*—to hurt or distress or worry Maeve, I will come for you." Then she slapped the hammer still hanging from her toolbelt.

Okay. That did it. Jonathan straightened and puffed out his chest, intentionally looming over the little hellcat. "Are you threatening me?" he asked in a growl that came out sounding a little more intimidating than he'd intended.

To her credit, Candy didn't back down. "Oh, yes, indeed, I am, Squatch. Your aunt has a community who loves her dearly, a found family because her own deserted her. And you should know that no one in Autumn Lake is going to stand by and let you cause trouble for Maeve. Got it?"

Jonathan wanted to slap back, to unleash a torrent of ultimatums on her head, too, but he'd heard the seed of truth in her words, and it shamed him into silence. What she'd said wasn't exactly accurate. He had his reasons for not coming before. But he could see her point, the way things looked from her perspective. From the whole town's perspective, he realized ruefully.

But that didn't mean he wasn't prepared to put up at least a modicum of a fight. He did have good reason to be here, and good reason to have come when he did, and right now, he wasn't sure if it was any of Ms. Needham's business.

On top of that, his aunt had given him a leg to stand on. He moved over to the design board for the upstairs bedrooms and pointed at the room labeled 'Home Office.' "This was my father's room."

"The one you were sleeping in."

"Yep." He'd known immediately, even though the shelves were empty and the walls were bare.

His dad had told him about the wall of windows that overlooked the lake. He'd told him how he'd lie in bed at night and in the dim glow of the nightlight, make out shapes and faces in the plaster pattern on the ceiling. He'd told him about the secret compartment behind the false back of the closet. Jonathan had stared at that same ceiling last night. He'd located the dog head, the ogre's face, the alien and his space ship in the swishing patterns overhead. He'd tapped on the back wall of the closet and was certain it was, indeed, hollow, although he hadn't been able to figure out how to open it. Was it possible there was something of his father's in there? And this morning, hours before Ms. Toolbelt showed up, Jonathan had woken up, awash in the color that filled the room, making him think, for just a moment, that he was lost in space and time. It had been unsettling, and then glorious, and then gut wrenching, and he'd curled in on himself in his sleeping bag and cried like a baby before falling back to sleep.

"What about it?" Candy asked warily, crossing her arms and narrowing her eyes at him.

"It's off-limits," he said firmly.

Candy's eyes widened. "Off-limits? What does that mean?"

"It means no renovation. No changes. Leave it exactly as it is."

Anger flashed across her face. "No. That room is supposed to be the showcase office. It has the best views of the lake, the best natural light—"

"It was my father's bedroom," Jonathan repeated, cutting her off. "And it's staying just the way it is."

"But I have plans for that room. I've already bought materials," she exclaimed.

"And I get to have input, remember?" That was the whole reason they were standing here having this conversation. "And I'm not on board with any plans for that room."

He could see her struggling to maintain her professional composure. The muscles in her jaw worked as she clenched her teeth, and her fingers curled into fists at her sides. "Well. We'll be talking to Maeve about that, won't we?" she said eventually, in a tone that suggested that she intended to have her way with that room, no matter how he felt about it. "She's got final say, after all."

But until she got the go-ahead from Maeve, her hands were tied, and she knew it.

"I guess we will," Jonathan agreed, feeling both victorious and uncomfortably petty. Was he being unreasonable?

Nope. Yes. Maybe?

Okay, probably. But right now, that room was his only tangible connection to his father's childhood, and he wasn't ready to see it transformed into something unrecognizable. "And I'll be staying in here in the house." He pointed toward the stairs.

"Great. I get to start my days with Mr. Grumpy Sasquatch." Candy rolled her eyes. "I take it you'll be sleeping in the shrine, then?"

The barb hit its mark, but Jonathan kept his expression neutral. "I will."

"Fine," she said, even though everything in that single word told him nothing was fine. She gave him a huge, fake smile that didn't reach her eyes. "Do you have any thoughts you'd like to contribute to the kitchen plans?" Her tone was so syrupy sweet that it made his teeth hurt.

He pretended to think about it for a little longer than was polite, just to goad her, then gave her a noncommittal, "Not so far."

Candy let out an impatient huff. "Well, then I have work to do, so why don't you head on up to your room and see if you can get a little more beauty sleep? You look like you could use some." She dismissed him with a shooing gesture.

Jonathan shook his head. "You are a bitter little thing, aren't you?"

The doorbell rang, cutting off whatever it was that Candy started to say back to him. She turned and marched to the door, her ponytail swishing so hard he thought it might start spinning at any minute. He ran a hand over his beard, wondering what exactly he'd gotten himself into.

But for the first time since his father's death, he felt a flicker of something that wasn't grief or guilt—a sense that maybe, just maybe, he was right where he was supposed to be, that perhaps this unexpected detour was exactly what he needed right now.

He flinched when Candy jerked open the door so hard that it banged against the wall.

Or maybe this would turn out to be the biggest mistake of his life.

7
Candy

"UM... HI. DELIVERY FOR Lewis?" said the nervous teenager on the porch, holding up an enormous food delivery box emblazoned with "Juno's Coffee Bar and Cafe." Candy didn't recognize the kid as one of Juno's regular baristas or servers, so maybe he'd hired on as a part-time driver. With her new cafe open, she was doing a lot more delivery orders.

"Thank you," she said, trying to inject some warmth back into her voice. The poor delivery guy hadn't done anything wrong. "Come on in. Let me get my wallet. What's your name?"

"Gene. It's already paid for, including a delivery tip," he assured her from the stoop. "It was a good one, too," he added with a bright grin. "Tell Mrs. Lewis thanks for me."

Candy promised him she would, then closed the door without the vehemence she'd opened it with. When she turned, Jonathan was still standing in the hallway, watching her with an unreadable expression.

"Food's here," she said unnecessarily, holding up the weighty box. There had to be more than a couple of breakfast sandwiches inside.

Jonathan nodded, and his stomach growled loudly in response, breaking some of the tension between them.

Despite herself, Candy laughed. "Well, your stomach has an opinion."

A ghost of a smile touched his lips. "It's been expressing itself pretty clearly all morning. Here. Let me take that for you." He stepped forward and held out his hands for the box.

"I got it," she insisted, more out of habit than because she didn't want his help. She worked hard to not be so defensive around guys, especially those who were so much bigger than she was, but this particular male brought out the feisty in her. His words echoed in her mind. *You're a bitter little thing, aren't you?*

Jonathan raised both hands like Candy had accused him of trying something offensive, but she ignored the gesture. In spite of her enormous breakfast, she was actually hungry again. Probably all the stress this guy was causing her. She wanted to enjoy Juno's sandwich, and being angry while eating was a good way to get heartburn. "It's not that heavy," she said, but in a nicer tone. "Come on. Let's not waste your aunt's generosity."

She slid the box onto the kitchen table, pulled open the top flaps and gasped when she saw the contents. There was enough food inside to feed a whole crew. But as she started pulling things out, she realized that Maeve had done more than buy breakfast for them. She'd included in the order a whole loaf of Juno's sourdough bread, a jar of Kimber Tate's delicious plum jam, a pound of freshly ground coffee, a small carton of cream, and a whole box of various pastries. Breakfast for days.

"I can't believe that woman," she said as she slid a wrapped sandwich toward Jonathan, who had taken a seat on the other side of the table. "Actually, I can. She is generous to a fault." She shot him a warning look. "So don't take advantage—"

"Don't take advantage of her or you'll come for me," he finished for her. He sounded like he was getting tired of her threats.

Actually, so was she. She'd been a little high on adrenaline after finding him, but now she was beginning to think she just sounded like a tin can with a pebble in it. All bark and no bite. She wasn't going to do Jonathan any physical harm, not now that she knew who he was and why he was there, and certainly not with her precious hammer. The thing had cost her a fortune. But besides that, she wasn't a violent person. She rescued spiders and took them outside rather than squashing them. She used humane traps when she encountered mice or other rodents and released them into the wild. The way, far away wild, of course.

No, she was bubbly. Sparkly. Optimistic. Little Miss Sunshine, even when she didn't feel like it. Somewhere along the line, someone—okay, her mother, who was just like her—had convinced her that it was her purpose in life to make the world a brighter, happier place. Which was one of the reasons the TV show fiasco had nearly destroyed her.

But that was behind her now. She was starting new. Thanks to Maeve and her cousin and her friends and this wonderful Autumn Lake community, she had a second chance, a new lease on life.

Maybe she ought to extend an olive branch to Squatch, too. He looked kind of miserable, she had to admit.

"Would you like some more coffee with your breakfast? Juno ground my favorite Robusta beans; they're from Ethiopia." She held up the bag, the aroma making her salivate.

"Uh, sure," he said, clearly surprised by her offer. "Can I help?"

"Nah." She pointed at the cream carton as she filled the electric kettle with water. "Juno sent cream, and there's real maple syrup in the fridge."

"I thought you said there was no sugar," he said, cocking his head at her, his eyebrows raised.

"There isn't," she quipped over her shoulder as she measured out the grounds into the French press. She shot him a capricious grin. "But there *is* maple syrup."

Jonathan made a noise in the back of his throat, but Candy didn't see his expression. She suddenly felt rather vulnerable with her back to him. Was he judging her backside in these jeans? She'd thought she looked pretty cute this morning when she'd left the house....

Stop! she silently reprimanded herself. But she brought the carafe and plunger top to the table while she waited for the water to boil. She wasn't quite ready to turn her back on the enemy, even if he was supposed to be her ally.

But Jonathan wasn't looking at her. He was completely focused on the sandwich he'd started to unwrap. His nose twitched as the aromas of bacon and buttery croissant wafted up from the packaging. He swallowed hard; the poor guy was practically drooling.

Candy bit back a grin. "I figured you'd probably want the basic eggs and bacon on a croissant, but there are two of the roasted pepper and asiago, so you're welcome to try that instead."

Jonathan's eyes were wide with anticipation. "Can I have both?"

The teakettle whistled. Candy shoved the delivery box his way, then got up to get the hot water. "Have at it, big guy. She sent six sandwiches."

As they settled at the kitchen table with fresh cups of coffee, Candy was grateful for the momentary truce over the food. Even so, she couldn't help wondering what she'd gotten herself into. Working with this man for the next two months was going to be a challenge, to say the least. But the thought of abandoning the project hurt more than the prospect of dealing with Jonathan Burkhardt.

She'd faced worse obstacles in her career. She'd rebuilt her reputation after the TV disaster; she could certainly handle one stubborn, grieving nephew. And maybe there was more to him than met the eye.

The thought brought her up short. It didn't matter what was beneath Jonathan's grumpy exterior. This was a business arrangement, nothing more. She'd work with him because she had to, but she wouldn't let herself get personally invested.

She unwrapped her sandwich, the aroma of roasted peppers and melted cheese filling the kitchen. "Maeve stocked you up," she observed, noting the three containers of fruit Jonathan had taken out with the sandwiches. "So, no touching my stash. Everything in the fridge has my name on it." She swirled her name in the air, holding an invisible pen, reminding herself all too well of the thousands of signatures she'd signed as Candy Mason.

"I wasn't going to touch your stash," he grunted, although the way he dropped his gaze made her wonder if he'd at least considered it.

Candy watched as Jonathan took an enormous bite, closed his eyes, and chewed with an expression of pure bliss. For a moment, he looked younger, less burdened. When he opened his eyes and caught her staring, she quickly looked away, focusing on her own meal.

They ate in silence for several minutes before Candy spoke again. "We need to come up with a workable arrangement if we're going to get through this renovation."

Jonathan nodded, swallowing a mouthful of coffee. "Agreed."

"I start work early," she warned. "By seven AM most days, soften earlier, rarely later."

"Not a problem," he said. "I'm used to being up before dawn."

"From the trail?" she asked around a delicious bite of her own, curiosity getting the better of her.

He nodded. "Best time to hike, before the heat of the day. Before the packs start moving."

"The packs?"

"The packs of hikers. They tend to form clumps as they go along. They might split up and go at their own paces during the day, but once the sun goes down, well, there's security in numbers, in tucking in with the same familiar faces, especially at night."

"That makes sense." She gave him a questioning look. "I take it you aren't a pack kind of guy?"

Jonathan took another large bite of his sandwich at that moment, and if she had to guess, it was to give himself time to come up with a response to her question. She didn't fill the silence, but instead, waited him out. She really wanted to know, especially since they'd apparently be spending a significant amount of time together over the next coming days. Weeks, maybe, depending on how long he was staying.

He finally said, "Not on the trail, I wasn't."

She lifted an eyebrow in question, but still said nothing. After another moment, it worked.

"I didn't do the trail as a social event." Then he took another bite, holding her gaze until she looked away. Clearly, he wasn't going to say anything more about that.

She found that she wanted to ask him more, wanted to know why he'd done it, what his motivation had been. Did he always look like a hairy, scrawny caveman or did he start off cleanshaven in fancy new hiking duds? Had he been a hiker before? And what did he do when he wasn't hiking? Did he have a 'Normal-Joe' job? A butcher? A baker? A candlestick maker? What about a relationship? He wasn't wearing a ring, but then, a lot of athletes didn't wear jewelry—

Don't get distracted, she reminded herself firmly. This is about the job, not the client. And speaking of the job...

"So, I don't know how much Maeve told you about this project, but I'm documenting everything for my social media accounts," she said, returning to business. "It's how I market my services." When he just looked at her like he didn't understand what she was getting at, she added, "I just thought you should know since you're going to be hanging around. In case you have an issue with being on camera."

"Just keep me out of the shot," he said. "I'm not exactly camera material."

Candy took in his wild hair, untamed beard, and worn clothes. "No argument there," she agreed, but there was no real bite to her words.

The truce was fragile, but it was a start. She had not quite two months to transform this house, and as long as Jonathan Burkhardt stayed out of her way and signed off on her plans, they'd find a way to work together without killing each other. Candy wasn't sure which would be the bigger challenge: him staying out of her way, or finishing the job with both of them alive and breathing.

But as she bit into her sandwich, she felt a flicker of her usual optimism returning. No matter what obstacles Jonathan threw in her path, she had faith in her abilities. This project would be extraordinary, and it would launch Hearth & Home Renovations into a new level of success.

She just had to survive working with Jonathan Burkhardt first.

8
Jonathan

JONATHAN WANDERED THROUGH THE house, his curiosity finally getting the best of him. He'd poked his head into a few of the rooms late last night when he'd gotten in just after midnight, but he'd felt a little like Goldilocks at the three bears' house looking for a comfortable bed to fall into. With Candy gone for a store run now, he was taking his time, opening closets and cupboards, peering out at the view from every window, and trying to get a sense of the place where his father grew up.

He'd heard stories about this house, about the lake, Troy's favorite fishing hole, and the trails through the woods surrounding the property. Although remarkable, the place wasn't quite what he'd imagined. The way his father had made it sound, the lake house was more like a mansion, but this two-story three-bedroom home couldn't be more than 2500 square feet at the most, not counting the garage, and everything about the property had a slightly listless feel to it.

The sound of a car pulling into the driveway caught his attention. Was Candy back already? In the master bedroom, he drew back the drape and watched Maeve's silver Buick roll to a stop in the driveway below. Her silver bob gleamed in the afternoon sun as she carefully exited the car, straightened her tailored linen pants, and moved out of sight toward the front door., smoothing her hands over her pale blue slacks.

Jonathan ran his fingers through his shaggy beard, suddenly self-conscious. Maeve Lewis was the epitome of elegance—well-dressed, well-groomed, and well-mannered. And here he was, looking like he'd just wandered out of the wilderness.

"Oh wait," he muttered dryly to himself as he hurried out of the room. "I did just wander out of the wilderness."

He made it to the bottom of the stairs just as she pushed open the front door and came in. She hesitated in the foyer when she saw him.

"Jonathan." Her smile was polite but guarded. "I wanted to check in this afternoon and see if I can be of service to you."

"Hi, Maeve," he said, wondering if he was supposed to call her 'Aunt Maeve.' Candy had called her by her first name, so until the woman said otherwise, he'd follow suit.

But now what? They were in a weird standoff with him gripping the stair rail and her just inside the front door. It was her house, but he was staying here; did she offer him a drink, or the other way around?

"If you don't mind," Maeve said into the awkward silence. "I could use a glass of water. I just came from running a few errands, and I never think to bring water with me, even in this heat."

He had a hard time picturing this classy lady carrying around a plastic water bottle. She was more of a crystal stemware kind of dame. But he nodded. "Sure. I heard the icemaker rumble a little bit ago, so I'm pretty sure there's ice, too."

"Lovely," Maeve said, moving ahead of him into the kitchen, a room she was probably far more comfortable in than he was. This whole situation was so bizarre.

"Would you like one?" Maeve asked as she took two glasses from the first cupboard she opened. She didn't wait for his response, but filled both with ice and water from the refrigerator dispenser and handed him one before settling into the same chair she'd sat in that morning. Maeve took a long sip of the cold water, and Jonathan did the same. Then she put down her glass, laced her fingers together on the table in front of her, and gave him a warm smile. She seemed much more composed than she had this morning, so hopefully, she was getting used to the idea of him being here.

"I'd like to extend another invitation to you," she finally said, although if he were to guess, she wasn't a hundred percent comfortable with what she was about to offer him. "This place has been empty for months, and now that Candy's going to be working her magic on it, the state of it is probably going to get a whole lot worse before it gets better." She glanced around the room, frowning as she sized up its current condition. She squared her shoulders and said, "I have a spare room in my condo, and you're welcome to it. I thought perhaps you might be more comfortable staying there while you're in town."

From her purse, she withdrew a keyring with a bright green tag on it and slid it toward him. "This is the key to my front door."

Jonathan glanced at it but made no move to take it. He sensed the reluctance in her offer, and he didn't blame her. He might be her nephew, but she knew very little about him. "That's very kind of you," he said. "But I'd rather stay here, if that's okay." He wanted answers from her, and being in her home might be a little too close for her comfort.

"Are you sure? My guest room is quite comfortable, and this place is...." She gestured vaguely at the half-dismantled kitchen. "Well, it's a work in progress, isn't it?"

"I've gotten used to roughing it." He gave a half smile. "This is paradise compared to some of the places I've slept in the last several months."

"I can only imagine," Maeve acknowledged. "You know, your father always talked about one day hiking the Appalachian Trail."

Ouch. Did she have any clue how hard-hitting her words were? Jonathan nodded, and as casually as he could manage, said, "Yes. We always meant to hike the trail together."

Maeve leaned forward. "Oh, Jonathan. I'm sorry." He could see in her compassionate gaze that she'd picked up on the regret in his statement. Thankfully, she changed the subject. "And where is Candy this afternoon? I thought she'd still be here."

"She left about an hour ago," Jonathan said. "She had to pick up some supplies from the hardware store, I believe."

Maeve frowned. "Charlie's? I thought they delivered."

Jonathan gave her a wry look. "I kinda got the feeling she needed an excuse to get out of the house for a bit."

"Ah." Maeve nodded slowly, then met his gaze again. "I want you to feel at home here, Jonathan, truly I do." She paused, considering her next words. "But please accept and respect Candy and the job I've hired her to do. This renovation means a lot to both of us, so unless you have serious issues with her plans, I'm asking you to do your best to not get in her way."

"I understand," he said stiffly. Was she chastising him? He had been a bit of a bear this morning, after all.

"Good. Candy is a dear, but she's also a bit of a whirling dervish, and once she gets cracking on something, it's best to stand clear." Maeve gave him a conspiratorial smile. "If you know what's good for you."

"Got it." He appreciated her attempt at levity; it gave him a glimpse into the lighter side of her. His father had once said his sister had a keen sense of humor. Jonathan wanted to know who this woman was beyond the stories he'd heard about her as a young woman. He wanted to know why she and his father had gone their separate ways, what they'd fallen out over. But he couldn't just jump into the deep end of things. He could see that she was wary of him, still trying to take his measure, just as he was with her.

Still, she'd stood by her invitation to him, even in the face of the feisty Miss Toolbelt's arguments, and that spoke volumes.

"And you're sure I can't tempt you with my guest room?" Maeve asked, pressing a little harder this time. "You might appreciate a place of your own with all of the activity that's going to be happening around here."

It occurred to Jonathan that maybe his aunt was more worried about Candy's wellbeing than his if he chose to stay here during the renovation. He needed to reassure her that he had no ill intentions. "If you are okay with it, I'd like to spend some time here. Get a feel for the place. I'm staying in my dad's old room, and Candy is okay with that." Well, that wasn't exactly true, was it? "At least, for now," he added.

Maeve studied him for a long moment, her blue-gray eyes, so like his father's, searching his face. "Very well," she finally said. "But the offer stands if you change your mind."

"Thank you," Jonathan said, meaning it.

Maeve's gaze drifted toward the window and out to the lake beyond. "Troy loved this house," she said softly. "Especially in the summer. He was a regular Tom Sawyer, swimming or fishing with his friends in the lake, carving trails through the woods, or just sitting out on that deck dreaming of big adventures." She turned back to Jonathan. "I have a photo of him sitting at the end of the dock with his feet dangling over the edge, his arm around his dog, Jack, the sun almost gone. It's very Norman Rockwell," she said with a little chuckle. "It's one of my favorite snapshots of him."

Jonathan tried to picture his father as a boy, sitting out there, contemplating life. The image wouldn't fully form; it was like trying to see through murky water.

"I never could get him to wear sunscreen or bug spray," Maeve continued with a faint smile. "Even though I made him do a full body tick check every time he came in the house. Stubborn, just like our father."

Jonathan filed away these small details about the man he thought he'd known completely. It was strange to hear about him from someone who had known him in an entirely different life. Troy had been raised by his much older sister after their parents died in a car accident when he was only five. Maeve, just twenty years old and fresh out of school with her Secretarial Studies degree, was newly engaged to Stan Lewis, an engineer at a chemical plant in Evansville. Stan, according to Jonathan's father, had stubbornly refused to back out of taking on both Maeve and Troy. He'd sold his home located only minutes from his work and moved into the Burkhardt home in Autumn Lake, making the 30-minute commute to work every day. Stan and Maeve never had children of their own.

"I have some photo albums at home," Maeve continued, as if following his train of thought. "Pictures of Troy growing up. You're welcome to look through them sometime."

"I'd like that," Jonathan said, surprised to find he meant it.

Maeve took another sip, then glanced at the watch bracelet on her wrist. "I was hoping to catch Candy this afternoon, but I really must get going. I have a few more stops to make before I call it a day. I don't like to drive once the sun starts to go down." She stood, smoothing her slacks, then carrying her glass to the sink where she washed it, dried it, and returned it to the cupboard. Then she asked, "Would you like to come to supper at my home this evening?"

Jonathan's fatigue was catching up with him and he wondered if he'd offend her if he turned down her offer. She picked up on his indecision. "Why don't we plan a meal for tomorrow night, instead. It's been quite a day for all of us, and a good night's rest might be just what we all need."

"That sounds like a good plan," Jonathan agreed. "And I promise to be better company tomorrow."

"Well, then," Maeve said, slipping her purse over her arm. "I'll let you get back to... whatever you were doing."

Jonathan couldn't help wondering if all their encounters would be this stilted, this formal. Related or not, they were still strangers, connected only by a man who was no longer here to bridge the gap between them.

As Maeve's car disappeared down the driveway, Jonathan returned to the kitchen, now at a loss for how to fill his time. He could go back upstairs and take a nap, but he wasn't sure how he felt about trying to sleep while Candy worked. Besides, he wanted to make sure he'd sleep hard tonight. He rooted around the kitchen, realizing as he did so that most of the drawers and cupboards were empty. So whatever was here—the few dishes, the single shelf of protein bars and popcorn, the produce and condiments in the fridge—must all belong to Candy, stuff that she'd stocked the kitchen with in preparation for this job. He'd better make a store run soon, but the thought made his head hurt. Thankfully, his aunt had brought enough food to last well into tomorrow; he'd stop by the supermarket on his way home from dinner with Maeve.

In one drawer, he found a couple of Hearth & Home Renovations notepads and assorted colored pens. Surely, she wouldn't mind if he used some of the paper. List-making had become his life line over the last several months. Supply lists, gear lists, to-do lists—he would make a list of tasks that he could do while he was here. A list of repairs he could work on, things he could fix so that Candy didn't have to.

The stuck window in his room. The dripping shower and the loose cabinet hinge in the upstairs bathroom. Small stuff in the grand scheme of things, but it would make him feel like he was contributing rather than just taking up space.

He headed upstairs to better assess the shower problem. The bathroom was outdated but functional, with pale yellow tiles and a shower bath, the tub having seen better days. Not only did the shower head drip, but when he'd been using it the night before, he'd realized that water was also coming out of the faucet. Something needed to be tightened up or a gasket replaced, he thought, nudging the jiggly lever up and down, certain he could figure it out. That's what YouTube was for, right?

He'd need some tools of his own; he certainly wasn't going to ask to borrow any of Candy's. Maybe he'd make a run to a home improvement store tomorrow and set himself up with essentials. Some new power tools would be kinda nice, a socket set, a couple of screwdrivers, a pipe wrench. "And a big hammer of my own," he added with a snort.

As Jonathan turned to leave, he caught his reflection in the bathroom mirror and paused. His beard had grown out wild and untamed on the trail, and his hair hung almost to his shoulders in a ragged mess, not quite covering that ugly scar that he was still getting used to. He was almost gaunt, having pushed himself beyond what he'd thought possible for more than 2000 miles from Maine to Georgia. He chuckled dryly, shaking his head at the figure in the mirror. No wonder Candy had looked at him with such alarm this morning. He looked like a stranger, even to himself.

But then he straightened and flexed his bicep, pulling up his sleeve to view the sinewy definition of his muscles. "A lean, mean hiking machine," he declared. He might look like he'd just crawled out of a cave, but he'd earned it. And he certainly smelled better than a caveman. Or a sasquatch.

He pulled the rubber band from his hair and ran his fingers through it. It really was a mess, and honestly, most of the time, it drove him crazy. But if Ms. Toolbelt didn't like it? Well, maybe he'd let it grow just to give her something to be riled up about.

He slipped the hair tie back onto his wrist and shook his head like a shaggy dog, then he headed downstairs, singing softly to himself, "Let it grow, let it grow, won't tie it back anymore...."

9
Candy

CANDY PULLED INTO THE driveway of the little bungalow she shared with Liz and parked beside her cousin's pickup. She turned off the engine but didn't move, allowing herself one long, deep sigh before gathering her energy to go inside.

What a day.

When she'd left her house this morning—was it really just this morning?—she'd been brimming with excitement, ready to tackle her dream project. She certainly hadn't expected to find a big grump sleeping in one of the bedrooms, much less discover he was Maeve's long-lost nephew with an actual claim to the property.

Her phone chimed with a notification. Her morning livestream had already racked up thousands of views, more than triple her usual numbers. The moment she'd awakened Jonathan while wielding her hammer was preserved for all her followers to see. And apparently, they loved it.

They didn't just love it; they wanted more of it.

"More Squatch," she muttered miserably. "Just what I need."

She headed inside, hoping to slip past Liz and straight into a hot shower. The house was quiet as she entered, but the delicious scent of something simmering on the stove told her Liz was home.

"Hey, Cuz," Liz called from the kitchen. "I thought you'd be demolishing things until midnight."

"Change of plans," Candy replied, dropping her bag on the entryway bench. So much for sneaking in unnoticed.

She found Liz stirring a pot of homemade chili, her red hair pulled back in a practical French braid. In her cargo pants and baseball shirt, Liz was Candy's opposite in almost every way. She was practical where Candy was whimsical, pragmatic where Candy was often overly optimistic. Yet somehow, they balanced each other perfectly.

"You're never going to believe what happened today," Candy said, sinking into a kitchen chair.

Liz turned, spoon still in hand, one eyebrow raised. "Try me."

"I found a squa—a squatter sleeping in one of the bedrooms at Maeve's house." She'd almost said 'squatch,' but caught herself in time.

Liz's eyes widened, and she set down her spoon with deliberate care. "Did you call the police? You're okay, right?"

"I'm fine, yes," Candy said, holding her arms out at her sides to demonstrate. "And of course, I called the police." She smoothed her hand over the woven placemat in front of her on the farmhouse table. "Bobby Wayne showed up and questioned the guy. Turns out he's a long-lost nephew. You've lived here your whole life; did you know Maeve had a brother? Or a nephew, for that matter?"

Liz frowned. "I was not aware of either."

"Yeah, well, neither was I. Turns out Maeve had written to him and asked him if he was interested in the family house, but then his dad died, and he hiked the Appalachian Trail, and just decided to show up unannounced several months later."

Liz was shaking her head, both hands held up in an effort to stop the flow of words coming out of Candy's mouth. "Whoa, whoa, whoa, cuz. You lost me at 'dead dad.'" She crossed her arm and leaned against the counter. "Start from the beginning and pause for breaths so that I can ask for clarification, if necessary."

Candy gave her a sheepish look. "Sorry." She closed her eyes, took a deep, dramatic breath, then blew it out through pursed lips. "Maeve had a brother, Troy, who died last April. Apparently, they'd parted on bad terms and haven't spoken in decades."

"Oh, geez. How sad," Liz offered.

Candy nodded. "It is. And I can tell Maeve is very sad about it, too. Plus, it doesn't seem like something Maeve would have done, so I'm blaming it on Troy."

Liz cocked an eyebrow. "Okay."

"So, I guess Maeve somehow learned about Troy's death, and she somehow knew there was a Jonathan—"

"Um, what's a Jonathan?" Liz crossed her arms, and Candy had a sneaking suspicion that her cousin was starting to find this whole thing a little funny.

"Jonathan is the nephew," she clarified, giving Liz a stern look. "And don't laugh. None of this is funny."

"I'm not laughing," Liz declared, eyes wide and falsely innocent.

"Yeah, but you want to. I can see your eyebrow twitching."

Liz pressed two fingertips to her left eyebrow. "It's not twitching."

Candy rolled her eyes. "Anyway," she said, drawing the word out. "So even though Troy and Maeve haven't spoken in thirty-something years, she knew about Jonathan and she found out about Troy's death, and she sent Jonathan a letter asking him if he was interested in the lake house. Apparently, it's where Troy grew up. Are you sure you didn't know about any of this?"

Liz shook her head again. "I'm positive. My parents might remember all of this, but I probably wasn't even born when all of this went down." Her folks had moved to Florida a few years ago after her father retired. "Want me to call them and ask?"

"Right, It was at least thirty years ago." Candy chewed her lip as she tried to guess at Jonathan's age. It was hard to tell under all that hair. "But no, don't call them. It's not really important to this story."

"Okay. So then what happened? Maeve sent Jonathan a letter, and then..." Liz prompted.

"So Jonathan goes off on some kind pilgrimage on the Appalachian Trail, and when he gets home, he finds Maeve's letter waiting for him."

Liz held up her hands again. "Hold up. I'm struggling with the timeline here. Dad dies in April, right? It's August. Even if he started mid-April, that's only four months and some change. I've heard it usually takes six or seven months to do the whole trail."

Candy shrugged. "He said he arrived back in Atlanta last week."

"Whoa," Liz interrupted. She pulled out her phone and started tapping. "So he hiked south bound, as in from Maine to Georgia?" She held the phone up to show Candy, as if she could read it from across the room.

"The trail head in Baxter State Park didn't even open until May 23rd this year because of snow. Dude, that means he would have done it in three months. That's close to twenty-five miles of hiking a day." She narrowed her eyes at Candy. "Is he some kind of super athlete or something?"

"I don't know," Candy said, starting to get frustrated. "Why does it matter? The point is, his dad died, and he went hiking, that's all I know. I mean, it sure looks like he's been hiking for months. Or like he's been living under a bridge."

"Is he hot?"

Candy gaped at her cousin. "Really? That's what you want to know?"

"Yeah. What's he look like?" Liz was grinning now.

"I just said he looks like he's been living under a bridge. He looks like a sasquatch, that's what he looks like." Candy pushed back her chair and stood. "I'm going to go take a shower."

Liz crossed the room and took Candy by the shoulders. "Stop. Sorry. Please tell me the rest of the story. I won't interrupt again."

Candy sighed and sat back down. "Fine. So when he gets back to Atlanta, he reads Maeve's letter."

Liz nodded. "The one she wrote back in April."

"Right. So a four-month-old letter." Candy mimed holding a phone to her ear. "And instead of calling her up and saying, 'Hey, Aunt Maeve, it's me, your long-lost nephew, whom you've never met or even exchanged a single word with in person, even though I only live four hundred miles away, and I couldn't be bothered to make the trip before, but I just read your letter, and now that you're offering me a sweet lake house, I'd like to come check it out and see if you all are good enough for me.'"

"Wow," Liz interjects, her voice laced with sarcasm. "That would have been quite a greeting."

"Yeah, well, he really should have started with all of that. Atlanta, Liz? It's like a seven-hour drive. Why has he never visited his aunt before now?" Then she waved her hands. "Never mind. I'm getting distracted again. He should have called her and said all of that, but no. He just hops in his dad's old sports car—"

"Ooh. What kind of sports car?"

"He just hops in his dad's old sports car," Candy repeated slowly, glaring at her cousin, who sheepishly drew her thumb and finger across her lips like she was zipping her mouth closed. "And then he drives up here unannounced, like it's no big deal."

"Well, that's a little assumptive," Liz unzipped her lips to say, turning back to her chili. "How'd Maeve take it?"

"She was shocked at first, but then..." Candy paused, remembering the poignant moment in the kitchen when Maeve had first set eyes on Jonathan. "I mean, it was super awkward. Neither of them really knew how to interact, having just met, but she said he looks just like his father, and that she was glad he'd come."

Liz whistled low. "So what does this mean for you?" Leave it to her cousin to get right to the point.

Candy let out a huff of disgust. "Technically, nothing has changed, other than that I don't get to work in an empty house. Apparently Squatch has decided to stay at the house rather than in Maeve's guest room."

"Squatch?" Liz didn't even try to pretend she wasn't laughing.

"Yep. I've named him Squatch. He looks like a sasquatch and acts like a squatter. Jonathan is too nice a name for him."

"Works for me," Liz said, nodding slowly. She pulled two bowls from the cabinet and began dishing chili into each of them. "You said, 'technically.'"

Candy accepted one of the bowls of chili, then waited for Liz to add shredded cheese and a huge dollop of sour cream into hers before passing the fixings to her. Then Liz pulled out a skillet of cornbread from the oven and set it on a trivet on the table. Candy got up to grab two small plates, butter, and honey.

"Technically, nothing has changed," she repeated. "Because technically, Maeve owns the house and she's the one I've contracted with. But she says she wants him to have input on my renovation plans, since he'll be the owner eventually." The words made her throat constrict painfully. *He'll be the owner eventually.* Not her. Not someday. Not ever. It was his family home; why *wouldn't* he want it?

"Ouch." Liz winced sympathetically, as if reacting to the pain in Candy's heart. "That's not what you signed up for."

"Not even close." Candy stirred sour cream into her chili. "He's already declared his dad's old bedroom off-limits, a room that was going to be an amazing home office. But nope. No renovation allowed."

"And you say he's staying at the house?"

"Yep. In that very room, actually." Candy got up again and filled a glass with ice water. "Which means that every morning, I get to be greeted by Mr. Grumpy Sasquatch instead of the glorious rays of morning sunshine streaming in through the windows of my favorite room in the house."

"I see." Liz blew on a bite of the hot stew. "Are you comfortable being alone there with him?" She looked genuinely concerned.

"No. I'm not comfortable with him there."

Liz frowned. "Then you need to talk to Maeve about that, cuz."

Candy shook her head. "It's not that. I'm not afraid of him like that. I really do think he's not going to jump me or try anything illegal."

"How can you be so sure?" Liz challenged.

Candy shrugged. "I'm used to working with mostly men, remember? He doesn't have that—that nasty vibe, you know?"

Liz did, indeed, know what Candy was talking about. She, too, worked in a field dominated by male workers. As a plumber working for the county's water department, she was the only woman on an all male crew.

"Besides, the police know he's here—Bobby spent some time with him and gave him a whole 'don't mess with Candy' spiel."

"I like that Bobby Wayne," Liz said. "So why are you not comfortable with Squatch?"

Candy grinned at Liz's quick adoption of the nickname, but then she quickly sobered. "It's just going to be different now, that's all. I was going to have that place all to myself for the two months to do with as I please. Now not only do I have to deal with him creeping around the place at all hours, but I have to give him access to my plans and let him give me input on them."

She didn't add what was really twisting the knife: that each of those plans had been created with not just any client in mind, but with her own preferences. The soft gray and blue palette for the master bedroom, the built-in bookshelves in the living room, the expanded deck facing the lake—all choices she'd made thinking that maybe, just maybe, this could one day be her home. Having Jonathan weigh in on decisions that felt so personal was like having a stranger rearrange her furniture.

Liz set down her spoon and looked sympathetically at her. In a quiet voice, she asked, "You're not thinking about bailing, are you?"

"Absolutely not," Candy said firmly. "Maeve still wants me to do the renovation, and she has final say. I'm not letting some grumpy sasquatch ruin this opportunity for me."

"That's my girl," Liz grinned. "So, what else do you know about this guy? What does he do for a living?"

Candy shook her head. "I have no idea. Something that would allow him to take several months off to go wandering in the woods, I suppose. Or maybe he's unemployed and homeless and that's why he's here."

"Does he have any skills? As in, free labor? Can he swing a hammer?"

"I don't know that, either. He didn't offer to help today, but then, we pretty much avoided each other most of the day after he nixed my plans for the office."

"Yikes."

Candy sighed. "He's grieving, I'm sure, and I kinda think that maybe he's here to get some closure. I don't know if it's even about the house at all."

"So you have to be nice to him, right?"

"Yep." Candy sighed with resignation. "Even though I think he's going to make this project ten times harder than it needs to be."

Liz laughed, the sound warm and familiar in the cozy kitchen. "Well, you've faced worse obstacles with 'Drills and Thrills' and yet, you prevailed," Liz pointed out. "I believe in you, Cuz. Don't let the grumpy mythical creature stand in your way."

They ate in comfortable silence for a few minutes, the chili warming Candy from the inside out. As exhausted as she was, the steady presence of her cousin was exactly what she needed after such a chaotic day.

"Why don't you go shower, and then we can watch a new episode or two of that British baking show," Liz said when they were finished eating.

"Seriously?" Candy asked, trying not to sound too exuberant about Liz's offer. She didn't want to make her change her mind, after all. Getting Liz to watch cooking shows was like pulling teeth. But Candy could do with something sweet and wholesome, and having company would be the extra cherry on top for her.

As Candy headed off to her room, her thoughts drifted back to Jonathan. Despite her frustration, she couldn't help but wonder about him. What was his story? His job? Why was he here? How did he get that scar on his face? And most importantly, what did he plan to do with the house once the renovation was complete.

As she joined Liz on the couch, sinking into the cushions with a contented sigh, Candy pushed those questions aside. But she made a silent promise to herself: this renovation would be a success, no matter what. She'd make sure of it.

10
Jonathan

JONATHAN STUDIED THE DRIPPING showerhead with a critical eye. He'd watched a couple of how-to videos on his phone after Candy had left for the day. According to the videos, he'd need to remove the faceplate and replace the washer inside—a simple fix requiring only a screwdriver and a new washer, maybe a wrench if the fittings were stubborn. Spurred on by how straightforward the fix looked, he'd headed over to the hardware store and purchased a tool set that came with the basic home repair essentials, plus a variety pack of rubber washers, and a hefty pipe wrench.

When he'd woken up this morning, he'd felt confident he could tackle the minor repair.

Now, however, he wasn't so sure. The drip was still there, and now there was water trickling out from around the water diverter lever on the tub spout even though the faucets were turned off. One of the videos had mentioned something about diverter gates and how they could get stuck or clogged with mineral deposits over time.

That had to be the problem. The diverter gate in the tub spout wasn't sealing properly, causing the leak. Another simple fix, according to the video. Just unscrew the tub spout and replace the whole part with a new tub spout kit.

He'd heard Candy's car pull up a few minutes ago, and now he was determined to have something to show for the last hour he'd spent working in this bathroom. He'd seen replacement kits at Charlie's—he'd take this one off and head over there with it this morning so he'd be sure and get the right replacement spout.

First things first, though. He needed to shut off the water. The shower wall butted up to one end of the vanity, so Jonathan crawled under the sink and located two shut-off valves, one for hot and one for cold. He turned both knobs clockwise until they were firmly closed, then tested the sink faucet. No water came out.

Back in the tub, Jonathan knelt down and examined the spout. The thing was ancient, the caulking around it cracked and yellowed with age. He couldn't feel an anchor screw on the underside of it, which meant it was likely a standard screw-on model, just like in the video.

Using a utility knife from his kit, he scraped away the old caulking, then gripped the spout with both hands and tried to unscrew it, but it refused to budge. Jonathan positioned his new pipe wrench on the spout and began to turn it counterclockwise, his biceps straining. Finally, he felt it give with a satisfying creak.

"Success," he muttered, continuing to twist the wrench. The spout rotated freely now, and after a few more turns, it came loose in his hand.

That's when everything went wrong.

Water erupted from the exposed pipe with shocking force, hitting him square in the face. Jonathan gasped, inhaling a mouthful, and fell backward, and the spout clattered into the tub as he frantically tried to shield himself from the spray.

"What the—" he sputtered, scrambling to his knees. Water was gushed everywhere, spraying the shower walls, soaking him from head to toe, and splashing out onto the floor. He desperately tried to jam the spout back onto the pipe, but the threads wouldn't catch, and the water pressure kept pushing it away.

Jonathan then tried blocking the flow with his hand, but the pressure was too strong, and the water simply sprayed in every direction, making an even bigger mess.

"Candy!" he yelled, hoping she was already in the house. He grabbed his towel from a hook nearby and wrapped it around the end of the pipe to at least try to slow the deluge, but then he realized that he was forcing water back into the wall, so he just draped the towel over the pipe, holding it in place with one hand, while wiping the water from his face with the other.

He hollered again, this time at the top of his lungs. "Candy, help!"

The tub was filling quickly around him, the already slow drain unable to keep up with the volume of water. If he didn't get this stopped soon, it would start spilling over the edge, adding to the flood on the floor.

He heard rapid footsteps on the stairs, then Candy appeared in the doorway, her expression shifting from curious to horrified in an instant.

Without a word, she spun on her heels and fled the scene.

"Where are you going?" he shouted, the towel slipping off the pipe for a moment, pummeling him with another blast. "I'm getting drenched here!" Jonathan remained in the tub, clutching the towel over the pipe, praying Candy would return soon. He'd really messed up this time.

Less than a minute later, the water pressure dropped dramatically, then stopped altogether. He slumped in the tub, soaked and defeated.

Candy reappeared in the doorway, breathless, her face flushed with exertion. "What on earth just happened?" she gasped, her gaze scanning the room, taking in the chaos.

"I was trying to fix the shower," Jonathan growled, mortification making him impatient.

"Without turning off the water first?"

"I *did* turn off the water!" he snapped, pointing at the open doors of the vanity. "Under the sink. Both of them."

"Those don't control the tub!" she exclaimed. "The main water shut-off is in the basement." She shook her head disbelievingly. "What were you thinking?"

Jonathan drew his knees up, hesitant to try to stand in front of her, lest he slip and fall and make an even bigger fool of himself. He plucked at his sodden shirt. His towel lay in a crumpled heap next to the drain, completely drenched and useless. "I thought it would be a simple fix, okay? I was just trying to help."

"Nothing's simple with old plumbing," Candy said, shaking her head. She crossed the wet floor to the tub and picked up the fallen spout, examining it. "This is a 1970s retrofit on a 1930s tub. See that copper pipe?" She pointed at the water line that stuck out of the hole in the shower wall. It sure looked innocent right now, docilely drip-drip-dripping away. "The plumbing in this house is a patchwork from at least three decades."

Jonathan pushed his wet hair out of his face. "I didn't know."

"Clearly," she replied, but her tone lacked the edge he'd expected. She seemed more resigned than angry. "You can't just watch a YouTube video and suddenly be a plumber."

Well. She pegged him, didn't she? "I was only trying to help," he said quietly, a little defensively.

Candy sighed, then unexpectedly extended her hand to him. "Come on, get up. We need to deal with this before the water seeps into the subflooring and causes even more damage."

Jonathan took her hand, surprised by the strength in her grip as she helped him to his feet. "I'm sorry," he said, the words feeling inadequate given the destruction around them.

"Out of the tub with you," she replied, but there was a hint of humor in her voice. "Sorry doesn't sop up this mess, but apology accepted. Why don't you change out of your wet things, and I'll run down and grab some shop towels."

"I can get them for you," he offered as he started to peel off his shirt. "I'll clean up in here."

"Whoa, there, Squatch," Candy said, putting a hand up to cover her eyes. "You can at least wait until I'm out of the room, okay?"

Jonathan had to press his lips together so as not to smirk at her obvious discomfort. "I wasn't going to strip down to my skivvies in front of you," he insisted, clutching his shirt around his neck.

"Good to know." She rolled her eyes, then left the room.

Jonathan toed off his soggy sneakers and socks, and left them in the tub. In his room, he quickly changed, then returned to the bathroom to hang his things over the shower curtain rod. He'd seen a washer and dryer in the garage, but he didn't know if they worked or were even hooked up.

Candy returned several minutes later, looking relieved to see Jonathan in dry clothes. She was carrying an armload of light blue towels. "Use these on the floor," she said, tossing him several. "I'm going to see if I can get this spout to stay in place for now so we can turn the water back on." She pulled a roll of Teflon tape from her toolbelt and climbed into the tub.

She made quick work of the task, then used a couple of the towels on the shower walls before climbing out of the tub again. "I'm going to go turn the water back on. Stand by and holler if that starts leaking, okay?"

Jonathan nodded, not thrilled at the thought of getting hosed again if her repair malfunctioned, but of course, not only had she gotten the spout back on, the leak had also stopped from both the shower and from around the diverter lever.

Candy returned, tested the faucet knobs to make sure everything worked, turned the water valves back on under the sink, then joined him in mopping up the rest of the mess.

She didn't say a word.

Jonathan felt the need to explain himself. He considered telling her about his list of jobs to do, but he thought better of it, seeing as how badly he'd handled things so far. "I just... I don't like feeling useless," he admitted. "Sitting around while you're working doesn't feel right."

Candy paused, studying him. "I get that," she said after a moment. "But maybe next time, ask before you start dismantling anything."

"Noted," Jonathan agreed, wringing out a soaked towel into the tub. "Is there anything I can do to help that won't flood the house?"

She seemed to consider his question seriously. "Maybe. What are you good at? Do you have any useful skills? Can you use a cordless drill?"

Despite everything, Jonathan found himself smiling. "I can swing a hammer," he teased.

Candy eyed his still-open tool set where it was perched on the toilet seat. It had somehow avoided getting rained on. "Maybe you can swing a hammer, but can you actually hit whatever it is you're aiming for?" So she gave as good as she got. "We don't want you leaving dents in the woodwork."

Jonathan held up his hands in surrender. "I can lift heavy things. And I can build a pretty mean campfire."

Candy surprised him by giggling. No, it was more of a chortle. A sound he found he liked. "I'll remember that when we get the deck done and the new furniture out there. I've ordered a really sweet patio fire pit, and you can prove your fire-making skills to me then." She started gathering up the wet towels in a plastic trash bag she'd brought with her. "But the lifting heavy things might come in handy before then."

They finished the cleanup in what was beginning to feel like comfortable silence before Candy spoke again. "Look, I understand wanting to contribute. But this is my project, my reputation on the line. I can't have you going rogue on repairs."

"Fair enough," Jonathan acknowledged.

She waved one hand around to indicate the whole bathroom. "I'm redoing most of this in here, so none of these fixtures need to be repaired. They're all going to be replaced."

"Right."

"And only when I'm ready to do the work in here," she added, putting the screws to him just the tiniest bit more.

"Of course." Jonathan did not care for the humble pie she was serving up, but he probably deserved it.

"But," she continued, setting the trash bag of towels by the door. "If you really want to help, I could use an extra pair of hands for some of the grunt work." She pointed at the bag. "Starting with that. Wet towels get heavy. You can take them down to the garage and throw the whole lot into the dryer for me." She paused and narrowed her eyes at him. "You do know how to use a dryer, don't you?"

"Yes, I know how to use a dryer. And a washer," Jonathan added dryly. "But then, maybe I should stay away from anything with water."

"As long as you're not trying to repair the washer, I think you're good," Candy replied, the ghost of a smile playing at her lips. "Now finish up in here while I check the ceiling downstairs. The dining room is right under this bathroom, and I need to make sure water isn't dripping through."

As she left, Jonathan surveyed the disaster he'd created. He'd made a mess of things, literally and figuratively, but at least Candy hadn't thrown him out on his ear.

That evening, over pork chops, fried potatoes, and green beans, Jonathan told Maeve about the morning's flood disaster. He'd been reluctant to do so at first, but then his aunt had shared one story after another about Troy getting in and out of trouble during his childhood at the lake. "A regular Tom Sawyer," she'd said again, and Jonathan could almost picture his father in a scruffy straw hat, ducking out of chores to go spend a day at his favorite fishing hole.

So Jonathan told her about the day, about his terrible error in judgement, and about Candy's surprising display of grace under fire, and Maeve had laughed so hard, tears had welled in her eyes.

As Jonathan lay in bed, gazing out over the moonlit lake, he couldn't hold back another round of laughter. Two days in a row, now, he'd made a real banger of a morning for Ms. Toolbelt. "You'd better get your act together," he chided himself. He was supposed to trying to make things better for her, not worse.

11
Candy

CANDY PULLED INTO THE driveway of the lake house, wondering what catastrophe would be awaiting her this morning. After yesterday's plumbing disaster, she'd half-expected to find the place flooded again, or perhaps on fire, considering that was one of his self-proclaimed skills. She'd spent an extra twenty minutes checking the dining room ceiling for water damage before leaving yesterday, relieved to find that their quick clean-up had prevented any serious issues.

The aroma of fresh coffee greeted her as she pushed open the front door. Inside the kitchen, Jonathan was standing at the counter, his back to her, working the plunger on her French press. He'd tied a bandana around his head to keep his hair back from his face, and he was humming something under his breath that she couldn't quite make out.

He glanced over his shoulder as she set her bag down on the table. "Morning," he said, his voice still rough with sleep. "Hope you don't mind, but I found your coffee. Figured I'd make enough for both of us."

Candy raised an eyebrow. He was using her precious French press without asking. Still, if that was as bad as it got today, she'd take it.

"I don't mind," she said, pulling out her phone. "Actually, would you mind if I film you making that? It would be great content for my daily update. I don't know why, but my fans are slightly enamored by you." Now why on earth had she shared that? Her cheeks warmed, but she made a show of opening her camera app, hoping he wouldn't notice.

Jonathan hesitated, his hand pausing on the coffee plunger. "You want to film me making coffee?"

"My followers love seeing the little day-to-day stuff," she explained. "And the morning coffee ritual is kind of a tradition on my renovation sites. It's how I start every day, so if you're going to commandeer the task...." She left the sentence hanging, hoping he wouldn't refuse.

He looked uncomfortable but nodded. "Uh, okay, I guess."

"Great!" Candy beamed. "Just let me set up the shot." She stepped back out of the kitchen and positioned herself in the foyer like she'd just come in the front door. She raised her phone, pointing it through the door into the kitchen, framing Jonathan dead center. His beard didn't seem quite as scruffy today, she thought, peering at his image on her screen. Had he trimmed it? Probably not, but the bandana made a surprising difference in his appearance.

"Ready when you are," she called to him.

Jonathan mimed pushing the plunger down into the carafe again, but this time, he stood to the side a bit, keeping his scarred cheek turned away from the camera. She hadn't realized he was self-conscious about it. In fact, she'd almost stopped noticing it, herself. He poured coffee into two mugs, the morning sunlight turning the liquid translucent and illuminating whisps of steam above each cup. It also gave his beard a coppery glow that contrasted nicely with the blue bandana. It was a perfect shot; her fans would rave about it.

When he glanced up and smiled directly into the camera, Candy she made out a dimple hiding under all that facial hair. The thought was so unexpected that she almost fumbled her phone.

"Sweet," she said quickly, ending the recording. "That'll be great for this morning's update."

Jonathan slid a mug across the counter to her. "Glad I could help provide you with content. See, I'm good for something, right?"

Was that sarcasm in his voice? Candy chose to ignore it, moving to the kitchen table where she'd already set out her planner. "Thanks for the coffee," she said, the aroma making her mouth water.

She opened her planner to today's date, uncapping a teal marker to start color-coding her tasks for the day. The planner was a riot of rainbow colors, each task category assigned its own shade: green for demolition, blue for plumbing, orange for electrical, purple for carpentry. It might look chaotic to an outsider, but the system worked perfectly for her.

Plus, the colorful pages photographed beautifully for social media and her followers loved the behind-the-scenes glimpses of her process.

She could feel Jonathan's eyes on her as she wrote. When she glanced up, he was definitely smirking.

"What?" she asked, her hackles rising.

"Nothing," he said, but the grin remained. "Just... that's a lot of colors."

Candy narrowed her eyes. "It's a system. It helps me stay organized. How do you manage your time?"

Jonathan set his mug down in front of the chair next to her, then peered over her shoulder at the day's two-page spread. Candy fought the sudden urge to snap the planner shut. She had nothing to hide, and in fact, if he'd learn her system, working together might be a whole lot easier.

He shook his head and sat down beside her, reaching into his back pocket for his phone. "I use a project management app," he said. "Everything's digital – tasks, deadlines, reminders."

"Well, I prefer analog," Candy said defensively. "And my followers like seeing the—"

Her words cut off as Jonathan's elbow bumped his mug, sending it toppling over. Dark coffee splattered the open pages of her planner. The pool of liquid spread rapidly across the table toward her planner, seeping underneath it before she could scoop it up.

"No!" she cried, jumping to her feet and lifting it up off the table. Coffee dripped from the colorful cover, and at least the first week's worth of pages were soaked through, the carefully color-coded tasks blurring into indistinguishable smudges.

Jonathan grabbed a roll of paper towels and started mopping up the spill. "I'm so sorry," he said, sounding genuinely contrite. He ripped off several and thrust them at her. "Here."

"It's fine," Candy said automatically, but she felt like crying. She shook the planner over the table, trying not to splatter her light blue t-shirt, trying to assess the damage. She created a new planner for every job, complete with a custom cover, pockets and dividers, tabs and stickers. She didn't care if it was girlie; she'd been a planner girl all her life, and having these project portfolio planners lined up on a shelf in her room motivated her to keep adding more. They were her badges of honor, her written testament to overcoming the odds. She spent a lot of time setting them up, and right now, she was watching hours of planning disappear before her eyes.

"Let me help," Jonathan offered, reaching for the dripping book. "Maybe if we put it in the sun, it'll dry out."

"The ink is water-soluble," Candy explained, trying to keep the disappointment from her voice. "It's not salvageable. I'll have to redo it." She carefully set the planner over on the counter and blotted the pages as best she could. At least maybe she could read some of it enough to transfer the important information to a new one.

"It's only a notebook, right?" Jonathan asked, sounding hopeful. "Can you copy your schedule into another one?"

Candy stiffened. "It's not only a notebook." She made air quotes around the word 'only' and glared at him over her shoulder. "This is a custom planner. I make a new one for every project, and my followers expect to see it in my daily updates."

Jonathan's expression shifted from apologetic to skeptical. "Your followers care about what your planner looks like?"

"Yes," Candy insisted, feeling her cheeks flush. "It's part of my aesthetic, my personal brand. It helps me stand out in a crowded field, and it appeals to my target audience. Women, especially, love my planners. I actually do whole posts on how I put these things together."

"Wow," Jonathan intoned, and she didn't miss the subtle eye roll that accompanied the word. "Look, I'm sorry I messed up your... aesthetic."

The way he said it made the word sound ridiculous, as if cultivating a professional image was somehow shallow or insincere. Candy pressed her lips together, biting back a sharp retort.

The morning without a mishap had been too good to be true.

"It's fine," she said again, her tone making it clear it was anything but. "I'll figure something out."

She turned back to the planner, pulling salvageable pages from it and setting them aside, refusing to let him see how much the incident, and his dismissive attitude, had upset her. The day was just beginning, and already they were off to a rocky start.

♥ ∙ ♥ ∙ ♥ ∙ ♥ ∙ ♥

OVER THE NEXT FEW days, Candy and Jonathan established a tentative working routine. They started each morning over coffee, but Candy no longer laid out her plans on the table. After a brief discussion of the day's priorities, they'd go their separate ways, with Candy tackling her carefully plotted renovation tasks, and Jonathan working on his Candy-approved list of minor repairs.

Sometimes they met again at lunch, each with their own food, to discuss what they'd accomplished. The conversations were polite but strained, neither quite sure how to move past their rough start. Once Jonathan's tasks were complete, instead of asking if there was anything else he could do, he'd excuse himself and disappear inside his room for the rest of the day. Then, at the end of each day, he would come out so they could exchange awkward goodbyes before Candy headed home.

It was tolerable, but not fun. Candy missed the excitement and joy she usually felt at the beginning of a big project. She'd recreated her planner, which had helped her feel more in control of things. She'd even spent extra time including tasks for Jonathan, spitefully using a brown marker.

But instead of eagerly documenting each step of the renovation for her followers, she found herself going through the motions, her updates more perfunctory than passionate.

By Friday afternoon, Candy was mentally drained. She wrapped up her work a little earlier than usual, packing her tools away with a sense of relief. The weekend would give her some much-needed distance from the lake house, and from Jonathan.

"Heading out?" Jonathan asked, appearing in the kitchen doorway as she gathered her things.

"Yeah," Candy replied. "I'm meeting some friends for supper."

"Sounds fun," he said, leaning in the doorframe. "Have a good weekend."

"You too," she replied automatically, slinging her messenger bag over her shoulder. "Don't flood anything while I'm gone."

A small smile cracked through his beard. "I'll try to restrain myself."

The drive to Juno's Coffee Bar and Cafe took only ten minutes. The familiar shop with its cheerful teal awning was a welcome sight after the tense week. Candy parked and hurried inside, instantly spotting her friends at their usual corner table.

"There she is!" Juno called, waving her over. She must've had enough coverage to be able to sit down for a meal with them. "We were just about to send out a search party."

"Sorry I'm late," Candy said, dropping into the empty chair between Claire and Addison, unusually happy to see her friends this evening.

"How's the renovation going?" Penny asked, passing Candy a menu. "Any more flooded bathrooms?"

"You told them?" Candy asked Liz, who just shrugged unapologetically.

"Of course she did," Juno said. "The saga of Candy and the Sasquatch is the most entertainment we've had in months."

"He's not that bad," Candy found herself saying, surprising even herself with the defensive tone. "I mean, he's trying to be helpful." She snorted. "He's just not very good at it."

"Sounds like someone's warming up to the hairy intruder," Claire teased, her blue eyes twinkling.

"Not really," Candy protested. "He's still a pain in my backside. Last night after I left, he took it upon himself to organize the workbench out in the garage where I've been keeping all my tools."

"Uh-oh," Liz muttered, not quite under her breath.

"Yeah, uh-oh," Candy concurred. "It may have looked a little chaotic to him, but I had everything right where I wanted it."

"Did he break anything?" Addison asked, sounding worried.

"No. Everything was there. It just felt—I don't know. Like an invasion of my privacy. He's got his own tools; why does he have to touch mine?" Candy added, knowing she sounded like a petulant teenager. "Then on Wednesday morning, he spilled a whole cup of coffee on my planner, soaking the thing. It was a mess."

Claire touched her hand in sympathy. "Your project planner?" Candy bought her supplies from The Cracked Spine, Claire's bookshop, so she knew exactly what kind of a mess Candy was talking about. All of her friends knew how important the books were, and everyone wore similar expressions of concern for her.

"Hey," Liz said, nudging her foot under the table. She sat across from her. "Maeve hasn't taken the project from you. Nothing has changed about the renovation itself. You still get to transform that beautiful house exactly how you planned."

"Except for Troy's old bedroom," Candy pointed out.

"One room," Claire said firmly, apparently having heard about that, too. "Out of an entire house. You can work around that."

Penny added, "At least he has his mancave to hide out in so he's not just roaming the rooms while you're trying to work."

Candy couldn't help but laugh at that. "True. He does spend a lot of time up there."

"See?" Juno said, gathering up the menus and handing them to one of her wait staff who'd come over to take their orders. "You can do this, Candy Needham. We believe in you. And when this is all done, you'll have an amazing showcase for your business."

Candy nodded, feeling some of the week's tension begin to ease as she sat surrounded by the unshakeable support of her loyal friends. They were right. The essentials of the project remained unchanged. She could work around the off-limits bedroom and one grumpy sasquatch.

"Now," the happily married Addison said, leaning forward conspiratorially. "What we really want to know is... under all that hair, is he hot? Single?"

The table erupted in laughter as Candy groaned and poked Addison in the arm. "*Et tu*, Brute?"

12
Jonathan

Jonathan wandered through the house early Monday morning, taking note of all that Candy had accomplished in just one week. The half bath in the hallway off the living room had been turned into a peaceful paradise with sky blue paint above white beadboard trimmed with a decorative chair rail. The toilet was shiny and new, and Candy had replaced the old vanity with a pedestal sink and an enormous vintage mirror with an etched delicate ivy border that made the room look twice its size.

On the opposite end of the house near the garage, she'd taken out a non-weight bearing wall to expand the size of the existing tiny mudroom, and, according to the design boards, planned to convert the space into a multifunction laundry room and bathroom, complete with a door that opened onto the deck so swimmer could access a bathroom without having to traipse through the living room. She hadn't started framing it up yet, so he had a hard time imagining how she was going to fit everything.

He ran his hand along the smooth surface of the freshly sanded butcher block island she'd constructed, impressed by Candy's expertise. She'd known exactly what to do at every turn, never hesitating or second-guessing herself. It was a stark contrast to his own fumbling attempts at helping.

At doing almost anything these days.

The weekend had dragged on longer than he'd expected. He'd spent all of Saturday taking advantage of having the place to himself and no expectations of him, and taken stock of where he was on his current projects. Candy had inspired him with her planner, as loathe as he was to admit it, and he'd set some new goals, both short- and long-term. He'd ended the day at Maeve's for supper, feeling a new sense of accomplishment as he sat across the table from his aunt, a woman who was quickly becoming less and less a stranger to him.

He'd opted out of attending church with her on Sunday morning, suddenly self-conscious of his appearance. He had decent clothes to wear, but he really needed a haircut and a shave before he sat through a small town church service. Especially sitting next to the classy Maeve Lewis. So Sunday had stretched endlessly before him. He'd tried to work on his hiking app, but found himself distracted, his mind wandering to the renovation and to Candy more often than he cared to admit.

He'd actually missed the sound of her humming to herself as she worked, the tap-tap-tap of her hammer, even her colorful commentary when something wasn't going quite right.

Jonathan shook his head at the direction of his thoughts. He wasn't here to make friends, just to figure out how he felt about this house and to sort through his father's things. Getting attached to the perky contractor was not part of the plan.

He glanced at the clock. Candy would arrive any minute. As had become their routine, he moved to the kitchen to brew a fresh carafe of coffee. He'd paid attention to how she liked it. Strong, but not bitter, with the water just below boiling point when it hit the coarse grounds.

As he measured out the coffee beans into the grinder, his mind wandered back to Wednesday morning and the planner incident. He still felt a twist of guilt whenever he thought about it. Candy hadn't seemed upset about it since, and he'd seen her pull out a new one, all filled out in an array of colors, on Friday, but that didn't make him feel any better.

Last night, unable to sleep, he'd finally given in to his curiosity and had gone online to check out her social media channels. He'd wanted to see for himself what her aesthetic was, exactly, and to find out what kind of following she had.

What he discovered had surprised him.

Her channels were professional and well-curated, a perfect blend of informative content and engaging personality. And her followers—tens of thousands across multiple platforms—clearly adored her. They asked detailed questions about her renovation techniques, praised her design choices, and seemed genuinely invested in her success.

And there was the planner, exactly as she'd described it. She shared an image of it every morning with her fresh task list and schedule, and every evening with what she'd accomplished checked off, followed by a brief note about how she felt about the day's progress. Her planner posts were some of her most popular, often generating hundreds of comments.

Jonathan had felt especially ashamed when he came across the post about the coffee spill. There was the coffee-stained cover next to an image of him making the coffee that morning. The caption read: *Someone spilled coffee on my planner this morning. Can't even be mad because he made me a cup of my favorite Robusta and it was simply luscious!* She'd added the 'chef's kiss' emoji at the end.

No snarky quip about him being a klutzy caveman, no complaining about what a mess the spill had made of things. Just... grace. And her followers had eaten it up, many commenting about how they were enjoying the "Squatch Saga" and asking for more updates about the "mysterious mountain man" helping with her renovation.

After the coffee spill, things had changed between them. He had a feeling it was because of his reaction to her social media marketing, his disregard for the effort she put into establishing her image, building her brand, and defining her identity as a skilled contractor and talented designer.

What Candy didn't know was that during his time on the Appalachian Trail, he'd encountered far too many people—women, in particular—filming their hikes for social media, making themselves look all female-empowered and tough, but then leaning heavily on their peers or even other hikers they didn't know to make up for their ineptitude or lack of preparation for the harsh conditions in the wild. Their constant filming had often interfered with everyone's enjoyment of the great outdoors, intrusive cameras capturing moments that should have been private. He'd heard the word "aesthetic" a thousand times too many during those months, and when Candy had said it, his reaction had been almost visceral.

Jonathan reached up and touched his scar, the raised ridge of tissue a constant reminder of one particularly harrowing encounter with an Instagram "adventuress" who'd been more concerned with getting the perfect shot than with basic safety. Then he tamped down the rising anger. He wasn't going to dwell on that.

He'd been around Candy for a week now. He'd seen her work ethic, her skill, her knowledge, and her dedication to going above and beyond. She wasn't just the pretty face of a DIY TV show; she was the real deal.

The front door opened, and he heard Candy's cheerful "Good morning!" before he saw her. She breezed into the kitchen, bringing with her the fresh scent of something floral and a little spicy that made him go momentarily blank. No one had smelled anything close to that good on the trail, that was for sure.

Her hair was still down around her shoulders, damp like she'd just gotten out of the shower. She wore a fitted pink t-shirt with her company logo embroidered on the pocket, and her usual work jeans and boots. She looked tanned and rested, and more relaxed than she'd been all last week.

"Sorry I'm running late," she said, setting her bag down on the table. "There was actually traffic downtown this morning."

Jonathan handed her a mug. "No problem. Coffee's still hot."

She took a sip and closed her eyes in appreciation. "Mmm, this is perfect. So good." She even did the chef's kiss gesture with her fingers, and Jonathan was glad for his beard, knowing it hid the flush he felt creeping up his neck.

"It's the least I can do," he said, watching as she pulled out her planner—the new one with a fresh cover—and set it on the table. "How was your weekend?" he asked, staying where he was with his own coffee. He leaned against the counter and crossed one ankle over the other.

"It was great," she said, flipping open to the day's page. "Liz finally convinced me to binge-watch 'The Last of Us' all day Saturday. Have you seen it?"

Jonathan shook his head. "I've played the game, but I haven't watched the show yet."

"It was so good," she enthused, her eyes lighting up. "Creepy as all get-out, and generally not my cup of tea, but the story was really great, and I got so invested in the characters."

"Nice," Jonathan said. "Maybe I'll have to watch it after all. I usually don't care for movies made from games, but since you've given it your stamp of approval, I'll give it a go."

"So you're one of those film snobs." She pushed the tip of her nose up with one finger, nearly poking herself in the eye with the purple pen she held. "I take it you don't like movies made from books, either?"

Jonathan shrugged. "If the shoe fits," he said good-naturedly. "So what about yesterday?" he asked, finding himself genuinely interested in how she spent her time away from the renovation. "You must have been outside; you've got some nice color." He pointed at her bare arms below the cuffs of her t-shirt.

"Thank you." She preened a little, brushing her fingertips over her forearm. "Church in the morning, then out on the lake all afternoon out at The Garden Gate B&B," she said. "A couple of my friends have boats and jet skis, so we all packed picnics and just spent the day on the water. I slept like the dead last night," she added. "Which is why I'm late; I must have turned off my alarm in my sleep."

It sounded amazing to Jonathan, from the television show of the popular shooter game to a lazy afternoon at the lake, but most of all, the thought of just hanging out with Candy Needham and *not* in work mode. It would sure be nice to not have her watching him with wary anticipation all the time.

13
Candy

"WHAT ABOUT YOU?" CANDY asked, looking up at him over her mug. "What did you do this weekend?"

Jonathan shifted his weight. "Not much," he said vaguely, almost like he didn't want to tell her, especially after hearing about her great weekend. "I spent most of Saturday catching up on some work projects."

"So you disappeared into your mancave all weekend," Candy teased. "That's very on-brand for a mythical creature like yourself."

A reluctant smile tugged at the corner of his mouth and he stroked his beard. "A mythical creature, huh?"

Candy's face grew warm and she tried to brush off her embarrassment. She waved a hand in the air like she was swatting the comment away. "That's what Liz is calling you. I told her you looked like a sasquatch with all that—" She broke off and made a circle with her finger, indicating his overgrown locks. "You know, all that hair." She was certain her cheeks were turning hot pink.

"Yeah, the hair." Jonathan said, shoving his hair back from his face, a gesture he'd made several times since she'd arrived. He hadn't yet tied it back today and it looked like it might be driving him crazy. "It's a little out of control. I know."

Candy smirked. "A little? When was your last haircut? Or shave?"

Jonathan pretended to count back on his fingers, then said, "Last trim for both was in April."

A flicker of pain crossed his face, and she knew without him having to say that he'd probably done it for his father's funeral. "It all grows pretty fast, doesn't it?" she asked, trying to keep the conversation from veering into deep waters.

"Well, I didn't have a buzz cut." He cupped the back of his neck and gave her a bittersweet look. "My dad liked to call it a mullet."

"You had a mullet?" Candy's eyes went round with delight. She tried to imagine it but to no avail.

Jonathan chuckled. "Nah. But he used to tease me about how it curls when it starts to grow out."

Candy bit back a laugh of her own. He was actually getting embarrassed by this conversation. "I'm having trouble picturing you with anything but this, Squatch."

"Hey, now. I even wear suits to my day job," he countered.

"Like that Neanderthal caveman on those insurance commercials?" she teased. "You know, I don't even know what it is you do for a living. When you're not hiking across the country or flooding bathrooms, I mean."

That drew another chuckle from him. "Software development," he replied. "I work for a company called SyncTech back in Atlanta. Before the trail, I mean."

Candy cocked her head. "Before the trail?" she repeated. "Does that mean you don't work there anymore?"

"I still do. Technically. I'm just on extended leave right now."

Technically. What did that mean? Had he come here expecting to just move into the family home? If so, she'd really disrupted his plans. But then, he'd disrupted hers, too. And why was he so cagey about it all? Did his standoffishness really all just stem from whatever it was that had driven Troy and Maeve apart?

Did she really want to know?

Yeah, she kind of did. Maeve had put her foot down about allowing Candy to do what she'd come to do, so this project was safe. Well, except for the office. But Candy had designed every aspect of the renovation with someone like herself in mind... because she'd secretly started entertaining the notion of buying it. She'd grown to love Autumn Lake over the last few years while living with Liz, and even though her cousin had made it clear that she was a welcome roommate, Candy eventually wanted a place of her own, a place where she could maybe start a family one day. *That would require a husband,* a snippy little voice in her head reminded her.

But if Jonathan now had designs on the lake house, then she had no leg to stand on. He was family, this was a the family home, and Maeve had already offered it to him.

Time to change the subject. She didn't want to think about that.

"Software development?" Candy asked. "What exactly is that? It sounds like one of those catch-all labels. Like a general contractor," she said, pointing at herself.

He nodded. "You're right. It's a pretty broad field, but most of us specialize in one or two areas. I came out of school hoping to design and develop, but it's a pretty competitive landscape. I landed a decent job with SyncTech, one that would allow me to move up in the ranks, but I'm still doing a lot of coding and troubleshooting stuff. Not very exciting, I know," he said with a shrug. "But I've been working on a few apps of my own on the side."

"Really? Like what?" She downed the last of her coffee and closed her planner, turning her attention fully to him. He was warming to the topic, and she recognized that flair of excitement in his voice, the sound of someone who enjoyed what they were doing.

"I've designed one based on my AT experience," he explained, setting his cup down. "Real-time trail conditions, water sources, shelter availability, that kind of thing. It also has a ton of prep resources, including task lists, timelines, goal trackers, budget plans, meal plans, and more."

"That sounds really useful," Candy said, genuinely impressed. "Is it available yet, or still in development?"

"It's still in development," he said. "That's what I spent the weekend working on. But I'm already running beta testing on it, and so far, I'm getting some pretty positive feedback."

"Wow. You must be really proud of yourself." Candy rose and brought her coffee cup to the sink to rinse it out. "Do you design games too?"

Jonathan shook his head. "No, but I know a guy who works on The Last of Us, actually. We went to college together."

"Seriously?" Candy perked up, her eyes widening. "That's so cool! The zombies in that show are absolutely disgusting—those fungus things growing out of their heads?" She shuddered dramatically. "But the story was amazing. I got so invested in Joel and Ellie's journey."

The kitchen window was open to the cool morning, and a light wafted in, stirring the air around them. It occurred to Candy just how close they were standing when she caught of whiff of whatever scent Jonathan had on. Woods and moss, a hint of spice. It wasn't strong, so maybe it was just his shampoo, but she decided she liked it a little too much.

She pulled her phone out of her back pocket and glanced at her time. "But speaking of relationships, I need to build one with that living room floor. How strong are you feeling today?" Without thinking, she reached over and squeezed his rock-hard bicep. She froze, realizing what she'd just done, then dropped her hand to her side in abject mortification. "Sorry about that," she murmured, putting a few steps between them.

Jonathan, too, looked a little flustered, but he gathered his wits before she did and raised his arm to flex playfully for her. "I'm ready and willing. What kind of heavy lifting do you have in mind for me?"

She wanted to press her palms to her flaming cheeks, to hit rewind and go back thirty seconds in time. But he was making light of it, so she would, too. She took a steadying breath. "We're going to pull up that nasty old carpet and roll it on out of the house. I'm having a dumpster delivered, but they can't get it here until this afternoon, so we'll just pile it up out in the driveway for now. I parked on the street so it's clear." Wow. Those words just tumbled right on out of there.

"We're going to work together?" Jonathan asked, like he wasn't sure he'd heard correctly.

"Unless you have other plans?" Candy raised an eyebrow. "It will go much faster with two people."

"I'd be happy to help," he said quickly. "Just tell me what to do."

"I have lots of masks, and I insist that you wear one. Who knows what kind of stuff we're going to stir up. I think that carpet's been down for a good thirty years." She led the way out of the kitchen, pausing in the foyer to set her planner next to the design boards. She eyed the office panel, but said nothing. She was holding onto hope that at some point, maybe once he'd seen what she was capable of, that Jonathan would change his mind about that bedroom and let her have her way with it.

"Should I grab my tools?" he asked, pointing toward the stairs.

She shook her head. "I've got everything we need."

"Then show me the masks, Miss Toolbelt," he declared, pulling a bandana from his back jeans pocket and tying it around his hair. "Ready when you are."

His earnestness was unexpectedly charming, and Candy didn't even mind the nickname he'd given her. She found herself looking forward to working with him today, a stark contrast to how she'd felt just a week ago. Maybe the grumpy sasquatch was starting to come around.

"Then, let's get to it," she said, pointing toward the living room. "That carpet isn't going to rip itself up."

14

Jonathan

THEY STARTED AT THE corner nearest the fireplace, where Candy had already cut a square of carpet free. She showed Jonathan how to grip the edge and pull steadily to separate it from the tack strips holding it in place.

"Like this," she demonstrated, gripping the edge of the carpet and peeling back a large enough section so that Jonathan could grab on, too. Her words were a little muffled behind her mask. "It can be a bit of a bear with these older carpets, especially if the nails in the tack strips are old and rusty, but it'll come up easier and go a lot faster if we work together."

Jonathan nodded, rolling the edge to give him something to grip. The carpet was heavier than he expected, stubborn in its resistance to being dislodged after decades in place. He gave it a hard pull, putting the strength of his shoulders into it.

The carpet suddenly released with unexpected force. Jonathan stumbled back, taking the carpet with him. Candy, still holding on beside him, tumbled backward with a yelp, landing hard on her backside.

"Candy!" Jonathan dropped the carpet and reached for her. "Are—are you okay?"

She winced, holding up a hand to stop him. "I'm fine," she insisted, though her grimace told a different story. "Just give me a minute." But she'd gone a little pale.

"Let me help you up," he offered, extending his hand.

"No, I'm good." Candy gingerly got to her feet on her own, brushing dust from her jeans. She shot him a smile that didn't reach her eyes.

"You sure?" he asked, mortified, and praying that he hadn't really hurt her. "I'm so sorry." Her ponytail was a little askew, but he thought better of saying anything to her about it.

She nodded, giving him a momentary wave of relief, but then said, "I think I'm going to run to the restroom for a minute. Just... maybe don't pull anything else up until I get back, okay?"

Jonathan nodded miserably, watching her walk away. Nope. She was limping. He watched her limp away. Great. "You hurt her, you big buffoon," he muttered under his breath. And now she didn't even trust him to continue without supervision.

He stood in the middle of the partially-exposed, nasty-looking carpet padding, debating whether he should just leave her to work alone. Maybe his presence was causing more problems than it was solving. Just as he was considering slipping out the side door and driving off into the wide blue yonder, the doorbell rang. Before Jonathan could cross the room to get it, the front door swung open and a portly middle-aged man walked in like he owned the place. He was dressed in a limp button-down shirt tucked into the low-riding waistband of a pair of pants that were too small for him, and on his feet were a pair of old school pointy-toed cowboy boots.

"Hello?" the man called out, his eyes scanning the open space until he spotted Jonathan. "Ah. Good morning." He marched across the foyer, one hand extended, a clipboard clutched in his other one.

Candy emerged from the bathroom, looking a little more composed, her ponytail back in place, her mask pulled down under her chin. She paused when she saw the stranger, but then recognition flashed in her eyes.

"Building inspector," the newcomer said by way of introduction, his hand still proffered. Jonathan took it and did his best not to grit his teeth when the guy squeezed way too hard for a handshake. "I'm Tad Rodgers," he said, then glanced down at his clipboard and back up at Jonathan, a smarmy look on his face. "You're not Candy Needham, the television Queen of DIY, are you?" He guffawed like he'd just told the world's funniest joke.

"Uh, hi. I'm Jon. Jon Burkhardt." He turned to point at Candy, but Tad barreled on.

"Got a few questions about the permits filed for this renovation." Rodgers flipped through the papers on his clipboard, then narrowed his gaze on Jonathan again. "Some concerns about the structural modifications listed here."

"You should really talk to—" Jonathan began, gesturing toward Candy.

"Excuse me," Candy said, approaching confidently, removing her mask and shoving it into her back pocket. As far as Jonathan could tell, she wasn't limping now. "How can I help you?"

The inspector glanced at Candy, his jovial smile turning almost imperceptibly to a sneer. To Jonathan, he said, "You the owner?"

Jonathan stiffened, anger flaring at the inspector's blatant dismissal of her. He opened his mouth, ready to set the man straight, when Candy stepped forward.

"The owner is Maeve Lewis," Candy said, her voice deceptively calm. "And she's not on the property. What can I do for you?"

Tad Rodgers took a step back and made a show of sizing Candy up. "Well, you're a tiny little thing, aren't ya?" he said with an ugly chuckle. "You looked a lot taller on TV."

Candy shrugged. "Yes, well, they say the camera puts a good ten pounds on you."

Jonathan let out a surprised snort. Not wanting to offend either of them, he covered it up with a fake sneeze. "Sorry. Carpet dust," he said when Candy shot him a censorious look.

But Tad Rodgers wasn't finished being a patronizing lowlife. He pointed at her new work boots. "Got yourself some fancy shoes, there."

Candy played along, putting one foot out and turning it this way and that. She lifted wide eyes to the inspector. "I know. Aren't they the absolute cutest?" Then she pointed at his ridiculous boots and gasped. "But yours are so cute, too!"

Jonathan knew in that moment that Tad Rodgers, Building Inspector, had met his match. He stepped back, giving Candy room to work.

"I'm Candy Needham, by the way. I'm the contractor on record. My license number is on all the permit applications, along with my contact information." She extended her hand, but not to shake his. "Your name was Rodgers? I don't believe we've met before. May I see your license, please?"

The inspector seemed taken aback but recovered quickly, ignoring her request. "Yes, well, there are some questions about the proposed load-bearing modifications in your permits."

"Hold up," Candy said, turning to Jonathan. "Did Mr. Rogers here show you his license?"

Jonathan shook his head, thoroughly enjoying watching the scene play out in front of him.

"Did you invite him into the house? Onto the property?"

"Now, sweethear—"

Candy cut him off before he got the 't' out. She took a step closer to the inspector "I'm not sweet. And if you don't show me your license, I'm going to have to insist that you leave." She gestured for the door as if she expected him to go ahead of her. "You're welcome to come back with your license and after you've given me notice, and then you can knock on the front door, just like everyone else, and wait to be invited inside. Okay?" She said the last word with ridiculously false brightness.

"I have my license," the inspector declared, pulling his wallet from his back pocket and flipping it open. "Right here." He held it out to her.

Candy took it from him and studied it for much longer than was necessary, then gave it back. "See? That wasn't so hard, was it? I'm curious, though. How do you plan on inspecting anything with your vision trouble?"

Tad looked confused. "I see just fine."

"Really?" She pointed at Jonathan. "But you mistook this sasquatch here for tiny little me."

The inspector had the good grace to blush. "I was just joking, ma'am."

Candy said nothing; just stood there studying the man for so long, that Jonathan knew Tad wouldn't be able to keep his mouth shut.

"I didn't mean to offend you. Sheesh."

Finally, Candy spoke, changing the subject, her tone professional and confident. "Tell me which modifications specifically."

For a moment, Tad looked like he had no clue what she was talking about. Candy pointed at his clipboard.

"Oh. Right. The wall removal between the kitchen and dining area," the inspector said, scanning the room again. "That's a supporting wall for the second floor."

Candy smiled patiently. "If you'll look at page three of the submission, you'll see detailed plans for the LVL beam installation that will replace the wall's support function. We're using a 2-ply 11 7/8-inch beam, which exceeds the minimum requirements for the span."

The inspector flipped through his papers, frowning. "And the mud room expansion?"

"The wall being removed there is non-load-bearing," Candy explained. "It's just a partition wall from a 1970s remodel. The original blueprints show that space was originally open until the previous owners divided it."

Jonathan retreated and made his way to the kitchen. He'd been ready to defend her, to tell the misogynistic inspector off, but Candy didn't need his defense. She was handling the situation with more professionalism and restraint than he would have managed.

From the doorway, he watched as she pulled out her own copy of the permits from a folder in the drawer of the foyer table, pointing out specifications and explaining her plans in technical terms that had the inspector nodding along. Her knowledge was impressive and undeniable.

Jonathan felt a strange mix of emotions. On one hand, he was disappointed he hadn't gotten to be the hero, stepping in to rescue her. On the other hand, it was clear she didn't need rescuing, and watching her command the situation with such authority was far more satisfying. He leaned against the kitchen doorframe, content to observe as she systematically addressed each of the inspector's concerns. This was her domain, and she navigated it with expertise.

A truck engine rumbled outside, breaking his concentration. Jonathan glanced out the kitchen window to see a delivery truck pulling up.

"Looks like your dumpster delivery is here," he called to Candy, who was still deep in conversation with the inspector.

She glanced over her shoulder. "Would you mind signing for it? I need to finish up here."

"No problem," Jonathan replied, heading for the door. He could at least make himself useful in some small way.

Outside, a young man in a uniform skillfully backed his trailer into the driveway, dropped the dumpster like he'd done it a thousand times, then jumped down from the truck cab, a clipboard in hand. He held it out to Jonathan. "Hearth & Home Renovations?" he asked.

"Yep. I can sign for that," Jonathan offered.

The driver pointed at the bottom of the page. "Just need a signature and printed name."

Jonathan scrawled his signature on the line, then paused when he reached the space for his printed name. In clear block letters, he wrote: "SQUATCH BURKHARDT."

The driver glanced at the form, grinned, then handed Jonathan a copy of the receipt. "Thanks, Mr. Burkhardt."

As the driver pulled away, Jonathan hoped Candy would get a kick out of his little joke. At the very least, it might go a little ways toward helping her to forgive him for sending her flying across the floor earlier.

15
Candy

When Tad Rodgers finally left without finding a single legitimate issue with her permits, Candy waited until his car disappeared down the driveway before letting herself relax. She'd stood her ground professionally, but inside she'd been seething at his condescending attitude. Now that he was gone, she needed to release all that pent-up energy.

She pulled her phone from her pocket, scrolled through her playlist, and hit play. The opening notes of "Mr. Brightside" by The Killers filled the living room, and she cranked up the volume without hesitation.

"That's what I'm talking about!" she exclaimed to the empty room, doing a fist pump in the air. She spun in a circle, adding dramatic arm movements as she sang along at the top of her lungs. Her hip twinged slightly from her earlier tumble, but the adrenaline of her victory over the inspector pushed any discomfort aside.

Candy had no idea where Jonathan had disappeared to, and honestly, she didn't care. She could finish pulling up the carpet herself, but first, she was going to celebrate putting that pompous inspector in his place. She danced across the half-exposed floor, hamming it up with air guitar during the instrumental break, completely lost in her moment of triumph.

As the song reached its crescendo, Candy whirled around—and froze. Jonathan stood in the doorframe between the kitchen and living room, arms crossed, watching her with an unreadable expression.

Heat rushed to her face, but she laughed off her embarrassment. Let him judge her; why should she care? She was sick of having people treat her like she was incapable just because of her diminutive stature and her blonde, blue-eyed looks. She pointed a finger at him and said, "Go ahead and laugh, but I showed him who's boss!"

To her surprise, Jonathan's mouth quirked into something resembling a smile. "You certainly did," he agreed. "That was impressive. I've never seen someone shut down a condescending jerk so professionally."

Candy blinked, not quite sure how to respond to the unexpected compliment. "Thanks. I've had plenty of practice."

"I bet you have." Jonathan pushed away from the doorframe and shoved his hands in his pocket. He looked a little sheepish—probably still feeling bad for knocking her on her backside—but she also saw a gleam of respect in his eyes.

"I know I'm 'a tiny little thing,'" she said, making air quotes around the phrase the inspector had used. "I don't need anyone telling me as much. And most of time, I like being my size." Should she stop? Was she sharing too much? Did Jonathan even care how she felt about this? Did it matter? It felt good to say this stuff out loud to someone. "My size is often a handicap in this industry, but I bend over backward to not let it hold me back, and I *more* than compensate for any shortcomings—" She broke off and snickered at her unintentional pun.

"Nice," Jonathan commented, nodding slowly, appreciatively.

"I more than make up for my shortcomings by being the best in my business," she finished, knowing that sounded conceited. But if she didn't believe she was the best, why should clients hire her? "And do you know what the crazy thing is?" She didn't wait for his response. "I actually *am* sweet. But don't condescendingly call me 'Sweetheart' or I'll—I'll—" There were all kinds of things she wanted to say, but truth be told, she wouldn't do any of them. "Or I'll set you straight," she finally finished lamely.

Jonathan cocked his head at her. "So, when you threatened me with that hammer, it was all bark and no bite?"

Candy jabbed a finger toward him. "Oh, no. That was a very, very real threat, Squatch. You haven't see what I can do with a hammer, yet."

Jonathan grinned. "I can't wait." He took a step into the room. "You hungry? I was thinking we could order some lunch. My treat."

"Your treat?" Candy repeated, momentarily thrown off by the change in subject, as well as by his offer. But yes, she was suddenly ravenous. Was it too early for lunch?

"Consider it my way of saying sorry for sending you flying across the room," he said, his face flushing slightly beneath his beard.

Candy hesitated only for a moment before nodding. "Okay. Sure. I'm actually starving."

"Chinese food okay?" Jonathan asked, already pulling out his phone. "I drove by a place called Dragon Garden this weekend. Maeve said they're pretty good."

"They're great," Candy agreed, a little surprised at how quickly she'd accepted his olive branch. She gave him her order and her mouth watered with anticipation at the thought of the tangy General Tsao's chicken meal, and even more so when Jonathan added crab rangoons and egg rolls to their order. Yum.

When he finished, he pulled a folded piece of paper from his back pocket and handed it to her. "By the way, I signed for the dumpster delivery."

"Great, thanks," Candy said, accepting the invoice. She unfolded it, checking the details, then her eyes widened when she spotted the signature line. In block letters beneath his signature, he'd written "SQUATCH BURKHARDT."

She pressed her lips together to suppress a grin, but failed miserably. Something about seeing her nickname for him written in his own hand made her ridiculously happy. She glanced up to find Jonathan watching her reaction, a hopeful look in his eyes.

"I'll head into town to pick up the food," he said before she could comment. "Should be ready in about twenty minutes."

Candy nodded, feeling more lighthearted than she had since her first day on the project. "Sounds good. I'll clear off the table."

After Jonathan left, Candy found herself humming as she set out paper napkins and a couple of Mason jar glasses for the tall pitcher of sweet tea she found in the fridge. Probably a gift from Maeve, she decided. She was startled by her own good mood. Just this morning, she'd been dreading another week of tension and awkwardness, and now here she was, practically giddy about sharing lunch with the same man who'd knocked her flat on her behind just hours ago.

She'd probably been a little too hard on the inspector, and part of her worried that she'd made an enemy of someone who could cause trouble for her down the line. But it had felt good to stand up for herself, to not pander to the unfair assumptions of people like Tad Rodgers.

Maybe she should take him one of Juno's scones, see if she could smooth things over a little. She didn't need or want any more hiccups on this job than she already had.

By the time Jonathan returned with the food, Candy was ravenous. It had taken every ounce of her willpower not to start nibbling on some of the spaghetti leftovers she'd discovered in the fridge along with the sweet tea. She'd had to leave the kitchen altogether after getting a whiff of the meaty marinara sauce.

She started to fill his glass with tea, then paused. "Do you want sweet tea or water?" she asked as he set the takeout bags on the table.

Jonathan eyed the pitcher she held. "Tea sounds good, but I have to warn you. It's sweet enough to make your teeth hurt."

"Just the way I like it," Candy grinned, flashing her pearly whites at him the way she used to do when the camera was right in her face.

Chill, Candy, she told herself when Jonathan gave her a bemused look. Was she being too friendly, too eager to be chummy? Was he suspicious of her changed demeanor? She felt a flutter of uncertainty and pulled back, reining in her enthusiasm.

"So, how long have you been a contractor?" Jonathan asked as they settled in to eat. "Were you one before the TV show?"

Candy shook her head, grateful for the neutral topic. "No, I went back to school after the show ended. Got my contractor's license, did apprentice work with some really great builders in the area."

He nodded, digging into his kung pao chicken. "You really know what you're talking about. I'm impressed, Candy."

"Because I'm a tiny little thing with a face for television and a girl brain?" The moment the words were out, she regretted voicing to them. She hated that it still smarted to not be taken seriously, but Jonathan wasn't doing that. He was acknowledging her accomplishments, not belittling her. "Sorry," she said, then let out a long sigh. "That was uncalled for."

"I get it," Jonathan said, meeting her gaze. "Especially after today with Tad. You don't have to apologize."

"Thanks," she said, touched by his graciousness.

The meal was delicious, and Candy ate with abandon. Between the carpet wrestling and the inspector stand-off, the morning had burned through a lot of energy.

As they finished up, Jonathan cleared his throat. "Listen, I feel bad about what happened with the carpet. Maybe I should tackle something else this afternoon. Something where I'm less likely to cause bodily harm."

Candy felt a twinge of guilt. Had she made him feel bad? She'd hurried to the bathroom so she wouldn't embarrass herself further by crying in front of him, not because she was angry at him. Or was he intimidated by her knowledge? Surely not. "The carpet thing was just an accident," she assured him. "No harm done."

"Still," he insisted, dropping his chopsticks into his empty rice container. "Maybe I'd be more useful doing something else."

"If you're sure," Candy said, thinking quickly. "I've been meaning to sort through the garage—separating items for donation versus trash. Could you do that? There are some boxes out there already. Just throw the trash in the dumpster.""

Jonathan nodded, looking relieved. "I can handle that. But let me help haul out the carpet pieces once they're up, since I know those will be heavy."

"Thanks. I'd appreciate that." Candy stood, gathering their empty containers, confused by the way the meal was ending. What had happened to bring back the awkwardness between them? It was probably her fault. Probably her projecting her bitterness onto him. She didn't want to be that kind of a person, and she hated the idea that he might think she was.

It was good that Jonathan spent the next few hours out in the garage. Candy turned up her music and took out her frustration on the carpet, cutting it up into manageable sections. Then she pulled up the filthy pad, and using her heavy duty pry bar, ripped up the carpet tack strips and the staples used to hold the pad in place. She ended the afternoon with heartburn, but was assuaged by the release of endorphins that came with hard work.

As she and Jonathan tag-teamed on hauling the carpet scraps out to the dumpster, she mentally made a note to herself to stop trying to create camaraderie where there wasn't any. She was here in this house to do a job, not to fraternize with the owner's nephew. If Squatch wanted to put his muscles to work, she'd take the help. If he didn't, she wouldn't be offended or hurt or anything. After all, she'd originally planned to manage almost everything on her own before he showed up.

16
Jonathan

"WHAT IF YOU EXTEND the bench all the way to the corner?" Jonathan ventured to ask on Tuesday afternoon. Candy had surprised him by asking him for his opinion. She'd been mapping out the new mudroom's storage system on her tablet at the kitchen counter, and a large element was the built-in bench with its shoe shelf under the seat and the coat hooks and shelves above. "I like the big plant in that corner, but not everyone is a plant person. Without the plant there, it might end up becoming a dumping ground for stuff that doesn't get put away." He'd been thinking about kids, for some reason, which was a little out of left field, but he'd soldiered on. "It's just a thought. Either way, that custom bench is amazing."

She'd considered his suggestion for a moment, head tilted, then nodded. "Actually, that works. I can shift the whole unit over, leaving a little more space on the other end. That gives the door extra clearance, too. Good call."

Small victories like these became more frequent, yet Jonathan was very aware of the fact that Candy had become more guarded since their lunch on Monday. Gone was the animated woman who'd danced with abandon to The Killers and passionately defended her work to the building inspector. In her place was a consummate professional who kept conversations centered firmly on the renovation.

He missed that other Candy. That was the Candy he wanted to get to know better.

On Wednesday evening, Jonathan arrived at Maeve's condo for dinner as promised. The baked chicken on a bed of Basmati rice and roasted vegetables was delicious as he'd come to expect, and he made a point to compliment her on her cooking.

"It's just such a pleasure to get to cook for someone else again," Maeve told him. "Most of the time, it was only Stan and me, but he always made me feel like I'd laid a king's banquet before him when I laid the table. That man was an enthusiastic eater."

Jonathan chuckled, thinking of another enthusiastic eater he knew. He got a kick out of how much Candy enjoyed her meals. She always put aside her phone and her planner and made a point to take a break and appreciate the act of nourishing her body.

"So how's the renovation coming along?" Maeve passed him a basket of dinner rolls. They were still warm, fresh from the oven.

"Your contractor is pretty amazing," Jonathan admitted. "She's transformed one of the downstairs bathrooms already, and we've exposed the original hardwood floors in the living room, kitchen, and dining room, and I can't wait to see what that will look like once its refinished. You should come see the progress." He eyed her, curious as to why she hadn't been by the place once since the day he'd come to town. Was she purposely staying away to force him and Candy to work things out without interfering? Or... hm. Was it some kind of a matchmaking attempt?

The thought didn't bother him nearly as much as it should have.

Maeve smiled enigmatically as she took her seat. "Oh, I don't think so. Candy specifically asked that I not visit until the end. She wants me to get the full impact, the 'wow effect,' as she called it."

"That sounds just like her." Jonathan nodded, not quite sure why he felt let down. It wasn't as if he needed his aunt to orchestrate more time alone with Candy. They spent all day together anyway. "And you're good with that? You're not worried about the process?" He quickly added, "Not that you should be. Like I said, she's really good at what she does."

"I'm not worried," Maeve insisted. "Not in the slightest. I've seen her work, I've seen her plans, and I trust her." She pointed at her cell phone on its charger over on the counter. "Besides, I'm an official Hearth Breaker, so I get to watch it unfold along with everyone else."

Jonathan's eyes widened. "Nice," he said. "A Hearth and Home groupie." Then he asked, "Is it hard watching it all get taken apart?"

Maeve didn't respond immediately, but then said, "I think if I had to be there seeing it happen in person, it might be. But watching it online gives me a degree of separation that makes it easier."

"Sure, that makes sense."

"She's very clever about not showing too much as she finishes up the different projects, isn't she? That's something she must have learned from her TV show; how to save the big reveal until last."

Jonathan mentally scrolled through all the images and videos on her channels. Maeve was right. Candy kept her followers' attention by feeding that anticipation for the finished product. Very clever, indeed.

"So, tell me more about this app you're developing," Maeve said, changing the subject. "The one for hikers."

Jonathan latched onto the familiar topic. He'd gotten a lot done since coming to Autumn Lake. It had been an unexpected benefit of extending his leave, and he was excited with all the upgrades he'd configured into the app. "It's coming together quickly," he told her. "I think because so much of what I'm putting into the app is a result of firsthand experience with the trail. I'm making sure to incorporate everything that I dealt with before, during, and even after."

"After?" Maeve questioned, a slight frown forming between her brows.

"Yes," Jonathan said. "The body goes through quite an ordeal on that trail, especially if someone hikes it all in one stretch in such a short time. So does the mind. And when it's over and you're back home after several months of pushing yourself? Well, I wasn't exactly prepared for the let down. I thought I'd feel more... accomplished, I guess." There was a lot more to it than that, but he wasn't yet ready to talk about the disillusionment he'd experienced after coming home.

Maeve nodded. "I see." The way she said it made him think that maybe she understood more than he gave her credit for.

"All I wanted to do was sleep and eat and heal, but my muscle memory wouldn't let me. I still can't seem to sleep past first light, and it took me a while to get used to a soft mattress again. I'd wake up with a stiff back and neck and couldn't figure out why. I've quickly adapted back to civilization, don't get me wrong," he added with a chuckle. "But it makes me really appreciate meals like this, sitting at a table, drinking from a glass, eating off of nice dishes."

Maeve gave him a mischievous look. "Well, I don't know about civilized," she said, gesturing at his beard. "But you do look healthier. I believe you're putting a little meat on your bones. And that's good thing."

Jonathan grinned and wiped his mouth with his napkin, hoping he hadn't gotten any food in his facial hair. On the trail, he'd hardly cared about stuff like that, but sitting across from his classy aunt in her clean, elegantly decorated dining room, he was quite conscious of his wilderness look. "You're the one putting meat on my bones," he told her. "I haven't eaten this well in a very long time. It's nice to go to bed at night after a good meal. Thank you."

"It's my pleasure," Maeve said, nudging the platter of roast vegetables his way. "So are there no apps out there that help prepare and plan for a hike like this?" Maeve asked.

"Absolutely, and some pretty good ones, too." Jonathan gladly accepted a second helping of everything on the table. "The Appalachian Trail itself has a lot of resources for hikers, but they're scattered across different websites, guidebooks, and forums. My app centralizes everything and makes it specific to the individual hiker's experience. It also has real-time trail conditions, water sources, and shelter availability, but it also helps the hiker customize stuff like gear, meals, budget, and more according to their level of experience and personal needs."

"Things you wish you'd had when you started," Maeve observed.

"Exactly," Jonathan agreed. "Especially for the first section of the trail out of Maine. I opted to travel southbound so I'd end the hike back at home in Atlanta, but that was pretty rough."

In a moment, he was back in those early days on the trail, specifically the notorious 100-Mile Wilderness in Maine, the most remote section of the entire Appalachian Trail. He'd chosen to hike southbound, starting at Mount Katahdin in Maine rather than the more common northbound route from Georgia, which would have given him a chance to break in his gear, find his stride, and work up to the much more challenging part of the trail in good weather. It had been late May when they'd opened the trail head, and winter still held the Maine woods in its grip.

He remembered the bite of the cold as he'd stepped off the trail shuttle, his brand-new gear gleaming and untested. Oh, he'd had gone on a couple of short hikes in his expensive boots to make sure they were a good fit for his feet, but May in Georgia is very different than May in Maine, and the opportunities to really put his gear to the test simply weren't there. The ranger at the trailhead had eyed him skeptically, warning him about the conditions ahead. Deep snow was still packed into the higher elevations, stream crossings swollen with snowmelt, temperatures dropped below freezing at night.

Jonathan had assured the ranger that he was prepared, but the truth of the matter was that he really hadn't cared. In fact, he relished the challenge, was looking forward to going head to head with nature. He knew he was tempting fate by putting himself into the way of the whims of the elements, but the thought of coming to grips with his own mortality spurred him on. Even so, he hadn't expected the overwhelming isolation to affect him so intensely. The relentless difficulty of navigating snow-covered trails with no cell service, no bailout points, and 100 miles between him and the nearest town, which meant no way to replenish his supplies or seek medical attention. He was completely and utterly alone, which only served to remind him that it wasn't supposed to be that way.

This was supposed to be a hike he and his father took together.

By day three, his feet were a mass of blisters, his food calculations proving woefully inadequate for the calories he was burning. By day five, he'd run out of stove fuel, forcing him to eat cold, partially rehydrated meals. The nights were the worst, huddled in his sleeping bag as temperatures plummeted, listening to the wind howl through the trees, the sound of no other living thing stupid enough to be out in the wilderness with him.

On day seven, lost in a section where spring snowmelt had obscured the trail completely, he'd fallen into an ice-cold stream. Soaked and shivering, miles from the nearest shelter, Jonathan had experienced true fear for perhaps the first time in his life. He'd thought, with clarifying certainty: I'm going to die out here.

That night, he'd managed to make camp and start a fire with the last of his dry materials. As he'd sat there, watching the flames push back the darkness, something in him had shifted. The corporate executive with the corner office and the carefully plotted life trajectory had begun to fall away, revealing someone else beneath—someone more resilient, more humble, more alive.

"Jonathan?" Maeve's voice pulled him back to the present.

"Sorry," he said, blinking. "I was just thinking about the trail."

"The experience has deeply affected you, hasn't it?" she observed.

"It has," he acknowledged. "Though I'm not sure I fully understand how yet. I feel like I'm in an in-between place since getting home. I know I need to get back to my job. They've been very patient with me, but they won't hold my position forever. But I'm having a hard time seeing myself back there again. It feels like going back there would be like going backwards."

"Have you thought anymore about the lake house?" she prodded gently. "Perhaps you could work remotely for a season? The kind of work you do seems like it would be something you could do from anywhere, but I won't pretend to understand it, so I don't want to make assumptions, either." She was giving him time to sort things out, he knew, and part of him appreciated her for being so generous. The other part of him wanted her to give him an ultimatum, force his hand, make him choose. He felt stuck, caught in the web of indecision, unable to go back and unable to move forward on his own.

"My position at SyncTech isn't one I can do remotely, not long-term, anyway," he told her.

"What about your own projects? Could you make a business of designing your own apps?" She wasn't asking him any questions he hadn't already asked himself.

"Not at this point. I don't have the financial stability to go rogue yet. I mean, it's something I'd love to do, but I'm not there yet."

For several moments, neither of them spoke, then Maeve reached across the table and patted his hand. "I believe that there's a reason God sends us through the wilderness, Jonathan. Maybe it's to teach us to lean on Him to be our guide, but maybe it's because He wants to get us off the path we're on so that He can show us a better way."

Her sentiment might have been a little cliche, but her words kept replaying in his mind as he lay in bed that night. Even though he was safe and warm in the bedroom that used to be his father's, he felt soul-crushingly lost. Without intentionally setting about to do so, Jonathan found himself praying, asking God what he was supposed to do now, begging Him for guidance, for direction. He fell asleep with the words "Please help me," on his lips.

The rest of the week continued in much the same vein. Days were spent carefully navigating his working relationship with Candy, evenings split between dinner with Maeve and working on his app. By Friday, they'd settled into a comfortable routine, but Jonathan couldn't shake his frustration at the persistent wall Candy maintained between them.

His leave from SyncTech was nearly up, and he doubted he could get another extension. He needed to make some decisions, and soon. Part of him was tempted to just quit his job altogether, to walk away, so that he could see this renovation through to completion. Another part wanted to get back to the familiar rhythms of his life in Atlanta.

But something else nagged at him. There was unfinished business here, he thought, not just with the house or his aunt, but with Candy.

Not because of romantic notions, of course. He just wanted to make sure they were on the same page about the renovation progress.

At least, that's what he told himself.

As Friday afternoon wound down, Jonathan resolved to talk to Candy before he left for the day. He needed to tell her about his leave ending, to get her input on whether his presence was actually helpful or just a hindrance. He'd planned what to say, how to phrase it casually, as he walked through the house looking for her.

He checked the kitchen first, then the living room. Finally, he heard movement upstairs and headed up to the second floor. He found Candy in the master suite, but not in the mode he'd grown accustomed to seeing her in all week. She wasn't focused on measurements or paint swatches or carefully studying her tablet. Instead, she was practically bouncing in her boots, phone in hand, filming, her entire being radiating excitement.

When she spotted him in the doorway, her face lit up in a way he hadn't seen in what felt like forever. "Jonathan! You have to see this!" She turned her camera toward him.

Before he could respond, she'd crossed the room and grabbed his hand, pulling him toward the built-in bookcase in the master bedroom.

"I found something amazing," she said, her blue eyes sparkling.

Jonathan allowed himself to be led, acutely aware of her small hand gripping his, her excitement infectious. She reminded him of Tigger from Winnie the Pooh, though he kept the observation to himself. Whatever had her so animated, he couldn't wait to see it, and not just for the discovery itself, but for the chance to spend time with this version of Candy again.

17
Candy

"LOOK AT THIS!" CANDY exclaimed, her voice rising with enthusiasm. She showed Jonathan how the ornate wooden bookcase, which she had assumed was permanently attached to the wall, actually had a section that swung outward when one end of a shelf was pressed, releasing a latch. She could barely contain her excitement as she panned her camera to capture his reaction.

"I was measuring because I wanted to extend the built-ins, and I noticed this section had different dimensions." She moved her fingers along the lip of the fourth shelf up. "When I pushed here, the whole thing swung out!"

Jonathan leaned in closer, his eyes widening in surprise. Inside the compartment were several neatly organized items: a stack of important-looking documents in a leather portfolio, a few small velvet jewelry pouches and boxes, an envelope that appeared to contain cash, and most notably, a framed family photograph showing a young couple with two children, a girl and a much younger boy. The compartment wasn't large—just a small niche in the wall with enough space for important documents and a few treasured items—but finding it felt like uncovering a time capsule from the past.

"That must be your grandparents," Candy said, focusing her camera on the photograph. "And your dad, right? With Maeve?" She sighed at the nostalgia the image evoked in her. "Your aunt was so beautiful," she gushed. "I mean, she still is, but wow. Look at those eyes."

She panned the camera up to Jonathan again, thrilled to see that he seemed genuinely excited by the family history she'd unearthed. "They're obviously a family trait; you have them too, Squatch." She zoomed in on his rather pretty eyes, she suddenly noticed, and made every effort to remain professional.

"This is amazing," Jonathan murmured, reaching out hesitantly to touch the frame of the old photograph. "Dad never mentioned a hidden compartment in here."

The way he said it made Candy's ears perk up. "You say that like he might have mentioned others?"

Jonathan nodded. "Yeah. There's one in the back of the closet in his bedroom. I checked in there, hoping to find something of his, but it's empty." He looked right into the camera, surprising Candy. He'd reluctantly agreed to be on film, but he rarely spoke directly to her audience like this. "I was hoping to find old comic books or trading cards, a real treasure, you know? But it's still pretty cool. He said he used to go read comics in there whenever he got sent to his room, pretend he was a superhero and could bust right through the walls." He offered a rather dashing half-grin. "I don't think he minded being sent to his room."

"Wow," Candy whispered, her excitement building. "I wonder just how many secret compartments and cubbyholes there are in this house. Do you think there's one in Maeve's old room?" Then she pressed her hand to her cheek. "Oh, goodness, Jonathan. Do you think Maeve knows about this?"

"I don't know," he said with a shrug. "She and Stan moved in here after they were married, but I can't imagine she would have left all of this stuff behind if she did." He gingerly touched one of the jewelry pouches. "This stuff must be pretty old, and probably valuable, don't you think?"

Candy watched Jonathan's face carefully. His expression had softened in a way she hadn't seen before, making him look younger, less guarded. He carefully lifted the photograph, studying the faces of his family members. "They look so happy," he said quietly.

She lowered her phone, stopping the recording. This moment felt too personal to share with her followers. She couldn't help but feel a little intrusive, witnessing this private encounter with Jonathan's past.

"I should..." she began, taking a step back. "I can give you some privacy to look through these things."

"No," Jonathan said quickly, looking up at her. A genuine, unguarded smile transformed his face. "Stay. Please. You found it. You should be part of this discovery."

The warmth in his voice caught her off guard. She'd grown so accustomed to the walls between them that his sudden openness had her feeling a little befuddled. "Are you sure?" she asked, gesturing toward the items. "These look pretty personal."

"I'm sure," he replied, setting the photo back in its place. He picked up the envelope of cash and thumbed through the bills without taking them out. "There are five hundred dollars here. That was probably a good little rainy-day stash for my grandparents." He returned it to the cubby, too. "I think I'd like Maeve to see this before I go through anything else. Especially the jewelry; maybe some of it is stuff she'd remember."

"That's a great idea. I wonder if she'd let me film her going through it."

"She might. She's pretty supportive of what you're doing here," he said, then added with a wry grin, "She warned me not to get in your way."

"Oh. She said that to you?" Candy was intrigued. She'd known Maeve was completely on board with the renovation plans, but Jonathan's admission was a surprise.

"She sure did. Said if I knew what was good for me, I'd keep a low profile."

Candy snorted and held up her fingers to tick things off. "So low profile to you means pouring coffee on my planner, flooding a bathroom, and tossing me end-over-end on a magic carpet ride?"

Jonathan guffawed. "You should see how I act when I'm *trying* to get your attention," he quipped. His eyes were bright with excitement as he met her gaze. "You know what? This calls for a celebration. Let me take you out to dinner tonight."

The invitation was so unexpected that Candy blinked. "Dinner?"

"Yes, dinner," Jonathan repeated, his rare smile still lighting up his face. "You know, that meal people eat in the evening?"

Candy couldn't help but smile back at his gentle teasing. "I know what dinner is, Squatch."

She considered his offer for a moment. Was this a good idea? They'd finally reached a comfortable working relationship, and socializing outside of the renovation could complicate things. On the other hand, she couldn't deny that she was curious about him, about his story. And the idea of spending an evening with this more relaxed version of Jonathan was strangely appealing.

But then she remembered. "I actually already have plans with Liz tonight," she admitted, feeling oddly disappointed to turn him down. "We're meeting at Juno's. It's French Toast Friday. Juno uses up her leftover breads and makes the most amazing French toast."

"Ah," Jonathan said, his smile dimming slightly. "Of course. Another time, then."

"But," Candy found herself saying, "you're welcome to join us, if you'd like. Liz has been dying to meet you anyway. Though I've warned her about your predisposition to scowl," she teased.

Jonathan chuckled, the sound warm and rich. "I think I can manage to be civil for one evening."

"I wouldn't want to put you out," Candy added, enjoying the back and forth with him. "I know how difficult human interaction is for mythical creatures."

"I'll risk it," he countered, his eyes crinkling at the corners. "What time should I be ready?"

Candy checked her watch. "Six? I need to go home and shower first. I've been working on some of the plumbing in there." She pointed at the master bathroom. "And I'm afraid I might be wearing a hint of eau de toilet, and I don't meant eau de toilette. Very different fragrances, if you know what I mean."

"You smell good to me," Jonathan said, then immediately looked embarrassed by his own comment. "I mean—well, you don't smell like a toilet." He squeezed his eyes shut and rubbed his brow. "That wasn't any better, was it?"

"It's okay," Candy laughed, saving him from his floundering. "But I still want to clean up. I can give you my address if you want to pick me up, or we can just meet at Juno's."

"I'll pick you up," Jonathan offered readily, almost like he'd already been planning to suggest it.

Candy noted how different the energy between them felt now. The discovery had somehow broken through the professional barriers they'd carefully maintained all week. There seemed to be a new sense of ease, a warmth that she found she liked. Things had definitely shifted. From squaring off across the bedroom that first morning to this moment of shared discovery and connection—it was like they'd entered a new phase in their relationship.

Not that they had a relationship, she reminded herself firmly. They had a professional arrangement, complicated by circumstances neither of them had anticipated.

But now they also had dinner plans, and Candy wasn't quite sure what to make of that.

"Six o'clock," Jonathan confirmed as they headed toward the stairs. "Juno's is pretty casual, right?"

"Definitely casual," Candy assured him. "You'll fit in just fine, as long as you don't show up in your threadbare trail clothes." She shot a quick glance at his hair, but swallowed the suggestion—that he might want to do something with the mop on top—on the tip of her tongue.

Jonathan hadn't missed the look she'd given it, though. He ran a hand through his wild hair. "I'll try not to embarrass you," he said with a wink.

18
Jonathan

When Jonathan pulled up outside the address Candy had given him, she was already on the front porch, sitting on the steps. The little cottage-style home was exactly what he would have imagined for her with its quaint white siding and cornflower blue shutters, window boxes brimming with petunias and trailing ivy, and a welcoming porch swing decorated with plump floral cushions. It was undeniably feminine.

"Beautiful place," he said, getting out of the car. "Looks just like you."

Candy chuckled as she stood up. "Oh, this is all Liz's doing. She's the cottage-core freak, not me." She glanced around with affection. "But it *is* beautiful, isn't it?"

"Liz, huh?" *You're beautiful,* is what he wanted to say. She wore a loose, fluttery pale blue top that complemented her sun-kissed skin, paired with fitted jeans and ankle boots that added a couple of inches to her petite frame. Her blonde hair fell in loose waves around her shoulders. "I'd have never guessed."

Candy grinned as she came down the steps. "Right? All those flannel shirts and Carhartts? You should see her fairy garden out back." She put a hand up to the side of her mouth and whispered, "I'll see if I can finagle an invitation for you." Then she straightened and gave him an impudent look. "You clean up nice. For a sasquatch."

"Thank you," he said, as he walked her around to the passenger door of his car. He'd spent more time than he cared to admit getting ready for tonight. He hadn't trimmed his beard—he wasn't quite ready for that yet—but he had showered, combed his hair back from his face so that it dried in a semblance of order, and put on a teal button-down shirt and a pair of dark jeans. "So do you, Miss Toolbelt. So do you."

"Wow," Candy breathed as they approached the car, her eyes wide with genuine admiration. "This is seriously gorgeous."

A surge of pride rose inside of him as he held the door for her.

She slid into the low-slung seat, her fingers tracing the contours of the pristine blue leather interior. "Original leather?" she asked after he'd circled the car and climbed in behind the wheel.

"Everything's original. Dad and I restored it together," he explained, running his hands almost reverently over the dashboard. "We spent hundreds of hours working on this car. Took us almost three years."

"It shows," Candy said, her eyes taking in every detail. "I've never seen a restoration this perfect. The color is stunning."

"Montreux Blue," Jonathan told her as he started the engine. The familiar rumble filled the air, and he grinned at the appreciative look on Candy's face. "It was Dad's favorite of the original colors. I pushed for Regimental Red or Starlight Black, but he insisted on the blue."

As they headed toward the heart of Autumn Lake, Jonathan found himself sharing stories about the restoration process. There were weekends spent hunting down vintage parts at swap meets, arguments over period-correct details, late nights in the garage that would mean two grumpy guys sharing breakfast before work and school the next morning.

"Wait. What?" Candy interjected, a note of feigned disbelief in her voice. "You, grumpy?"

Jonathan shot her a grin. "Right? Can you believe it?" For the first time since his father died, he found himself happy to be driving the GTO with someone else beside him.

He held that thought close, not wanting to examine too carefully how nice it felt to have this particular someone riding in the car with him, her eyes bright with interest, laughing at his stories.

"Did you always know this much about cars?" she asked as they drove down Camellia Court toward the Juno's Coffee Bar on the corner.

"Not really," Jonathan admitted. "Dad was the expert. I was just the kid holding the flashlight and handing him tools at first." He smiled at the memory. "But he taught me a lot. Said every man should know how to rebuild an engine, even if he never had to. I don't know about other cars, but I could tell you a whole lot about what's under the hood of this beauty." He patted the dashboard affectionately.

When they arrived at Juno's, the parking lot was already full. Jonathan found a spot on the street and walked around to open Candy's door again.

"Such a gentleman," she teased as she climbed out.

"I have my moments," he replied with a half-smile. "Don't tell anyone—it might ruin my reputation."

Candy leaned in close, bringing with her whatever fragrance she was wearing. Orange blossoms and vanilla, he thought, resisting the sudden wild urge to breathe her in. "Your secret's safe with me, Squatch." So distracted was he by how good she smelled, it took him a minute to recall what secret she was referring to.

As they approached the entrance to Juno's, Jonathan felt a familiar twinge of social anxiety. He was about to meet Candy's cousin, Liz, and another one of her friends, Juno, the proprietress of the cafe. These women clearly mattered to her. Had he imposed on her personal time by coming this evening? Had Candy felt obligated to invite him? He hoped not, but he couldn't help wondering if he should be here.

It was too late to back out now. Candy pushed open the door, and the warm scent of coffee and fresh-baked goods enveloped them. The café was busy but not crowded, with soft lighting and mismatched vintage furniture creating a cozy atmosphere.

"Oh." Candy paused on the threshold, surprise in her voice. "Over there," she said, waving toward a corner table. Jonathan followed her gaze, surprised to see not just one person but a whole group of women seated around a large farmhouse table.

"That's more than Liz," he observed warily.

"I wasn't expecting the whole gang," she murmured, pasting on a bright smile and leading the way toward the table.

A tall woman with coppery hair—Liz, he assumed—spotted them first and broke into a wide grin. "Look who's here!" she called, drawing the attention of the entire group.

Candy leaned in close to Jonathan before they reached the table. "I'm sorry," she whispered. "I had no idea they'd all be here."

"It's okay," he assured her, though his stomach had tightened into a knot. He was perfectly comfortable in his own skin sitting behind a desk in his cubicle or tinkering under the hood of the GTO with his dad. But being put on the spot in public was another thing altogether. He hoped he wouldn't come across as aloof or awkward, even though it was his awkwardness that gave people the perception that he was aloof. He found that he really wanted Candy's friends to be okay with him, maybe to even like him.

"Hey, everyone!" Candy's voice was almost back to its usual cheerful lilt. "This is Jonathan. Jonathan, this is... well, everyone."

Liz stood up first, offering her hand. "Nice to finally meet you, Squatch," she said with a mischievous grin. "I'm Liz, Candy's cousin and the best roomy in the world."

"Pleasure," Jonathan replied, shaking her hand.

Candy snorted. "Well, I might have agreed until now. Is this your doing?" she asked, making a sweeping gesture with her hand to include all of the women around the table.

"You wouldn't have expected any less from me," Liz countered, giving Candy a quick hug. Jonathan saw through the ribbing to their closeness, and, as he often did, he wondered what kind of relationships he might have enjoyed if he'd had cousins of his own, or even a sibling or two.

"I'm Claire," offered a woman wearing square dark-rimmed glasses, her pale blonde hair falling down her back in a messy braid. And was that a red wig beside her plate? Jonathan frowned and tried to avert his gaze from the thing while he shook her hand. She pointed out the cafe window to the bookstore on the opposite corner. "I own The Cracked Spine."

She must have noticed him eyeing the wig. She held it up, settled it onto her head, then straightened the collar of her orange turtleneck and fluffed her maroon pleated miniskirt. "Velma Dinkley," she said, holding out her hand to him again. "The rest of the gang are riding around in the Mystery Machine somewhere."

"Claire dresses up like characters from books and movies," Candy explained to Jonathan. To Claire, she said, "Nice knee socks, Velma."

Claire rolled her eyes and tugged the wig off again. She dropped it into her oversized handbag on the floor by her feet and fluffed her own hair again. "That thing looks great, but it's too hot for wigs this time of year."

"I'm Addison," added a pretty brunette with shoulder-length curls. "My place is Addison's Arbor. I sell plants and flowers," she clarified with a smile. "And we deliver, if you ever feel like sending that darling auntie of yours a pretty bouquet."

"Nice sales segue," Candy declared, holding up a hand for a high-five from Addison.

"I'm learning," the brunette said, her cheeks coloring prettily. "But honestly, I'd be happy just to keep all the plants and flowers to myself."

Juno had just approached the table with a tray of drinks. "Your handsome hubby might not be so happy about that idea."

Addison let out a light-hearted, "Ha! No, he would not. He already calls me The Crazy Plant Lady. In fact, he thinks that's what I should have called the shop."

"I'm Penny," said a pretty woman from across the table. "I'm co-owner of The Garden Gate Bed and Breakfast. I have a rare Friday evening off, so when Liz put out the bat signal, I was out the door before anyone could stop me." She held up her phone. "I'm on call, though, so I'm glad you two got here before I got called away."

Juno circled the table and extended her hand toward Jonathan. "Juno Thomas. This is my place," she said with a hint of pride. "And you must be Maeve's nephew. We've heard a lot about you."

"All terrible things, I bet," Jonathan joked, trying to relax.

"Absolutely," Liz confirmed with a smirk. "According to Candy, you're part caveman, part natural disaster."

Candy groaned, her cheeks flushing pink. "Liz!"

Liz began to hum softly, her eyes wide with feigned innocence. A moment later, Jonathan recognized the song from Disney's *Aladdin*, the one that Aladdin sang to Princess Jasmine as they soared over the city on his magic carpet.

"Did you really dump coffee on her planner?" Claire asked, eyes twinkling. "I keep telling her she needs to use smear-proof pigment pens."

"And did you really launch her across the room with the carpet?" Penny chimed in, not even bothering to hold back her giggles at the notion.

Jonathan's face grew warm. "I see my reputation precedes me."

"Don't worry," Juno said, pulling out two empty chairs. "You've got extra points with us as we all adore your aunt."

"She's one of our favorite people in Autumn Lake," Claire added.

Jonathan nodded, touched by their obvious affection for Maeve. "That's good to know," he said. "The point system, and that Maeve has a community that looks out for her." The moment the words were out, he realized what he'd unwittingly left unsaid... that her family, which meant him, *wasn't* looking out for her. It was a sobering thought.

Juno eyed him, an unusually keen look on her face. "It's been good for her to have you here, you know. I hope you're not taking this whole endeavor lightly."

"You'd better mind your manners, Squatch," Liz added in a deceptively casual tone, a broad smile softening her strong features. "No one takes advantage of one of our own without recourse."

From beside him, he sensed Candy grow still. To quickly diffuse the tension, Jonathan held up his hands in mock surrender. "I know, I know. If I do, you'll all come for me." He glanced at Candy with a grin. "Armed with hammers instead of pitchforks, I assume."

The women burst into laughter, and Jonathan's shoulders loosened as he let out a relieved breath. Maybe this wouldn't be so bad after all.

"So, Jonathan," Addison began as Juno went to get them menus. "Candy tells us you hiked the entire Appalachian Trail. That's impressive."

"Thank you," he replied, his wariness back. He wasn't sure he wanted to talk about it right now. He was still trying to process the whole experience himself. "It was..." He searched for the right answer. An ordeal? An act of self-flagellation? A practice in penance? "It was an experience," he finally landed on.

"Is that how you got your scar?" Juno asked bluntly, pointing at his face. The woman was direct.

Jonathan's hand automatically rose to touch the jagged line that ran from his temple down over his cheekbone. He was used to people pretending *not* to notice it, so having Juno point it out—literally—was a new experience for him. He glanced at Candy; she looked like she might be holding her breath.

"Or did Candy do that to you?" Liz spoke into the hush that had fallen at the table, and Jonathan shot her an appreciative grin. Humor often took the edge off of a situation, and this was no exception.

He leaned sideways and bumped shoulders with Candy. "She'd probably like to take credit for it," he joked, and when Candy's friends laughed, he continued with the real story. "I actually got it while helping to rescue a woman on the trail."

"So you're a mythical creature *and* a hero," Liz exclaimed, flapping a hand in front of her face as if she might faint. "Be still my heart."

"Hardly," Jonathan insisted, starting to be embarrassed by the attention. "She was filming herself and the view behind her, and took one too many steps backward. She slipped over the edge of a rock face and couldn't get back up on her own, so I had to climb down to help her."

The women collectively leaned in, captivated by his story.

"While helping her scale back up, her phone slipped out of her pocket. She tried to grab for it and nearly took us both off the ledge." Jonathan shook his head at the memory. "I slipped and caught my cheek on dead tree sticking out of ground. Ripped part of my ear off, too." He touched his mangled lobe. "The phone was a goner, but we both made it back up."

"You're lucky you didn't lose an eye," Claire said, wincing sympathetically.

Liz snorted. "You're lucky you both weren't goners."

"Extremely lucky," Jonathan agreed. "To add insult to injury, the girl was more upset about losing her expensive camera than grateful for being rescued. She didn't even thank me. I don't think she even knew I was hurt."

"Some people." Liz shook her head in disgust. "Don't tell me. Was she doing a live feed for her followers?" Then she laid a hand on Candy's arm. "Nothing against you, cuz. I know your live feeds are just for your business. And you already know this, but I just think too many people live too much of their lives in front of a live audience of strangers these days."

Amen to that, Jonathan thought, the memory of that moment on the rock face making his scar tingle. "I agree," he simply said.

"Were you able to get medical attention?" Candy asked quietly.

Jonathan shook his head. "I was about three days from the nearest town. I cleaned it as best I could and kept going." He shrugged, trying to downplay it. "It probably could have used stitches, but it healed okay."

A hush fell as the women regarded him, each of them with varying degrees of respect and curiosity on their faces. Jonathan shifted uncomfortably under their scrutiny, unaccustomed to being the center of attention.

"So," he said, eager to change the subject. "Candy mentioned something about your amazing French toast, Juno?"

Juno's face lit up. "The best in Indiana," she declared. "I use up the leftover artisan breads from the week—sourdough, cinnamon swirl, cranberry walnut—soak them in a custard with vanilla bean and a hint of orange zest, then top them with local maple syrup and seasonal berries."

"Or peanut butter, if you're classy like me," Liz quipped, breathing on her knuckles, then rubbing them on her shoulder.

Juno shook her head. "Why you insist on defiling my fine wares by piling on peanut butter is beyond me," she said with a long-suffering sigh.

Liz elbowed her. "Oh, please. Everyone likes peanut butter and maple syrup on French toast." She pointed at Jonathan and one eyebrow hitched up in challenge. "Right, Squatch?"

"It all sounds incredible," Jonathan said diplomatically, his stomach growling at the descriptions.

"It is," Candy confirmed with enthusiasm. "Juno could open a restaurant with this French toast alone and make a fortune."

As the conversation shifted to other topics, Jonathan found his tension easing. Candy's friends were warm, funny, and refreshingly direct. They teased each other mercilessly, included him in their inside jokes, and treated him like he belonged at their table despite having just met him.

For the first time in a very long time—since before his father's death, certainly—Jonathan felt the simple pleasure of being part of a group, of normal social interaction without the weight of grief and isolation pressing down on him. In fact, he couldn't remember the last time he felt so comfortable out in public, surrounded by people and chatter and the clinks and clatters from the kitchen beyond the counter. This kind of setting often wore thin for him, especially in the evenings after a long work day, but tonight, none of it seemed to get to him.

And as loathe as he was to admit as much, he was pretty sure it had a lot to do with the bright-eyed woman beside him. His knee bumped hers under the table, and the brief contact made his pulse ratchet up. Was it all one-sided?

19
Candy

Candy's initial embarrassment at finding her entire friend group waiting for them quickly faded as the evening progressed. She'd been worried about how Jonathan would react to the ambush. After all, she'd only invited him to join her and Liz, not the entire Garden Variety Lovers Club. But to her surprise and relief, Jonathan seemed to be holding his own quite well.

She watched him from the corner of her eye as he engaged in conversation with her friends, his deep voice a contrast to their softer tones. There was something different about him tonight. He was more relaxed, more present. The perpetual furrow between his brows had softened, and he'd even laughed a few times, the sound making her smile.

"Hey, Juno," Claire said, steering the conversation to a new topic. "I've got that lace washed and ready. Can you come by my place this evening after closing? Or tomorrow evening?" Most of the group of friends owned and operated their own businesses, and late night after-hour get-togethers were well understood. Turning to Jonathan, Claire explained, "Juno's getting married this fall out at the Garden Gate B&B."

"Claire found this amazing vintage lace for the veil," Juno said to the group. "It's got this perfect golden undertone, and I just love it so much."

He nodded slowly, the topic of weddings making him a little wary. It was a bit of a foreign language to him, having never even come close to laying eyes on the altar himself. He and his father were both confirmed bachelors, as far as Jonathan was concerned. And with very few friends close enough for him to be invited to such events, he'd only attended maybe three of them in the last decade.

Juno's face softened into an almost dreamy smile. "Ten weeks from tomorrow," she confirmed, a hint of nervousness creeping into her voice. "And yes," she said to Claire. "I can do either one. You choose."

"I'm so excited to have our first fall wedding," Penny said, rubbing her hands together. "The dahlias and mums will be in their full glory, and the crabapples, redbuds, and dogwoods will already be in full autumn color. Oh, and the firebushes along the back border; we're hoping they'll be at their brightest."

"It'll be amazing," Juno said. "The rusts and gold, deep burgundies. They're my favorites, and Alex doesn't care either way, as long as he gets to leave the garden as my husband when the day is over."

"I get to do the wedding flowers," Addison explained to Jonathan. "Sugar maple leaves, big double dahlias, and Odessa calla lilies for Juno's bouquet, along with some fall-hued chrysanthemums and snapdragons."

"Odessa calla lilies are a deep inky purple," Juno added. "They're almost black, but they're so elegant on the long green stems."

"And Candy made a custom wedding arch for them," Addison said, reaching over and squeezing Candy's hand. "It's absolutely stunning as it is, but I can't wait to decorate it to match the bouquets."

Candy had built Juno a special wedding arbor last month and had surprised her with it at her bridal shower. Juno had once commented on how beautiful they were, but that the only way she'd get married under one is if she could take it home and put it in her own garden. Since Alex and his daughter, Lena, would be moving into her second story apartment after they were married, she'd decided against one, insisting that the bower of redbuds and dogwoods and other fall-colored trees and shrubs would be a stunning enough backdrop without one.

Liz snorted. "While you all handle the pretty stuff, I'll be making sure the toilets are functioning properly at the B&B." She turned to Jonathan with a wink. "I work for the water and sewer company," she explained. "And speaking of plumbing, how's it going at the renovation project? Candy tells me you've had some... *adventures* in that department."

Candy nudged her cousin's foot under the table and mouthed 'thank you' in silent appreciation. She'd noticed Jonathan's eyes starting to glaze over slightly during the wedding talk, and she'd been trying to figure out a way to steer the conversation elsewhere. He wasn't being rude, but detailed discussions of floral arrangements and veils weren't exactly riveting for most men, and she could tell that Jonathan fell into that category.

"Oh, you could definitely say that," Jonathan replied with a self-deprecating smile. "If there was an Olympic event for flooding bathrooms, I'd be a gold medalist."

Candy laughed. "He tried to fix a leaky shower faucet without turning off the water main."

"In my defense," Jonathan protested, "I did turn off what I thought were the right valves. How was I supposed to know there were separate shut-offs for the tub?"

"Did the water go everywhere?" Penny asked, eyes wide.

"Everywhere," Candy confirmed. "I heard him yelling for help, and when I got upstairs, he was soaked from head to toe, trying to stop the spray with a towel."

"Please, please, please tell us about the carpet incident," Liz prompted with a mischievous grin, pressing her hands together in a prayer-like gesture. "I want to hear it from your perspective, Squatch."

Jonathan groaned good-naturedly. "Ah yes, my other moment of glory. We were pulling up old carpet in the living room, and I may have used a bit too much force."

"A bit?" Candy exclaimed. "You practically launched me across the room!"

"A whole new world," Liz crooned loudly, and the table erupted in laughter, Candy and Jonathan both joining in. There was something endearing about watching Jonathan make fun of himself, admitting his mistakes without defensiveness. It was so different from the grumpy, closed-off man she'd met that first morning.

"Honestly," she admitted when they'd settled down, "having Jonathan around has made the renovation more interesting, if not exactly easier."

"That may be so," he countered. "But you have to admit that I've been good for your aesthetic, right? I've seen the comments, and I think your fans kinda like me, Miss Toolbelt."

"I'll admit that they do. You've grown on them, Squatch." Candy felt a pang in her chest when he'd used the word 'aesthetic,' reminding her of the story he'd just told about how he'd gotten that scar on his cheek. Suddenly, his initial dismissiveness of her social media made more sense. If his experience with content creators on the trail had been with self-absorbed people who valued their online presence over real-life safety and courtesy, no wonder he'd been skeptical of her work.

In response to a question about what he did for a living, he explained his job as a software developer, but then started talking about the hiking app he was working on. He seemed to have a new enthusiasm for it that she hadn't heard in his voice when he'd told her about it. In fact, he was sharing stuff with her friends that he hadn't mentioned to her, and she found herself genuinely wanting to understand him better.

"I've been developing app ideas for a few years, hoping to one day go into business for myself."

"Really?" Juno asked, relaxing back in her seat. "I bet you could make a mint doing artisan coffee shop apps. I'd love something that was custom-built just for my shop, especially since I now have both the coffee bar and the cafe, plus the catering side, too. The generic app we use is hosted by another company, and it seems we're always dealing with issues."

Jonathan's eyes widened with interest. "I'd be happy to take a look at it with you," he offered. Candy thought he sounded surprised, and she wondered why. Was he just being modest, or did he struggle with self-worth issues?

"You know what I'd love?" she asked, eager to bolster his confidence, if that's what this was about. "I'd love to have a custom app for my less-DIY-inclined followers who won't go into the big home improvement stores for fear of being embarrassed by their lack of know-how. I love places like that, but even with all my knowledge, sometimes I can't for the life of me figure out where to find a specific hinge or bolt or odd supply, and inevitably, the person I ask to help me treats me like an airheaded little lady. I'd love to be able to punch in my question about what I need, have the app give me the nearest location where that thing is in stock, tell me what aisle and shelf it's on, and then check to see who's manning the service desk so I'll know if I need to go to self-checkout to avoid the know-it-all old geezer who thinks I should be barefoot and pregnant in the kitchen rather than installing a new kitchen."

Claire said dryly, "That's very specific."

"Ha." Candy made a self-deprecating sound. "Yeah, well, when was the last time you set foot in a home improvement store?"

Claire shook her head. "You wouldn't catch me dead in a place like that. It's why I have friends like you, Candy, darling."

"So what are your plans?" Juno asked, bringing the question back around to Jonathan. "Are you moving to Autumn Lake?"

How did she do that? Juno just came right out and asked the question that Candy had been circling since the day she met Jonathan Burkhardt.

He seemed a little taken aback by the question, too. "Um, well, I—I haven't made any big decisions yet," he said, stumbling over his noncommittal words. "I'm currently on an extended leave from SyncTech, the company I work for."

"That's good of them," Juno commented, nodding slowly. "How long did they give you?"

Jonathan grimaced. "They didn't really *give* me more than a five-day bereavement leave. I requested a six-month personal leave. Unpaid, of course. Fortunately, they were happy enough with my work that they were willing to hold my job for me. It helped that I was willing to check in once a week and do any emergency trouble-shooting remotely."

"When do you go back?" Juno was like a dog with a bone, but Candy didn't dare shut her down. She wanted to know, too.

Jonathan straightened in his seat and took a sip of water before answering. "I'm heading back—" His voice cracked and he cleared his throat and tried again. "I'm leaving town on Sunday."

Candy felt the blood drain from her face. What? *What?* And he didn't think that was something he should share with her? "This weekend?" she repeated, trying to keep her voice casual. Did he truly disregard her feelings so much? "I had no idea you were leaving so soon."

"Yeah," Jonathan confirmed, looking slightly uncomfortable. " I have to be back in the office on Monday."

"Oh," Candy said, unable to think of anything more eloquent. "Well, that's... I mean, I'm sure they'll be glad to have you back."

An awkward silence fell over the table until Liz, bless her, jumped in with a question for Penny about her mother's health, smoothly transitioning the conversation to safer territory.

Much to Candy's relief, the evening wound down soon after that. She couldn't stop thinking about the fact that Jonathan was leaving town and hadn't bothered to say anything to her. Had Maeve known he was leaving so soon? Would he be coming back to check on the project, or was this it? What were his future plans for the house? Why hadn't Juno pushed for answers on *that* question?

"Ready to head out?" Liz asked, touching Candy's arm. It was obvious that her cousin was a little worried about her. Candy had been pretty quiet since Jonathan had shared his travel plans with everyone. "I can give you a ride home."

"Yeah, that'd be—" Candy began, but Jonathan spoke up first.

"I can take you home," he said firmly. "I was hoping to discuss the house plans over dinner. Can we talk about it on the way back instead?"

"I don't want to put you out," Candy protested weakly.

"It's no trouble at all," Jonathan insisted, his eyes meeting hers with an intensity that made her pulse quicken. "I'd like to."

With all her friends watching, Candy felt suddenly put on the spot. "Okay then," she agreed, hoping her cheeks weren't as pink as they felt. "I'll see you at home soon," she said to her cousin.

They said their goodbyes and headed out into the balmy evening, Candy's mixed emotions putting her on edge. The evening had gone better than she could have hoped. Her friends had made Jonathan feel welcome, and he seemed to have genuinely enjoyed their company. But the knowledge that he was leaving in two days had her feeling a little bereft, maybe even angry.

"Your friends are great," Jonathan said as they walked to his car. "Thanks for sharing them with me tonight."

"They liked you too," Candy replied honestly. "And it sounds like Juno might want to hire you to build her an app."

Jonathan nodded. "I'd be honored. Small businesses really benefit when they have custom apps for their clients."

As he opened the passenger door for her, their eyes met briefly. Candy quickly looked away, sliding into the seat and busying herself with her seatbelt. She didn't want him to see how his departure made her feel, especially since she didn't fully understand it herself.

What was happening to her? This was Squatch, the grumpy intruder who'd thrown her renovation plans into disarray. She should be glad he was going to be gone, leaving her to do what she loved so much.

But at that moment, the thought of showing up to an empty lake house on Monday morning held no appeal for her at all.

20
Jonathan

As they pulled away from the cafe, Jonathan glanced at Candy in the passenger seat. She was staring out the window, and she'd gone unusually quiet since his announcement about returning to Atlanta. He felt awful about the way it had come out; he'd really meant to tell her in private, but they'd both been surprised by the presence of her whole group of friends. Then there was Juno with her direct, no-nonsense questions. There was no way he could have avoided answering her without being rude, especially after they'd so warmly welcomed him at their table.

When he'd seen the bevy of women gathered there, he'd felt a bit like being stood before a firing squad, but he'd been pleasantly surprised to find that he really enjoyed his time with them. How he wished he'd made the effort to tell Candy about having to return to Atlanta first. He really hated the tension that hung between them, and it was all his fault.

"It's a beautiful night," he said, breaking the silence. He hesitated, then took a chance. "Would you like to take a drive? Maybe around the lake before I take you home?"

He half-expected her to decline, to insist he just take her straight home. To his surprise, she turned to him with a small smile.

"Sure," she said. "That sounds nice."

Relieved, Jonathan turned onto Lakeside Drive, the winding road that skirted the south shore of Autumn Lake. He didn't want to rush their conversation, and the drive to Candy's place took maybe fifteen minutes. This would give them a chance to warm up to each other again, he hoped.

The moonlight silvered the surface of the water where they glimpsed it between trees or in the open stretches between homes. The air outside was just cool enough that they could have rolled the windows down and been comfortable, but the rumble of the GTO's engine would have prevented conversation.

"I should have told you about Atlanta before we got to the coffee shop," he said after they'd driven in silence for a few minutes.

"I should have asked," Candy replied with a shrug that seemed a bit too forced to be casual.

Jonathan nodded, slowing the car as they approached a curve. "I was hoping to take you out to dinner and telling you about all of this over supper...." He left the sentence unfinished. He wasn't blaming her friends, but it was their presence at the table that had prevented him from talking to her about it the way he'd planned. "

"I hadn't expected anyone but Liz to be there." Candy acknowledged his unspoken sentiment. "Though I should have known better. When one Garden Variety Lover shows up, the rest usually follow."

"I was glad to meet them," Jonathan assured her. "They're great. It just meant I didn't get a chance to talk to you about my plans first. When Juno asked, I couldn't come up with a quick dodge on the spot."

They crossed a narrow bridge that spanned an inlet, the GTO's engine echoing off the water below. On the other side, they entered the North Shore development, a stark contrast to the older, more established south shore where the lake house stood. Here, impressive modern homes with perfectly manicured lawns lined the street, many with boat docks extending into the water.

"I imagine these houses cost a fortune," Jonathan remarked, eyeing a particularly massive glass and stone structure.

"We locals call the owners 'WOOTs'," Candy said with a hint of her usual sparkle returning.

"WOOTs?"

"Wealthy Out Of Towners," she explained. "Most of them are vacation homes or time shares. Not many year-round residents up here."

Jonathan smiled, grateful for the lighter mood. "And what does that make you and your friends? Locals?"

"Townies, of course," she said proudly. "Though I'm technically a transplant. Liz is the true townie."

They continued along the curving road, passing the high-end Carpe Diem Resort with its imposing gates and elegant landscaping. As they rounded the northern tip of the lake, Jonathan gathered his courage for what he wanted to say next.

"I wanted to talk about our future together," he said, then immediately realized how that sounded when Candy's head whipped toward him, her eyes wide. "The renovation, I mean. The future of the renovation," he clarified quickly, feeling his face grow warm. "I didn't mean... I was referring to the house."

"Right," Candy said, looking away again. "Of course."

"What I'm trying to say," he pressed on, "is that I've been thinking about how to handle things with my job. I need to go back on Monday—that's non-negotiable at this point—but I was wondering if you could use my help if I came back after that."

He glanced at her profile, illuminated by the dashboard lights. "I know my DIY limitations, and I don't want to foist myself on you, but if you need or could use my help, I can talk to my boss and see what arrangements can be made." He was being unrealistically optimistic, but he found that he wanted to come back. He wanted to work on the house with her.

Candy was quiet for a long moment, and Jonathan focused on driving, giving her time to think. They were looping back through the North Shore development again and heading back toward town. Soon they began to see older cottages and cabins dotting the shoreline, the lights in the windows a warm welcome after the austerity of the WOOT neighborhoods.

"I never planned on having your help," she finally said, her voice measured. "So do what's best for you, Jonathan. I have the renovation under control." She shifted in her seat to face him. "With your help, I'm actually a couple of days ahead of schedule, so don't worry about me."

Jonathan couldn't decide how to take that. Was she brushing him off? Letting him know he wasn't needed? Or was she genuinely trying to reassure him?

"I'm not worried about you," he said, perhaps a bit more defensively than he'd intended. "I was just offering my help if you need it. I trust you to do a great job."

Candy's mouth dropped open, and he could see immediately that his words had offended her.

"*You* trust me?" she repeated, her voice oddly calm. "Need I remind you that it was Maeve who hired me, not you? I don't need your stamp of approval."

"That's not—" Jonathan tried to interject, but Candy wasn't finished.

"I've been doing this professionally for years. Just because you showed up doesn't mean I suddenly need your validation." He could now hear the challenge in her tone.

"I know that," Jonathan said, frustration creeping into his voice. "But Maeve did say you're supposed to have my input on your plans, remember?"

Candy crossed her arms, her eyes boring into the side of his face. "And do you have any input you'd like to share with me?"

"No," Jonathan admitted. "I'm good with everything. All of it." He hesitated, then clarified, "Other than my dad's room, I mean. Please don't touch it while I'm gone, okay?"

Candy's expression shifted from indignation to hurt, then settled into a weary sadness that made him feel worse than if she'd yelled at him. Once again, he'd stuck his big old sasquatch foot in his mouth.

"I won't touch it while you're gone," she said quietly, repeating his words back to him, making him feel even smaller than he already did. She turned to gaze out the window. "Please take me home now."

They drove the rest of the way in tense silence, the beauty of the moonlit lake lost on both of them. Jonathan mentally kicked himself for ruining what had started as a pleasant evening. Why was it so difficult to say the right thing around her?

As he pulled into her driveway, he was floundering for something to say that would reset things between them. But before he could even put the car in park, she had her seatbelt unbuckled and the door open.

"Candy, wait," he called after her as she hurried up the walkway to her front door. He quickly parked and rushed to catch up.

"Candy," he said again, gently catching her hand to stop her. "Please."

She paused, turning to face him with a carefully neutral expression. "What is it, Jonathan?"

His name on her lips sounded wrong to him; he wanted her to call him Squatch again, which almost made him laugh.

"Thank you," he said earnestly, "for letting me intrude on your renovation these past two weeks. I know I haven't made things easy, but I've learned a lot from you."

The sincerity in his voice must have gotten through to her, because her expression softened slightly. "I've enjoyed getting to know you too," she said with a smile that didn't quite reach her eyes. Then again, the moonlight cast shadows across her face, and the porchlight backlit her features, making it hard for him to make out what she was feeling. "Good luck in Atlanta."

Before he could respond, she slipped her hand from his and disappeared into the cottage, the porch light switching off moments later.

Jonathan stood for a long moment, staring at the darkened door, then slowly made his way back to his car. As he drove away, he couldn't shake the feeling that her parting smile was the same practiced, camera-ready expression he'd seen during the last few episodes of her DIY television show, back when she'd known things were going belly up, and she'd had to show up and pretend to the world that everything was just fine.

Because of course he'd watched every single episode of 'Drills and Thrills with Candy Mason', and he'd gotten to know her well enough over the last two weeks to recognize that smile. Bright and cheerful on the surface, but hollow underneath.

It wasn't until he was halfway back to the lake house that he realized she hadn't actually answered whether his return the following week would be welcome or not.

21
Candy

CANDY PUSHED OPEN THE front door, the familiar creak echoing through the empty rooms, and felt a pang of loneliness. The house was far too quiet, and she found herself pausing in the foyer every morning, listening for the sound of Jonathan moving around the kitchen, knowing full well that she'd only hear the sound of his absence.

While he'd been around, the house had been a whirlwind of activity. Arguments and laughter, mishaps and discoveries, and, dare she admit, an aversion that had slowly become attraction. Now there was no aromatic smell of freshly-brewed coffee meeting her at the door, no shaggy-haired companion telling her good morning in his sleep-gruff voice. With Jonathan gone, she was left with only her own thoughts in this big old, hollowed out, half-renovated house.

She'd spent the last nine days with her head down, pushing herself to surpass her goals, to check things off her list ahead of time. She'd gotten a lot accomplished, too, staying well past dark, sometimes not making it home until after midnight. She'd painted the whole downstairs, sprayed and installed the new kitchen cabinets, completed the custom butcher block island, replaced windows, finalized her furniture orders, and so much more.

She wanted to be able to enjoy her open house event, and because of Jonathan's help, she was well ahead of her schedule, which meant she'd have some breathing room at the end. Maybe she'd even take a day away, to rest and rejuvenate so that she could be clear-headed when talking with potential clients. She wasn't going to lose that edge, just because he was no longer there to make her coffee.

She shook off the feeling, squared her shoulders, and pulled out her phone.

"Good morning, Hearth Breakers!" she said brightly, slipping into her camera persona with practiced ease as she began recording. "It's a brand-new week here at our Hollyhock Hill renovation, and although we're several days ahead of schedule, we've still got some tedious tasks to tackle." She flipped the camera to show her face. "Try saying that three times fast!" Then she panned the camera around the foyer and into the kitchen, careful not to show the stunning ocean blue cabinetry. "We've exposed the original hardwood floors, but as you can see, they're looking pretty rough, but promising. Today, we're starting with the kitchen floor, since that one needs the most attention."

She'd promised a live feed this morning, assuring everyone that she'd give them a quick visual rundown of what they'd accomplished so far, but she was careful not to show too much. One of her trademarks moves with big projects like this was to wait until the end for the big reveal. Sometimes she even brought in a drone so she could capture everything from a birds-eye view, especially when her renovations included outside remodels and landscaping changes, too.

She moved through the house, filming as she went, carefully avoiding any mention of Jonathan's absence. Her followers had grown quite fond of the "Squatch Saga," as they called it, and the comments in her feed were already filling with questions about where he was, if he was hiding out in one of the bedrooms again, why he wasn't making her coffee in the mornings anymore. She'd given vague responses in the comments, but had said very little about him in her live feeds, ignoring most of the more direct questions, and instead simply repeating that he had business to attend to and would return when he could.

Now here it was, another Monday morning, and she had work to do.

A few weeks ago, Candy had cut out a tiny sample of the linoleum flooring and the backing and sent it in to have it tested for asbestos. Maeve had said she and Stan had it tested back in the 1980s when the general public became aware of the hazardous material, and she was certain that the results had come back negative. But she hadn't been able to find documentation on it, so Candy had opted to have it all tested again.

As Maeve had said, the tests for the flooring materials came back negative, much to Candy's relief, but she still took extra precautions as she started pulling up the discolored and brittle flooring. She worked in small sections, scoring the tile first, then pouring boiling hot water over the surface and letting it soak in for several minutes before working up the linoleum and backing with a heavy duty scraper. In some places, where it was really stuck fast, she had to work orange oil into the backing to break it up. Even with all the doors and windows open for ventilation, she wore a heavy duty respirator that covered her nose and mouth, and a pair of custom fit goggles that she'd been issued for the television show. On the last day she'd been on set, she'd snatched them off the hook where she kept them and strapped them on her head like a pair of vintage pilot goggles, and she'd walked out of the building without looking back.

It took her most of two hot and sweaty, very long days of shoulder-burning, knee-bruising grunt work to get everything up, but by Wednesday morning, the old was out and the wood floor was ready to be prepped. She'd sent in several more tests over the last two days, and so far, the lab she worked with had found no trace of asbestos, so she was gearing up to take a drum sander to the whole thing.

Candy was thrilled to find that the beautiful oak floor she'd uncovered in the living room continued into the kitchen, but here it was in much worse condition. Decades of adhesive from the first layer of linoleum, applied sometime in the 1940s from what she could tell, had left the wood stained and rough, and in some places, splintered from where shards of wood had come up with the stuff. But Candy was certain it could be salvaged with the right tools, a high-quality polyurethane sealer, and plenty of elbow grease.

She spent Wednesday morning carefully masking everything off with plastic and tape, creating a sealed workspace to contain the inevitable dust storm. The prep work was tedious but necessary; rushing would only lead to mistakes, and with floors this old, she couldn't afford any.

Her shoulders ached from the last couple of days, but she was eager to get started with the actual sanding. She pulled on her coveralls, strapped on her heavy-duty respirator mask, and fired up the drum sander. The machine vibrated powerfully in her hands as she guided it carefully across the floor, making slow, methodical passes over the damaged wood. The top layer of finish and decades of grime came away first, revealing glimpses of the unstained oak beneath. It was painstaking work, requiring absolute focus to keep the sander level and prevent it from gouging, but the beauty of old wood floors like this was that the planks were solid, not veneer, and she could afford to go a little deeper, as long as she kept it even.

Hours passed as she worked, stopping only to change the sandpaper or to step outside for fresh air breaks. The materials used in adhesives and finishes during the first half of the 20th century were often toxic, even when they didn't have asbestos in them, so she wasn't taking any chances.

During her breaks, she sat on the front porch steps, gulping fresh air, chugging water, and letting her mind wander. Without Jonathan around, she found herself mentally reviewing her vision for the master bathroom—the double vanity with marble countertops, the walk-in shower with its rainfall showerhead, all elements she'd once dared to imagine using herself someday.

It was foolish, this renewed hope that somehow the house might still become hers. Jonathan hadn't given a straight answer about returning, which meant there was a possibility of him choosing to stay in Atlanta. And if he did that, then there was also a possibility that she could still put an offer on this place, could still make it her own.

If Jonathan, however, chose to move back to Autumn Lake, to make this house his home?

Well, when he'd said he wanted to talk about "their future together" during that moonlit drive they'd shared, even though he'd quickly clarified he meant the renovation, a door had been opened to let out a tiny smidgeon of hope that maybe, just maybe, there might be room for both of them in his place. And once out in the light, no matter how hard she tried, the idea wouldn't go back to the shadows.

Candy shook her head, trying to dispel the thought. Jonathan was probably settling comfortably back into his real life. She knew he was still grieving deeply over the loss of his father. She saw it in his eyes when he didn't know she was watching, the way he ducked his head as if his thoughts suddenly became too heavy to bear. The way his fingertips brushed the images of his father in the photo albums he sometimes shared with her. Speaking about Troy had him swallowing hard against the knot of pain that made his words come out tight, strangled. Even so, Jonathan must be feeling a sense of relief and comfort in the familiar, now that he was back at work among people who valued him for the skills and knowledge he brought to the table at a place like SyncTech.

No, whatever tenuous connection they'd formed over the two weeks they'd been practically forced to work alongside each other, it wasn't enough to build future dreams on. At least not dreams that included the two of them together.

By Thursday noon, her shoulders and back were screaming in protest as she finished the last section of the kitchen floor. The oak gleamed golden beneath her feet, free of adhesive and old finish, ready for staining. She still needed to go over it with progressively finer grits of sandpaper to smooth everything to a silky finish, but the hardest part was done. When she locked the front door behind her that night, the entire downstairs was prepped and ready for staining in the morning.

Candy dragged herself home, exhausted but satisfied with her progress. It was the earliest she'd left the job site in almost days, and Liz took one look at her slumped form on the couch and handed her a small envelope.

"What's this?" Candy asked, opening it to find a gift certificate inside.

"Tip Top Talons," Liz announced drolly. "For a mani-pedi and a massage. I was going to give it to you when this whole thing was finished, but you look like you need it now. You're about to keel over, Cuz, and your hands are a disaster."

Candy glanced down at her rough, scraped knuckles and broken nails. They were, indeed, a mess. "Since when do you care about fingernails and toenails?" she asked, holding up her hands for her cousin to see.

Liz waved a hand like she was batting the question out of the air. "Oh, I don't care about that stuff at all. But I know you have an aesthetic to tend to, and I know your followers will call you out on those ragged nails. Yikes."

There was that word again. Candy sobered and dropped her hands to her lap. "Do you think it's ridiculous?" she asked, hoping Liz would understand without having to explain.

"That you have a brand? That you cater yourself to that aesthetic?" Liz lifted Candy's legs off the couch and dropped down beside her, taking her feet in her lap. She pressed her thumbs into the arch of her feet, and Candy moaned with a mixture of pain and pleasure. "Absolutely not, Candy Needham. You've built a career on working hard and looking good while doing it." She continued to knead the bottom of Candy's feet. "You are a beautiful woman, cousin of mine, and that's not bad thing. You know what I wish?"

Candy rolled her eyes, half expected Liz to say that she wished she'd been born beautiful, too, and she braced herself for it. How many times had she heard that sentiment from other women in her industry, women who insinuated that Candy's success was a result of her good looks rather than her skill or know-how? In her opinion, the women she rubbed shoulders with in the home improvement world were much more likely to look down on her because of her blonde hair and curvy petite figure than any man. Sure, the guys treated her like she had fluff for brains, but women could be the cruelest of all with their snide remarks and their petty looks.

"I wish that you would stop worrying about how you look, Candy. I wish that you would stop worrying and instead, be stinkin' proud of it. You're beautiful, but you're also brilliant. Who convinced you that you can only be one or the other? It's like you're always trying to prove your worth to someone, and I'm starting to believe that someone is you."

If Liz hadn't been rubbing her feet, Candy might have been tempted to kick her in the shin. Because she didn't want Liz to stop, however, that meant she was forced to hear her out.

"Listen, I know you got the raw end of the deal with that stupid TV show. But you are so much more than a television personality. You actually *have* a personality, and you aren't embarrassed to use it. You have brains and you're not ashamed to use them. You have beauty, but you're constantly second-guessing yourself about using it." Liz gave one of her bit toes a painful pinch. "Just stop it. Now."

"Ouch!" Candy pulled her feet off of Liz's lap and swiveled on the couch to sit up. "I've had a brutal week. Why are you being so mean to me?"

Liz shook her head. "And after I just gave you a gift certificate to have your talons tip-topped."

Candy sighed and leaned her head on Liz's shoulder. "Thank you," she murmured. "For the certificate, for the foot massage, and yes, even for the pep talk. I just want everyone to take me seriously, you know?"

"But why?" Liz rolled her eyes. "That doesn't sound like any fun at all."

Candy sat up and met her cousin's eyes. "You're right. You're always right. But right now, I just need to go to bed." She held up the gift certificate. "Thank you, Liz. This was very thoughtful, and believe me, when the floors are done, I'm calling this in." She took one more look at her ugly nails. "I can do a before and after of these beauties for my aesthetic."

She went to bed that night planning her attack on the master bedroom, which she'd be starting next week. For now, she'd focus on getting the downstairs floors stained and sealed, which would need the weekend to fully cure before furniture could be moved back in. Candy had packed up all the contents of the secret compartment and taken them to Maeve, who was shocked to learn of the existence of the hidden cubby. She'd known about the one in Troy's closet, said there was on in the closet of her childhood bedroom, too, and had told Candy where to look for it and how to open it.

"I emptied it, of course, years ago, but it's still there. I never once imagined, however, that Dad and Mother would also have a secret hiding place." She'd been brought to tears at the sight of the photo, and several of the jewels were precious to her, too, not so much for their monetary value, but because she remembered her mother wearing each piece.

Friday morning dawned clear and cool, a perfect day for applying stain. Candy arrived at the house a little earlier than usual, eager to get started. As she pushed open the front door, she stopped dead in her tracks.

Someone was in the house.

The smell of freshly brewed coffee had her lifting her nose instinctively.

Through the foyer and kitchen doorway, she could see a man standing at the counter, his back to her. He wore a pair of jeans and a gray Henley that emphasized the breadth of his shoulders. His neck was pale above the collar of the shirt, and as he turned toward her, Candy gasped.

22
Jonathan

JONATHAN REACHED UP TO touch the back of his bare neck, the prickling sensation of being watched making him smile. Miss Toolbelt was here.

He'd just finished brewing the coffee and now poured it into two mugs, his movements deliberate and unhurried despite the sudden acceleration of his pulse. Taking a deep breath, he turned around.

Candy stood in the middle of the empty foyer, planner in one hand, toolbelt slung low on her hips, the morning sunlight streaming through the windows behind her creating a halo effect around her blonde hair. She looked like she'd been frozen mid-step, her blue eyes wide with shock.

And unless he was mistaken, after the initial surprise faded, she looked glad to see him. The realization made him smile, momentarily forgetting the discomfort of their last encounter.

"Morning," he said, his voice still a little rough from the short night's sleep after the long drive back to Autumn Lake last night.

Candy made a funny sound in the back of her throat, something between a gasp and a laugh. "Well, hey there, Squatch," she finally managed in a breathy voice that sounded nothing like her usual confident tone.

Jonathan's grin widened. He knew she was shocked by his transformation, probably even more so than he had been when he'd sat in the barber's chair in Atlanta and watched months of growth fall away. At least he'd known what was under all that hair. She'd never seen the Jonathan he'd been before the trail.

Before his dad died.

Aaaand, time to change the subject.

"Coffee?" he offered, lifting one of the mugs. "I brought some beans from my favorite coffee place in Atlanta. Thought you'd like to try them."

That seemed to break her out of her trance. She nodded and walked toward him, her eyes never leaving his face. She took the offered mug but remained silent, studying him with an intensity that might have made him uncomfortable a few weeks ago.

"These floors are amazing," he said, gesturing around them with his free hand. "Oak, right? You've done so much while I've been gone."

Candy still didn't respond, just kept staring. Jonathan reached up self-consciously to touch the scar on his face, wondering if it looked worse now without his beard to partially conceal it. But he was pretty sure that wasn't what she was looking at.

Finally, she shook her head slightly, as if clearing it. "You're so handsome," she said, the words tumbling out like she couldn't stop them. She didn't even seem embarrassed by the admission. "Wow. Who would have known?"

Jonathan felt warmth creep up his neck and into his cheeks, knowing she could definitely see his cheeks flush, now that his beard was gone. But contrary to what he might have expected, he wasn't embarrassed by her praise. It pleased him, especially coming from her.

"Thank you," he said simply, then asked, "What's on the agenda for today? The floors? Are we staining them?"

"When did you get in?" Candy asked instead of answering his question. "And what are your plans? I mean, how long are you staying?"

"I got in late last night," Jonathan explained, taking a sip of his coffee. Mm. It was so good. "And I'm here at least through to the end of the job."

He didn't elaborate further, not wanting to overwhelm her with everything at once. The truth was, he had a lot to tell her; about the up-and-coming tech company interested in his AT app, about his decision to take a leap of faith and launch his own business, about how he'd walked into his boss's office on Monday morning and handed in his resignation.

But those details could wait. He was worried he might fail, that his plans might fall through, and he didn't want to make promises he couldn't keep. For now, it was enough that he was back, ready to work hard alongside Candy, but also ready to put his dreams to the test and launch his own business. He hoped to finalize the sale of the app by the time the house renovation was finished. Once that happened, then he'd tell her everything, and maybe they could celebrate both of their accomplishments together.

"I see," Candy said, finally taking a sip of her coffee. "Well, that's... good." She seemed to be processing his return, her initial shock giving way to a more measured response. "And yes, I've been working on the floors pretty much all week. Got all the linoleum up—there was no asbestos, thankfully—and I've spent the last few days sanding. This morning, I'm applying the first coat of stain, then second one will go down last thing before I leave, then I'll be back tomorrow to do two coats of sealer. I hadn't planned on anyone being in the house this weekend."

"Will I be in the way?" he asked, attempting to keep up with her plan.

Candy eyed him like he might be a little thick. "If you don't plan to come downstairs for the next three days, then no, you won't be in the way."

Jonathan nodded slowly, considering her words. Then he stated the obvious. "You don't want me walking on the floors."

"Bingo," she said, pointing at him. "I start at one door and work my way out the other. The products I use are all water based, but they still need at least 4-6 hours to cure enough to walk on them, and even then, nothing with heavy tread, unless you have shoe covers."

Jonathan nodded. Maeve had offered him her guestroom more than once, so if she was still open to it, he'd take her up on it for the next few days. "I can probably crash at Maeve's place this weekend. Will you still let me help?"

She moved to the table and set her planner down, opening it to the day's page. She positioned her full coffee cup beside it, then took a few colored pens from the planner's zipper pouch, aligning them in a neat row next to the coffee cup. She pulled a case of drill bits out of her toolbelt, took two bits out and arranged the yellow case along with the bits beside the planner. Jonathan watched her set up what was obviously a staged shot for social media, and he marveled at how quickly she worked. "Sure, you can help," she said, finally looking up at him. "If you can go stand over there and lean against the counter... Yes, right there." She circled the table and approached him. "Hold your cup about chest high. A little higher." She positioned his arm just so, then stepped back. "Perfect. Can you hold that pose for a few seconds?"

"This is how I can help you? By posing?"

"Yep," Candy quipped, shooting him a capricious grin as she moved back around the table to the doorway of the kitchen. "Now give me a fresh-out-of-bed smolder. Mess up your hair a little."

"You're serious."

"As a heart attack." She wiggled her fingers above the top of her head, simulating a motion she wanted him to make. "Mess it up. Bedhead messy."

Jonathan shook his head, but did as he was told. He could hardly believe that he'd come all the way back to Autumn Lake just to model for Candy's morning coffee ritual. "How's this?" he asked, giving her his best brooding alpha male look.

Candy snorted. "Wow. Please tone down the duck lips, dude. You look like you just bit into a lemon."

"Hey, now," Jonathan shot back, unable to keep from laughing at her reaction. "That was my sexy smolder face."

But Candy was shaking her head. "Nope. Let's nix the smolder. You need to look like you're at least enjoying the coffee you made, not like it's too bitter to drink. Now I'm going to walk in the door, act surprised to see you standing there, and zoom in on you. I want you to be staring out that window, then turn when I gasp. Grin at me the way you did just a few minutes ago, like you know something I don't, and then take a sip of your coffee. I'll pan the camera down to my planner and end the shot here." She pointed at the tableau she'd just arranged. "Got it?"

Jonathan nodded. "Got it." Grin at her like he knew something she didn't. Well, he knew a lot of things she didn't right now. Like that he was planning on staying. Or that he was glad that she seemed glad to see him. The he was really glad that she thought he was handsome. Or that he'd missed her. Even more than he'd realized until this moment.

She narrowed her eyes like she didn't quite believe him. "Let's give it a practice run," she said, turning to leave the room. Then she came back in, directing him through what she envisioned from start to finish. "Now wash, rinse, and repeat."

He did exactly as she'd instructed, turning to greet her with a grin when she gasped softly, and took a careful sip of the hot coffee. He waited until she'd gotten her final shot of her planner, then asked, "How was that?"

Candy shook her head again, but the grin on her face told him she was rather pleased. "Perfect. The light coming in the window caught a bit of steam from your coffee and made the tips of your hair look almost gold." She made the chef's kiss gesture, what he was quickly recognizing as her favorite stamp of approval, and added, "Lookin' good, Sasquatch. My followers are going to eat you for breakfast." She dropped into her chair and started editing the video. "Now, hush," she said, not bothering to look up at him. "I need to record a voice over."

He watched her in silence while she manipulated the video on her phone, her thumbs moving at lightning speed. "It's Freaky Friday, Hearth Breakers, and here's why. Look who I found in the kitchen, brewing fresh coffee. Is it a raccoon? A squatter? Bigfoot? Why no! It's none other than our very own mythical creature, Squatch! He's been to the big city, Hearth Breakers; can you tell? Shave and a haircut—" Then she rapped her knuckles twice on the table. "And here's today's plan. Let's see if we can't get a little sweat equity out of him, shall we? I'll keep you posted!" She replayed it a few times, lining up her recording so that it was exactly how she wanted it, and a few moments later, she uploaded the clip.

"There," she said, grinning up at him. "Shave and a haircut." She held up the two drill bits before tucking them back into the case. "Two bits."

"Nice," Jonathan said with a chuckle. He didn't have to see the clip to know that she'd timed it perfectly, but of course, he'd watch it the first chance he got.

Candy closed her planner with a snap of the pages, then sat back in her chair and picked up her coffee cup. "Okay. So I vacuumed and mopped last night, but we're going to start with a barely damp mopping, followed by wiping down with tack cloths to pick up any remaining dust that's settled since then. With two of us, we'll get through that pretty quickly." She eyed his clothes with skepticism. "You have anything to wear that isn't quite so nice? Maybe some of those fresh-off-the-trail duds?"

"I actually brought work clothes," Jonathan assured her, pointing toward the stairs.

"Now that's using your not so hairy noggin, Squatch." Candy tapped one temple, a small smile tugging at the corner of her mouth.

The familiar nickname warmed his chest. There was a shift in her demeanor, an acceptance that he hadn't expected so quickly. He was shocked at how relieved it made him feel. He pushed away from the counter and set his mug down. "I'll go change."

"First, finish your coffee," Candy insisted. "Then we'll get started. With two of us, we've got a little more breathing room." Her eyes kept darting to his face, a look he couldn't quite read.

"What is it?" he asked, brushing his fingertips across his mouth. Did he have a coffee mustache? Or was she ogling his scar?

"I still can't believe it," she said, gesturing toward his chin. "It's like this floor. Pull up the carpet and linoleum to find these beautiful oak planks underneath. I mean, there was a whole different you under all of that."

"Same me," he assured her with a soft laugh. "Just... easier to find."

That earned him a genuine smile, and Jonathan felt something settle inside him. Coming back had been the right decision. Whatever happened with his app, with his new business venture, with this house, being here, seeing that smile, felt right in a way that sitting in his SyncTech office space or wandering around his nondescript, utilitarian apartment had not.

Jonathan emptied his mug, rinsed it out, and set it on the drainer in the sink. "I need to call Maeve and see if the offer of her spare room is still on the table. I haven't unpacked yet, so when I go change, I'll bring my suitcase down and toss it in my car. Then I'll be all yours."

To his delight, Candy's cheeks colored at his words, but she gave him a brusque nod. "I'll start mopping. You can follow me with the tack cloth when you're ready."

23
Candy

CANDY COULDN'T STOP LOOKING at him. She didn't even care when he caught her staring.

They'd been working on the floor for the past few hours, meticulously applying stain in a coordinated pattern. Jonathan spread it with a long-handled applicator while Candy followed up with a brush to ensure even coverage and work the stain into the grain. The system worked perfectly, allowing them to move through the rooms much faster than she would have alone.

But every few minutes, her eyes would drift back to his face, taking in the sharp line of his jaw, the defined cheekbones that had been hidden beneath his beard. Even the scar looked different now. It seemed less like a rugged battle wound and more like an interesting character mark on an otherwise classically handsome face.

Jonathan seemed to still be getting accustomed to it too. He kept stroking his jaw self-consciously and rubbing the back of his neck where his hair had been cut. His hair was still long enough to curl at the ends, but it must feel strange to him to have all that weight gone.

"What?" he asked finally, catching her mid-stare as they paused to refill their applicators.

"Sorry," Candy said, not sorry at all. "It's just... such a dramatic change."

"Too much?" He cupped his jaw and smoothed his palm down the column of his neck, a self-conscious gesture she found endearing. "Should I have kept the beard? I haven't been completely clean-shaven in years."

"No, not at all. It looks really good. You have a great jawline, Squatch." She bent back to her work, hiding her smile. "I can still call you Squatch, right? Shave and a haircut, you're still Squatch to me."

Jonathan chuckled. "I've gotten used to it. It would feel weird if you called me anything else."

"I have a feeling you'll always be Squatch to my followers, too." She'd seen the comments that had been pouring in all morning. *Squatch is back! Happy Squatch Day! Squatch for president! Return of the Squatch Saga! We love our mythical creature! Rainbows and unicorns and sasquatches, oh my! Breakfast with Squatch – yummy! Hey Squatch – you can make me coffee any day or night! Come renovate me, Squatch!*

And that was the PG-rated ones. Candy had never seen so many exclamation points under one post before. She knew Jonathan now followed her channels, but she hoped he didn't read the comments.

As they worked their way across the kitchen floor toward the doorway, Candy found her thoughts drifting. The man beside her looked so different from the wild-haired intruder she'd found sleeping in the bedroom her first day on the job. She could see this clean-cut conventional-looking guy living in this house, cooking in this kitchen, reading by the fireplace, working in that office she still hoped to create.

He looked like an upstanding member of society now, someone who could take care of and nurture a home like this. Like a man who might want to share this amazing home with a family, with a woman...

Maybe even a woman like me, whispered a quiet little voice in her head.

The thought made her feel like a teenager with a crush, and she quickly pushed it away, focusing back on the task at hand. She was being ridiculous. Jonathan had just come back to help finish the renovation; she shouldn't read anything more into it.

"You're pulling ahead of me," she called out to him. "Slow down a little or we'll get uneven coverage."

"Sorry," Jonathan said, looking back at her. "I didn't realize I'd sped up."

Candy grimaced. "You didn't. I'm moving a little slower, that's all." She'd been distracted by inappropriate thoughts about him, but she couldn't tell him that. "I've been giving my knees a workout all week, and they've just about had enough."

Jonathan stopped mopping, concerned. "I can brush for a while. Here," he said, holding the mop out toward her. "Let's switch."

"I'm fine," she promised him. She waved her brush at the front door. "We're so close. Let's just keep going." What she didn't say was that she wasn't sure she could trust him to do the brushwork. He was more than willing to give it a go, but she was extremely particular about her finishes, and with oak having such a porous grain, it was imperative that the stain go on smooth and even.

For a moment, Candy thought he might argue, but he didn't. Between the two of them, they made remarkable time, and before noon, they were out the front door. "I have lunch in my car," she told Jonathan, stretching her back and relishing the pop of her spine as she did so. "Chicken salad sandwiches, if you feel like sharing. I brought enough for supper, too, in case I had to stay late," she said, although that wasn't exactly true. She'd expected to be ravenous by lunch and had prepared accordingly. She pointed at her car. "I've got everything in a cooler since I knew I wouldn't be able to get to the fridge."

Jonathan hesitated, and Candy wondered if she'd overstepped. Then he said, "Sure, but I'm buying pizza after the second coat. According to Maeve, Patsy's Pizza is supposed to be pretty good."

"It is," Candy confirmed. "She's got a Chicago-style bacon and mushroom pie that's ridiculously messy and even more ridiculously delicious."

"Then it's settled," Jonathan declared. He patted the hood of her SUV. "Sandwiches for lunch at your place, pizza for supper at mine."

Candy actually flinched, his words finding their mark, even though she knew they hadn't been spoken with malice. A reminder that she had to keep her head clear, that once she wrapped up this renovation, she'd be handing over the keys to the man beside her and walking away from all of this. She flashed him a brave smile and popped open her trunk to grab her cooler. "Sounds like a plan."

That evening, with the second coat of stain complete, a pizza box open on the deck between them, Candy and Jonathan sat in comfortable silence and watched the early evening breeze ripple the surface of the lake. In spite of the late August heat, the breeze that came off the water brought with it cooler air, and Candy lifted her face to it.

"Can you use my help tomorrow applying the sealer coat?" Jonathan asked between bites. "Maeve is fine with me crashing there for a few days, but she and a few of her friends are spending the morning yard-saling and then having lunch at a famous German restaurant in Evansville, so I'm available if you can use me."

"Is yard-saling really a verb?" Candy asked, not quite ready to start thinking about working again tomorrow.

Jonathan chuckled. "I'm not going to challenge my aunt on that. If she used it as a verb, I'm going to assume it's a verb."

"Good call, Squatch." Candy sat forward and carefully slid another slice of pizza onto her plate. Had she been alone, she'd have been on her third piece by now, but she was pacing herself, not wanting to out-eat Jonathan, who was, apparently, a very slow eater. "And yes, if you'd like to come over tomorrow, I'll be here by eight to get started. We'll do two coats tomorrow, then I'll be back early Sunday morning to put a third coat, at least in the kitchen where the traffic is heavy."

"I can help with that, too," he offered.

Candy shrugged, the warm afternoon sun on her skin coupled with a full belly lulling her into a bit of a stupor. She'd pushed herself hard the last two weeks, and suddenly, all she wanted to do was lay back on the deck and close her eyes, just for a few minutes. "Maybe make sure Maeve isn't expecting you to spend the afternoon with her, but if you're free, come on over." She plucked a mushroom off her plate and popped it in her mouth.

They sat in comfortable silence while they ate, watching the sun begin its slow descent. Across the lake, the pale walls of the Carpe Diem Resort turned to gold.

"So," Jonathan said finally, "I have a proposition for you."

Candy turned toward him. "Oh, yeah?"

He nodded, a spark of enthusiasm in his eyes. "What if we come back in a couple of hours and put the first coat of sealer on tonight?"

She narrowed her eyes at him. "And why would we do that? I'm pooped."

"I know," he said quickly, wiping his hands on a napkin. "But hear me out. If we do the first coat tonight, we could be out of here by ten, right?"

Candy calculated the time in her head. "Yeah. I figure it will take us about three hours per coat. If we start soon, sure. But again, why?"

"So if we do our first coat of the sealant tonight, we can take tomorrow morning off, then come back in the evening for the second coat."

Candy nodded, the idea of sleeping in sounding delightfully decadent. "You're starting to win me over. Go on."

He grinned and tossed the napkin onto his plate. "And if we have the morning off, then maybe we can go for a drive. Take a ride in the GTO, get lunch somewhere nice. You can tell me why you love Autumn Lake so much."

Candy hesitated. The invitation was tempting—very tempting. She was wary of turning their work relationship into anything else, though, especially after a day of no mishaps, a day they'd spent getting along.

But she wanted to go. Very much.

"I'd like that," she said finally. "But if we do the sealer tonight, we'll need to be back tomorrow evening to do the second coat, and we'll still have to do a third on Sunday, particularly in the kitchen where the traffic is heavy."

"Deal," Jonathan said, his smile warming her more than the evening sun.

"And if we do the first coat now, you won't be able to stay tonight. In fact, you might as well stay at Maeve's the whole weekend. It won't be set up enough to walk on until Monday."

"Got it. I'll call Maeve now and ask if I can take her up on the offer of her guestroom." He was being very agreeable. Should she be suspicious?

"Good." She set down her plate and took a long drink, the bubbles in the carbonated water tickling her nose. "Do you have a destination in mind?" She hoped he wasn't expecting her to come up with a plan. As much as she loved people and getting out and about, the idea of taking a day off to just rest and recover sounded ridiculously appealing. A busy tourist location or a crowded restaurant didn't exactly conjure up a relaxing vibe.

"Actually, I was thinking maybe we just get in the car and drive. I looked at the map, and there are roads that follow the Ohio River pretty closely for miles." He glanced over at her. "We can just head in one direction and see where they take us."

Candy was typically a well-mapped-out plan kind of girl. A destination person. It always helped when the journey along the way was nice, but usually, what was more important was where she'd end up and what she'd do when she got there. Now, however, the idea of having no plans at all, other than heading east or west and ending up back where they started sounded enticing. Intriguing. Inspiring.

"Okay," she said, giving him a curious look. Of course, Jonathan was a lone wolf trailblazer kind of guy. Hadn't he just hiked the Appalachian Trail all by himself? Sure, he'd most certainly come across others on the way—the girl who'd given him that scar, for one—but to undertake a task like that without a rallying support system at your side was quite a feat. "Which way should we go?"

Jonathan grabbed a twig off the deck near his feet. He snapped it two and held up one, then the other. "This one is east, and this one is west." Then he put them behind his back and made a show of switching the sticks around. "Your call."

Candy shimmied her shoulders indecisively for a moment, then pointed at his right arm.

"East it is," he declared, holding up the short knobby stick he'd designated for east. "What time should I pick you up? Nine? Ten?"

Candy hedged a little, not wanting to dampen his enthusiasm. "I get up pretty early," she told him. "I'll probably have breakfast around seven. How about nine, or even earlier?"

Jonathan laughed. "A woman after my own heart. Since being on the trail, I've had a hard time sleeping in past sunrise most mornings."

"Except a few Mondays ago when you were snoring loud enough to make the house shake," she teased, nudging him with her elbow. "You scared the living daylights out of me, you know. I thought maybe a rabid raccoon had gotten in the house. Or worse."

Jonathan grinned sideways at her. "Like a filthy, stinkin' sasquatch?"

"Exactly!" Candy exclaimed, trying to ignore the pleasant flutter in her stomach at the thought of spending a whole day with the man. "Should I pack us a picnic lunch?"

He shook his head. "Let's just see what little hole-in-the-wall we find along the way. Is that okay?"

Eventually, they cleaned up their pizza dinner and went back inside to apply the first sealer coat. As they worked side by side in comfortable rhythm, Candy wondered if this outing tomorrow was meant to be a date. If she were Juno, she'd just come right out and ask.

They both seemed to be energized by the thought of tomorrow's excursion, and the first coat went on without a hiccup. By nine-thirty, they were stepping outside the front door and heading their separate ways for the night.

"Those floors are going to be beautiful," Jonathan said, genuine admiration in his voice as he waited while she locked up. "I mean, they already are, but with another coat or two? Wow."

"Right?" Candy agreed, feeling a surge of pride. She was glad Jonathan liked it, especially since he would likely be the person living her and making these floors his own.

He walked with her to her car. "Thank you," he said unexpectedly.

"For what?"

"For letting me help," he replied. "For not kicking me out when I showed up this morning. For agreeing to tomorrow."

Candy felt her cheeks warm. "I was glad to see you," she admitted, the words slipping out before she could stop them. "Honestly, I'd gotten accustomed to having you around." Then she grinned and added, "It's been far too quiet around here without your grumpy grumblings."

Jonathan's eyes softened. "I missed you, too, Miss Toolbelt. I'll see you tomorrow, then. Eight o'clock?"

"Eight o'clock is perfect," she confirmed, opening her door before she could do something foolish, like invite him to come even earlier and have breakfast with her.

On her drive home, Candy tried to make sense of the conflicting emotions swirling inside her. She was excited about tomorrow, nervous about what it meant, and still trying to process the transformation in Jonathan. Not just his appearance, but something deeper.

When she walked into her house with her cooler, Liz was curled up on the couch with a book.

"You're home early," her cousin observed, looking up.

"Early? It's almost ten o'clock," she said with a laugh.

"Yeah, but the way you made it sound this morning, I thought you might be pulling an all-nighter over there."

"Change of plans," Candy replied, dropping her keys on the entry table, then shooting Liz a sideways glance. "I had help today."

Liz's eyebrows shot up. "Squatch is back?"

Candy couldn't hold back her grin. "Squatch is back. And guess what? He's taking me for a drive in his car tomorrow morning."

Liz closed her book with a snap. "Well, well, well. Sounds like someone has a date."

"It's not a date," Candy protested, even as her stomach fluttered again. "It's just... a drive. Maybe lunch."

"Uh-huh," Liz smirked, pointing at the other end of the sofa. "Sit and tell me all about it."

Candy flopped down beside her cousin and leaned her head against the back of the couch. "That's it. There's nothing more to tell."

"And you're good with being seen in public with a caveman?"

"Oh, just wait until you see him." She rolled her head to the side and grinned at Liz.

Her cousin's eyes widened. "Why? What happened?"

Candy let out a rather girlish sigh, but this was Liz, and the moment her cousin laid eyes on the guy, she'd understand. "He got a haircut. And shaved. He's..." She trailed off, struggling to find the right words.

"Hot?" Liz supplied.

"Criminally," Candy admitted with a moan of surrender. "I couldn't stop staring at him. You'll see for yourself if you get up early enough. He's picking me up at eight."

Liz whistled low. "Oh, I'll be up. This I have to see." She rubbed her hands together gleefully. "It's been a long time since you've had that look on your face, Cuz."

Candy made a dismissive sound. "Whatever. Just because he's ridiculously handsome doesn't mean I don't still hate him."

"Love and hate," Liz quipped. "Two sides of the same coin."

Candy threw a cushion at her cousin, but Liz's laughter only confirmed what she already knew. She was in trouble. Deep trouble. And the worst part was, she didn't mind one bit.

24
Jonathan

Jonathan pulled into Candy and Liz's driveway. Five minutes early. He debated waiting until exactly eight, not wanting to seem too eager, but decided against it. He'd been up since before six anyway, too wired about the day ahead to sleep much longer.

As he turned off the engine, the front door of the house swung open. But instead of Candy, Liz stepped onto the porch.

She wore a pair of cutoff jean shorts and a faded Autumn Lake Fire Department t-shirt, her hair loose around her shoulders instead of pulled back in the severe French braid he remembered from Juno's. It changed her whole appearance, softening her features and making her look younger, less like the no-nonsense tomboy he'd met before.

"Nice car, Squatch," she called out, descending the porch steps and circling the GTO with an appreciative eye. "Good to see you back in town."

"Thanks," Jonathan replied. It was a relief to hear Candy's cousin say so. "You like classic cars?"

"My dad restored a sixty-nine Chevelle when I was a kid. I handed him tools and eventually graduated to helping with replacing spark plugs and hoses." She peered at the gleaming blue finish. "Is the paint original?"

"We had to repaint it, but it's the original color. Montreux Blue. Everything else is, though," Jonathan confirmed, warming to the subject. "Check out the leather interior."

Liz whistled low, then jerked her head toward the hood. "Mind if I take a look under there?"

Jonathan grinned, popping the hood for her. They were both leaning over the engine, Liz asking questions about the 400 V8, when the front door opened again.

He straightened up too quickly, banging his head on the raised hood. Rubbing the spot, he turned to see Candy stepping onto the porch, and his breath caught.

The pretty yellow sundress she had on fell just above her knees. She wore a light denim jacket over it and simple white sneakers on her feet. Her blonde hair was down, framing her face in soft waves, and a pair of oversized sunglasses perched on top of her head. She looked nothing like the toolbelt-wearing contractor he'd worked with the day before.

His immediate pleasure at seeing her—combined with the embarrassment of hitting his head—made him blurt the first thing that came to mind. "You're late."

Candy looked at her watch, then rolled her eyes. "It's exactly eight o'clock, Mr. Grumpy. And good morning to you too."

"Charming, Squatch," Liz teased, closing the hood with a solid thunk. She stepped back, giving him an exaggerated once-over. She pointed at his face. "The new look suits you, though I'm still calling you Squatch."

Jonathan rubbed his neck self-consciously. "Your cousin warned me that the name would stick."

Candy joined them in the driveway carrying her cooler. He gave her a questioning look.

"Just some drinks and snacks," she said defensively, holding it behind her like he might try to snatch it. "I wasn't sure how long we'd be out."

"Good thinking," he said, moving to take it from her and placing it carefully in the backseat. He held the passenger door open for her, and she slid in with a murmured thanks.

As Jonathan pulled away from the curb, he caught a glimpse of Liz in the rearview mirror, giving Candy a thumbs-up behind his back. He pretended not to notice.

They headed east out of town, taking the scenic route that ran alongside the Ohio River as planned. The day was perfect with clear blue skies, a light breeze, and temperatures that hadn't yet reached the heat of midday. The GTO's engine purred as they cruised along the winding roads, passing through farmland dotted with rustic barns and fields of late summer crops.

Beside him, Candy was quiet, but not uncomfortably so. She'd brought a real camera, not just her phone, and occasionally snapped photos of the passing scenery.

"Are you documenting our day out of the house?" Jonathan asked after she'd taken a particularly lovely shot of sunlight filtering through a stand of trees.

"No, this is just for me," Candy replied, lowering the camera to her lap. "It's been a long time since I've taken a day off, or even used this camera. I just want to capture a few memories of the day."

Something in her voice made Jonathan glance over. She was looking at him, not the scenery, and quickly averted her gaze when their eyes met. He felt a warmth spread through his chest.

"Besides," she added, "my followers might get jealous if they knew I was spending the whole day with you. You've become quite popular."

Jonathan groaned. "I saw some of the comments yesterday. They're..."

"Enthusiastic?" Candy suggested with a laugh.

"That's one word for it," he agreed, though he'd been thinking 'terrifying' might be more accurate.

They drove through several small river towns, each with its own character. There were historic main streets with brick buildings, diners advertising the best pie or waffles or biscuits and gravy in the county, community centers, school houses, and churches.

"Look," Candy said suddenly, pointing to a small white church on a hill overlooking the river. "Isn't that beautiful? And look at the cemetery. It looks like something out of a movie with all those huge trees and ancient headstones. Can we stop?" she turned to him and asked. "I'd love to take a few pictures."

Jonathan hesitated. He hadn't been to a cemetery since his father's funeral, and the thought of walking among gravestones made something tighten in his chest. But the hope in Candy's eyes made it impossible to refuse.

"Sure." He pulled into the small gravel parking lot beside the church.

The cemetery was peaceful, with the river visible in the distance and massive maples providing shade over many of the gravestones. They wandered silently among the markers, Candy occasionally stopping to photograph an interesting headstone or a particularly beautiful view.

"Some of these dates go back to the 1820s," she noted, kneeling to examine one weathered stone. "Imagine all the history here."

Jonathan nodded, but he grew quieter as they moved through the rows. Candy seemed to sense his change in mood, glancing at him with increasing concern until finally, she stopped and touched his arm.

"It's getting hot," she said, though the temperature was still pleasant. "Let's sit in the shade for a bit."

They sat with their backs against the massive trunk, looking out over the peaceful scene. After a few moments of silence, Candy spoke softly.

"I was insensitive," she began. "I didn't think about how hard this might be for you."

Jonathan wanted to reassure her, to tell her that she hadn't done anything wrong, that he was fine. But what came out instead was, "It was a heart attack."

Candy only nodded; maybe she already knew. But he found that he wanted to talk about it. "It just came out of left field," he said, picking at a blade of grass. "Completely unexpected. He was fit, so active. Always hiking, biking, staying busy." He shook his head. "It was a surprise to everyone."

"I'm so sorry," Candy murmured.

"I found him," Jonathan went on, his voice tight with tamped down emotion. She squeezed his hand in empathy. He pointed across the graveyard at the GTO where it was parked, glistening in the sunshine. "He died on a roller cart under that car. When I first pulled up to his place, the garage was open, the hood was up, but when I didn't see him, I headed inside. I searched the whole house before I headed back out to the garage and there he was, his feet sticking out from under the front of the car. I'd walked right by him."

The memory of seeing his father's limp legs... For a moment, Jonathan had almost convinced himself that Troy had just fallen asleep under the hood, or maybe he'd passed out from fumes. But with the garage door open for ventilation and the motor not even running? Besides, he'd made an increasing amount of noise as he'd grown more and more frantic in his search, and when he'd burst into the garage, he'd been hollering loud enough to alert the neighbor. Tom Larkin called 9-1-1 as he came up the sidewalk, his expression grim, knowing without asking that something was terribly wrong.

Jonathan had gently slid the trolley out from under the car, grabbing for Troy's hands first, but they'd already been cool to the touch, inanimate. Then he took in the blue-tinged lips, his half-open, unseeing his eyes. Jonathan had pressed his cheek to his father's mouth, desperate for the faintest hint of a breath, for the tiniest bit of hope, then to his chest to listen for a heartbeat, holding back his cries of, "Oh, Dad. No, no. Dad, no," until he was certain there were no signs of life.

He took a steadying breath now, taking a moment to collect himself. "At the hospital, the doctor told me he'd recently been diagnosed with Familial Hypercholesterolemia—FH—a genetic heart disorder." Jonathan swallowed hard. "Dad never said a thing to me. I had no idea."

Candy reached over and took his hand. For several moments, she said nothing. Then turning to study his face, she asked, "Familial. Does that mean it's hereditary?"

Jonathan nodded slowly. "It means it runs in the family. But it's not automatically passed on."

Beside him, Candy took a deep breath, then let it out in a long, quiet exhale that ended with an, "And what about you?"

"I had blood tests and a genetic test done shortly after Dad died. Everything came back negative." He closed his eyes for a moment, remembering the appointment when they went over his test results. He'd sat in that chair and wept, not from relief, but from what he now understood was a form of survivor's guilt. "Dad drew the short stick and I got lucky, and I still can't figure out why."

Candy stared down at their clasped hands, a frown marring her profile. "Oh, Jonathan," she whispered. "That's a lot to carry around with you. I'm glad you told me."

It was exactly what he needed to hear, he realized. Having braced himself for a barrage of questions, to have her simply listen was a gift.

They sat that way for several minutes, not speaking, just holding hands as the breeze rustled the leaves above them. Her hand was warm and soft in his, and despite the heat, Jonathan found he didn't want to let go.

Finally, Candy broke the silence. "Okay, but this is getting a little gross," she said, pulling away dramatically. "Why are your hands so sweaty? Don't tell me you tried to fix another leak on your own."

The shift in tone was so unexpected that Jonathan burst out laughing, the tension broken.

"Are you hungry yet?" she asked, nudging his shoulder with hers. "Because I'm starving."

"I've never met a woman who proudly eats as much as you do," Jonathan observed with a smile.

Candy punched his arm, not entirely gently. "For that, you're paying for lunch. And I'm definitely getting dessert."

As they stood and brushed grass from their clothes, heading back to the car, Jonathan realized he would have happily kept holding her hand all day, sweaty palms or not.

25
Candy

Monday morning arrived with a renewed sense of anticipation that Candy couldn't ignore. After their day trip on Saturday that included lunch at a quaint riverfront café, a leisurely drive back to Autumn Lake, and then the remainder of the weekend spent finishing up the wood floors, she found herself looking forward to getting back to work.

Or maybe, she admitted to herself as she pulled into the driveway, she was just looking forward to seeing Jonathan again.

Apparently, he was looking forward to seeing her this morning, too, because when she pulled in the driveway, Jonathan was waiting for her on the porch, two mugs of coffee in hand. Without his beard, his smile was even more devastating in the morning light.

Candy took out her phone and filmed him as she climbed from her SUV and headed up the front walk toward him.

"Good morning," he said, ignoring the camera and handing her a steaming cup as she approached. There was still a hint of that guarded look in his eyes that she'd seen since their intimate conversation in the graveyard on Saturday, but he also seemed genuinely happy to see her. Which made her genuinely happy to see him.

"Good morning, Squatch," she replied, trying to ignore the flutter in her stomach when their fingers brushed during the handoff. She took a sip and sighed dreamily. It was already her third cup of coffee this morning, but she and Liz had made pancakes for breakfast before they both left for work, and one simply couldn't have pancakes without the bite of coffee to cut the sweetness of the maple syrup. She peered at Jonathan over her cup. "How'd you sleep last night?"

She hadn't seen him since Sunday morning when they'd applied the last coat of sealer. They'd opted to do all of the wood floors, not just the kitchen, so it had taken a little longer than planned. Which meant starting a couple of hours later this morning. It was almost ten o'clock, and even though she hadn't slept in, she felt well-rested, both in body and mind.

Jonathan chuckled dryly. "I'm thinking Aunt Maeve might have spent a little more money on the queen-size mattress in her guestroom than she did on the twin bed in my dad's old room. It's been like sleeping on a cloud the last few nights. I feel amazing." He turned this way and that, preening theatrically for the camera.

"Excellent," Candy said with a laugh, then turned the camera to face her. "Happy Monday, Hearth Breakers! We're ready, as you just heard Squatch say. Are you?"

Over the next few days, they fell into a comfortable working rhythm that surprised her. In spite of his lack of natural ability, Jonathan was a quick learner, and soon he was anticipating what she needed before she asked and adapting to her methods without complaint. Before long, they were moving around each other with an easy familiarity that made the work flow smoothly.

"Your fans are crazy," Jonathan remarked during their lunch break on Tuesday, scrolling through the comments on her latest video. "They apparently can't get enough of 'Hot Squatch.'"

Candy beamed with pleasure. "I know, right?"

"Should I be offended or flattered?" he asked with a wry smile.

"Definitely flattered," Candy assured him, pulling out her phone to record a quick update. "The transformation reveal has been my most-watched video ever. People love a good makeover story."

She had indeed been playing up Jonathan's presence in her videos, calling him "Hot Squatch" and capturing his reactions to her teasing. For his part, Jonathan had leaned into his grumpy persona, delivering deadpan comebacks that had her followers in stitches. His natural dry wit, once unleashed, was surprisingly hilarious. Every video featuring Jonathan brought in more views, more followers, more engagement. Her subscriber count had nearly doubled in the past few weeks.

It should have been cause for celebration, but a nagging worry had begun to take root. What would happen when the project was over? Would Jonathan stay in Autumn Lake or return to Atlanta? And if he left, would all these new followers, clearly drawn to his presence as much as her renovation skills, abandon her channel?

She tried to push these thoughts aside as they tackled the non-loadbearing wall between the mudroom and small back entry on Wednesday. They'd set up plastic sheeting to contain the dust, but by the time they'd removed the drywall, they were both covered in white powder despite their protective gear.

"Hold still," Jonathan said, reaching toward her after they'd stepped outside and removed their masks and goggles. His fingertips brushed her cheek, gently wiping away dust that had gotten close to her eye. "You look like a raccoon."

The touch was so unexpected, so tender, that Candy felt her breath catch. "So do you," she managed to say, hoping he couldn't hear the slight tremor in her voice.

Their only real disagreement came on Thursday over the tile selection for the upstairs Jack and Jill bathroom, the one Jonathan had flooded. Candy had chosen a classic subway tile with a thin accent strip of mosaic glass. She wanted to retain the room's vintage appeal, but still give it clean lines and smooth surfaces. There was nothing worse than hard-to-clean bathroom tile.

"What about something bolder?" Jonathan suggested, pulling up images on his phone. "Like this hexagon pattern?"

"Too trendy," Candy countered. "It'll look dated in five years."

"But this is timeless," Jonathan argued, showing her a different pattern. "A basketweave in marble would add texture while still feeling classic."

They debated back and forth, presenting options and counterarguments, until they finally landed on a compromise of larger subway tiles in a herringbone pattern with the glass mosaic as a shower niche accent. It was better than either of their original ideas, and Candy found herself admiring how they'd pushed each other toward a more creative solution.

Driving home to Liz's that evening, Candy realized just how much she'd come to enjoy starting her days with Jonathan. Their morning coffee ritual, the easy banter, the way he listened to her ideas with genuine interest—it had all become a highlight of her daily routine.

But beneath the comfortable partnership they'd established, she couldn't ignore the lingering questions about his future plans. Despite his mention of staying until the job was finished, he still hadn't said anything about what came after.

She replayed his revelation in the cemetery, the raw grief still evident in his voice as he'd described finding his father. The uncertainty about his own health that he carried. She understood now why he might be hesitant to make definitive plans, why he might need time and space to figure things out. He seemed in much better spirits now than he had when he'd first come to Autumn Lake, and she liked to think that maybe she'd had something to do with his transformation. Despite her early misgivings about him, if she could have things her way, he'd choose Autumn Lake over Atlanta. He'd choose this home over his fancy big city apartment.

He'd choose her.

As much as she wanted answers, she wouldn't press him. For now, she would enjoy their working relationship and try not to think too much about what might happen when the renovation was complete.

26
Jonathan

JONATHAN SAT CROSS-LEGGED ON the carpet in his father's old bedroom, his back against the side of the bed, laptop balanced on his knees. He'd been up working since five, making adjustments based on the latest round of beta testing feedback.

The interest in his hiking app had far exceeded his expectations. Five thousand users were now actively testing it, and their enthusiasm fueled his own. Annually, there were an estimated three million visitors to the Appalachian Trail, but only about three thousand of them managed a full hike-through each year. So to have so many users giving his app a try was very exciting for him.

But it was the new projects that occupied his thoughts this morning. One in particular; the app he'd started sketching out after Candy had voiced her desire for a DIY app for women.

"What if," he murmured to himself, typing notes rapidly, "users could take a photo of a part they need replaced, and the app identifies it and tells them exactly where to find it in the store?"

He'd been brainstorming features for days now, building on Candy's initial concept. A directory of women-owned hardware stores and contract businesses. Video tutorials organized by skill level. A community forum where users could share their projects and ask questions. This could be a real boon for his real business launch, something with much broader appeal than his niche hiking app.

And then there was Juno's Coffee Bar app, too. It wasn't anything she was ready to start on, at least not until after her wedding, but they'd volleyed emails back and forth with conceptual ideas, and Jonathan thought he had a good notion of what she needed.

Glancing at his watch, Jonathan saved his work and closed the laptop. Candy would be arriving soon, and they had a full day of hanging drywall ahead of them. He'd promised to have coffee ready, but this morning she was bringing breakfast.

Just as he reached the bottom of the stairs, he heard her car pull into the driveway. Through the window, he watched her gather a paper bag from the passenger seat and make her way to the door, her blonde ponytail swinging with each step.

"Morning," she called as she entered, holding up the bag. "I brought breakfast sandwiches from Juno's. She's got a new one on the menu that I haven't tried. Its egg, bacon, and avocado on ciabatta with a Sriracha mayonnaise."

"Sounds perfect," Jonathan replied, taking the food bag from her while she divested herself of her armful of other items. "Coffee's ready."

They settled at the kitchen table, unwrapping their sandwiches and discussing the day's plans. The mudroom demolition was complete, the framing was in place, and now they needed to hang drywall before they could begin the tile work in what would soon be a stunning new laundry, bathroom, and mudroom combo.

"How'd you sleep last night?" Candy asked as she filmed him unwrapping the gorgeous sandwich. "You look like you've been up for awhile."

Jonathan nodded and looked directly into the camera. "Absolutely. I've only rolled off the bed once since being back upstairs, but that was two nights ago. Slept like a fat cat last night." He patted his flat stomach and took an enormous bite before she rolled her eyes and stopped filming.

It had been more than a month since he'd come off the trail, and he finally felt almost back to his normal self. He was no longer ravenous all the time, he slept better, although he'd grown to love the quiet of the morning before the rest of the world woke up, and he'd kept that new habit. He'd put on a good ten pounds since he'd left the trail, his clothes didn't hang off of him anymore, he no longer got the uncomfortable headaches that had plagued him the whole second half of the hike, and the scar on his face was almost unnoticeable. "The truth is, I'm starting to feel at home here. This is a good place to wake up in."

"That's nice," Candy said softly. "I'm glad."

They finished breakfast in companionable silence, both aware of the work awaiting them. Drywall installation was physically demanding, requiring precision and teamwork, especially in the awkward spaces of a small room.

By midmorning, they had established an efficient system. Jonathan would hold each sheet in place while Candy secured it with the screw gun. Their height difference made them a good team—he could reach the top portions easily, while she handled the lower sections.

"Hold it steady," Candy directed as they positioned a sheet around a newly framed window. She was right beside him, her arm occasionally brushing against his as she worked the power tools.

Jonathan was acutely aware of her proximity. The faint scent of her shampoo, the warmth of her body next to his, and the look of concentration on her face as she measured and marked cut lines were constant distractions. He found himself having to consciously refocus on the task at hand.

"You're getting pretty good at this," she remarked as they finished another section. "For a software guy, you're not half bad with your hands."

"High praise from Miss Toolbelt herself," he replied with a mock bow.

Candy laughed, the sound echoing in the half-finished room. "Don't let it go to your head. We still have the ceiling to do after lunch."

The ceiling proved more challenging than the walls. They had to work in even closer proximity, arms raised overhead, their bodies pressed together as they maneuvered each heavy sheet into place. By late afternoon, Jonathan's shoulders ached from the effort, but there was a satisfaction in seeing the room take shape around them.

"We did good work today," Candy said as they cleaned up their tools outside with the garden hose. "All the new fixtures and cabinets should be here sometime on Monday, fingers crossed. I can't wait to get this room all put together."

She'd told him about the shipping delay with the materials, her concerns that it would be cutting things close with them arriving so late. But they'd pushed to get the rest of the downstairs finished so they could spend the last couple of weeks upstairs, which would give them a little more flexibility to fit in the mudroom as needed.

"We'll get it done," he reassured her. "It's all coming together."

Although, that wasn't exactly something he wanted to celebrate, he realized. Each completed room meant they were one step closer to the end of the renovation, to her moving on to another project, to him having to make a decision about where he was going to put down his roots.

After they cleaned up for the day, Jonathan walked Candy out to her car. Even though he had a full evening of work ahead of him, he was reluctant to see her leave. He wanted to ask her to stay and have dinner with him, watch the sunset on the lake from the back deck, or sit close together on the floor in his room and watch a movie on his laptop like a couple of teenagers. But he had calls to make, codes to update, and hundreds of comments to respond to on his app.

"So," Candy said, pausing by her driver's door. "Got big plans for the weekend?"

Jonathan shook his head. "Just work stuff," he said noncommittally. "I've got some big deadlines coming up." He still hadn't told her that if all went well, and it looked like it might just be happening, that he'd be making Autumn Lake and this home his permanent residence, and he didn't mention now the online meeting he had tomorrow afternoon, the possibility that this could be the break he'd been hoping for.

"Oh." Was that disappointment in her voice? She let her car door drift shut and gave him a beseeching look. "I was thinking about coming in tomorrow. There's that wallpaper in the master bedroom and upstairs hallway—I'd like to get it down so we can start prepping for paint next week. Is that okay with you? I'll try not to make too much noise outside your room."

The thought of seeing her tomorrow, of not having to wait until Monday, made him smile. "That would be great," he said, perhaps too quickly. "I could help."

Candy's face brightened, relief and pleasure evident in her smile. "Really? I don't want to take you away from your work."

He took a step closer and reached past her to open her door again. "Really. You can take me away any time."

"Oh, good," she gushed, her cheeks turning a pretty pink. She didn't move to get in the car. "That could save me hours."

She looked up at him then, her blue eyes sparkling, and something there—hope, warmth, possibility—broke through his careful reserve.

Before he could overthink it, Jonathan leaned down and pressed his lips gently to hers. The kiss was tentative at first, almost a question, but he felt it down to his toes.

When he pulled back, Candy's eyes were wide, her cheeks flushed. For a moment, neither of them spoke, the air between them charged.

"I'll see you tomorrow, then," she finally said, her voice slightly breathless as she turned away from him and climbed in behind the wheel of her SUV.

"Tomorrow," Jonathan echoed, before closing the door after her.

As she drove away, he pressed his lips together, still feeling the soft pressure of hers. What had he just done? What did it mean for them, for his plans, for everything he'd been carefully considering these past weeks?

He didn't have answers yet, but for the first time since his father's death, the uncertainty didn't feel like a weight dragging him down. Instead, it felt like the beginning of something new—something that might be worth rearranging his life for.

27
Candy

CANDY HAD BARELY SLEPT. Every time she closed her eyes, she felt Jonathan's lips on hers again, reliving that moment in the driveway when everything between them had shifted.

She'd driven home in a daze, unable to process what had happened. When Liz had asked her about her day, she'd mumbled something about drywall and escaped to her room, not trusting herself to speak without giving everything away.

Now, as she pulled up to the lake house, her stomach fluttered with nervous anticipation. What would she say to him? Would they talk about the kiss, or pretend it hadn't happened? Was it a one-time impulse, or the beginning of something more?

She found Jonathan in the kitchen. "Morning," he said, his voice carefully casual, though his eyes lingered on her face much longer than usual. He handed her a mug of coffee, their fingers brushing, sending a ripple of pleasure up her arm, but then he stepped away. So that was how it would be. Business as usual.

"Good morning," she said as breezily as possible. Her hands shook the tiniest bit, and she was glad she'd opted not to film this morning. She didn't want to give her followers motion sickness. She moved to the table where she opened her planner to the day's schedule showing "Wallpaper is coming down!" Then she withdrew three scraps of wallpaper she'd peeled from the upstairs rooms and arranged them next to the three correlating paint color swatches that would go up on the walls next week. She crisscrossed a scraper and a putty knife on top of the samples beside the planner, then she set her coffee cup close by and snapped a couple of shots, moving around the table to capture the best light.

She could feel Jonathan watching her work, but she stayed focused on the task at hand. When she crouched down and angled her camera so that he was in the background, he smiled lazily and lifted his mug in a salute. It was a lovely shot; she knew as much without even having to preview it.

"Thank you," she said softly, lowering her phone.

Jonathan raised an eyebrow. "For?"

"For being such a good sport about all of this. I know you're not a fan of social media, but my social media is a fan of yours," she added with an appreciative smile.

Jonathan beckoned her over. "Come here," he said, patting the counter beside him. "Give me your phone. Let's do a coffee selfie together."

With only a moment's hesitation—the thought of standing so close to him made it a little hard to breathe—she circled the table and moved to his side. She handed him her phone.

He patted the counter again. "You're too short. Up here."

Candy rolled her eyes. "As you just pointed out, I'm too short to just hop on up there," she said. "You know, maybe I'm not the problem. Maybe you're too tall, and you should crouch."

He was chuckling by the end of her little rant, and turning to face her, he put both hands at her waist and lifted her up. She squealed in surprise, grabbing his shoulders to steady herself. Their faces were suddenly only inches apart, and with her now perched on the new granite countertop, they were almost eye-to-eye.

"Hey, there," Jonathan said, his hands moving from her waist to the counter on either side of her. He leaned in, slowly, his gaze locked on hers. She hadn't let go of his shoulders, and when he pressed his lips to hers, her arms slid around his neck. She closed her eyes and kissed him back.

A few moments later, he lifted his head, his eyelids heavy as he studied her face. Her lips tingled, her cheeks were on fire, and her pulse raced, but she didn't look away. So maybe *not* business as usual.

"Good morning," Jonathan said again, his voice low and husky. One side of his mouth hitched up in what Candy could only describe as a smile of satisfaction. Self-congratulatory, even.

"Good morning, Squatch." He was too close for her to think clearly. "I thought we were doing a coffee selfie."

He chuckled, the sound a low rumble in his chest. "Just took a little detour." He pushed away from the counter and grabbed her mug off the table to give her. Then he picked up his own, along with her phone, and moved in close beside her. "Cups up," he said, raising his out in front of him. "And say, 'Cheers!'"

He smelled so good. Something light and clean, like fresh-cut grass with a hint of citrus and spice. She forced herself to relax, to smile as naturally as possible up at the camera he held out in front of them. He snapped several shots before straightening and handing her phone back to her.

"Ready to tackle that wallpaper?" Candy hopped off the counter before he could offer to help. Still a little lightheaded from that kiss, she wasn't sure how much work she'd get done if they started up again, and she needed to get that paper down.

"I'm ready," he replied, giving her that lazy smile. But he stood back and didn't touch her while she gathered her things from the table.

They spent the morning in the upstairs hallway, working side by side to remove the outdated floral wallpaper. The process was tedious. They started by peeling what they could of the top layer, which fortunately came down in large strips. Then they soaked the glue layer with hot soapy water and carefully scraped away the gummy residue so as not to damage the surface of the wall underneath. In the hallway, they ended up having to go through two layers of wallpaper.

"Whoever put this up wasn't messing around," Candy remarked, struggling with a particularly stubborn section. "They must have used industrial-strength adhesive."

Jonathan chuckled, working a few feet away from her. "I remember my dad once saying that he would never have wallpaper in our house. He said he had this core memory of his big sister manhandling huge rolls of wallpaper, and her husband begging her to hire a professional to do it. Maybe that's where the industrial-strength glue came from."

Candy got a chuckle over that. "I imagine you're right. Putting up wallpaper, especially back when materials weren't manufactured for convenience, is not a task for the fainthearted." She peeled off a surprisingly well-preserved strip of the second layer they'd come to. "Maeve has expensive taste, too," Candy added, examining the quality of the paper she was removing. "This isn't the cheap stuff."

The mundane conversation helped get them back to the easy camaraderie they'd shared before last night's kiss. For awhile, the only sounds in the house were the scrape of their tools against the wall and the occasional chit chat, and Candy found herself relaxing in Jonathan's presence. There was something soothing about working alongside him, their movements falling into an easy rhythm.

"Whoa," Jonathan said suddenly, his voice sharp with surprise. He was down on one knee, scraping residue off the wall around the doorframe by Troy's bedroom. "Check this out."

Candy moved to his side, peering over his shoulder. There, marked neatly on the wall was a series of horizontal pen lines with dates and measurements written beside them.

"Look," Jonathan said softly, tracing his finger just above the markings. "Troy, age 2. Troy, age 3. Troy, age 4..."

It was a height chart, carefully tracking the growth of Jonathan's father from childhood into his teenage years. The last mark was labeled "Troy, age 6." and must have been the last measurement before his parents died.

"Wow," Candy said, watching Jonathan's face as he studied this unexpected connection to his father's past.

"Dad did the same thing for me," Jonathan said quietly, his eyes never leaving the pencil marks. "Just like this, with a line, my name, my age, and the date, in our house in Atlanta. He measured me every birthday until I was eighteen." He smiled at the memory. "I outgrew him by the time I was sixteen. He pretended to be annoyed, but I could tell he was proud."

The tenderness in his voice made Candy's heart ache. "You two were close," she observed softly.

Jonathan nodded. "It was just the two of us for as long as I can remember."

Candy hesitated, then asked gently, "What happened to your mother?"

"She died when I was a baby," Jonathan replied, his voice matter-of-fact. "And since I didn't remember her at all, it wasn't really a pressing issue for me. I knew pretty young that Dad wasn't comfortable talking about her, so I didn't ask."

"Was there no other family? On her side?" Candy asked.

Jonathan shook his head. "Not that I knew of. No one other than Maeve, although I now wish I'd asked more about my mom. Who knows? I may have a cousin Liz out there somewhere." He gave her a sad smile. "My dad was a great parent. He did the best he could on his own."

"He sounds like an amazing man," Candy said, brushing her fingers over Troy's name on the wall. "I'm sorry about your mom."

"It's okay," Jonathan assured her. "I never knew any different." He looked back at the height chart.

She touched his arm gently. "We should save this. I can cut this section out," she offered. "You could frame it, preserve it properly."

Jonathan's eyes lit up. "You could do that?"

"Of course," she said with a smile. "Let me get my tools."

She retrieved what she needed from downstairs and carefully measured and marked the area around the height chart. Using her reciprocating saw, she cut the section of plaster away from the wall while Jonathan watched.

"We'll need to reinforce the back of this," she explained as she gently placed the section on a piece of heavy cardboard she'd laid out on the floor. "But it should frame up nicely."

"Thank you," Jonathan said, his hand covering hers as they both knelt beside the salvaged piece of wall.

Candy nodded, but she didn't want to make the moment about herself. She could see that he was still a little caught up in the emotions the find had stirred up, so she simply gave his hand a quick squeeze, then stood to unplug her saw. "I'm going to put this away."

But Jonathan followed shortly after, carrying the cardboard with its precious load out to the garage where he laid it gently on the old workbench. "Let's take a break for lunch," he suggested. "I'm hungry," he said with a teasing grin. "So I know you must be starving."

"You're going to give me a complex," Candy poked him in the ribs, then stuck out her tongue at him.

Jonathan grabbed her face in both hands and kissed her soundly. "Don't ever stop eating," he said when he came up for air.

In the kitchen, Jonathan pulled out sandwiches he'd prepared earlier and set them on plates while Candy washed up. As they sat at the table, he reached over and took her hand.

"Thank you," he said sincerely. "For going the extra mile to preserve that chart. I know it means more work for you."

Candy laughed lightly. "I'm used to you making more work for me."

"Hey now," he protested with a grin. "You're going to give me a complex."

"Then we're even," she declared, relishing in how natural it felt to be sharing a meal with him. "But," she continued, "I'll concede that you've more than made up for it by helping me around here." She met his eyes, and in a softer, more serious tone, told him, "I'm glad you came back, Jonathan. I missed you while you were gone. I'd gotten used to you greeting me at the door with coffee each morning."

The admission hung between them for a moment before Jonathan leaned forward and gently pressed his lips to hers. Unlike the almost aggressive kiss in the garage, the passionate kiss that morning, or the tentative first kiss the night before, this one was gentle, tender, his hand sliding around to cradle the back of her head.

The sweetness of it lingered when they pulled apart, and Candy relished the lightheaded sensation as her heart did a jig inside her ribcage.

"I missed you, too." Jonathan lifted her hand to plant another kiss in her palm. "Now eat. You're looking faint." He pointed at her face, and there was that self-satisfied grin again. "Like you might pass out."

Candy pressed her palms to her cheeks, embarrassed that he could see just how much his kisses affected her, but she wasn't the only one. Without his beard, the pulse fluttering rapidly at the side of his neck was more than enough evidence of that.

After lunch, they returned to the master bedroom to continue removing wallpaper. The air between them had changed, charged with a new awareness. They worked closer together than necessary, finding excuses to brush against each other, exchanging smiles and glances that had Candy's pulse racing. At one point, Jonathan playfully flicked water from his spray bottle at her, and she retaliated by draping a strip of damp wallpaper over his head. He grabbed her wrist, laughing, and pulled her close for yet another quick kiss.

"You're distracting me from my work, Squatch," she accused, pushing both hands against his chest to break out of his embrace.

By late afternoon, the wallpaper was gone, the hole where they'd cut out the growth chart was patched, and the walls sanded. They'd even had time to apply a coat of primer in preparation for painting next week.

As they packed up their tools, Jonathan looked over at her, his eyes bright with anticipation. "Hey, Miss Toolbelt. Can I take you out to dinner tonight? Somewhere that isn't road stop food or take out?"

Candy gave him a sad face. "I can't," she said. "It's our monthly Garden Variety Lovers Club get together. It's tradition."

"Monthly?" Jonathan asked, his question lighthearted, but she saw the disappointment in his eyes. "You all seem to gather more often than that."

"Yeah, I know. But that's because we're friends. This is an 'attendance required' supper." When he cocked an eyebrow at her, she explained. "You know how people always say they mean to get together, to take that trip, to have that cup of coffee, but then they never do? Well, that's why we—" Candy broke off, watching the color drain from his face. "Jonathan? Are you okay?"

He was nodding, quickly, but the frown that had formed between his brows was still there. "I'm fine. Yes, I know what you mean."

"Are you sure?" He didn't sound okay, and now he wasn't quite meeting her gaze.

"I'm sure," he said again, taking her hand. "I'm glad you ladies are making it a priority to get together. It's more important than you know." He finally looked at her and smiled, but she could still see the tension in the lines at his mouth. "I just wasn't quite ready for this day to end."

"What about tomorrow?" Candy suggested, wondering what she'd said that had triggered such a visceral reaction from him.

Jonathan shook his head. "I promised to spend the day with Maeve. Church in the morning, then lunch afterward. She's got more of my dad's stuff she wants to go through with me." He paused, then said, "And I'm hoping to finally hear from her what happened between her and my dad. I'm reluctant to commit to anything else tomorrow, just in case it opens a can of worms that can't be wrangled right away."

"That's probably best," Candy agreed. "Next week, then?"

Jonathan smiled, still holding her hand. "I'd like to take you out every single night next week," he said, pulling her slowly toward him.

When they finally broke apart, Candy said reluctantly, "I really should go. I do not want to keep the ladies waiting." She had a feeling there'd be no keeping secrets about Jonathan from her way too intuitive friends. She should probably warn him. "Um, just so you know," she began, hedging a little. "My friends are... well, they're intuitive, for lack of a better word."

Jonathan snorted. "Meaning, they're going to guess about this?" He pointed back and forth between them.

"And I'm a terrible liar," Candy admitted with a nod. "I blush easily."

"No, really?" he asked, feigning shock. "I thought you just applied heavy makeup for the camera."

"And now I don't feel bad at all for having other plans this evening," she shot back. But then he kissed her again, and she forgot to be offended by his teasing.

He walked her to her car, their fingers intertwined. "Have fun tonight," he said as she opened her door.

"I will," she promised. "See you Monday?"

"I'll be waiting with your coffee, Boss," he assured her, stealing one last quick kiss before she got into her car.

An hour later, freshly showered and changed, Candy hurried into the coffee shop and dropped into an empty chair beside Claire. Addison, Penny, and Liz were already seated across from them, and Juno was still behind the counter. But she was peeling off her apron and chatting with two of her servers, most likely instructing them to come get her if they needed help. Which they wouldn't. Juno's staff were not only well-trained, but they also loved their boss and would bend over backwards to make sure she could take an hour off to hang with her friends.

"Well, look who's glowing," Liz remarked, eyeing Candy's flushed cheeks. "How's life with the mythical creature these days?"

Juno bustled over with a tray of six glasses of icy raspberry lemonade. She set it down and took the last empty chair across at the head of the table. "Give us the details," she said as she started passing the drinks around.

Candy couldn't hold back her smile. "It's good," she said cryptically, even though she knew she wouldn't be able to hold her news in for much longer than it took for her to settle in. "The house is coming along great, and I can't wait for you all to see the transformation. The downstairs is pretty much done, other than the new mudroom cabinets and the washer and dryer that are all supposed to be here next week." She held up both hands and crossed her fingers. "Hopefully, no more shipping hang-ups with the cabinets. They're coming unfinished because I'm doing a custom stain and an oil-based topcoat. They'll need to air out for a few days before I install them so I don't asphyxiate anyone during the showing." She accepted the glass of lemonade Addison passed to her and took a sip before continuing. "We're tackling the upstairs this week, and with Jonathan's help, I should be finished—"

"Hold up," Liz interrupted, both hands out in front of her.

"Yeah, slow down, woman," Juno added. "My brain can't keep up with your mouth."

"I'm sorry, but who is this 'Jonathan' you speak of?" Liz asked, cocking her head at Candy.

Penny leaned forward, feigning ignorance. "Oh yes. Do tell."

Candy rolled her eyes. "Fine. Squatch, okay?"

Liz pointed at her. "The mythical creature I asked you about," she said, her tone dry. "I know the renovation is going great, and that it's going to be spectacular and blow our minds. I want to know about Squatch."

"We all do," Claire said, waving a hand around to include everyone at the table. "Squatch. Squatch. Squatch. Squatch," she began to chant, and pretty soon, they'd all joined in.

Candy raised both hands. "Hush, you guys! Seriously, how old are you?" But she was having a hard time not laughing, partly at their antics, but also because she was elated at how the last week with Jonathan had ended.

"Better spill the tea, sister," Juno said. "We're not typically a patient bunch, especially when we haven't eaten."

Candy bit her lip, then blurted out, "I've been kissed by a sasquatch."

Addison gasped and covered her mouth, Claire and Penny started clapping, Juno lifted her glass of lemonade in a toast, and Liz sat back in her chair and shook her head. "I should have known when I saw that car of his," she said drolly.

"When?" Penny wanted to know. "Just now? Like, when you left?"

Candy shrugged one shoulder. "Last night."

"Last night?" Liz asked, straightening in her seat. "You didn't tell me that. You walked in, freshly kissed, and didn't say a word."

"I wasn't sure if it was a real kiss or not," Candy defended.

Juno chuckled, and Claire held up a hand, ticking things off on her fingers. "Did his lips touch yours? Did you pucker up? Did either one or both of you close your eyes? Did it last more than—"

"Okay, okay," Candy cut in. "It was a real kiss. But I wanted to make sure it was going to still be real come morning, too."

Juno nodded, her expression solemn. "I get it. So was it?"

"Oh, yes," Candy gushed. "It was very real. This morning. At lunch. This afternoon. And it was still very, very real when we said goodbye to each other an hour ago."

Her friends erupted in excited exclamations and demands for details, which Candy provided, leaving out only the most personal moments.

"So, things are officially... something?" Addison asked when Candy finished.

"Well, we haven't really labeled it," Candy replied, unable to keep the hopeful note from her voice. "But he wants to take me out to dinner next week. Every night next week since I won't let him cook on the new stove until after the open house."

"Who would have thought?" Claire mused. "When you first met him, you were ready to brain him with your hammer."

"He was a different person then," Candy defended, surprising herself with her vehemence. "Or at least, I saw him differently."

"Love does that," Juno said wisely, pretending to put on a pair of glasses. "Helps you see the best in people."

"Love?" Candy sputtered. "I didn't say anything about love."

Claire leaned over and put an arm around her. She kissed her cheek and said, "It's written all over your face, sugar plum."

As they moved on to other topics, Candy found herself thinking about the day's events—the tenderness in Jonathan's eyes when he'd talked about his father, the warmth of her hand in his, the press of his lips against hers.

Her friends were right. She was falling for him. Hard. Despite all her initial reservations, despite the uncertainty of his plans, despite everything.

And for the first time since he'd shown up at the lake house that first morning, Candy allowed herself to hope that maybe, just maybe, Jonathan Burkhardt might be falling for her, too.

28
Jonathan

JONATHAN SHIFTED IN BED, studying the swirled patterns in the plaster on the ceiling in the early morning light seeping between the cracks in the window blinds. He'd been awake for some time, the evening with Candy playing on an endless loop in his mind. What was he doing? Why was he jumping ahead of himself with her?

Since coming to Autumn Lake, everything had shifted—his appearance, his career trajectory, his connection to family he'd never known. But the most significant change was how he felt about Candy.

He ran a hand over his face, feeling the still unfamiliar smoothness of his shaved jaw. The thought of pursuing something real with her was both exhilarating and terrifying. He'd come to Autumn Lake to sort through his grief and find answers about his family, not to lose his heart to a blonde spitfire with a hammer.

Oh, he wanted it all—to move to Autumn Lake, own his own business, pursue a relationship with Candy. But just because he wanted those things didn't mean they were his for the taking. He still didn't know why his father had cut ties with Maeve, why he'd only ever talked about her as a long-lost memory. When Jonathan had asked about her, Troy had always simply said, "Your Aunt Maeve and Uncle Stan are long gone, buddy. It's just you and me."

Before he could commit to permanent life choices, before he could even think about pursuing something real with Candy, he needed answers.

And Candy deserved better than half-measures or uncertainty.

With a sigh, Jonathan threw back the covers. He'd agreed to attend church with Maeve this morning and then spend the day with her. With the renovation winding down, it was time to ask the questions that had been haunting him.

• ❤ • ❤ • ❤ • ❤ • ❤ •

THE SMALL COUNTRY CHURCH buzzed with quiet conversation as Jonathan followed Maeve down the center aisle. The building was modest but well-maintained, with simple stained glass windows casting colorful patterns across the wooden pews.

Jonathan spotted Candy sitting with her friends about halfway down. His heart quickened at the sight of her in a pretty floral shirt, her hair swept up in a loose twist. As he and his aunt passed her pew, he turned and gave her a quick salute. She smiled broadly, her eyes bright and warm, and saluted back. He'd have like to sit with her and Liz, but Maeve pointed at a pew two rows from the front.

"This is my pew," she told him. He stepped back to let her slip in ahead of him and smiled at an elderly woman who was already seated further down the bench. Behind her hand, Maeve added, "And that's my friend, Lottie. I'll sit between you, or she'll talk your ear off through the whole service."

After the pastor's closing prayer, Maeve introduced him to what felt like half the congregation. Everyone welcomed him warmly, expressing delight at meeting "Maeve's nephew." It was strange, being embraced by a community he'd never known, one that had apparently held his aunt in high regard for decades

Outside, they finally made their way to where Candy stood with Liz and a few of their friends. Hazel Poleman, co-owner of the Garden Gate B&B, took his hand and held it firmly.

"My goodness, it's grand to meet you. I've heard so much about you over the years, young man," she gushed.

Jonathan looked in surprise at his aunt. Over the years? How had this energetic little woman heard of him?

"You look just like your father," Hazel added, reaching up to pat Jonathan's cheek. "Such a lovely young man, that Troy." She shot a smile at Maeve. "I bet this one takes after his father, doesn't he?"

Maeve nodded. "He certainly does. In all the best ways."

"So what are your plans for this lovely day?" Hazel asked them, finally releasing Jonathan's hand. "We're having Sunday brunch in an hour if you two would like to join us. The lovely Needham ladies are coming, too."

Maeve looped her arm through Jonathan's. "I'm kidnapping him for the day," she said in a conspiratorial tone. "Between the renovation and Fall Festival preparations, we've hardly had time together."

Jonathan felt a twinge of guilt. He'd had time; he'd just been giving his to Candy.

"Oh goodness, yes," Hazel agreed, nodding understandingly. "I forgot you were heading up the committee this year. You two certainly have a lot to catch up on. We'll catch you on another Sunday."

Jonathan thanked her, then made a point to connect with Candy. He wasn't sure how she felt about going public with what was happening between them, but because of his own conflicted thoughts, he wanted to be sensitive. He reached over and touched her shoulder, just the brush of his fingers. "And I'll see you in the morning, Miss Toolbelt."

"Bright and early, Squatch," she returned, her eyes twinkling with mischief.

Beside her, Liz smirked knowingly. "Hey, Mythical Creature."

Penny introduced her mother and husband to him, then Maeve reminded him that she had to put a chicken in the oven soon if they were going to eat in a timely manner. They said their goodbyes, but Jonathan was certain he could feel Candy's eyes on him the whole way across the parking lot. He didn't mind one bit.

BACK AT MAEVE'S CONDO, Jonathan found himself following his aunt around with his toolbox, tackling her list of small repairs—loose cabinet hinges, changing out decorative switch plates, replacing smoke detector batteries, and reprogramming the television remote that she'd somehow accidentally reset to factory settings.

"I miss my old lady game shows," she admitted with a conspiratorial whisper as he reprogrammed the remote. "But you didn't hear it from this youngster."

"I'll never tell," he promised, testing the remote to make sure everything worked.

"So tell me how things are going with Candy," Maeve said, once they'd returned to the kitchen where he began packing up his tools while she mashed potatoes on the stove top.

Jonathan glanced over at her, something in her tone making him think she was probing for more than just renovation news. "She's really good at what she does," he told her, opting for a vague response. "I'm learning a lot from her, and not just renovation stuff. She's teaching me how to take care of a home."

"She's such a delight," Maeve agreed. "Thank you for being flexible with all of this, Jonathan. I know I offered you the home, but I simply couldn't pull that project out from under her. She claims she's charging me her cost, but I am quite certain that she'd pulling funds out of her own pocket for upgrades. She won't admit it, of course, nor will she accept any more than what we agreed upon, so giving her your cooperation means a lot to me."

That sounded like something Candy would do. She'd mentioned having gotten a small settlement after the early cancellation of her contract, but he also remembered her saying she'd used it to pay for her contractor's schooling. He hoped the project wasn't bleeding her dry, and now, knowing how much she'd invested in it, he was that much more determined to be a help and not a hindrance.

"Are you hungry?" Maeve asked, opening the oven door to read the thermometer in the chicken's thigh. "This is ready to come out."

The smell wafting from the kitchen had been tantalizing him for the past hour. "You don't need to ask me twice."

After they'd eaten their fill, Maeve poured them each a cup of coffee and they moved into the living room. Jonathan settled into the comfortable armchair across from her, sensing a shift in her demeanor. She seemed to be gathering herself for something.

"I'd like to talk to you," she said finally, her fingers tracing the rim of her cup. "About your father. About what happened between us."

Jonathan set his own cup down. He'd been mulling over how to broach the topic himself, but Maeve had brought it up first. "I'd like that."

His aunt took a deep breath. "I suppose I need to start at the beginning."

"The beginning sounds good," he agreed, realizing that the classy, elegant Maeve Lewis was nervous.

"After our parents died, I became responsible for Troy when I was barely twenty myself. I was engaged to Stan at the time." She picked up a large manilla envelope from the end table beside her and opened the top flap. She withdrew a photo and handed it to him. It was of a very young Troy and a smiling wholesome-looking woman in a yellow top and denim shorts standing together on the lake house dock, fishing poles in hand, and holding a stringer of iridescent sunfish held up between them. "Your grandmother, Irene," she said. "That was from the summer before she died. Troy wasn't quite six."

Jonathan studied the beaming pride on the young Troy's face, the laughter on Irene's, recognizing Maeve in her mother. "What a great picture," he said.

"It's one of my favorites of those two," Maeve smiled softly. "Troy was their miracle child, having thought they couldn't have any others after me," Maeve said. "With our age gap, he was in many ways an only child, and Mom spoiled him rotten." She smiled sadly. "I know I was guilty of doing so, too. He was just so cute with those big blue eyes." She pointed at Jonathan. "You have the Burkhardt eyes."

His father had told him the same thing on more than one occasions.

"Needless to say, when Mother died, Troy simply didn't know how to channel his grief. He was a little terror for a while," she said with a sad chuckle. "My wonderful Stan essentially married us both and moved into the lake house with us so that Troy wouldn't lose the only home he'd ever known. Stan made the tedious commute to Evansville our whole marriage without a word of complaint."

This much Jonathan already knew. His father had said he'd been a handful after losing his parents.

"We settled into our new normal, but by high school, Troy showed signs that he was still struggling with the loss of our parents. He was such a nice young man, but he had few friends because he tended to dive in too quickly, too... *enthusiastically*, I suppose, and hold too tightly. Especially when he started dating."

She paused, toying with the cuff of her sleeve, and Jonathan could tell that his aunt was choosing her words carefully, trying to be objective as she talked about someone they'd both known and loved. It had him a little on edge, and he found that he was almost afraid of what she might say next.

"One young lady told her friends in the girls' restroom that Troy was stalking her, and a teacher overheard the conversation. Carrie—that was her name—assured the teacher that he wasn't actually stalking her, just that she'd noticed him sitting alone on a field trip and had invited him to join her group of friends, and Troy had mistaken her kindness as a romantic gesture. Apparently, he didn't believe her when she insisted she just wanted to be friends, and had asked her to go out with him on more than one occasion. The teacher had still followed up with us, just to be on the safe side. Troy was mortified, of course, and he grew noticeably withdrawn after that. He was on the track team all four years of high school, so he didn't close himself in his room every day, but running is a solitary sport, even when you're on a team. He did eventually end up dating a neighbor girl who was also on the track team, but she broke his heart right before their senior prom when she told him that he was too needy, that he was suffocating her." She shook her head at the memory. "Sadly, she was right. He was so afraid of rejection, that the people he cared about would leave him, that he wound up chasing them away."

This was all new to Jonathan, and he wasn't sure how to process what Maeve was saying. Troy had been a quiet, patient man, kind to everyone. Jonathan had never seen this clingy, needy almost obsessive version Maeve was painting.

"Abandonment issues, his counselor called it. I felt like I'd failed him." She sighed deeply. "At the counselor's advice, Troy started attending a community grief recovery group, hoping he'd connect with others going through similar struggles. I went with him for the first few times, but the folks were so warm and welcoming to him, and when he asked if he could continue attending alone, I had no qualms about agreeing." She pulled another photo from the envelope and slid it across the coffee table to him.

It was a picture of a sharp-looking teenage Troy in an auto shop bay, his hair tousled, a broad smile on his face, standing beside a car that was up on a lift. He had a smudge of grease on one cheek and both his hands were covered in the stuff. Jonathan flipped the photo over and read the date and the neat inscription. *First rebuilt engine.*

"Troy got an after-school job at a local garage and discovered a real passion for working on cars." The pride in her voice was unmistakable. "After he graduated from high school, he went full time there, saving every penny for college where he'd study mechanical engineering. Our parents had life insurance when they died, but as his guardian, I opted to put Jonathan's portion into a trust to preserve it for him for when he was an adult and could make his own decisions about it. His plan was to pay for college out of his own savings, then use that the life insurance money to open his own garage. I was so proud of the strides he'd made, and I could see that he was, too."

Her expression darkened. "It was right around then that he met Daisy. Your mother. She started attending the same grief group."

Jonathan sat straight. He set down the photos she'd handed him.

29
Jonathan

"DAISY JENSEN WAS THIRTY-TWO to Troy's very young twenty," Maeve continued. "A beautiful, but hardened woman who'd already had two marriages. She'd come back to town to care for her ailing mother."

"Thirty-two?" Troy had never mentioned this detail, or that she'd been married before. For a thirty-something woman twice divorced to go after a vulnerable twenty-year-old seemed downright immoral. "What was she doing at the grief group?"

"Daisy's mother was sick, and from what she told the group, supposedly dying. She joined preemptively, saying that she was there to learn coping skills." Maeve took a sip of her coffee, then continued, her tone grim. "I tried to warn Troy about her. Everyone did. She had a reputation for targeting men of means or, in your father's case, men who were about to come into money. I believe she went to the group to find her next husband. A nice well-off widower who would get her out of Autumn Lake. It was no secret that she hated small town life."

Jonathan put his hands up to stop her. "Wait, please. This is my mother you're talking about." He tried not to sound offended, but if what Maeve was saying was true, then everything he'd been led to believe about Daisy, everything his father had told him about her, no longer made sense. "I'm having a hard time correlating the version of both of my parents you're giving me. It doesn't add up to what I know of them."

"I thought that might be the case," she said, nodding slowly. She learned forward a little and said, "I'd like to ask you to let me tell you everything first. Then we can sort things out from there. Would that be okay? I'm certain it won't be easy to hear, and please know that none of this is easy

205

for me to talk about, but I want you to have the whole picture before you make up your mind about all of it."

He considered leaving, but after what she'd already shared, he was even more confused than ever. He needed answers. "I guess that's fair."

Maeve nodded again, then picked up where she'd left off. "Your father saw a damsel in distress who needed rescuing, and Troy fell for it, hook, line, and sinker. She painted herself as a woman alone in the great big world who would soon have to face life without her beloved mother."

"Something he related to," Jonathan said, forgetting for a moment that he'd agreed to listen first.

"Something he related to," his aunt echoed. "In no time at all, it seemed, they were a couple, and nothing we could say would persuade Troy to slow down. When he came to me and asked for our mother's ring so he could propose to her not even three months after meeting her, I refused. Troy stormed out and didn't come home for a whole week. I went by the garage where he worked, and Bill, his boss, told me Troy had taken the week off. The way he said it made me certain there was more going on, but Bill couldn't—or wouldn't—give me anymore details."

Jonathan's gut churned; he had a feeling he knew what was coming.

"They were sitting on the deck when we got home from church the following Sunday, her looking smug, and Troy looking like a besotted fool." Maeve released a sigh of frustration. "Stan and I were appalled when he boldly told us they were married, and that Daisy was moving in."

He tried to picture his father at twenty, in love with an older woman everyone disapproved of. It was hard to reconcile with the cautious, reserved man he'd known.

Maeve pinched the bridge of her nose as if dredging all of this up was causing her pain. Likely, it was. "I think Stan might have allowed it, but I knew that letting her into our home would be inviting chaos and division to live with us. I told Troy that he would always have a room to come home to, but that Daisy wasn't welcome."

"Well, Daisy started in on me, accusing me of trying to break up their marriage, of being jealous of her because he'd defied me and chosen her. She even went so far as to say that Troy owned fifty percent of the house so we couldn't keep them out. At that, Troy started nodding, like she'd already been filling his head with her claims, and now he was seeing all the proof he needed to believe her."

Maeve picked up her coffee cup, but it was empty.

Jonathan started to get to his feet. "I'll get you a refill."

His aunt shook her head. "No, no. I don't need any more caffeine. I'll be up half the night as it is." She set the cup aside. "Poor Stan. He was a problem-solver. He didn't mind conflict if the point of it was find solutions, but people like Daisy thrive on making scenes and stirring up trouble, and I could see that he was at a loss on how to proceed. She brazenly stood there, puffed up with her own self-importance, building her case against us on lies that she'd somehow convinced Troy to believe."

She took a deep breath and let it out slowly. "I refused to be intimidated in my own home, and I stood my ground. I demanded that she leave, that she wasn't welcome. She grabbed Troy's arm and said that they had become one in the sight of God, and that she wasn't going anywhere without him. So I turned to my brother who was practically hiding behind her by then. I'm mortified to admit this to you, Jonathan, but I told him to take out his trash, that she was stinking up our home."

Her hand trembled as she pressed a palm to her cheek. "That woman slapped me so hard, I saw stars."

"She what?" he gasped, the words hitting him like he was the one who'd just been struck.

"Stan stepped in, of course. He took Daisy by the arm and physically escorted her off the deck. When she tried to claw at him, he raised his voice loud enough to be heard above her shrieking and said he file an assault charge and get a restraining order against her if she ever showed up at the house again." She sighed. "For some reason, that threat did the trick. Maybe she'd already had trouble with the law. It was enough to take the edge off her fight, anyway."

"And... Dad? What did he do?"

Tears welled in his aunt's eyes, and she rubbed her cheek subconsciously. Maybe he didn't need to know. Maybe this was all too much for her. "It's okay. I think I can guess."

"No, no." Maeve pulled a tissue from a pocket in her skirt and dabbed gently at her eyes. "You need to hear everything so that you can make a well-informed decision about me, about the lake house, and about the past, too. It doesn't determine *who* we are, but it does influence our decisions, so the clearer the picture you have, the better."

He sat back, not so sure he wanted to hear more

"For a moment, Troy stared after Daisy like she'd gone crazy. I stood there, my cheek burning, certain he could see the outline of her hand there, waiting for him to realize what a mistake he'd made. But then she started crying, begging him to come with her, that they didn't need us, that we didn't understand their love and never would, that it was them against the world." Her voice quavered as she continued. "I saw him wavering, looking back and forth between us, so I drew a line in the sand. I told him that if he left with her, he wouldn't be welcome in our home, either."

Somewhere in this story, there had to be good news. After all, his parents had loved each other.

"I should have kept my mouth shut. If I had, Troy might have come home once Daisy was gone." Her tears were falling now, trickling slowly down her cheeks as she relived that terrible day. "He wouldn't meet my eyes. 'She's pregnant,' he told me, and I should be proud of him for doing the right thing. When I didn't respond, he straightened his shoulders and lifted his chin, and the last words he said to me were that they would never darken my doorstep again. Then he turned and walked away, following Daisy and Stan around the side of the house."

Jonathan frowned, doing the math. "But... that doesn't add up. I was born almost three years later."

Maeve nodded, but said nothing, waiting for him to puzzle things out.

He wanted to think the best of his parents. "Did she lose the baby?"

"The likely truth is that she wasn't pregnant, Jonathan," his aunt said, speaking the words he already knew in his heart were true. "They moved in with her mother for about seven months, but there was never any talk around town of a pregnancy. And in a place as small as Autumn Lake, talk is inevitable," she added with a wry look. "If she were pregnant, it would have gotten back to me."

He couldn't imagine how difficult it must have been for all of them to be living in such a small community with this huge wound between them.

"Then Troy turned twenty-one, they got access to his money, and they moved away without a word to us. I heard they'd left town from my hairdresser."

If the tale weren't so tragic, Jonathan would have chuckled at the cliché of the hairdresser being in the know before the main parties. Instead, he said, "This doesn't sound like my parents." He felt the need to defend them in their absence. The things Maeve was saying were a grievous malignment of them both. "You're suggesting she married him, maybe faked a pregnancy to make it happen, all for that money?"

Maeve nodded. "That's exactly what I'm suggesting." The finality of it hung heavy in the air between them.

"How did she even know about it?" he challenged.

"Everyone knew, Jonathan. It's a small town, remember? My brother was so excited about his future. Before she came along, he'd talk to anyone who would listen. It wasn't a lot of money, but it was more than enough to set them up in a nice little home with some financial breathing room if they were careful."

"Okay," he said, still not sure how to process it all. "But apparently, they figured it out. I mean, if my mom—"

"I'm sorry," his aunt said, holding up a hand to stop him. "But there's more you need to know."

From the envelope, she pulled out a couple of picture postcards. "Daisy sent us Christmas cards," Maeve continued. "Not to keep in touch, but to remind us of what we'd lost." She handed him the first one.

Jonathan stared down at it, a photo he'd never seen before. His handsome young father and startlingly beautiful mother embraced in front of a bright red door with an enormous pine bough wreath on it. They smiled at the camera, but suddenly, Jonathan saw something else in his mother's eyes. Something not quite wholesome. The age gap between his parents was unsettlingly obvious. As beautiful as she was, Daisy could have passed for Troy's mother.

"This came the the next year." The second postcard showed his beaming father holding a tiny baby, standing in front of a Christmas tree. Daisy sat in a chair beside them, wearing a flowing silk gown, her mouth turned up at the corners in a smile that didn't reach her eyes. She was still stunning, but like cut glass with sharp edges and hard lines. Jonathan had never seen this photo either, which was odd. It was likely their first family photo taken after his birth a few days before Thanksgiving, and exactly one month after his father had turned twenty-three.

"That's you," Maeve said, confirming what he already knew. "I sent a congratulations card and baby gifts, but the cards stopped coming after that, and then my letters and packages started getting returned."

Jonathan stared at pictures of his mother, moved by the change in her appearance between the two images. She was striking, with high cheekbones and a wide mouth with full lips, clinging possessively to his father's waist in the first picture, while in the second, her arms and legs were crossed almost defensively. She looked pale and almost gaunt, not like a woman who'd just given birth, but like someone fighting off an illness.

His father had kept only a few photos of his mother, photos he'd specifically saved for Jonathan, and when he'd asked why there weren't more, Troy had told him that seeing her pictures felt like reliving the pain of losing her all over again. "This would have been taken just a few months before she died," he said, touching her face and looking up at his aunt.

Maeve's eyes widened in surprise. "I'm—sorry?"

Jonathan gave her a curious look. "I guess I just figured you knew. She died the following May when I was about six months old. A car accident."

Maeve leaned forward, one hand pressed flat to the coffee table, her confusion turning to understanding and sorrow. "Oh, Jonathan. She didn't die."

His head snapped up. "What?"

"Honey, she left. Daisy... she eventually came back to Autumn Lake," she said gently.

Jonathan dropped the postcards like they burned his fingers. "No. No, that's not right. She died. In a car accident," he repeated. "My father was devastated. He couldn't bear to even have her pictures around—" He broke off, his thoughts whirling, rearranging the pieces of his memory into a completely different picture. All his life, he'd carried the narrative of his poor father, widowed young, raising his son alone after a tragic loss. The story had shaped how he saw his father—as a hero who'd persevered despite heartbreak.

"You're wrong. This is all wrong." But it explained so much... his father's reluctance to discuss his mother, Troy's wariness about new relationships, his occasional cryptic comments about trusting the wrong people. Jonathan pushed to his feet, going lightheaded for a moment, his knees weak. "Maybe my father didn't come back here for good reason. Maybe you turned this place against him, if this is what you're telling everyone in Autumn Lake."

Maeve met his gaze without flinching. "Why would I make any of this up, Jonathan? It would be so easy for you to prove me wrong."

Jonathan felt his breath leave him in a rush. "Is she—is she here? In Autumn Lake?"

"No, no," Maeve was quick to say, lifting both hands to stop his misinterpreting. "She's been gone for decades, now. She was only here for a few months before she left town again, but Sadie, her mother, eventually passed away several years later, and we saw Daisy at the funeral. She didn't speak to us, of course, and she was gone within days after the services. I think the house was sold shortly after that, so there isn't anything left here for her to come back to." She stood, too, but kept the coffee table between them. "But all you have to do is ask around town, Jonathan."

He shook his head, the enormity of this situation settling on his shoulders. "Everyone knows about this? That she walked away—she *abandoned* us? Hazel at church?" Did Candy and her friends all know his real history, too? Was he the last person in the world to know that he'd been lied to his whole life?

That his beloved father had lied to him?

He scanned the room, looking for the tie he'd pulled off while playing handyman, remembering only that he'd draped it over something. The back of a chair? He had to get out of here. He felt like he was betraying his father just by being there.

But what if his father had betrayed him?

His aunt reached out, her hand hovering in the space between them, palm up. "Oh, Jonathan. Won't you sit down? Please." She lowered her hand when he didn't move. "I wrote and asked him to come home, to bring you home to Autumn Lake. Many times. I begged him—" She broke off, her voice catching. She withdrew several letters, but she didn't try to give them to him. "He sent everything back to me, unopened."

The weight of it all pressed down on Jonathan. His father, his rock, his hero. He had lied to him his entire life, had chosen to invent a dead wife rather than admit to being abandoned. But that meant that his mother might still be alive out there somewhere. "Is she—is Daisy still—" He broke off, unable to finish the question.

Maeve shook her head. "She was only a couple of years younger than I am, Jonathan, and she led a hard life. I heard she passed away a few years ago, but I don't know where she ended up. I thought maybe your father, or even you might know, but now I see that wouldn't be possible. I'm so sorry." After a long moment of silence, she said, "It seems that all the women in Troy's life left him. Our mother when she died, Daisy when she walked away. And me when I issued that awful ultimatum."

"He walked away from you," he said dully, meeting her eyes briefly.

She smiled grimly. "But I forced his hand, didn't I? He really believed he loved Daisy, and that he was doing the right thing by marrying her. I saw it in his eyes, Jonathan. I saw how much he believed it would work."

Jonathan scrubbed a hand through his hair. In one fell swoop, his world had turned upside down. His father was a liar, and his mother was the villain, not the woman across from him. Daisy, whom Troy had painted as practically a saint, had turned the Burkhardt family inside out and then walked away, washing her hands of them all. And now, she was dead all over again, and his chest swelled with a confusing concoction of rage and grief and impotence.

Suddenly, a knot of tears gathered in the back of his throat, and he collapsed back onto the chair, dropping his face into his hands. What was he supposed to do now?

Finally, he lifted his head. "We moved a few years after Mom di—after she was gone," he amended, still reeling from the truth. "How did you know where to send that letter?"

Across from him, Maeve was seated again, too. "I found you online when you were twelve. Thank goodness for social media. I followed your accounts." She smiled softly. "You weren't very active. You mostly posted workout photos and computer game stuff that I didn't understand at all."

Despite everything, Jonathan nodded. "That was all that mattered to me back then."

"I was so happy when you started posting about hiking with your dad, and then fixing up that car together," she continued. "It gave me glimpses into your lives, even if from a distance."

Jonathan thought of his aunt secretly following his sparse social media presence, treasuring those small windows into his and his father's lives. It carved a deep sadness in his gut, realizing how much they'd missed out on because of his mother's selfishness, his father's pride.

"I don't know what to do." The words were out before he had time to reconsider admitting as much.

For a long time, they sat across in silence, each lost in their own ruminations. Finally, Maeve asked, "What about Candy?"

Jonathan stiffened, caught off guard by her question. "Cand? What about her?"

"Have the two of you made any plans for after the lake house is finished?" Her tone was careful, her words even more so, but he had a good idea what she was getting at.

"That obvious, huh?"

"You look at her the way your father looked at Daisy."

Jonathan flinched. "That doesn't sound like a good thing."

"He loved your mother, Jonathan. She just didn't love him back."

"Or me," he added, his stomach turning.

Maeve leaned forward. "Daisy didn't love anyone," she said. "Not even herself. No one could love themselves and do the things she did. Clearly, she was a deeply troubled woman."

Jonathan shook his head. "But Dad still made the choices he did, Aunt Maeve. And those choices damaged lives. What did you call him? A besotted fool? He let his head be turned by his feelings, even when he learned they were wrong. His lust, his love—if that's really what it was—his pride, his grief. A fool. Not a hero."

Maeve frowned, her gaze intent. "Jonathan, you listen to me. I may not have been around while you were growing up, and I may have only seen snippets of the life your father created for you, but what I saw was a man who loved his son, and a son who loved his father. Yes, he lied to you about

Daisy, and I won't defend that. But I believe he wanted to keep you from having to live under the dark cloud of abandonment that followed him around. It may even be why he chose not to come home, to bring you here. Maybe he simply couldn't bear to keep living under that shadow, himself, and by cutting off all ties to this life, it was his way of starting fresh. Of giving you a new beginning, too."

Jonathan wasn't so quick to explain away his father's decisions. "He chose wrong," he declared dully.

Maeve didn't argue, and he saw her words for what they were; a futile attempt to comfort him, to assuage him. She didn't really believe them herself, did she? He ran a hand through his hair, feeling suddenly vulnerable. "I do love the lake house," he acknowledged. "And Candy is a fine woman."

"A fine woman?" Maeve echoed, her brows creasing.

"She's great," Jonathan acknowledged. "But after everything you've just told me, I don't want to make the same mistakes my father did. I don't want to let my feelings—for a place, for a career, and especially for a woman—cloud my judgment."

Maeve studied him for a moment. "Have you considered that perhaps your father's judgment wasn't clouded by his *feelings* for Daisy, but by Daisy herself? She was manipulative, predatory. She targeted him specifically."

Jonathan frowned. "What difference does that make?"

"I'm saying," Maeve replied deliberately, "that Candy is nothing like Daisy. From where I sit, they couldn't be more different. So perhaps you should judge Candy on her own merits," she suggested. "Not on fears inherited from your father's experience."

She was right, of course. But the things he'd learned today had shaken the foundation of everything he thought he knew.

"You have a lot to think about," Maeve said, sitting back into the sofa to gather the small stack of letters and photos beside her. "Take your time, Jonathan. Pride can make you rash. Don't make impulsive decisions. That's where your father went wrong." She rose and circled the coffee table to rest a hand on his shoulder. "That house isn't going anywhere, and I have a strong feeling that Candy isn't, either. Use your discretion, and take your time, but don't throw away a chance at happiness because of someone else's mistakes."

His thoughts, as he left Maeve's condo later that evening, were deeply unsettled. His father had shaped his life around a lie, had raised him to believe a fiction that protected Troy's pride and covered up Daisy's treachery, but it had distorted Jonathan's understanding of his own history.

He and his aunt hadn't even discussed Troy's heart condition. He doubted she even knew about it. How could the man justify leaving his son to deal with so much in the wake in the wake of his death?

What other truths had his father sacrificed in service of a more palatable narrative?

Then there was Candy. Bright, honest Candy, who wore her heart on her sleeve and faced the world with unflinching courage. Surely, she was nothing like the calculating woman his mother had apparently been. But could Jonathan trust his judgment? Could he trust himself not to repeat his father's mistakes?

As the lake house came into view, Jonathan felt weighed down by Troy's shadow as it loomed over him, dark and complex. All he wanted to do was find a safe place to hide, where no one could witness his misery.

30
Candy

CANDY PULLED INTO THE driveway, anticipating a yummier greeting than her usual good morning coffee from Jonathan. After Saturday's sweet kisses, followed by only a brief exchange of greetings on Sunday, she could hardly wait to see his handsome face, especially since she could actually see the whole thing without his caveman hair. She wasn't going to film her entering the house; what they had was still a little too new, too personal, for her to share with her followers.

As she pushed through the front door, however, the house felt unusually quiet. She paused in the foyer, noticing that there were no lights on in the house, and no fresh coffee aroma wafted out to greet her.

"Jonathan?" she called out, trying not to be worried. Maybe he'd stayed late at his aunt's place and spent the night. "Are you here?"

In the kitchen, she pulled out the coffee supplies and filled the kettle with water. While it boiled, she stuck her head out into the garage and stilled. Jonathan's car was parked inside.

Candy headed out into the main room and called upstairs, "Squatch? You up there?" She didn't want to go knocking on his door, just in case he was still in bed or in the shower, but this wasn't like him.

"I'll make coffee first," she told herself. "If he doesn't wake up with me puttering around and the smell of coffee in the house, then I'll start knocking."

A few minutes later, she heard him on the stairs. She ducked her head around the opening of the kitchen to greet him, but when she saw him, her cheerful "Good morning," died in her throat.

He looked rough. His hair was disheveled, like he'd run his hands through it too many times, and there were dark circles under his eyes.

Barefoot, he wore a loose t-shirt and a pair of gym shorts, obviously what he'd slept in. If he'd slept at all.

He thrust his chin toward her in greeting, but said nothing.

"Hey," she said uncertainly.

Jonathan nodded as he entered the kitchen. "Sorry about no coffee. I didn't realize it was so late." He didn't smile at her, and he certainly didn't look like he was thinking about kissing her.

"Is everything okay?" she asked, warning bells clanging inside her head. What on earth had changed between Sunday morning and now? What could she have possibly done to have him scowling at her again? Weren't they past the whole Mr. Grumpy mornings?

Jonathan pulled out one of the new bar stools that had come in last week and sat at the breakfast counter. He rubbed his face with both hands. "I'm fine. Just didn't sleep much last night."

Candy went about making the coffee, hoping he'd expound without her having to ask.

His brow furrowed as he said, "I was going through some of my dad's things, stuff Maeve gave me." His voice was flat, distant, and he barely looked at her.

She nodded sympathetically and tried not to take it personally. She recognized the particular brand of exhaustion that came from emotional overload. She'd been there herself after the TV show fiasco, those long nights spent wondering if she'd ever feel normal again. "That must be difficult," she said gently.

Jonathan shrugged, accepting the cup of coffee she slid toward him. "It's fine. Just a lot to process," he said, effectively ending the conversation.

Candy moved to the table and sat down, pulling her schedule toward her and opening the page to today's plan. She was down to the last two weeks, and every day had a detailed checklist she had to get through if she was going to be ready for her big event. The Open House actually began Friday afternoon, so technically, she really only had ten days.

At the top of today's list was a starred question: What are we going to do about the office?

She'd have much preferred to address the topic after affectionate greetings and a good morning kiss, but obviously, that wasn't to be the case.

She still needed to broach the subject sooner than later. Even if he threw open the doors of his father's room to her today, she'd still have to alter her plans for the room in order to get it ready in time for the open house.

Candy took a fortifying gulp of coffee, grimacing a little at how hot it was, then straightened her shoulders. "Speaking of your dad..." she began. Jonathan narrowed his eyes, and for a moment, she hesitated. Maybe now wasn't the best time to do this. But no, she was on a strict schedule, and if he was going to relinquish the room, she needed to know sooner than later. "I know this is a sensitive subject, but have you given any thought to what you want to do with his room? Your room?"

The muscle in his jaw tightened, but he didn't respond immediately.

Undaunted, she continued, "I was thinking that instead of just an office, we could make it double as a guestroom. I found this really cool Murphy bed that looks like a built-in wardrobe when it's put away. It would go great with the new shelving units I have in mind, too." She opened her tablet where the image of the room schematic she'd been working on last night were still pulled up. She'd thought maybe if he saw it all put together, he'd be more receptive. "We'd be able to transform the room while still honoring his memory."

"No." The single word cut through the air like a blade. Jonathan was almost glaring at her, his shoulders rigid.

"Jonathan, I understand that room holds special meaning for you," she said, trying to stay patient. "Will you at least look at my design? I think you'd really appreciate—"

"I said no, Candy." His eyes flashed with an emotion between pain and anger. "What I'd really appreciate is for you to leave the room the way it is."

Candy felt her cheeks flush, part embarrassment and part frustration. But as she looked at his face—really looked—she saw the grief there, the exhaustion, the weight of whatever he'd discovered in his father's things. He wasn't really angry at her, she was fairly sure. Still, his words had stung.

She took a step back, both literally and figuratively. "Of course. I'm sorry for pushing."

An uncomfortable silence settled between them. Candy busied herself setting up a quick photo of her planner, aligning her pens, the tablet, and her coffee cup with her usual precision. Jonathan remained at the counter, his gaze fixed outside the window. His expression told her he wasn't appreciating the view, which meant he was probably envisioning something other than the morning sunlight making the surface of the lake look like it had been scattered with diamonds.

"I have a pretty full list of little things to check off today. Do you want to see it? Or is there a specific task you'd like to work on today?" she finally asked, hoping to restore some normalcy to their morning routine.

After a moment, Jonathan turned to meet her gaze, and Candy brought a hand to her mouth. He looked absolutely gutted, like the bottom of his world had dropped out from under him. Like he was about to break into tears at any moment. "Actually, I think I'm going to work in my room today," he said, his tone apologetic, his voice rough with what could have been fatigue or emotion. Or both. He rose and pushed the stool back under the counter. "I've got some phone calls to make, business stuff I need to attend to."

"Um, sure," Candy said, trying to keep the disappointment from her voice. She closed her planner. "That's fine, of course. I do have house painters coming this morning. it might be a little noisy for a bit; they have to pressure wash the eves and some of the siding first."

"I've got headphones." Jonathan was already moving toward the stairs. "I can work through it."

And just like that, he was gone.

Candy stood in the kitchen, listening to his footsteps on the stairs, the soft click of his door closing. "What happened?" she whispered into the ugly silence that he'd left in his wake. She wanted to go to him, to take his hands and look him in the eyes, to ask him to tell her what was hurting. She wanted to hold him and tell him everything was going to be all right, that they'd get through it together.

But what she wanted didn't matter, because right now, Jonathan just wanted to be alone. She'd give him his space and when he emerged from his cave ready to face the world again, she'd be waiting with another cup of coffee and a tender hug. And maybe a few sweet kisses.

Taking a deep breath, she scooped up her stuff and headed for the mudroom. Today she needed to get everything else done in there so she could focus on the new cabinets when they finally arrived on Wednesday.

Candy felt Jonathan's absence keenly. She'd gotten used to having him as her helper, their banter, the way they moved around each other with increasing ease. "You're going to have get used to working alone again, anyway," she reminded herself. Once this project was done, she'd be back to a one-woman show.

The sound of trucks pulling up outside interrupted her thoughts. Clint Sanner and his painting crew had arrived, and she headed out to greet them. Getting the exterior of the house painted was something she'd have preferred to schedule early, but Clint had assured her they could knock the whole job out in two days if she'd wait until he could get his whole team on site.

It meant the landscaping had to wait, too, but she'd ended up scoring an unexpected deal with Second Nature Landscaping by waiting. Ted was clearing out his end-of-season stock and had offered her a fantastic price by mixing and matching what was available. The design was perfect, and both jobs were scheduled to finish just in time for the Open House.

Back inside, she paused at the bottom of the stairs before heading back to the mudroom, but she heard nothing coming from Jonathan's room. It was unsettling to have him in the house and not shadowing her or at least popping in and out of whatever room she was working in. Her heart ached for him, and she wished she knew how to help him.

What had he discovered that had affected him so deeply, she wondered. Was it photographs that brought back memories? Letters he'd never seen? Whatever it was, it had clearly shaken him.

By noon, she'd made significant progress. The old cabinets were out, walls were primed and ready for paint, and the adjoining compact bathroom was almost done, too. All that was left to complete the mudroom was the bank of custom cabinets for the laundry area and the matching vanity in the bathroom. She wiped the sweat from her forehead, satisfied with the morning's accomplishments despite working alone.

The painting crew was on their lunch break, their equipment silent for the moment. Upstairs, the house remained quiet. Not even the sound of typing or phone conversations drifted down.

Candy climbed the stairs slowly, knocking gently on Jonathan's door. "Jonathan? I brought some pastrami and provolone sandwiches for lunch. Would you like one?"

A long pause, then: "No thanks. I'm good."

His voice sounded hollow, and Candy wanted to insist that he eat, that he couldn't afford to lose any of the precious weight he'd gained back, but she left him alone. Not wanting to eat alone in the kitchen she'd shared so many meals with Jonathan in, she headed home, leaving one of the pastrami sandwiches behind in the pretty new fridge, just in case he changed his mind and came looking for sustenance.

Outside on Liz's small back porch, Candy ate her sandwich and ruminated on how much the relationship between Jonathan and her had changed since their first meeting. They'd gone from adversaries to coworkers to... more. Or so she'd believed. The kisses they'd shared had meant something to her, but now she wondered if Jonathan was having second thoughts.

She couldn't shake the feeling that something fundamental had shifted today. The easy partnership they'd built over the past weeks felt fragile, uncertain. Maybe going through his father's things had reminded him of his own uncertainty about the future. Maybe he was realizing that getting involved with her wasn't the best idea when he hadn't even decided if he was staying in Autumn Lake.

Grief had a way of making everything else feel unstable when you were struggling to maintain your own emotional equilibrium. But was it just grief that had him isolating himself? Or was there more to his withdrawal than she knew?

When she returned to Hollyhock Hill, the painting crew was back at work. Jonathan was still holed up in his room, so Candy dove back into the mudroom, putting the first coat of lake blue paint on the walls.

31
Jonathan

JONATHAN SAT AT HIS father's old desk, staring at his laptop screen, unable to focus on the mind-numbing coding updates he needed to get done. The contents of the boxes Maeve had given him to go through were scattered haphazardly on his bed, drawing his attention away from the work he'd planned to do today.

A sepia-toned photo of grandparents he'd never meet, a birthday card signed with childish enthusiasm, a school paper marked with a teacher's red pen. Each artifact forced him to redraw the map of his life, to reconsider everything he thought he knew. Daisy hadn't died—she'd abandoned them. Maeve hadn't forgotten them—Troy had rejected her. Autumn Lake wasn't just some distant backdrop to his father's stories—it was his birthright, a home that had been waiting for him all along.

And Troy's heart condition? Especially since it was genetic... hadn't he cared that the diagnosis was also a potential death sentence for his son?

When Troy had died so unexpectedly, Jonathan had been almost relieved to learn of the heart condition that had taken him down. At least it had helped him make sense of it all. But then to discover that his father had known about it and had simply opted not to tell Jonathan? That had thrown a completely different lens over the whole situation. What if he'd been able to convince Troy to get treatment, to slow down, to adjust his lifestyle? Could they have had more years together? Would they have gotten the chance to do more of the things they'd always talked about?

Why had there been so much secrecy and deception? The weight of it crushed down on him.

His phone vibrated on the desk. He glanced at the screen, not recognizing the number. He almost let it go to voicemail, but then snatched it up, desperate for a distraction from his spiraling thoughts. "Jonathan Burkhardt."

"Jonathan, it's Warren Mitchell." His former boss's voice was crisp, professional. "How are you holding up?"

Jonathan straightened, surprised. "Warren. Hello. I'm doing all right," he lied. Warren Mitchell was the last person he'd expected to hear from. Why was he calling? Had Jonathan left behind some unfinished task? "How can I help you?"

"I'll get right to it. Hernandez is moving to the Washington office, so we need a new Senior Technical Director. The board is asking about you."

The information landed strangely, like a lifeline thrown toward a drowning man who wasn't sure he wanted to be saved.

"I realize you left to pursue other opportunities," Warren continued without pausing for a response, "but this isn't a lateral move. Twenty percent salary increase, premium benefits package, and genuine autonomy over your division. No more committee approvals for every decision."

"I see." Jonathan's free hand tightened on the edge of the desk. The endless bureaucratic hoops had been one of the department's biggest frustrations at SyncTech.

Just yesterday, he'd been sketching plans for his future here—his app business, the house, Candy. Now today, all of that felt like a dream. Maybe even someone else's dream.

"When would you need an answer?" he asked. Was he seriously going to consider it?

"Well, it's short notice, but the board meets Thursday. If you could come in before then to meet with me first, that would be ideal." Warren added, "Just a formality, of course."

"I see," Jonathan said. It was, indeed, short notice. It wouldn't be an issue to get there, but choosing to accept the position was not a small decision. Even so, he was surprised by how tempting the offer suddenly felt. He thought about Maeve, yesterday, encouraging him to take his time, to not make decisions impulsively.

But he knew SyncTech inside and out. The company had been his work home for years, and saying 'yes' to Warren would be far less impulsive than striking out on his own right now while his personal life was in such upheaval. Returning to Atlanta would be like heading back home after summer camp on the lake, he thought ruefully.

"Can you email me the details?" he asked, not wanting to make any commitment over the phone. "I'll take a look and get back to you by this time tomorrow at the latest."

"Of course. I'll have Joan send you the package now." The sound of a chair scooting back could be heard through the phone. "I look forward to hearing from you." And then he hung up.

Jonathan put down his phone and leaned back in his chair, clasping his hands behind his neck. The stretch felt good across his chest and shoulders; he'd been sitting too long. His stomach growled, too, reminding him he hadn't eaten since last night. He needed food, needed to clear his head.

Maybe Candy's offer of a pastrami sandwich still stood.

Downstairs, he paused on the last step when he heard her voice. She was in the kitchen, on speakerphone, talking animatedly.

"It's so good to hear from you," she was saying, her voice bright with that professional warmth she reserved for business calls. "And I'm thrilled that you thought of me."

Jonathan hesitated at the foot of the stairs, not wanting to interrupt.

"You'd be perfect for this, Candy," a man's voice enthused through the speaker. "After what happened with 'Drills and Thrills,' this would put you back on the map. National audience, prime time slot. Your Hearth Breakers will love it."

Jonathan's ears perked up at the mention of television. He took a silent step closer.

"But Chicago for six months?" Candy asked, a tiny note of resistance threading through her cheerfulness.

"A small price to pay for this kind of platform. Think about it. Your own show, creative control this time. And your contractor expertise front and center."

Jonathan felt something cold settle in his chest. Chicago.

"It's an offer that's too good to turn down," Candy said, and then she laughed, the sound one of anticipation and excitement.

He didn't wait to hear more. Silently, he retreated back up the stairs, no longer hungry, but feeling hollower than ever.

His mind raced as he paced the small room. Another television opportunity. Why *wouldn't* she say yes? This renovation was just a stepping stone, a way to rebuild her reputation. Had she ever really planned to stay in Autumn Lake permanently? She was living in Liz's home, not her own. Renting a room from family, probably getting a sweet deal, while she got her feet back under her.

All along, she'd been treating Hearth and Home Renovations like a performance, hadn't she? The TV-friendly name. The pretty pink branding. The crafty calendar and colorful aesthetics. The followers and fans – her Hearth Breakers. Now that he stepped back and looked at the big picture, he could see that she'd always had her sights set on something other than this small-town life.

And he'd been ready to rearrange his whole life around a woman he'd known for little more than a month. "Why are women so fickle?" he snapped, picking up the Christmas photo Maeve had shown him only yesterday, the one of him and his parents. Now that he knew what he did about Daisy, her dissatisfaction and malcontent just radiated off the image.

He was just like his father, wasn't he? Making the same mistakes. Letting his feelings cloud his judgment, letting himself believe in something because he wanted to, not because it made sense.

Candy is nothing like Daisy. From where I sit, they couldn't be more different, he heard Maeve say.

Maybe it wasn't women who were fickle. Maybe it was him. He was the one who had kissed her, initiated the shift from platonic to romantic in their relationship. He was the one who'd walked away from a great job to jump into a highly-competitive market with no track record, no safety net, and no guarantees.

It was time to get back to real life. "Summer camp at the lake is over," he declared, making up his mind.

Before he could second-guess himself, he grabbed his phone and dialed his old boss back. He hadn't even bothered to look at the email from Joan.

"That was quick," Warren answered.

"I'd like to schedule that interview," Jonathan said, his voice unnaturally calm despite the turmoil inside him.

Warren paused before asking, "What about your personal business in Indiana? Will you still need time to wrap that up? Can we count on you to be fully committed here?"

He cringed inwardly at his old boss's question. Apparently, even Warren thought Jonathan might be making an impulsive decision. "This isn't personal; it's just a job to get through, and then I'll be back in Atlanta permanently."

"That's good to hear. We'd be thrilled to have you back on SyncTech soil, Jonathan."

"I can be there to meet with you on Wednesday morning at nine," Jonathan said, ignoring the alarm bells going of his head.

"Excellent! I'll have Joan set everything up."

Hanging up, Jonathan tossed his phone onto the bed and reached up to stroke his beard, forgetting that it was yet one more thing he'd given up.

He thought of Candy downstairs, probably already mapping out her move to Chicago, her triumphant return to television.

He began packing his laptop and charger into his bag. It was time to return to reality. To the life he'd had before Autumn Lake had temporarily seduced him with its quiet beauty and promises of new beginnings.

It was time to go home to Atlanta where he truly belonged.

32
Candy

"It's an offer that's too good to turn down," Candy said and then laughed, shaking her head as she leaned against the kitchen counter. "But I'm going to pass anyway, Derek."

"You can't be serious," Derek's voice came through the speakerphone. "This is what you've been waiting for, Candy. A chance to rebrand yourself, to show everyone what you're really capable of."

"A year ago, you might have been right. But things are different now." She smiled, running her fingers along the edge of the new granite countertop she'd installed last week. She thought she heard footsteps on the stairs, but when she peered around the opening that led from the kitchen to the family room, she didn't see any sign of Jonathan.

"Different how?" Derek pressed. "Candy, do you know how many people would kill for this opportunity?"

"I'm building something real here in Autumn Lake," she explained, the certainty of her decision sitting comfortably in her chest. "Hearth and Home Renovations isn't just a stepping stone for me. It's my future."

She could hear Derek's frustration through the phone. "At least think about it for a few days."

"My answer won't change," she said, and offered him recommendations for other contractors who might be interested in the Chicago opportunity.

As she ended the call, Candy figured Jonathan had come down while she was talking, then retreated, not wanting to interrupt her call. She hadn't seen him since breakfast, and despite his mood, she was worried about him. He hadn't eaten lunch as far as she knew.

She gathered the remaining pastrami sandwich and a bottle of water, then headed upstairs. Approaching his door, she listened for any sound, not wanting to wake him if he was napping, but there was only what sounded like the squeak of the office chair. She was about to knock when his words stopped her cold.

"This isn't personal." His voice was clear through the door. "It's just a job to get through, and then I'll be back in Atlanta permanently."

Candy's hand froze midair, the sandwich suddenly feeling heavy in her grip. She took a step back, her chest tightening. Not personal? Just a job to get through? After everything they'd shared—the long days working side by side, the laughter, the *kisses*? Was that all this had been to him? All *she* had been to him?

She turned and hurried back down the hallway, moving carefully to ensure her footsteps wouldn't betray her presence. The last thing she wanted was for Jonathan to know she'd overheard him.

Back in the kitchen, she practically threw the sandwich back into the refrigerator. For a moment, she stood there, gripping the edge of the counter, trying to process what she'd just heard.

A *permanent* return to Atlanta. That's what he'd said. Not a trip, not a visit. He planned to head back to Atlanta permanently.

How had she so completely misread everything between them?

The remainder of the day passed in a blur. Candy buried herself in work, focusing on each task with an intensity that left no room for thoughts of Jonathan. When he finally emerged from his room that afternoon, she was on her hands and knees measuring for the baseboards in the dining room.

"I'm heading to Maeve's," he said from the doorway, his voice neutral. He held two good-sized cardboard boxes, both labeled 'Troy' in black marker. "She can store this stuff until I figure out what I'm going to do with it." He was dressed in dark jeans and a charcoal pearl button shirt, his jawline covered in a two-day stubble, his eyes still shadowed.

Rakish, she thought. *He looks disreputable.* The kind of man who would kiss a girl one day and walk away the next.

"Okay," she replied, only glancing up briefly from her tape measure. She kept her tone equally flat, betraying nothing of what she'd overheard.

By the time he returned, it was starting to get dark. She had packed up for the day and was heading out the door. They exchanged brief, impersonal goodbyes, and Candy hurried to her car, not wanting him to see the tears that fell over his rejection.

That night in bed, Candy replayed every moment of the time she'd spent with Jonathan, searching for signs she might have missed. Had she been projecting her own feelings onto him? Had those kisses meant nothing?

♥ · ♥ · ♥ · ♥ · ♥

TUESDAY MORNING DAWNED BRIGHT and clear, a perfect late summer day that seemed to mock her somber mood. Candy arrived at Hollyhock Hill earlier than usual, determined to stay focused on her work regardless of the awkwardness with Jonathan.

But when she pushed open the front door, the house felt different. Empty.

Even emptier than it had the day before.

"Jonathan?" she called, her tentative voice echoing through the foyer.

The kitchen was spotless, the counters wiped clean, and the gorgeous fireclay farmhouse sink was empty. But next to her electric kettle was a single mug and the French press, already loaded with coffee grounds and ready to brew. A folded note sat propped against the cup.

Her fingers trembled slightly as she opened it, something in her already knowing what it would say.

> *Candy,*
> *I've gone back to Atlanta. SyncTech offered me a new position that was <u>too good to turn down</u>. I'll be in touch about the lake house details later.*
>
> *—Jonathan*
>
> *P.S. The coffee was ground fresh this morning. Sorry I couldn't share a cup with you.*

Candy stared at the note, reading it three times as if the sparse words might somehow rearrange themselves into a different message. He'd underlined the phrase, 'too good to turn down' as if that would help her make sense of the note.

She flipped the paper over, like she might find an explanation on the back, something she'd missed. But there was nothing.

He'd gone. No goodbye, no details, just a perfunctory note and a pre-loaded coffee press.

She pushed the start button on the kettle mechanically, listening to the water gurgle and glug as it came to a boil. It was somehow the loneliest sound in the world to her. She'd known this was coming after overhearing his conversation, but the abruptness of his departure still stunned her.

Her phone buzzed with a text about her custom cabinets.

Sorry – a minor delay with your delivery. Engine trouble, but I'll be back on the road as soon as possible. If repairs go well, I might still make it late Wednesday, but it's looking like it's going to be Thursday morning.

Perfect. Just perfect.

She shoved Jonathan's note into her pocket and turned off the kettle, then slowly poured the hot water over the grounds in the carafe. She set her timer for four minutes, then pulled out her planner.

The open house was only a week and a half away. If the cabinets didn't arrive until Thursday, she'd have to completely rework her timeline to finish the mudroom. But even as she calculated new timeframes and alternative plans, a small, sensible voice in the back of her mind whispered: *Focus on what you can control.*

And right now, that wasn't Jonathan Burkhardt or his feelings or his sudden departure. It wasn't delayed cabinets or shifting timelines.

It was this house. This renovation. The work she had come here to do.

Her timer went off, and Candy pushed the coffee plunger down, breathing in the fortifying aroma of her favorite Robusta roast. Then she poured the dark amber liquid into the solitary mug and took it to the table where she opened her planner to today's tasks. One by one, she would check them off, just as she always did. The mudroom would have to wait, but there were plenty of other projects she could advance in the meantime.

"It's just a job to get through," she murmured, echoing Jonathan's words as she snapped a photo and posted it to her feed. "So, let's get through it."

33
Jonathan

JONATHAN'S HANDS TIGHTENED ON the steering wheel as he passed another mile marker. The speedometer remained steady, but his heart rate had been erratic since crossing the Georgia state line. Atlanta's skyline was still hours away, but already the weight of the city pressed against his chest—traffic patterns he'd memorized, cubicle walls that closed in a little more each year, the careful distance maintained between coworkers who'd never really known him.

He glanced over at the passenger seat, not for the first time wishing to see something other than a gas station coffee cup and his laptop bag. Some*one*, to be precise. Having Miss Toolbelt along for the ride, animatedly recounting some story about her latest social media mishap and calling him 'Squatch' would have made this trip much more enjoyable.

Except if Miss Toolbelt sat in his passenger seat, he wouldn't be driving them to Atlanta.

Her absence felt accusatory.

Don't make impulsive decisions, Maeve had warned him just three days ago. *That's where your father went wrong.*

The irony hit him like a physical blow. Here he was, fleeing Autumn Lake with the same haste his father had shown thirty years ago. But while Troy had been driven by reckless pride, Jonathan was manipulated by fear.

Fear of uncertainty. Fear of failure. Fear of rejection, of being hurt. Fear of complications he couldn't control.

He'd left without a word to Maeve, and he'd left Candy nothing but a cold, cryptic note and a cruel tableau of their shared mornings for her social media fans. He'd arranged it all in such an aesthetically pleasing display, with the water kettle in the background, the press with the coffee grounds in the carafe, the plunger propped up beside it... and the single mug to represent the choice she'd made to abandon him.

Jonathan cringed as he imagined how she must have felt, walking into that empty house. Eight weeks of starting their mornings together, of arguments that had turned to laughter, of words that had melted into kisses; he'd summed it all up in a few cutting lines.

How could he point fingers at his father? At least Troy had fought for what he'd believed in, what he'd wanted. Jonathan was nothing but a coward, a man who'd never fought for anything. How long had he been stuck in his SyncTech cubicle while those around him, like Hernandez, had risen in the ranks, not because they were better at the job than he was, but because they'd put themselves out there when Jonathan was too fearful to take a risk? How many times had he walked away from a budding relationship because he couldn't loosen his tight grip on the control reins?

How many times had he told his father, "Maybe soon, Dad," or "When I have time," or "I'm just too busy right now, Dad," not because he couldn't make adjustments, but because he was afraid to?

His aunt's voice echoed in his mind again. *Don't throw away a chance at happiness because of someone else's mistakes.* Right now, his dad's mistakes were becoming blurred with his own.

A truck stop ahead offered him a choice: keep driving south toward his old life, or take the exit. Jonathan found himself slowing, then turning into the parking lot without conscious decision. He needed to stretch his legs, he told himself. Clear his head.

But as he stood beside the GTO, watching eighteen-wheelers rumble past on the interstate, Jonathan knew he wasn't ready to return to Atlanta. Not like this. Not because he was running scared.

His phone buzzed with a text from Warren: *Looking forward to seeing you tomorrow morning. Conference room B at 9 AM.*

Tomorrow. Sixteen hours away. Sixteen hours to sit in his empty apartment, to stare at walls that held no memories of laughter or shared meals or morning coffee brewed just right. Sixteen hours to prepare for a meeting where he'd discuss salary adjustments and benefits packages and commit to another decade of predictable, contained existence.

What if he stuck his neck out, risked everything to pursue the life he wanted? The thought surfaced unbidden, radical in its simplicity. He could keep his appointment, but why not bring a few demands of his own? He could propose remote work; the technology existed, and half his team was scattered across time zones anyway. He could ask for what he needed, what he wanted, rather than accepting what they offered.

And then he would turn around and drive back to Autumn Lake. Back to the house where he'd discovered what home could feel like. Back to the woman who modeled what it meant to go after what she wanted.

Back to Maeve, who deserved better than a repeat of Troy's mistakes.

Jonathan pulled out his phone, scrolling past Warren's text to find a different number. As it rang, he found himself holding his breath.

"Hello, Jonathan," came his aunt's warm greeting. "How nice to hear from you this afternoon."

"Aunt Maeve," he began, hoping she couldn't hear the tremor in his voice. "I'd like to talk to you about the lake house."

A few minutes later, as he ended the call, Jonathan experienced a sense of certainty that he was exactly where he needed to be, making the choices that mattered most. Not impulsive choices driven by pride, by fear, or confusion. But choices motivated by the love and support of family, by the hope of a better future, and by the confidence that results from facing your darkest doubts and coming out on the other side victorious.

Jonathan couldn't control how tomorrow morning's interview would end, but he had a proposal to present, one that he believed would be beneficial for both parties. After that, he'd be back on the road to his new home town, and, with any luck, a woman to convince that maybe, just maybe, he was worth a second—or was it a third now?—chance.

The GTO's engine roared to life, but this time, he wasn't running away.

34
Candy

THE FIRST CRACK OF thunder just before midnight Wednesday night jolted Candy awake. She lay in an exhausted haze, listening to the sound of a building storm outside her bedroom window, rattling the panes with increasing intensity.

"No, no, no!" she cried, throwing back the covers and bolting out of bed.

The weather forecast had called for clear skies all week; not even a hint of a cloud in sight. Another flash of lightning was followed immediately by an earthshaking rumble of thunder. There was a very real and sudden squall right on top of them.

Her cabinets. The expensive, custom-built cabinets that had, to her surprise, arrived late that afternoon just as she was heading out for the day.

They were now sitting on the back deck, wrapped in the foam padding and plastic they'd been shipped in and draped with a blue tarp, but still ultimately exposed to the elements. This wasn't a light misting, but a late summer storm; rain blown sideways by the wind that swept across the lake.

Not bothering to change out of her pajamas, Candy shoved her arms into an oversized hooded windbreaker and her bare feet into her work boots. She hurried through the house, hoping her clomping footsteps wouldn't wake Liz, grabbed her purse and keys near the front door, and raced out into the storm.

The rain hit her face like cold needles as she ran to her SUV.

The drive to Hollyhock Hill was treacherous. Sheets of water pounded her windshield as fast as the wipers could clear it, and the wind jostled her vehicle with enough force to make her question whether the cabinets were worth risking her life and limb for. "I can't lose those," she wailed, watching for debris that littered the road. She was already working at a loss on this project, and even though she was sure she'd recoup it and more in jobs that came out of this one, right now, she didn't have a whole lot of financial wiggle room. She certainly couldn't replace them before showing the place. She swerved to avoid the top of a large branch that had splintered off a tree and lay splayed across half of her lane.

When she swung into the driveway, her heart nearly stopped, and she slammed on the brakes.

Jonathan's GTO was parked there, getting pummeled by the deluge.

She stared at it for a moment, disbelief mixing with something that felt dangerously like hope. He was back? But why? And when?

Lightning illuminated the house, startling her back to the dilemma at hand. She'd worry about Jonathan later; right now, she had a couple thousand dollars worth of product to try to salvage. Racing from her car, she barely felt the rain soaking through her clothes as she headed toward the back of the house.

She rounded the corner and there he was, wrestling with a large tarp that was fighting him in the gusting wind. He looked up at her approach, water streaming down his face.

"Help me get this secured!" he shouted over the tempest.

Candy grabbed one corner of the tarp, and together they managed to get it anchored over the few remaining cabinets. Jonathan had apparently already dragged several of the pieces inside before she got there.

He gestured at her, waving toward the mudroom door. "We need to get the rest of these inside!"

She nodded, and they bent to lift the first cabinet. The wood was heavy and awkward, made worse by the rain making everything slippery.

For the next hour, they worked together to salvage what they could. They quickly got the remaining sections inside, then Jonathan went to work unwrapping everything and toweling off the worst of the water that had seeped in under the protective plastic, while Candy grabbed her two high-powered air movers from the garage and set them up. It was loud in the small space with both blowers going, but they didn't speak beyond what was necessary. The urgency of the situation pushed aside all the hurt and confusion between them.

The unfinished wood had started to swell in places where the moisture had gotten to it directly, but to Candy's relief, she found that most of the pieces were salvageable. She'd set up a space heater in the mudroom and close the door to trap the dry heat in there, and between that and the fans, plus maybe a little sanding in the morning, her beautiful cabinets might come out of this mostly unscathed.

Thanks to Jonathan and his timely return to Autumn Lake and Hollyhock Hill.

By the time they'd done what they could, they were both soaked to the skin and shivering. Candy's hair hung in wet ropes around her face, and Jonathan's white t-shirt was translucent with water, clinging to his shoulders and chest.

"Thank you," she said, her voice raised to be heard above the sound of the fans inside and the downpour outside. She took a step toward him, intending to give him a quick hug of gratitude, but her waning adrenaline now that the crisis had passed, coupled with exhaustion, made her movements clumsy. She slipped on the slick floor and stumbled forward, crashing into him.

His arms shot out to catch her, pulling her against his chest to steady her.

They stood like that for a heartbeat, her hands pressed against his wet shirt, his arms wrapped around her. The storm continued its assault outside, but inside the mudroom, the air was charged with more than electricity.

Then his mouth was on hers.

The kiss was desperate and hungry, tasting of ozone and relief and all the words they hadn't said to each other. Candy felt herself melting into him, her exhaustion forgotten as she kissed him back with equal fervor.

When they finally broke apart, they stared at each other, breathing hard. Rain continued to pelt the window behind them, and thunder rumbled in the distance, but the storm seemed to be starting to lose its fervor.

Jonathan's eyes searched her face, his hands still resting on her waist.

She waited for him to say something. Anything. To explain why he'd left. Why he was back. Why he'd just kissed her like he never wanted to stop.

But he just continued to look at her, his gaze tracing a droplet of water down her cheek to the corner of her mouth.

"Jonathan—" she started.

The crack of a branch snapping off a tree outside made them both jump, breaking the spell. Jonathan's hands fell away, and he stepped back.

Candy's emotions crashed over her all at once. Relief, gratitude, anger, confusion; she stood there before him feeling raw and exposed. Why didn't he speak? Why didn't he say something?

"I—" she began, then shook her head. "I can't do this."

She pushed past him and dashed back out into the rain, desperate to put distance between them. Behind her, she heard him call her name, but she didn't stop.

She made it to her car and sat there, engine running, hands shaking on the steering wheel as she composed herself enough to drive safely.

He'd come back. He'd saved her cabinets. He'd kissed her like he couldn't get enough of her.

But then he'd just stood there, guarded and distant, like he'd been trying to figure out how to pretend it hadn't happened.

He was still just playing with her heart.

Candy put her SUV in reverse and backed out of the driveway, her headlights careening off his beautiful blue car. If she never saw his GTO again, she might just die a happy woman.

35
Jonathan

JONATHAN STOOD IN HIS upstairs window staring out at the deceptively serene lake. Other than the murkiness of the churned up water and some scattered debris on the lawn, he'd be hard-pressed to believe there'd been a raging storm the night before.

He'd hardly slept. Every time he closed his eyes, he felt Candy's body against his, tasted the rain on her lips, saw the confusion and hurt in her eyes when he'd stepped away, struck dumb by that kiss.

He'd made it back to Autumn lake just after eight last night, his emotions in turmoil after having said his final farewell to SyncTech. Warren had taken the morning to consider Jonathan's proposal, but when they'd met for lunch to discuss it, he'd turned it down. "This proposal is excellent except for your desire to work remote. I have to question your long-term commitment to this company," Warren had said. "Would you be willing to give us a ten-year commitment?"

Warren Mitchell hadn't become CEO of the company because he lacked intuition. Jonathan slowly shook his head. "I'm afraid that's more than I can give you."

They'd parted on amicable terms. Though the finality had stung during the drive, he felt relief too. The decision was made. No more looking back. Now he'd be free to dedicate his undivided attention to his own business, and the anticipation of that had eclipsed any lingering worry over whether he'd made the right decision to walk away from SyncTech.

As he'd pulled into the driveway of the lake house on Hollyhock Hill, he'd truly felt like he was coming home, the elation only marred slightly when he didn't see Candy's SUV still parked out front. He knew the next two weeks would have her keeping long hours to make sure every last detail of the renovation was mopped up, and he'd been almost hoping to find her there, still touching up baseboards or changing out fixtures.

He'd wandered around the house, taking in everything she'd accomplished already, imagining calling this place that was so filled with Candy's presence his own, then he'd headed upstairs with his suitcase. For a moment, he'd wondered if she'd ignored his decree to leave the bedroom untouched, and he'd pushed open the door, half-expecting to find brand new built-in shelves and a Murphy bed, but it looked exactly the same as it had when he left two days ago.

Dated. Like a time capsule, he realized. With his new perspective on facing fear and embracing change, he suddenly saw the room for what he'd made it into. A cage that would keep him trapped in the past. A prison cell with manacles made of fear. Even his father would tell him to let go and move on.

He'd opened the windows wide, expecting a cool lake breeze to sweep away the things that haunted him, but the night was surprisingly still. Quiet. As he'd settled into the now familiar bed, he'd lain awake, pondering what he'd say to Candy when he handed her a freshly-brewed cup of coffee in the morning.

Then the storm swept in, and he'd bolted upright, recalling the sight of the stacked cabinets on the deck outside. There'd been a tarp over them, but one look out his window showed the edges of the blue plastic cover flapping in the rising gusts, completely ineffective against the fast-moving gale. He'd thrown on a pair of pants over his boxers and raced outside to start hauling sections inside as quickly as he could. He'd be her hero, her champion. She'd see what he'd done, how he'd saved the day and rescued her investment, and she'd welcome him back with open arms.

Except that's not exactly how it had happened. Instead of telling her how he felt, that he'd stand by her, be there for her, he'd rescue her from the storms of life, he'd stood there like a moron, mute, unable to meet her gaze, after that kiss seared its way through his bloodstream.

Now, in the early gray light of morning, all his old insecurities swarmed around him again.

He wanted to stay in Autumn Lake, wanted to see where things with Candy could go. But the thought of taking that plunge terrified him. What if he was wrong about her? What if she became a superstar TV personality and couldn't be bothered with small town life? What if he rearranged his entire life and she walked away?

What if his business failed?

What if he let his aunt down the way he'd let his father down?

What if, what if, what if... What was he really afraid of?

Afraid to fail, afraid to disappoint, afraid to take a risk on anything or anyone, especially myself, he thought bitterly.

And now he'd made Candy a victim of his fear and uncertainty, too. Last night, he'd seen it on her face, how desperately she'd needed him to say something, anything. To explain himself, to tell her what he was feeling. But he'd just stayed silent, paralyzed by his own cowardice.

Trying not to feel defeated already, he made his way downstairs to the kitchen. He had a sneaking suspicion that she might find an excuse not to show up today, knowing that he'd be here. He wasn't going to be thwarted though. Not yet. He'd make her coffee, just as he'd been planning before the storm crashed over them, and he'd tell her that he was back to stay, that he wanted the house, is business. Her, if she'd have him.

At seven-fifteen, he heard her SUV pull into the driveway.

At the window, Jonathan watched her climb out of her car with the careful precision of someone running on fumes. Dark circles shadowed her eyes, and her usually vibrant energy was replaced by a grim determination. She went directly around the side of the house and out of his line of sight. Presumably toward the deck and the back door to the mudroom where the rescued cabinets awaited her inspection.

He grabbed the coffee he'd already brewed and headed through the living room to meet her coming in.

He found her crouched on the floor next to one of the cabinets, running her fingers along the top edge of a door where the wood had swelled from water damage. The air movers were still running, and the space heater hummed in the corner.

"Coffee?" he offered, holding out the mug.

She looked up briefly, her expression carefully neutral. "Thank you." Her voice was polite but distant.

Candy stood and accepted the coffee, then immediately turned back to the cabinet. "I'll need to replace a door on this corner unit, but everything else is salvageable. I can work around it for the open house and order a replacement afterward."

"That's good news," Jonathan said carefully.

"Yes, it is." She moved to the next cabinet, clearly dismissing him. "Thank you for your help last night. I'm not sure what I would have done without you." The formal tone cut deeper than if she'd yelled at him.

"Candy, about last night—"

"There's nothing to discuss," she interrupted, not looking at him. "I need to get back to work. The clock is ticking."

She busied herself examining each cabinet, making notes on her tablet with mechanical efficiency. Jonathan lingered for a moment, wanting to push the conversation, but the rigid set of her shoulders warned him off.

He went upstairs and made a futile attempt to set up a work station at his father's old desk again, but the room around him felt stifling, suffocating, as if it no longer welcomed him. He didn't belong locked away up here, not in this... this shrine to his father. He should be at her side, helping her wrap this renovation up, getting this house into top showing condition, not sitting up here, locking her out, standing in her way.

No matter how hard he tried to stay productive, concentration eluded him. Every sound from downstairs reminded him of her presence and his failure. The whir of tools, her footsteps on the polished wood floors, the occasional thump of something being moved, it all mocked him.

By noon, he couldn't stand it anymore. He had to talk to her, had to explain himself somehow. He couldn't let things continue like this.

Jonathan closed his laptop and headed downstairs. As he approached the mudroom, he heard Candy talking and he halted.

"He kissed me, Liz," she was saying, her voice choked with emotion. "Like he needed me as much as I needed him," she continued. "And then he just stood there. Glaring at me, like he was already regretting it."

He started to turn away, but he bumped his elbow against the wall and froze when she stopped talking.

"But why did he have to kiss me like that?" she continued in response to something her cousin said, and Jonathan let out a quiet breath of relief that she hadn't heard him. "Why didn't he just give me a hug and tell me everything was going to be okay?"

Jonathan held his breath, listening to her pain. Pain *he'd* caused.

"I can't keep doing this," she said, her voice breaking. She sniffed loudly. "I can't keep hoping he'll... I just can't."

Hearing her cry because of him was unbearable. He'd thought she needed an explanation last night, a declaration. But what she'd really needed was simple human comfort. Someone to hold her and tell her it would be okay. Instead, he'd given her passion and confusion and then retreated into his own fears.

How had he made such a mess of things again? He hadn't even been back in town a day yet.

Jonathan quietly backed away and climbed the stairs to his room. He sat down heavily in the desk chair and stared at his unmade single bed, the loneliness and isolation it so clearly represented.

He had to come up with a plan. He had to find a way to make her see that she could trust him, that he could be counted on to be the kind of person she needed. If she needed muscles to manhandle furniture, he was her man. If she needed a hug and to be told everything would be fine, he'd be the guy to hold her. If she needed passionate kisses—in the rain or out of the rain—he wanted to be the only one to give them to her.

He wanted to give her the world.

His gaze swept the room one more time, settling on the empty bookshelf against the far wall. He replayed all the times Candy had mentioned her vision for this room. The way her eyes lit up when she talked about the natural light, the huge windows with the stunning lake view. He thought about her willingness to give up her plans because he'd demanded it. But what had he given her in return? Nothing but messes, and emotional upheaval, and mixed signals.

An idea struck him. It wasn't exactly the world, but there was something he could give her. Something that might show her how much he believed in her. How much he trusted her with what was precious to him.

It wouldn't fix everything. It might not fix anything. But it would be a start in the right direction.

She might see it as too little, too late. But he had to try. It was a risk he had to take.

He would start by giving her this room with his whole-hearted blessing.

36
Candy

CANDY SQUARED HER SHOULDERS with grim determination. She'd tossed and turned all night, but somewhere in the early morning hours, clarity had finally come. She had too much riding on this project to let Jonathan's personal chaos get in the way. Whatever he was doing with his life, coming or going, staying or leaving, hating or loving, she had to do whatever it took to get him out of her head.

Her open house was less than a week away. She had six days and a few hours to put the finishing touches on what was to be her triumphant return to the industry, and she simply could not afford to let her feelings for Jonathan and whatever games he was playing stand in the way of that.

Which meant that one of them had to go, and it wasn't going to be her.

She'd dressed carefully, choosing her most professional work clothes like armor. Navy cargo pants, a pale blue collared shirt with her logo on the front pocket. An outfit designed to show that this was business.

With each mile on the drive to Hollyhock Hill, her resolve strengthened. She would walk into that house, tell Jonathan to pack his things and go to Maeve's, and spend her final week working in peace.

She pulled into the driveway nearly an hour early, wanting to get this confrontation over with before he had a chance to make her coffee or make her mad; one or the other. The house standing beautiful and serene in the morning light. From the outside, it looked perfect—exactly like the dream home it had always been meant to be. The pale marine blue of the siding complimented the woods and lake in the backdrop, and the beige and cream Indiana limestone foundation and cladding gave the home an organic elegance. She had grown to love this house, having poured so much of herself into it.

Too bad she'd also grown to care too much for the man inside the house.

"He has to go," she declared. Taking a steadying breath, Candy climbed out of her SUV and headed for the front door. Time to take back control of her life.

She climbed the stairs, her footsteps echoing in the hallway, each one building her resolve. He'd told her he woke with the dawn, so she doubted she'd wake him up, but she wanted to catch him by surprise before his defenses were up. Before she lost her nerve.

At the top of the landing, Jonathan's bedroom door stood wide open.

Candy didn't look inside, just in case he wasn't prepared for company, but knocked on the doorframe. "Jonathan?" Her voice sounded breathy, nervous, and she cleared her throat and said his name again.

There was still no response, so she allowed herself to peek inside. The room was empty, but his laptop sat open on the desk. Her heart plummeted as she registered what filled the screen: an Atlanta real estate website, with several property listings bookmarked. Condos downtown. Modern apartments.

"Candy?" Jonathan's voice made her jump.

She turned to find him in the bathroom doorway, hair damp from the shower, surprise written across his face as he pulled a t-shirt over his head.

"You're early. I don't have coffee ready yet—"

"That's not necessary." The words came out sharper than she'd intended. She took a breath, forced herself to look unaffected by the situation, to remain detached. Her eyes flicked back to the laptop screen, then returned to his face. "We need to talk."

Jonathan followed her gaze and went very still. "Hold up. That's not what it looks like. I can explain."

"You don't need to explain anything." Candy's voice sounded steadier than she felt. "I understand perfectly."

"Candy, listen—"

She held up a hand to stop him, stood straighter, and called on every ounce of professionalism she possessed. "I'm on track to have everything ready well before the open house, so I won't need your help between now and then. And since there's nothing left for you to do here, I'd appreciate it if you could stay at Maeve's until then so I can focus on all the final details without—" She broke off, unsure how to finish that sentence.

"Without me underfoot?" he asked, crossing his arms and glaring at her.

"I have a cleaning crew coming early next week," she said, not backing down. "I need to have things ready for them, and it'll be easier for everyone if you're not in the house."

Jonathan's mouth opened as if to protest, but she forged on.

"I've already talked to Maeve and explained the situation." She'd called her this morning before she'd left the cottage, and Maeve had been happy to oblige, seemingly not at all suspicious of her request. "She's expecting you for breakfast."

When Jonathan looked like he might still argue, she said, "I *need* to focus, Jonathan. I n*eed* to have my head a hundred and ten percent in the game so that I don't miss any detail." She emphasized every 'need' in an effort to convince him that she wasn't going to change her mind. "I *need* this to be the absolute best showing possible, and I just can't afford any distractions."

The word 'distractions' hung between them, loaded with everything she hadn't said.

"Look, Candy—"

"Of course, I hope you'll join us for the open house next weekend," she said, talking over him. She didn't want to hear whatever he thought he had to say, the explanations he seemed so ready to offer her. "If you want to get here early to see it before guests start coming, that's fine, too. The showing begins Friday afternoon, but I'll be here all day."

"Okay," he said, dragging the word out a little, almost like he was expecting her to interrupt him again.

"In fact, if all goes according to schedule," she said, tapping the pretty planner she held. "I'm expecting to have everything completely ready by the end of the day on Wednesday." Her nerves were starting to show; she was talking too much. *Wrap it up, Candy.* "So, if you want to come before Friday, that would be fine, too. But maybe text to let me know first. I know it's your house—or it will be—but for now, to get through the next week, I just need...." She drifted off, waving her hand in a vague gesture.

"No distractions," he supplied.

Candy nodded and turned to head back downstairs. He stopped her before she'd crossed the landing.

"Can we talk after your open house? Please?"

She should say no. She should tell him it wasn't a good idea. But she heard herself say, "Okay. But right now, I've got to focus on this house before I think about anything else."

"Right, of course," he said, looking relieved that she'd left the door open, even if she hadn't committed to anything. He looked like he wanted to say more, but Candy was growing impatient. She just wanted to get downstairs and start attacking her to do list, and she needed him to leave her alone so she could.

"I've got to get to work." She started forward, then paused, feeling obligated to acknowledge his efforts. "Thank you for all you've done to help me around here. Especially for saving my cabinets." She felt the flush creeping up her neck; she couldn't think about the storm without also thinking about how marvelous it felt to be crushed against him, his mouth on hers, her blood thrumming in her ears— She cleared her throat. "Thank you," she said again, then made her way down the stairs, her head high, her chin up. At the bottom, she made a beeline for the mudroom. There was still plenty to do in there to keep her occupied until Jonathan had left the premises.

She closed the new pocket door behind her and collapsed against it. The tears came, hot and angry, full of disappointment and the death of hope she'd been foolish to harbor in the first place.

She'd grown to love this house, every corner shaped by her hands and dreams. But now she couldn't imagine living in it, surrounded by memories of what might have been.

Candy pushed away from the door and ducked into the pretty little attached bathroom where she grabbed a handful of tissue. She dabbed at her eyes, then gave her reflection a stern look. "Enough," she murmured. "You have a job to finish and you will finish it well."

That, at least, was something she could control.

37
Jonathan

JONATHAN STARED AT THE Atlanta real estate website still open on his laptop. He'd been researching property values, trying to gauge what his dad's Atlanta house might sell for—not looking for a place to buy. But Candy hadn't let him explain.

This wasn't how he'd imagined the conversation going. Not at all.

He'd planned to tell her about the interview, about turning down the remote position because it still tied him to someone else's timeline. About putting his father's Atlanta house on the market. About making his move to Autumn Lake permanent—not just the house, but the life, the community.

Instead, she'd walked away believing the worst.

And she hadn't let him tell her about the room. About his decision to give her the office she'd always wanted.

He couldn't tell if he was the problem right now, or her. "Why does love have to be so complicated?" he muttered.

Jonathan froze as the word echoed around the nearly-empty room. Love. Love? Did he love Candy Needham? Miss Toolbelt?

He shook his head in frustration. It didn't really matter if he did or not; it was obvious that she didn't share his feelings. She was kicking him out. Giving him the boot without a backward glance.

Jonathan closed the laptop without bothering to shut it down. He gathered his things mechanically, tossing clothes into his suitcase without bothering to fold them. He'd be unpacking again in little more than the time it would take to drive across town to Maeve's condo.

Twenty minutes later, he stood on his aunt's doorstep with his suitcase in one hand and a small carton of groceries he'd emptied out of the fridge at the lake house.

"Jonathan!" Maeve opened the door before he could knock and stepped back to welcome him inside. "Come in, come in. I'm so glad I get to have you here for a few days. Your room is ready for you, if you would like to go put your things down." She reached out and squeezed his forearm. "I still can't get over how much you look like your father with your beard gone. I saw the resemblance before, but now when I look at you—" Her words broke off and her eyes glistened with pleasure. "It's just so good to have you here. I'll stop rattling on like a little old lady now."

He knew she didn't intend it to be a negative thing, but her comparing him to his father made his stomach clench. He pushed the thought away and said, "You're too classy to ever rattle on, Aunt Maeve."

She pressed a hand to her sternum. "Why, that's the nicest thing anyone has said to me all week. You go get settled, then how about some breakfast? Or have you eaten already?"

His stomach rumbled, and Maeve chuckled. "Fried egg sandwiches coming up. And I'll put the coffee on," she added. "You look like you could use a little pick-me-up."

When Jonathan stepped out of the guestroom, the aromas of grilled sandwiches and coffee assailed him, a wave of nostalgia made him pause in the short hall. This was how his father's house always smelled in the mornings. Troy had been the king of fried eggs, sourdough toast, and coffee breakfasts, and rarely did he detour from that routine.

It was such a little thing, this reminder of his father's consistency, his determination to be a presence in Jonathan's life, to provide for his needs, to encourage his dreams, to be a source of counsel when his son needed it.

Maybe that's all Troy had been trying to give him – a simple, stable life without the complications of Autumn Lake and its painful history.

The notion didn't make the secrets right, but it made them feel less like betrayal and more like misguided protection

He found his aunt in the kitchen just dishing up pretty plates with sandwiches that were far prettier than his father's had ever been. They moved to the table where she'd already put out place settings and mugs of steaming coffee, along with a bottle of Louisiana hot sauce. "A household favorite," she'd told him the first time he'd had breakfast at her table, but it wasn't news to him. He couldn't remember there ever *not* being a bottle of the stuff in Troy's refrigerator.

After Maeve said a blessing over the food, they dug in. His first bite of the sandwich had him closing his eyes with pleasure at the bouquet of flavors. Sourdough, fresh garlic and herbs, the spicy tang of the hot sauce melding with the egg and Provolone cheese she'd use. It was perfection on buttered toast. "Wow," he said after he'd swallowed. "This is amazing, and I'm not just saying that because I'm hungry."

They made small talk about the Autumn Lake Fall Festival committee Maeve was heading up this year. "It's quite an endeavor, even for our small town, and it can truly take it out of me. This is my sixth time chairing the committee, and every year when it's over, I tell myself that it will be my last." She gave a wry chuckle. "Then by the time it rolls around again, I'm ready to jump on board."

"You're remarkable, Aunt Maeve. I hope I'm as full of life as you are when I'm your age."

She gave him a tender look. "You don't know how nice it is to be called 'Aunt Maeve' by you, Jonathan Burkhardt."

They'd finished their sandwiches and were on a second cup of coffee when Maeve, in what he could only call a guarded tone, asked, "Tell me, Jonathan. How is Candy holding up? I imagine she's feeling the pressure with the open house so close."

He felt certain there was more to her question, but she just eyed him patiently over the rim of her cup.

"Candy is..." He paused to choose his words carefully. "She's amazing. I'm floored by how much she's done in such a short time. And most of it by herself." He wiped his mouth with his napkin, suddenly nervous. "Of course, I've tried to help, but I don't think I've done anything she couldn't have figured out how to do on her own. She's hired crews for the big stuff: the landscaping, exterior paint, expanding the deck."

Maeve was nodding slowly, but she stayed quiet, and Jonathan felt compelled to fill the silence.

"I think she's feeling the pressure, but in a good way. She told me this morning that she's actually ahead of schedule and didn't my help anymore." He tried to make it sound like a positive thing, but by the look on his aunt's face, he didn't think he'd succeeded. "So thanks for letting me crash here for the week. I feel like I was starting to get in her way. Like you said when I first got here. She's a whirling dervish."

"I see." Maeve's tone suggested she saw more than what he was telling her. "Well, she's certainly got a lot on her plate right now." She set down her cup and studied him, her expression one of growing concern. "Was this her idea or yours?"

"This?" Jonathan asked for clarification, but he had a feeling he knew exactly what she was asking.

"You staying with me this week. Out of her way, as you put it."

His cheeks warmed and looked down at his empty plate. Could he call it a mutual agreement? Hardly. Not only had it *not* been his idea; he'd also disagreed with it. He met his aunt's probing gaze and admitted, "She asked me to leave this morning." It came out sounding almost sordid. "That she needed to focus." *I just can't afford any distractions*, she'd said, but he kept that part to himself.

"I see," Maeve said again.

"I guess I thought she'd be happy to have me back," he said magnanimously, then instantly wanted to delete the notion. He sounded like a pompous jerk. But then he felt defensive, so he kept going. "I mean, it's a big project, and I know I just said she's got it all under control, but I'm available. I could take out the trash. Pick up meals. Put up yard signs around town, you know? She just doesn't need me—my help, I guess."

"That's a lot of guessing." Her brow furrowed and her expression grew serious. She folded her hands, elbows on the table, and leaned forward. "I have to ask, Jonathan. Did you do or say anything to make her feel uncomfortable having you there?"

Jonathan stiffened at her insinuation. What had Candy said to Maeve when she'd called his aunt that morning? Had she indicated that she was uncomfortable around him? The thought made his chest tight. He shook his head. "No. No, I would never...." But as the intensity of that stormy night kiss and her tearful conversation with her cousin the next morning replayed in his mind, he knew he wasn't being honest. Not with his aunt, and not with himself.

"I came back," he said lamely. "I thought that was a step in the right direction."

"Why?" Maeve asked. "And which time are you talking about?"

So she'd gotten wind of his impulsive escape flight earlier that week, the one he'd known in his heart was a mistake before he even made it to Atlanta. "Both times," he said, hating that he sounded defensive. "And why did I come back? Is that what you're asking?" He started to shrug, then thought better of the casual, dismissive gesture. He wasn't a sullen teenager trying to avoid talking to an adult.

"Yes, Jonathan," Maeve said, her tone almost grave. "Why are you here? Have you made your mind up about us? About that beautiful home and this wonderful town? About that incredible woman you've had the privilege of working with over the last several weeks?"

"Um, I—" He faltered. This was the Maeve Lewis who had drawn a line in the sand for Troy all those years ago. Still elegant, still composed, but clearly a woman not to be trifled with.

"You've really left things to the last moment, haven't you?" Maeve continued when his words failed him. "Have you considered the rest of us in your decision making process? Me, my friends, this community who has never forgotten Troy and would love nothing more than to welcome you home? My attorney, who wants to get my paperwork finalized and off his desk. That precious, incredible, talented Candy Needham? I don't know all of what has transpired between you, but I heard the change in her voice this morning, Jonathan, and I'm afraid I'm holding you responsible for that." She toyed with the handle of her cup, then added in a softer, more vulnerable voice, "Have you given any thought to those of us who have been waiting for you to make up your mind, wondering if you'll like us enough to stay?"

Jonathan attempted to swallow the lump of shame that had risen in his throat. Honestly, he hadn't. Not once had he given thought to how difficult his indecisiveness and ambivalence must have been for Maeve. In blind faith, because he was her estranged little brother's son and she longed for restoration between them, she'd offered him the family home, invited him into her life. Then he'd shown up as if the whole thing were an inconvenience for him, and then proceeded to essentially freeload off of her hospitality for almost two months now, while languishing in his inability to commit to anything.

What was wrong with him?

"I'm a fool," he murmured, speaking more to himself than to his aunt. Maybe not a besotted fool like his father, but a fool nonetheless. Why had he kept all his thoughts, all his struggles, his grief and uncertainties to himself? Just because his father was gone didn't mean he was alone in the world. In fact, here was a woman who had a lifetime of decisions under her belt; surely, she could impart some wisdom into his life. He lifted his eyes to meet hers. "What do I do now?"

After a beat, Maeve sighed. "Well, let's see if we can sort through this and determine what can be salvaged."

Jonathan couldn't help thinking of Candy the night of the storm, saying pretty much the same thing. There hadn't been a whole lot of hope in her voice, either, but after they'd worked so hard together to rescue the beautiful custom crafted cabinets, they'd succeeded. They'd had to wait until the morning to be sure, but Candy had told him that they'd managed to save all of it.

Maybe, like with those cabinets, if they worked hard together, this could all be salvaged. Not just what had started between him and Candy, but also his relationship with Maeve. With this community who seemed so ready to embrace him as one of their own.

"I'm sorry I've been so focused on myself," he began, humbled by his new awareness. "Thank you for setting me straight. I'm embarrassed by—" He broke off, not sure how to encapsulate everything he was feeling right now. "My dad would be so ashamed of me."

Maeve put up a hand to stop him. "Your father would be proud of you, for what you're doing right now. For the amends you're going to make, starting today. You've been grieving, Jonathan, and that's okay. Grief is a very personal journey, but that doesn't mean you have to travel it alone."

He blinked back the sting of sudden tears. "Thank you."

Maeve nodded, then straightened her shoulders and pressed both hands flat to the table. "Now. Let's talk about action steps. Why don't you tell me where things stand while we do dishes?"

They both rose, and Jonathan followed her into the kitchen. He explained how the morning had started, with Candy arriving early, her mind clearly already made up about him moving out. "I think any possibility of her being talked out of it ended when she saw my laptop. It was open on my desk to some real estate listings. She assumed I was buying a place in Atlanta."

Maeve raised an eyebrow. "Were you considering it?"

"No. I was looking at comps for Dad's house. I'm putting it on the market."

Maeve's lips softened into a hopeful smile. "So, does that mean you're moving to Autumn Lake?"

Jonathan blinked. Wait. How was it that he still hadn't told her? "Yes," he declared, much more vehemently than necessary. "Yes, Aunt Maeve. I'm moving to Autumn Lake. And yes, if your offer still stand, I would be honored to buy the Burkhardt family home from you. I may not be able to afford it yet, but I have big plans for my own business, so maybe you'd consider renting it to me at first."

With uncharacteristic exuberance, Maeve grabbed Jonathan's face between her soapy, rubber-gloved hands, and said, "Welcome home, darling boy." Then she threw her arms around him and hugged him hard. "And the house is yours. It's our family home, and you're the next family member in line to have it. So no more talk of buying or renting, you hear?"

Jonathan hugged her back, not even caring about the sudsy water dripping off his chin or that she was getting the back of his shirt damp where she was clutching his shoulders. "Thank you," he whispered, overwhelmed by the whole situation.

Then she stepped back, patted his cheek, and went back to the dishes. Without even glancing his way, she asked, "Do you love her? Our Candy?"

He gaped at her, then snapped his mouth shut. He was going to have to get used to this woman's ability to blindside him.

"Do you love her?" she asked again in a more demanding tone. But it wasn't really a question; she was clearly just waiting for him to confirm something she already believed was true.

"I... I guess I'm falling in love with her," he admitted.

"There you go guessing again," his aunt admonished, elbowing him in the side. "Are you in love with her or not?"

Face your fears, man. He nodded. "I'm in love with her," he declared. "I've already fallen in love with her. Hard, it seems."

"And that frightens you. Why?"

Jonathan shrugged, feeling very much like a teenage boy trying to sort through his unstable emotions. "I guess— No, I know I've never really felt this way about anyone before. And it's very possible that she's taking on a new TV show after this."

Maeve looked up sharply. "That doesn't sound right. She told me she's already booked out into next spring with projects on the North Shore."

Jonathan frowned. "I heard her talking to someone about it. The guy said she'd be perfect for it, and she told him it was an offer too good to turn down."

His aunt shook her head. "That makes no sense at all. Talk to her, Jonathan. You need to talk to each other," she declared.

"She makes me crazy, Aunt Maeve; you should know that."

"Well, I'm sure you make her just as crazy, with all your back and forthing."

Jonathan grinned and pretended to pull an arrow from his chest. "Ouch. Brutal, Aunt Maeve. And I don't know if 'forthing' is a real word."

"Did you understand it?" she challenged, shaking a finger at him.

"I did." He chuckled, and then hesitantly said, "I just don't know how she feels about me anymore."

Maeve cocked her head. "Are you sure about that? Or are you just guessing, avoiding what you know is true so you don't have to face it?"

Candy had kissed him back. Every single time. She'd said yes to spending time with him away from the jobsite. Her eyes had lit up every morning when she'd walked in the front door to find him waiting with her coffee just the way she liked it. He knew how she felt about him.

At least, he knew how she'd felt before he'd forced her to draw a line in the sand this morning, because he couldn't seem to think about anyone but himself.

He wasn't going to make the same mistake his father had. He wasn't going to walk away just because he'd made mistakes and now things were complicated and uncomfortable.

He was going to stay and work things out.

"Candy loves me, too," he said, and the statement sounded so good, so true, he said it again. "She loves me, too."

Maeve gave a satisfied chuckle beside him, but she said nothing for a few moments, letting the words hang in the air like a proclamation.

"So what do I do now?" Jonathan prodded, desperate to know how to move forward from here.

Maeve turned to him. "Candy's scared," she said, gently. "Just like you are. Start by facing your fears, instead of running from them. Tell her the truth. Tell her how you feel." She rolled her eyes dramatically and added, "And for the love of Pete, tell her you're staying."

"Maybe I should start with that," Jonathan said, grinning at her antics.

"Maybe you should," she concurred with a laugh. But then she sobered. "But choose your timing carefully, Jonathan. This renovation means so much to her. Make sure whatever you decide to do won't interfere with her plans. She's not going anywhere," she insisted. "No matter what you thought you heard. Small town, remember? News like that would have spread like wildfire by now."

Candy had seemed so excited about the prospect. But he would ask her himself. None of this conjecturing and guessing, which apparently, he did a lot of, as his aunt kept pointing out.

This renovation means so much to her. As he headed to his room to try to get in a few hours of work, his aunt's words looped through his mind. The renovation wasn't just a project to Candy. It was her comeback, her proving ground, her chance to show everyone, including herself, what she was truly capable of.

And he'd been standing in her way, putting his grief ahead of her dreams. She'd shown him what this house could become, and in the process, what *he* could become. Now it was his turn to show her that he was ready to break out of the prison of the past and build something new.

He could picture her there in that kitchen, sitting at the table with her planner open. He saw her standing in front of the hidden compartment in the master bedroom, and lounging on the deck with a slice of pizza and a cold can of sparkling water. He imagined her in every room of that house, and how perfectly she belonged there.

They belonged there. Together.

38
Candy

Candy unbuckled her toolbelt and set it on the new hardwood workbench in the garage. Friday night, nearly nine o'clock, and she had made real progress on her To Do list.

A full day of uninterrupted focused work had been exactly what she needed. No Jonathan hovering, no confusing emotions to navigate. Just her, her tools, and the satisfaction of checking items off her list. The touch-up paint around the new door trims was complete, the cabinet hardware had been polished to a shine, and if she continued at this pace, she could ask the cleaning crew if they could come a couple of days early, which would mean she could start the final staging of the house early, too.

Her phone buzzed with a text from Liz: *Coming over. Bringing food. Don't argue.*

Despite her exhaustion, Candy smiled. Liz knew her too well. She'd have worked through the night, if necessary.

Twenty minutes later, Candy heard her cousin's truck pull in the driveway, and she hurried to meet her at the front door. It wasn't just Maeve she'd told to stay away in order to experience the big reveal at the end, but also her Garden Variety Lovers Club friends. And that included Liz. Her cousin had honored Candy's wishes... up until now.

Tonight, however, Candy decided she didn't mind. She'd been in the house alone all day once Jonathan left, and suddenly, a little company sounded good. Besides, letting Liz in would be like having one of Jonathan's beta users. Liz's response to the renovation would give Candy a fairly good idea of the kind of response to expect at her Open House. Besides, the place was almost ready, and what still needed her attention, like rewiring the master bedroom with dimmer switches and replacing the threshold of the garage doorway, wouldn't be on Liz's radar.

Candy opened the door and stepped back to let Liz in. "Ta-da!" she exclaimed, ushering her into the foyer and taking the tote Liz carried from her. The fragrance of spaghetti and garlic bread wafted out of it, making her mouth water.

Liz stood frozen in the entry, her eyes wide, taking everything in. "Holy moly, Cuz!" she whispered, finally turning to look at Candy. "This place is unrecognizable. I mean, wow. The floor. That stair rail—that's new, right?" She started wandering around the open space, touching surfaces, turning on and off lights, opening drawers. Then she flopped onto one of the soft leather sofas and started bouncing up and down. "I want one of these in my house. What do you think?"

Candy laughed and shook her head. "You are such a child, Liz. And that couch wouldn't even fit in your front door, no less in that darling little sitting room." Liz's cottage looked like something out of a fairytale, and an enormous leather recliner sofa had no place in that enchanted croft. She pointed at the buttons on the outside of one of the armrests. "Check out the recliner," she told her cousin, and watched with delight as Liz sprawled lazily and sighed with pleasure.

"I am sleeping here tonight," she declared, closing her eyes and pretending to snore.

"I'm going to dig into this food," Candy told her, heading into the kitchen. "Go take a look around and I'll plate things up."

Several minutes later, just as she was about to go looking for her, Liz's voice drifted down from the second floor. "Um... Cuz? You need to come up here."

Something in Liz's tone made Candy drop her cloth and hurry upstairs. She found Liz standing in the hallway, staring at Jonathan's open bedroom door.

"Why is his door open?" Candy demanded. She'd been going through her list methodically, from one room to the next, starting with the main floor. She hadn't come upstairs all day.

Liz frowned at her. "Uh, it was standing wide open when I came up here. I didn't open it, if that's what you're asking."

Candy peered inside the room, grimacing at the eyesore it now was compared to the rest of the house. "Did you go in there? He doesn't want anyone in—."

"Look at the desk," Liz interrupted, practically shoving her inside.

On the clean surface where Jonathan's laptop usually sat was a folded piece of paper with her name on it.

With trembling fingers, she unfolded the note.

> *Candy,*
> *This room should be part of your masterpiece, not my grumpy man cave. Make it everything you dreamed it could be. I don't know if you have time to get it done before the Open House, and I'm sorry for being such a jerk about it. Please let me know if I can help you with this. I'll be at Maeve's all week.*
>
> *I hope it's not too presumptuous of me, but I really liked that Murphy bed you suggested, so I ordered it and had them expedite shipping. It should be here on Tuesday.*
>
> *I'm looking forward to seeing you and this house in a few days.*
> *- Squatch*

"Oh," Candy breathed, sinking onto the edge of the bed and reading the note again. "He's still here, then."

Liz sat beside her, reading over her shoulder. "What do you mean?" she asked. "It says he's staying at Maeve's."

"He's giving me his dad's room," Candy whispered, not processing Liz's question, her mind spinning in too many directions. She pointed at his signature. "Look. He signed it Squatch." The sight of it made her heart swell and break at the same time. "And the bed. I—I don't get it."

"I'm having trouble getting it, too, Cuz," Liz cut in. "Want to fill me in?"

"He's leaving," Candy said, her voice cracking. "I was afraid it might be before the open house." She flapped the note in the air. "This note is so nice, and I was horrible to him this morning, Liz. I basically threw him out because I was scared and hurt and... and... mean."

"Hey," Liz wrapped an arm around her shoulders. "Take a breath. Tell me what happened."

The story poured out. Jonathan's return, his dramatic rescue of her cabinets, the storm, their kiss, his apartment hunting website, his decision to leave and go back to Atlanta.

"You're an idiot," Liz said gently.

"Thanks for the pep talk."

"No, listen." Liz turned to face her. "Do you know what this note says to me? It says that man is so crazy about you, he's willing to give up this room, his homage to his father. I don't know what you saw on that laptop, but even if he is making plans to go back, I have a feeling that all you'd have to do is ask him to stay."

"I can't do that," she murmured. "He's obviously got his whole life out in Atlanta. Autumn Lake is probably a huge step down for him."

"Hey," Liz said, pretending to be offended. "That's my home town you're maligning. Autumn Lake is better known in these parts as 'Awesome Lake,' I'll have you know."

Candy gave a snort. It was a name she'd dubbed the town when she was a teenager visiting Liz one summer. She'd fallen in love with the town way back then. She sighed and looked down at the note again. "It doesn't say he's not leaving. Just that he'll be here for my Open House."

"Don't make assumptions," Liz insisted. "You need to talk to that man. Sheesh." Liz got to her feet and held out a hand to Candy. "Come on. We've got our work cut out for us if we're going to get this room done by Friday."

Candy gasped. "I—I have too much to do. There's no way I can get it done in time."

"Maybe not by yourself. But I'll help, and I bet if we put the word out, the rest of the gang will show up, too."

It was true, Candy thought. Her Garden Variety Lovers Club friends would be there in a heartbeat if she asked for help. They'd all been chomping at the bit for a peek inside the lake house. Maybe it was time to let them in. Why was she so adamant about doing everything herself? \

As if reading her thoughts, Liz said, "Accepting help isn't a bad thing, you know. Especially now, when you've done so much already. I mean, look at this place." She grimaced. "Well, don't look at this room. Other than the view, it's hideous. But the rest of it?" She made an explosion gesture at her forehead. "Mind blown, woman."

"You'll help?" Candy asked, her voice as small as she felt. "I would love to get this office done in time to show it." She let her gaze move around the room, calculating projects and plans and hours needed to do the work. "Since Jonathan already ordered the bed, and I already have the materials for the shelving..." She narrowed her eyes at the desk, then the window. "That desk is solid wood. It's not my first choice, but I can strip it and refinish it so it will at least work for now. That way, if Jonathan is staying, he'll still have his father's desk."

"If?" Liz prompted. "You mean, *since* he's staying. Because you know he is. At least he will be after you tell him you love him and want to marry him and have all of his babies and that you're sorry for being such a stubborn, scared fool."

"Wow. That's a lot," Candy said, giving Liz a censorious look. "I think if I dumped all of that on him, he'd run off the end of the dock and throw himself in the lake."

"Then you could jump in after him," Liz suggested with a wicked grin. "Pretend you can't swim, fake like you're drowning, and he'd have no choice but to rescue you, and drag you back to shore, where he'd give you mouth-to-mouth, and—"

"Liz!" Candy cut her off, trying unsuccessfully not to smile. She looked down at the note again, and sobered, seeing it through new eyes. "What if he can't swim and we both drown?"

Liz squeezed her hand. "Tell him how you feel. It's the only thing to do. Tell him you love him and you want him to stay and you're sorry for being such a stubborn, scared fool." She swept her gaze around the room. "And then you beat this room into submission and transform it into the most spectacular man cave office that Jonathan Squatch Burkhardt, Mythical Creature Extraordinaire and Nerdy Tech Genius, will want nothing other than to claim as his own. And where he'll want to claim you as his own, too, of course," she added out of the side of her mouth.

"Oh my word, Liz. You are incorrigible."

"I have no clue what that means, but it must be awesome if it's what I am." Liz took the note from Candy's hand and set it on the bed beside her. "Look at me, Cuz." She waited until Candy did. "All kidding aside, your open house will be amazing with or without this room finished. A huge success. Launch-you-into-outer-space success. But it's not this room, or even this renovation, that's going to fill you up in here." She tapped Candy's chest. "It's time to renovate your heart, and you need Squatch's help to do it."

Candy stared at her cousin, her heart hammering. Jonathan had faced his fears. He'd given her something precious, shown her he trusted her completely. Now it was her turn to be brave.

"You're right," she whispered. "Do you really think I can convince him to stay?"

"Well," Liz said, standing and pulling Candy up with her, "there's only one way to find out."

39
Jonathan

JONATHAN PULLED INTO THE driveway and just sat in the car for a moment, marveling at the changes that had taken place in just a week. The house looked like something out of a magazine. The landscapers had worked their magic, with burgundy and gold mums flanking the walkway, and a buffet of colorful dinner-plate dahlias, coneflowers, and spikes of blue Agastache in the garden beds under the front windows. At the corner of the house, camouflaging the downspout, was a stand of ornamental grasses with plump seedheads swaying in the evening breeze behind. The freshly painted siding seemed to glow in the setting sun, and an enormous wreath of autumn leaves and berries adorned the blue front door, completing the picture of fall perfection.

He'd stayed away just as she'd asked, keeping himself busy with the tasks of finalizing his move from Atlanta, listing his father's home, setting up his business as an Indiana S-Corp, and meeting with Maeve's attorney to process the documents that would transfer ownership of the lake house from Maeve to him. Jonathan had accomplished more in the last week than he had since his father died, and every day that passed added to his certainty that he'd made the right decision to start his new life in Autumn Lake.

He just had one more fear to face down. The fear of rejection. But he'd come ready to fight for true love, and he planned on leaving Hollyhock Hill victorious tonight.

A soft light glowed in the front window, but Candy's SUV wasn't in the driveway. As she'd requested, he'd texted to let her know he wanted to come by and see the house before the event tomorrow. She'd responded with a thumbs up and had said she'd be there all evening. Maybe she'd run out for something and planned to be back shortly.

Jonathan grabbed the small bag from his passenger seat and headed up the walkway, his heart hammering in his chest. He hadn't seen Candy since last week when she'd asked him to leave.

He let himself in and paused in the foyer, marveling at everything he saw. He noted the plastic runners protecting the newly refinished floors. She must be expecting large crowds this weekend, and the thought filled him with pride. She'd done something extraordinary here.

Walking through the house was like seeing it for the first time. Every surface gleamed, every detail had been perfected. The sunlight filtering through the woven shades at the windows illuminated the rooms, giving everything a warm, welcome glow.

But it wasn't just Candy's work that made the house feel alive. He saw evidence of her friends everywhere—lush plants from Addison's Arbor in pretty ceramic pots, several beautiful glass cake plates with covers that must be for treats Juno was preparing, books arranged on the built-in shelves that surely came from Claire's bookshop. There were fresh flowers in simple vases, throws artfully draped over furniture, and small decorative touches that spoke of care and community.

This was where Candy belonged, among people who loved her and appreciated her talents and wanted the best for her. The thought made his chest tight with something between pride and longing.

He'd saved his father's room for last, and now stood outside the door, his hand on the knob. Part of him wanted to find it exactly as he'd left it—untouched and unchanged, a shrine to his grief and guilt. But the other part of him was almost breathless with anticipation. What had she created with the space he'd finally given her?

Jonathan steeled himself, turned the knob, and stepped inside.

The transformation took his breath away.

Gone was the dingy gray carpet, replaced with a plush, coffee-colored rug over hardwood that matched the rest of the house. His father's desk had been stripped and refinished to a rich mahogany and repositioned to face the enormous windows overlooking the lake. A new leather chair sat behind it, something substantial and inviting that looked like it belonged in a gentleman's study.

Electrical outlets had been installed in the floor near the desk, eliminating the need for cords snaking across the room. Below the windows sat a cushioned window seat with built-in storage under the bench, perfect for reading or just gazing out at the water.

It was the wall behind the desk, however, that brought tears to his eyes.

In simple black frames were photographs, a progression of images that told the story of his father's life. Troy as a chubby-cheeked baby in his mother's arms. Then as a beaming toddler being tossed in the air by his strapping father. A gap-toothed boy on a tricycle, grinning at the camera. Troy and his mother on the dock with their fish; the photo Maeve had shown him that day he'd learned the truth about his parents. It really was a beautiful shot. Troy sitting at the end of the dock with his feet dangling over the edge, his arm around a dog, and Jonathan recalled Maeve saying it was one of her favorites. Then he was a pre-teen in a baseball uniform. A teenager in track shorts crossing a finish line. A young man in a suit, probably at graduation, and the photo of Troy at the auto shop where he'd worked, his smile of satisfaction over his first successful rebuilt engine.

These weren't shrine pictures. They were celebration pictures. A life fully lived, captured in moments of joy and achievement and love.

On the shelves were photos that Maeve must have downloaded over the years from Jonathan's social media accounts; pictures from his birthdays, snapshots of him and his father fishing or hiking or working on the GTO. One of the two of them on Father's Day from just over a year ago. Jonathan picked it up and turned it toward the light from the window, smiling down at the face of his father, and the expression of contentment on his face.

They'd had a good life together, he and his father. Just the two of them. He would be grateful for every moment of it.

"What do you think?"

Jonathan spun to find Candy standing in the doorway. She looked beautiful, her hair loose around her shoulders, fresh and relaxed in a blue polka dot dress.

He opened his mouth to speak but found he had no words. The room was perfect. A space that honored his father's memory without feeling like the time capsule it had been. A room that looked forward while remembering the past.

"Sit," Candy said gently, pointing to the leather chair. "Try it out."

Jonathan moved around the desk on unsteady legs and sank into the chair. It molded to his body perfectly, supportive and comfortable. From this angle, he could see the lake through the windows, imagine morning coffee and evening sunsets, quiet work and peaceful contemplation.

Candy perched on the window seat, smoothing her fluttery skirt over her legs. She smiled as she watched him take it all in.

Jonathan finally found his voice. "The photographs are incredible. And these?" He pointed at the shelves. "Were you stalking me on social media, Miss Toolbelt?"

"Maeve is the stalker, Squatch. That woman has compiled more pictures of you than most mom's have of their firstborn. I asked her to choose a dozen of her favorites of each of you and this is what she gave me. Of course, there are many more, and she said you can always exchange them any time you want." Candy stood and beckoned for him to join her. "Come look," she said, crossing the room to the closet door. She pulled it open and stepped back to let him peer inside.

"You kept the cubby," he said, relief washing over him.

"Look inside," she instructed.

Jonathan gasped when he slid open the panel to reveal not a tiny hiding space, but the opening of a tunnel. "Where does this go?" he asked, dropping to a crouch to peer inside.

"See for yourself," she told him with a mischievous smile. "I'll meet you on the other side."

For just a moment, Jonathan hesitated, but as soon as Candy ducked out of the room, he got to his hands and knees and started crawling. She'd put down the same dark carpet on the floor in the tunnel, which made the crawl easier on his knees, and shortly, he came to a dead end with a panel like the one in the closet of the office. Just as he reached out to push on it, the panel slid away. Candy stood in a closet almost identical to the one in Troy's room.

"This was Maeve's room," she said, her eyes bright with excitement. "When I told her about the secret space we found in the master bedroom, she said she'd had one in her close, too."

"But a tunnel?" Jonathan asked, getting to his feet and looking around the bright, airy bedroom that had also been completely redone.

"When I checked it out on this end, I realized the cubbies were positioned opposite each other, and that got me thinking about your bathroom." She'd been calling it his bathroom ever since he'd flooded it. "It always seemed a little smaller than it should to me, and sure enough, behind the vanity was a false wall. So Liz and I did a little excavating one night and discovered that at one time, the cubbies were opposite ends of a tunnel." Her cheeks were pink with excitement, her eyes sparkled, and he didn't think he'd ever seen a more beautiful woman. "Isn't it the coolest thing ever?"

"This is wild," he agreed, crouching down again to look inside. "I'm going back through. Want to come with me?"

Candy grinned, then fluffed her skirt. "Not in this. But I'll meet you on the other end again."

Back in the office, Jonathan emerged from the closet to find Candy waiting for him by the desk. "And here's this," she said, bending over to pick up another framed item. She turned it around to show him the growth chart they'd cut out of the hallway wall a few weeks ago. He'd totally forgotten about it, but she hadn't.

"I didn't know if you'd want this in here, too, or in the mudroom, or somewhere else. It's kinda unique, so I thought I'd let you decide."

He took it from her and studied it, hoping his voice wouldn't betray just how close to tears he was. "Thank you," he said, the words completely inadequate for what he was feeling. "Candy, this is... it's all so much more than I could possibly have imagined." He pointed at the closet. "That tunnel? What a find." He gazed around the room, taking it all in again. "I'm overwhelmed. In the best way possible."

Tears sprang to her eyes, but unlike him, she didn't try to hide it. "I'm so glad," she said softly. "I wanted to honor your father, but I also wanted you to actually be able to use this space. To live in it, not just preserve it."

Jonathan moved to sit beside her on the window seat. He took her hand and lifted it to his lips. "You have done what I could not, Candy."

"WHAT DO YOU MEAN?" Candy asked softly. He didn't seem angry or terribly sad; more like he was coming to terms with something.

Jonathan set down the growth chart and ran his hands through his hair, a gesture she'd come to recognize when he was struggling with something difficult. He was quiet for so long that she thought he might not answer.

Finally, he looked up at her, his eyes haunted by pain. "My dad always wanted to hike the Appalachian Trail with me. We'd been talking about it since I was in high school. Over the last five or six years, though, we'd finally started getting pretty serious about it. Bought gear together, planned routes, discussed the best time to go." His voice grew tight. "But I kept putting it off. Work was always too busy, there was always some project that couldn't wait, some deadline that was more important than spending time with him."

Candy felt her heart clench as the pieces began falling into place.

"Last year, we were finally going to do it. Start in Maine and hike our way home, since the trailhead in Georgia was only about sixty-five miles from where we lived. We were ready. We were both in good shape, we were hiking every weekend to train, and we'd done our research."

He sighed, and she watched his changing expression as the memories washed over him. "We cancelled that trip because I decided that I needed to work. One of our big clients had a project with a looming deadline, and instead of telling him it would have to wait, I took on that extra project, hoping to win favor with my boss. All it did was win me long hours and a nominal bump in my paycheck that month. And a disappointed dad." Jonathan said with a bitter laugh. "I couldn't say 'no' to my boss, but for some reason, I had no trouble saying 'no' to my father."

"Jonathan," she began.

"When he died," he continued, not letting her cut in. Candy could see that he needed to talk, so she closed her mouth and listened. "I was so angry. At him for dying, at myself for wasting all that time, for choosing the wrong priorities, and at God for not giving me more time with my father." He met her eyes. "I decided we were going to hike it this year, that I wasn't going to let another summer go by without doing it. With Dad." His voice cracked on the word, but he cleared his throat and kept going.

"As soon as I wrapped up the rotten business of his death, I headed to Maine with Dad's ashes. We had to wait an extra week and a half because of extra heavy snow and ice, but the day they opened the trail head on Katahdin, Dad and I were waiting."

Candy could only imagine Jonathan, alone and ferocious, driven by grief and regret, desperate to make amends for his perceived wrongs. What could she possibly say to him?

"That first stretch up in Maine..." He shook his head like he was trying to shake loose the memory. "The 100 Mile Wilderness, it's called. I thought I might die. I was so cold and hungry and exhausted all the time. At one point, I lost the trail and ended up going through some ice into water. I honestly don't know why I didn't freeze to death that night, and it's a miracle I came out of there with all my fingers and toes. I've never been so cold for so long in my life." He let out a long sigh. "I spread Dad's ashes as I went, talking to him like a crazy man, like I could make up for that time with him after all. I know other hikers often made wide berths around me, but I didn't care. I was on a mission, and I think had it not been for Dad, I might not have made it home."

Tears were streaming down Candy's face by the time he finished. "Oh, Jonathan. I'm so sorry. I had no idea. I'm sorry for how I treated you when you first got here. If I'd known—"

"Hey," he said, reaching out to wipe away her tears. "You had no way of knowing. And besides, it was you who started filling up that empty place in me again."

"I what?"

Jonathan smiled softly at her, making her breath catch. "I came here because of Aunt Maeve's invitation, mainly because I didn't know what else to do. I was in no condition to return to work. I'd terminated the lease on my apartment and moved all my stuff into dad's place before I left, but there was no way I could go back there without him. So I came here."

"And you got stuck with me," Candy murmured. "I'm sorry."

"Stop. I'm the one who should be apologizing to you. You were supposed to be here; I wasn't. But you gave me a reason to get out of bed every morning, Miss Toolbelt." His smile broadened. "Sure, reluctantly at first—you were pretty scary with that hammer."

Candy made a face at him. "Yeah, well, you were pretty scary yourself with all that crazy caveman hair and mean old scowl."

Jonathan nodded. "I know. I was a mess when I got here. I'd hoped taking Dad on the trail would have helped. It was penance, you know? That's why I pushed myself so hard. I think it ended up being more about punishing myself than honoring Dad, and that's what I meant earlier." He stroked the back of her hand with his thumb. "This room, created with thoughtfulness and care and selflessness, honors him so much more effectively than my self-destructive rampage through the woods." He let out a wry chuckle.

"Oh, Jonathan, what you did was pretty amazing, too, you know. I bet your dad is up in heaven telling everyone how remarkable you are. I mean, you saved a complete stranger, right? If you hadn't been there, that influencer girl with the phone might have died. You were supposed to be on the trail on that day because you were supposed to save her." She reached over and touched the slowly-fading jagged line across his cheekbone. "I hope you look at this scar and remember how amazing you are."

Jonathan looked dubious at that, but he didn't argue. Instead, he said, "But you also inspired me to get back to something I'd given up on. The AT app? That a was another project Dad and I had been doing together for a couple of years while we planned our trip. After he died, I stopped working on it. I was able to experiment with the prototype firsthand on the trail, but other than that, I'd lost interest in doing any more with it. Until I came here and watched you give your all to make your dreams come to life." He tenderly cupped her cheek, his thumb brushing away a stray tear. "You've inspired me, Candy Needham."

"And have you finished it, yet?" she whispered, leaning into his touch.

"Actually, I sold it. Last week." His eyes were bright now, excited. "To a company that specializes in outdoor apps. It's going to help thousands of people have safer, better experiences on the trail."

Candy felt her breath catch. "Jonathan, that's incredible. Your Dad would have loved that."

He nodded. "He would, and I can hardly believe it myself. My first sale. It was a good one, too, and it's because of you." He took both her hands now and turned on the bench so that he was facing her. "You brought the light back into my dark and dreary life, Candy. With all your sunshine and ferocious cheer, your determination to see the best in everything—even grumpy sasquatches who camp out in the middle of your renovation."

She looked at him, waiting for him to say more, her heart hammering so loudly she was sure he could hear it. When he didn't continue, she realized he was waiting for her to speak. She took a shaky breath.

"I want you to stay," she said in a rush. "I don't want you to move back to Atlanta. As soon as Maeve said she'd offered you the house, I stopped imagining anyone else in it but you." She pressed her lips together to stop herself from adding, *and me.* "Please stay, Jonathan."

"You want me to stay for the house?" he asked quietly. "Or for something—or someone—else?"

A smile tugged at her lips despite her tears. "Well, Maeve would be heartbroken if you didn't stay." Then her voice grew serious. "I would be heartbroken, too, if you left all of this behind. If you left me."

Jonathan pressed a kiss in the palm of first one hand, then the other. "I wasn't planning on going back to Atlanta, Candy."

"But you had all those listings pulled up..." Her words faded as he shook his head to what she was saying.

"Comps. I was looking at what comparable sales were for my dad's place."

"Oh," she said in a small voice.

Jonathan's eyes searched hers. "What about you? What are your plans for Chicago?"

Candy blinked in confusion. "Chicago? What are you talking about?"

"The new TV show." Jonathan said, beginning to sound unsure of himself. "I heard you on the phone. The guy said you'd be perfect for it, and you said that it was an offer too good to pass up."

Understanding dawned on Candy's face. "Oh, Jonathan. I *did* pass it up. Without a second thought." She shook her head, comprehension dawning. "I mean, it was too good to pass up if I'd been looking for a TV show again, but I'm not in the market for one. I don't want to be Candy Mason or Candy Handywoman or some fake television personality. I turned him down because I'm building something real here in Autumn Lake."

"Oh." He looked rather abashed.

She wrinkled her nose at him. "That's why you wrote that in that awful note, isn't it? You even underlined it."

They stared at each other for a moment, then both burst into laughter.

"We're idiots," Jonathan said, shaking his head. "Both of us so afraid of a good thing that we jumped to conclusions out of fear."

"Speak for yourself," Candy said with mock indignation. "I'm a very intelligent woman who just happened to get tangled up with a very scary grumpy sasquatch."

"Well, it's good you're sticking around," Jonathan said, his voice growing serious again. "Because I'm officially homeless and jobless and wondering if your business is hiring."

Candy grinned. "I pay in good coffee and sweet kisses."

"Sounds perfect," he murmured, pulling her to her feet. "But you'd better not be looking for anyone else to fill that position."

"Never," she whispered as he drew her to him. With Jonathan's arms around her and his lips pressed to hers, Candy thought of nothing else but the sunshine happiness radiating through every fiber of her being.

When they finally broke apart, Jonathan rested his forehead against hers. "I love you, Candy 'Miss Toolbelt' Needham."

"I love you too, Jonathan 'Squatch' Burkhardt."

The lake house renovation stood ready for tomorrow's open house, every detail perfect, every room telling its own story, including, and especially, Jonathan's new office.

But the story that mattered most was the quiet transformation of two wounded hearts as Candy and Jonathan began building their future.

Together.

♥ • ♥ • ♥ • ♥ • ♥

Isn't it remarkable how easy it can be to let the past keep you from embracing the promise of new beginnings? And didn't you love the Mr. Grumpy/Ms. Sunshine trope? I hope you got a kick out of Candy and Jonathan's enemies to friends adventure, and how they each learned to trust themselves and those around them on their journey toward finding home. Together.

It's always a pleasure to have you read along as we walk with these characters through life-altering events and see them through to the other side where hope and love prevail.

There are more Autumn Lake Romances!

Visit me at **BeckyDoughty.com** and **subscribe to my mailing list** so you'll be the first to know when another book releases.

~ ~ ~

From the Author

An Excerpt: The Goodbye Girl

"Wait up! Please!"

The man standing at the back of the old-fashioned lift just stared at me as I careened through the small lobby, two bulging canvas grocery bags slung over my shoulder and dragging my overloaded luggage trolley behind me.

"Thanks for your help," I muttered under my breath as I turned and wedged myself through the narrow opening. I wasn't worried about him picking up on my sarcasm; earbud cords hung down either side of his neck and disappeared inside the collar of his coat. But I was so relieved there was someone else riding up with me that I didn't care. It was Christmas Eve, for Saint Nick's sake, and I wasn't going to let some rude guy in an elevator get to me.

Okay. It wasn't an elevator. Not by a long shot. As far as I was concerned, it barely qualified as a lift. An ancient Otis manual traction elevator, it was operated by a hand crank set into one wall of the cab...move the lever clockwise to go up, counterclockwise to go down, bring it to 12 o'clock to stop. And it was not self-leveling. It took a bit of finesse to line the bottom of the lift up with whatever floor you were stopping at.

The first time I'd braved it—and only after Sarah's relentless badgering—it had gotten stuck just past the second floor. My sister had laughed at my mini panic and casually slid open the accordion cage door and then slammed it shut again, latching it back into place. "Sometimes it does that," she explained as I stared in horror at the gaping opening between the threshold of the lift and the brick wall of the shaft.

"What if I got my leg stuck in there right as the thing started up again?" I asked, horrified at the grisly images that flooded my over-active imagination. "How can this thing even be legal?"

Sarah rolled her eyes. "You sound like one of my kids. Always suggesting the most improbable scenarios." She eyed me over her shoulder as she slid the door latch in place before reaching for the crank again. "Not only would your leg not even fit in there, Gracie, but why on earth would you put it in there in the first place?"

She had a point, but thankfully, I didn't have to acknowledge her superior reasoning skills because the elevator had responded with a clank and a shudder, and then lurched its way up the shaft until Sarah brought it to a stop in perfect position at the third-floor level. The screeching of the sliding door grated against my nerves, and for just a moment, I experienced a visceral sympathy for domesticated birds living in their pretty little cages. I clamped my teeth together and didn't say another word as I waited for her to push open the security door to let us out.

The security door that supposedly kept folks from tumbling to their deaths into the shaft when the elevator was on a different floor.

"Why do you even take it if it gets stuck all the time?" I asked her.

"It doesn't get stuck all the time, only every once in a while. And then you just have to reset it. No big deal." Maybe no big deal to her, but her brain didn't work the way mine did. "Besides, there's just something about this old Otis; it's one of the reasons I chose to rent an apartment here. I think it gives Pemberton Manor character, don't you?"

Character or not, here I was, launching myself back into the leg-crushing death trap, this time with someone who clearly couldn't care less about the fact that I might be a bit of a nervy co-passenger. In fact, he looked right past me, as though I wasn't even worth the effort to acknowledge. Must be some good music he was listening to.

The cheesy old song about love and elevators popped into my head against my will, making me feel even more uncomfortable. But I consoled myself with the certainty that there would be no love lost in this elevator.

I smiled politely at the guy anyway—he didn't smile back—and then realized I'd effectively boxed him in and now I would have to be responsible for operating the lift. I spun around, a brief futile hope rising up in me that the brass plated crank mechanism had been upgraded to a backlit numbered panel....

"Oh!" I said as I took in the tiny woman in the corner and the even tinier little girl at her side. Her tiny little girl hands gripped the crank, and her tiny little girl face was lit up with anticipation. The only thing that wasn't tiny about the duo was the woman's belly bulging out from the front of her unbuttoned coat. She looked like she was due to give birth at any moment.

The woman's hand on the girl's shoulder wasn't resting there lightly, I noticed. If not for the child's puffy jacket, she might have left bruises with her white-knuckled grip. I forced my mouth to soften into a gentler smile than the one I'd given the guy, but the woman spared me only a quick glance before shifting her gaze back to the floor at her feet.

Was she all right? In pain? Oh geez. Was she in labor?

Please let us not get stuck tonight! The thought raced through my head.

"Is this it?" I asked, my words bursting out of my mouth in feigned excitement the way Sarah's did when she was trying to get the attention of all twenty-one of her first grade students. I cleared my throat and tried again in a calmer, more non-teacher tone. "Are we waiting for anyone else?"

"Nope!" the child declared in her tiny little girl voice, bouncing up and down on her tiny little girl toes—or at least I assumed they were, since they were hidden inside tiny little girl ladybug rain boots. "Let's go, let's go!"

I swallowed hard and looked away; every time she bounced, her head bumped against her mother's belly

Please don't pop. Please don't pop. Please don't pop.

I looked over my shoulder at the man who was now studying a section of the decorative molding that ran along the top of the paneled walls of the cab. Apparently, he hadn't heard my question.

"Sir?" I said a little louder, resisting the urge to jerk one of the speakers from his ears. "Are you waiting for anyone else?" Why I'd taken it upon myself to make sure no one else was joining us, I had no idea. Maybe I was subconsciously hoping I'd have to get off the lift to make room.

The man turned and met my eyes, albeit only briefly, but then in a quiet voice replied, "I am not," before looking beyond me again. What was with these people and the whole no-eye-contact thing?

"Well." And once again, I was channeling Sarah. Her chipper voice inside my head bolstered me, however, and I needed all the courage I could amass at the moment. "I'm not quite sure how to do this, but there's a first time for everything, right?" I reached for the handle of the cage door and began to tug on it.

It didn't budge.

"You ha'ta lock the other door and push the button on the floor first," said the child, who couldn't have been more than four or five years old. "Want me to show you?"

I glanced at the girl's mother for cues, but the woman just withdrew her hand from her daughter's shoulder and rested back against the wood-paneling behind her.

"Careful, Itsy," she said. Her voice was husky, not like a smoker's, but like that of someone who didn't speak a lot. There were dark circles under her eyes and the slump of her shoulders led me to believe she was taking the elevator because she might just be too weary to take the stairs today. Although the child appeared well cared for with her rosy cheeks and shiny blond hair, the bones in the woman's face seemed too close to the surface, and her hands, now folded over her distended belly, showed no signs of late pregnancy weight gain or water retention. She looked too skinny to be healthy. Was it just a difficult pregnancy? Or worse?

A creepy sci-fi movie I'd watched with my brothers years ago flashed through my mind. In it, aliens came to earth to live in peace among humans, but to their dismay, their babies kept dying before they were born. Through a series of ridiculously contrived circumstances, the aliens discovered that if their babies had humans as surrogate mothers, they acclimated to life on earth. The movie got weird then because the combination of healthy human prenatal care and advanced alien development created these alien super babies that got a little too aggressive *in utero*. They essentially turned into little parasites that ate their way out of their surrogates...

I coughed and swallowed hard, willing away the mental images, but when I saw the woman's belly twitch and roll under her laced fingers, I looked away quickly and focused instead on Itsy. She clearly was no alien super baby, but a sweet normal human child.

Itsy. For some reason, the name delighted me. Was it a *Fried Green Tomatoes* reference? An "Itsy Bitsy Spider" tribute? Short for something like Isabella or Elisabeth? Wherever it derived from, it fit the diminutive child perfectly, and I grinned down at her. "Sure. Why don't you show me how the door works."

I bit back a warning to make sure she didn't get her leg stuck in the gap.

Itsy instructed me on how to make certain the safety door was latched first, and then squatted and pointed at the foot release on the floor at the edge of the threshold. "Step on that button first. Then you can close the pretty door."

The pretty door. Not a label I'd use to describe the bars that would lock us in. I wondered if the wee duo had ever gotten stuck inside the old Otis.

"Got it," I said and waited until Itsy had popped back up and stepped away before I slid my foot forward. I hesitated briefly, giving only a moment's air time to the vision of me pushing the lever the wrong way and sending us all plummeting to our deaths. Then I squared my shoulders, pressed down on the foot release mechanism, and slid the metal cage shut.

"Can I turn the handle now?" Itsy asked, bouncing in place again. At her mother's nod, she applied herself to the task with great concentration, the tiny tip of her tongue protruding from between her pursed lips.

She took us down first. I hadn't even been aware there was a basement in the old place.

My oldest sister lived on the third floor of a stately, 100-year-old home that had been converted into apartment living sometime in the last twenty or thirty years. Pemberton Manor was one of many old Victorians in our area that had met such a fate. Midtown residents took great pride in their city with its prestigious Southern California University, the registered historical district, and the quaint downtown Main Street. There was an open air amphitheater that housed class-act performances every summer, and the streets that meandered through delightfully varied neighborhoods marked the routes for annual bicycle races, marathons, holiday parades, and more. But over the last several years, Midtown had seen a surge of growth and development, which meant the old blue bloods had to make way for the up-and-comers with their hybrid transportation and dual-income-no-kids lifestyles. Now, instead of these old, converted Victorians housing college students who opted to live off campus, more often than not, the studio apartments were being filled with renters like Sarah who had steady jobs and no plans to move anytime soon.

I supposed the owners of places like Pemberton Manor were fine with that. They didn't have to worry about finding new renters every semester, or having to clean up after university students who saved up their laundry for summer vacation. But every time I set foot inside Pemberton Manor, I couldn't help feeling just a little bit sorry for the old dame. At one time, I imagined she'd been a tall and elegant beauty with her gabled windows and sharply angled roof lines, the spindled balconies and wide covered porch. But now, the house just felt weary to me. Tired. Not quite taken care of the way she once was. Too many people coming and going, taking bits and pieces of her soul with them, and leaving less and less of her behind.

It didn't help that the maintenance guy, Sean Something-or-other, didn't maintain much of anything around the place. Sean lived on the property in a detached converted garage, and Sarah insisted he had to be a distant relative of the homeowner. There was no other explanation for him being able to keep the job he never performed. She only called him when she was in dire straits and couldn't figure out how to repair something by Googling it. Those calls typically ended with her contacting a professional—at Sean's advice, of course—which is the only reason she even called him in the first place. If he recommended a professional, then it was paid for by the landlord.

The Otis elevator jolted to a stop and Itsy cried out, "B is for basement!"

Itsy's mother clapped softly, so I joined in. After a few moments of uncomfortable silence while Itsy beamed at the oblivious man in the corner, I added encouragingly, still using my Sarah voice, "That's right. And what floor are you and your mommy going to tonight?"

"Three!" she proclaimed, and I clapped with much greater enthusiasm.

~ ~ ~

Read the rest of Grace's story in **The Goodbye Girl: Pemberton Manor Book 1**